Eclipse Gate

Laura Cole

Published by Laura Cole, 2024.

This is a work of fiction. Similarities to real people, places, or events are entirely coincidental.

ECLIPSE GATE

First edition. November 17, 2024.

Copyright © 2024 Laura Cole.

ISBN: 979-8230636380

Written by Laura Cole.

Chapter 1: The Sands Beneath My Feet

I could feel the heat radiating from the cracked stone beneath my boots, the dust clinging to my skin like an unwanted second layer. The wind stirred the sand in lazy spirals, and the distant hum of the crew going about their work was the only sound, save for Gabriel's voice, which still seemed to echo louder than everything else.

"You can't just stand there, Lyra, and pretend everything's fine," he continued, the low rumble of his frustration gnawing at me. His eyes, dark and narrow under the weight of his frustration, scanned me like I was the problem, as if I had been the one to unleash whatever dark force was waiting inside that chamber. "I'm trying to save this expedition from disaster."

"I don't need saving," I muttered, just low enough that he wouldn't catch it, but I knew better than to think the words didn't land. Gabriel had a way of hearing what he wanted, and he had a way of using it against you.

His gaze lingered on me, sharp, piercing, as if he could unravel me with just one more look. I squared my shoulders, wishing my heart would stop pounding in my chest, that it would stop betraying the small flicker of fear I couldn't quite push down. The site was alive with a kind of ancient energy, the ground itself humming with a low, almost imperceptible vibration. It had been there ever since we'd cracked through the final barrier, unlocking a world beneath the earth's surface. It should've felt like triumph, but there was a hollowness to it now, a gnawing unease that no one seemed willing to admit except for me.

Gabriel, of course, was oblivious. Too consumed with being the hero, the self-appointed savior of everything that lay in that chamber. To him, I was just another challenge to be dominated, and if I could be sacrificed for his precious ego, so be it. I could see it in the curl of his lips, in the slight cock of his head, as though I was nothing more than an obstacle to his greater glory.

"I don't know why I'm even bothering with this," Gabriel grumbled, his hand slamming against the edge of the stone, the sound ringing out like a warning bell. His anger had always been volatile, quick to spark and just as quick to fizzle out. But something in his tone made it clear this was different. The heat between us wasn't just the oppressive desert sun. It was something deeper, something unspoken that had lingered long before we'd ever set foot in this forsaken place.

I took a step forward, unwilling to back down. The others were too far away, caught up in their own preparations, too busy to hear the quiet exchange happening between us.

"You're making a mistake," I said, my voice a careful thread of calm. "If you keep pushing this, you'll regret it."

Gabriel's lips tightened, his jaw clenching. "Regret? You think I'll regret protecting this team?" He pointed at the excavation site, his eyes narrowing with a fervor I knew all too well. "You're playing with things you don't understand, Lyra. You've seen it too—the changes, the energy. The pull. It's not just in your head."

I didn't answer immediately, letting the silence settle like the desert air around us. He was right about one thing—the pull had been undeniable the moment we'd unearthed the ancient chamber. But that didn't mean I had tampered with it.

"You don't understand," I finally said, my voice steady now, though I could feel the pressure of the moment building around me. "This isn't just about ancient relics or treasures. There's something else here, something that doesn't want to be disturbed. And I know you don't believe me, but you'll see soon enough."

I didn't wait for him to respond. His disbelief, his arrogance, it wasn't worth the effort. I turned on my heel, pushing through the crowd of workers and making my way toward the crumbling stone steps that led down into the chamber. The others had already set up their equipment, but the air down there was thick with a kind of charged silence that made my skin crawl.

The moment my feet hit the first step, a wave of cold swept over me, the air in the chamber thick with an ancient, heavy presence. The walls seemed to pulse, vibrating under my fingers as I traced the edges of the intricate carvings that adorned the chamber. Something was waiting, just beneath the surface—something I couldn't yet name but could feel down to the marrow in my bones.

I hadn't been lying when I told Gabriel I hadn't tampered with it. But that didn't mean it hadn't recognized me. That didn't mean it hadn't started to turn its gaze in my direction, like a lion eyeing the wounded gazelle.

I swallowed, pushing the thought away. The chamber had been sealed for thousands of years, untouched by the hands of men, but something about it felt wrong. We had breached it, but not in the way we'd anticipated. Gabriel could yell at me all he wanted; the truth was, we had all just walked into something far bigger than any of us had realized.

As I moved deeper into the shadows of the chamber, I could hear the subtle hum of the air, the faintest whisper like a voice on the wind. It was calling me, or maybe it was warning me. Either way, I couldn't turn back. Not now. Not when we were already so far down the rabbit hole. The question was no longer whether or not we would escape, but if we would make it out with our minds intact.

The tension between Gabriel and me crackled like static, but I refused to let his bluster rattle me. There were plenty of things I hated about Gabriel—his condescending tone, his hair that looked like it belonged on a 1980s action hero, the way he threw around terms like "disaster" with the same confidence he might use to order a coffee at Starbucks. He'd spent his career collecting treasures, earning accolades, and making people believe he was a man who could do anything. What he didn't realize was that people like him were never the ones who truly understood the risks. They didn't respect the power in the earth, the weight of what had been buried beneath it. But I did.

"You need to stop pretending you know what's going on here, Gabriel." I didn't raise my voice; I didn't need to. There was something in the quiet authority of my words that always managed to get under his skin. "I understand exactly what we're dealing with, and it's not about relics or gold. It's about the very thing we just unearthed. You've only scratched the surface."

He scoffed. "And what, you think I haven't been down here? You think I don't know this site as well as you do?"

The silence that followed was thick with unsaid things. Gabriel had been here, but only in the way someone reads a book and thinks they've understood it. I had felt it from the moment we breached the chamber: a pulse beneath the stone, a vibration that wasn't just the earth settling, but something ancient reaching back into the present, hungry and aware.

"I think you're too busy looking for treasure to see what's right in front of you," I said, taking a step closer to him, enough to make him shift uncomfortably. "And if you don't listen, this entire expedition is going to end badly. I don't need you to believe me; I need you to listen."

Gabriel stared at me for a moment, his lips pressed tight as though deciding whether or not to dismiss me entirely. He chose the latter, of course. "I'll be down there in a few minutes. But if you've caused even the slightest disturbance—"

"I haven't," I cut in sharply. "And I won't. But I can't promise that whatever's down there won't do something to us."

His eyes flickered with something between curiosity and doubt. "Fine. Do whatever it is you think you need to do, but don't make me regret letting you have free rein here."

I watched him walk off, disappearing into the dust, his boots crunching over the dry ground. His words stuck with me, though. He had no idea how right he was. Whatever was in that chamber, it wasn't just waiting for us to leave. It was waiting for something. Me, perhaps. Or maybe it had been waiting for centuries for someone to wake it from its slumber.

I shook the thought off and descended into the chamber, taking the steps with an ease that belied the uncertainty rolling in my gut. It wasn't as if I was afraid of the dark; I was afraid of what had been buried for so long, and what it might do to us now that it had been disturbed. The walls of the chamber felt colder than they had a few hours ago, like the stone itself had taken a deep breath and was holding it. The air, heavy with dust, tasted faintly of earth and something… older. My fingers brushed against the carvings again, tracing the ancient symbols as though they could offer some explanation. The hieroglyphs, I knew, were warning signs. I had no idea how long this chamber had been sealed, but judging by the layers of dust and the untouched perfection of the walls, it had been more than long enough to form a kind of power, a current, an awareness.

I heard the faintest sound, a whisper so low it could have been the wind—only the air down here hadn't moved in days. My skin prickled, my breath catching. Something was watching. I spun around, but nothing was there. No one. Just the cold stone and the uneasy hum of an unseen presence.

I didn't have much time to dwell on it. The workers above were starting to stir, their voices rising in a mix of murmurs and excited chatter. I could feel them, all of them, waiting for me to return with whatever news would lead them to treasure, to fortune. They wouldn't be so excited if they knew what I'd felt down here. If they could see the shadows that stretched a little too long on the walls, curling like something alive.

A sound—a shuffling, almost imperceptible—came from the far corner. I froze. Someone was here. But it was no one from the team. The figure that stepped out of the shadows wasn't human; it was a shape, a blur of movement too fast for my eyes to catch.

Then it spoke, its voice low, gravelly, but unmistakably familiar.

"Lyra," it said, and my blood ran cold. "You should've left when you had the chance."

I spun toward the voice, heart slamming against my ribs, but all I saw was the same cold stone, the same intricate carvings. No one was there.

The whisper came again, louder this time, though it didn't feel like sound. It felt like it was being pulled from the air itself, curling around me like smoke, thick and suffocating.

"Too late, Lyra. Too late."

I swallowed hard, my pulse hammering in my throat. Whoever—or whatever—was speaking wasn't from the team. It wasn't Gabriel. And it definitely wasn't human. It had been here long before any of us, watching, waiting.

It wasn't just the past that was alive down here. It was something else—something far more dangerous.

The air down here, in the bowels of the earth, was suffocating. It clung to my skin like sweat, thick with the scent of stone, dust, and something... older. Older than the city that lay above us, older than the people who believed themselves masters of the land. My heart raced, each beat echoing in the silence, but there was no comforting rhythm to cling to, no familiar heartbeat to ground me. Instead, the world around me seemed to pulse with a life of its own, a deep, hidden thrum I couldn't ignore.

I wasn't alone. Not in the way you think, not in any physical sense, but the presence was unmistakable. My skin prickled, my breath caught in my throat, and I tried not to shudder as the shadows seemed to stretch toward me, tendrils of darkness curling like fingers. If Gabriel had been right about one thing, it was the feeling of being watched. Something—someone—was waiting.

I wasn't sure how much longer I could keep my composure. I had no plan, no blueprint for how to survive whatever this was. And I certainly didn't know how to explain it to the others without sounding like I'd finally cracked. I glanced toward the entrance to the chamber, half expecting to see Gabriel and his smug face staring down at me, but there was nothing. Just darkness and stone, untouched by the world outside.

I took a breath, steadying myself. It wasn't fear that had me frozen; it was a deep, suffocating sense of unease. Like the room was waiting for something. For me. For the others. Maybe it was hoping we'd all make a mistake.

I stepped further in, my boots heavy against the cold, hard stone. The symbols on the walls shifted in the dim light, though I knew it was only the play of shadows. Or was it? A flicker of movement caught my eye, just beyond the edges of my vision. A figure, tall, cloaked in the dark. But when I blinked, nothing was there. Only the carvings, ancient and unreadable, stretching across the walls.

I couldn't shake the feeling that they were watching me, following my every movement, as though they knew who I was and what I had come here to do. My fingers brushed over the carvings again, as though they could offer some kind of reassurance, some kind of answer to the growing dread in my chest.

The whispers came again, low and insistent, winding their way around my thoughts like smoke. *Too late...* it hissed, the sound curling into my brain. *You shouldn't have come.*

I shook my head, trying to dispel the creeping sensation, but it only intensified. The walls, the very air around me, felt too close, too suffocating. I pulled my hand away from the stone, but the pressure didn't lift. Instead, it deepened. Something was stirring in the dark corners of the room, a thing that had been waiting, hidden in plain sight, for a long, long time.

"Lyra."

The voice was a hiss, cold and familiar, wrapping around my name like a snare. My pulse stuttered, my eyes snapping to the far corner of the room where the shadows seemed to deepen. This time, there was no mistaking it. The figure was real.

A silhouette, tall and broad, standing still as if waiting for me to notice it. I wasn't sure if I was imagining it or if I was just losing my mind, but the presence of the figure felt unmistakably real.

I stepped backward, my breath hitching in my throat. "Who's there?" I demanded, my voice suddenly sounding small, insignificant in the face of the looming darkness.

No answer.

Just the soft rustling of fabric against stone.

"Show yourself," I ordered, my voice firm, though my hands trembled at my sides. I was trained for situations like this. I knew how to face danger—how to confront it with the cold, logical precision I'd been taught. But this? This wasn't danger in the way I understood it. This was something else entirely.

The figure remained still, too still, as though it had no intention of answering, no intention of letting me control the moment. I took another step back, my heartbeat hammering in my chest, until I bumped into something solid, something I hadn't noticed before. I spun around, my breath catching as I faced an enormous stone slab, one that had been partially uncovered by the crew earlier. It wasn't just a slab; it was a door. An ancient door, sealed with symbols I couldn't read.

The figure in the corner shifted, and I turned back toward it. The air was thick, like the world itself was holding its breath, waiting for something to happen.

"Lyra," it whispered again, this time so close I could feel the chill of it on my skin.

A cold dread settled over me. The whisper wasn't just a sound; it was a presence, filling my head, choking my thoughts. My legs were trembling beneath me, but I forced myself to stand tall. "What do you want?" I asked, though I already knew the answer. It wasn't me it was after. It was the chamber. The power inside it. And I had made the mistake of unlocking it.

Before I could react, the door behind me groaned, its massive stone surface grinding against the earth as though something deep within it was waking, responding to the figure's presence. The ground trembled beneath my feet, and for a split second, I feared the entire chamber would collapse.

The figure stepped forward, its form sharpening in the darkness, and my breath caught. I should've known it wasn't just a voice. It wasn't just an ancient presence lurking in the shadows.

It was someone—or something—waiting for me to open the door.

And now that I had, there was no going back.

Chapter 2: A Glimpse of Shadows

I could taste the sand in my mouth, gritty and sharp, like a thousand tiny needles against my tongue. The air, thick with salt and the heady scent of earth, clung to my skin, making every breath feel a little too shallow. The moonlight spilled across the excavation site, casting long shadows that twisted unnaturally across the ground. Each one seemed to curl and writhe, like something waiting to spring to life, and I couldn't shake the feeling that I was not alone.

Gabriel stood a few feet away, his back straight and rigid, staring into the darkness. The tension in his body was palpable, like a wire stretched too tight. I could tell he was trying to keep it together, but there was something in the way his eyes darted around—searching, uncertain—that made the hairs on the back of my neck stand at attention.

"You hear it, don't you?" His voice was strained, a whisper that barely made it past his lips.

The question lingered in the air like smoke. It wasn't just the wind I'd heard earlier—the singing, haunting and distant—it was something else. Something raw. A hum in the earth beneath our feet. It rattled in my chest, vibrating through the soles of my boots and sinking into my bones. My heart picked up a beat. I nodded, though my throat felt dry, like I was choking on something unsaid.

"Yeah," I managed, my voice cracking like an old record. "But... what is it? What's down there?"

Gabriel didn't answer. He couldn't. His eyes were wide now, and his jaw tightened like he was trying to hold back whatever was clawing at the edge of his composure. The silence between us grew thick, the only sound the rhythmic rustle of the wind as it teased the fabric of my tent. But even that seemed too loud, too alive, in the stillness of the night.

Then, the ground beneath us shook again. It was subtle at first—just a tremor in the dirt—but then it came in waves. The sand shifted, a ripple that traveled outward, pushing up from beneath as if the earth itself was exhaling in a slow, deliberate sigh. My stomach churned, an instinctive warning that whatever was happening wasn't natural.

"Gabriel," I said, my voice barely more than a breath. "We need to get out of here."

But he didn't move. His eyes were fixed on the sand, watching it undulate like water, the way it parted in odd patterns as if something was pushing its way to the surface. His lips barely moved, but I caught the mutter—something under his breath, an incantation, a prayer maybe. The words were foreign, a string of syllables I couldn't place, but they rang in the air, thick with a sense of urgency.

I stepped closer, the heat from his body radiating off him in waves. "What's going on, Gabriel? What did we uncover?" I knew it was a dangerous question, but I couldn't help myself. The fear was a slow burn in my chest, a creeping dread that had nothing to do with the tremors in the earth and everything to do with Gabriel's silence.

He turned to face me then, his eyes wide, not with fear but something darker. There was something unsettling in the way his gaze met mine, a depth I'd never seen before, like he was looking at me but not seeing me.

"You shouldn't have come here," he said, his voice low and grim. "None of us should have."

Before I could respond, a low growl, like the rumbling of a distant storm, echoed from the pit. It was deep, primal, and it sent a chill down my spine. I turned to look at the excavation site, my eyes darting over the jagged edges of the hole we'd dug so recklessly.

In the shadows of the pit, I could see something move—something big.

The air around us thickened, the very atmosphere seemingly pressing in. My heart raced, a drumbeat in my chest that drowned out the wind and the eerie hum of the earth.

"Gabriel, what is that?" I asked, my voice shaking now.

He didn't respond immediately. Instead, he stepped forward, moving with a sudden intensity I wasn't prepared for. He reached down into the sand, fingers digging into the earth, as though trying to grasp something just beneath the surface. His knuckles were white, his jaw clenched tight.

"Don't—" I started, but it was too late. He yanked his hand back, and in the faint glow of the moon, I saw it.

A shard of something, dark and glistening, slick with what looked like oil—or blood—stuck to his fingertips. He stared at it, his breath coming out in harsh gasps.

"It's... it's too late," he murmured to himself, as if I weren't even there.

I swallowed hard, forcing myself to take a step back, away from him. "Gabriel, tell me what's going on. Tell me what's in that pit."

For a moment, he didn't look at me. Then, slowly, he raised his eyes, and the look in them made my blood run cold.

"It's not just history we're digging up," he said, his voice barely above a whisper. "It's a curse. A thing that's been waiting... a thing that shouldn't have been awakened."

The words hit me like a punch to the gut, and for the first time, I realized the weight of our discovery. This wasn't just an archaeological site. It wasn't just a dig for old bones or artifacts. What we had uncovered was something ancient, something that was never meant to see the light of day.

And now, whatever it was, it was coming for us.

I should have known something was wrong when Gabriel didn't even flinch at the sudden tremor in the ground. His eyes stayed fixed on the spot beneath our feet, a quiet intensity in them that made my stomach churn. I didn't want to know what it was that made him look like that, but I was already too deep into this mess to back out now.

The singing had stopped. The soft hum of whatever was waiting beneath the surface now felt more like a growl, low and warning, a pulse vibrating through the sand. I couldn't tell if it was my nerves or something else that made the air feel thicker, heavier, but it was like the world was holding its breath.

"What did we uncover, Gabriel?" I whispered, trying to sound calm, but the tremble in my voice betrayed me.

Gabriel slowly turned toward me, his face pale in the moonlight, a sheen of sweat making his skin gleam. His lips barely moved as he spoke, but his words hit me like a slap to the face.

"Something... not meant to be found." He paused, his gaze flicking toward the pit. "I don't know what it is, but whatever it is, it's angry."

I felt a tightness in my chest, like the space inside me had suddenly been squeezed out of all air. I wanted to reach for him, to shake him and demand he tell me more, but his expression told me everything I needed to know: he was just as lost as I was, if not more. The look in his eyes was enough to make my heart race, but it was the distance between us that made me uneasy. He wasn't just standing further away—he was pulling back, emotionally, physically, like he was already bracing for something bigger than either of us.

We stood there in silence, listening to the soft creak of the earth beneath us. My fingers twitched at my side, itching to grab something—anything—to ground myself, but there was nothing.

Just sand. Sand that seemed to shift and shudder every time the wind passed through it.

I stepped forward, not knowing why I did it, but something in me needed to see what was happening. Whatever it was. And there it was, just beneath the surface—a glimmer of something that wasn't earth. It looked metallic, but darker, like it had absorbed the light around it.

I couldn't help myself. I knelt down, brushing the sand aside with my hands. It was smooth to the touch, but there was a strange heat to it. I jerked my hand back, blinking. The spot was colder than the rest of the sand. How could something buried so deep be colder than its surroundings?

Gabriel was beside me in an instant, his hand on my shoulder. He didn't push me away, but there was a tightness in the way he gripped me. He wasn't just holding me to guide me; he was holding me to stop me from doing something reckless.

"You don't know what you're dealing with," he muttered, and for the first time, I could hear the true strain in his voice. He was holding something in, something that was about to burst.

I stared at the object again, squinting in the dim light. It was too large to be just a rock, too uniform to be a part of the natural landscape. It was an artifact, I realized. But not like any I'd ever seen. It was almost... alive, somehow. The way it shimmered in the light, the way it seemed to pulse with an energy that shouldn't have existed.

"What do you think it is?" I asked, even though I already knew that he didn't have an answer. Gabriel was the expert here, but even his expertise hadn't prepared him for whatever this was.

He didn't answer right away. Instead, he looked at the object with a mix of fascination and dread. "I've heard stories," he said slowly. "Whispers, really. About things buried beneath the earth. Ancient things. Things that can change the course of everything."

His gaze flicked to mine, and there was an almost desperate urgency in his eyes now. "We shouldn't be here."

I frowned. The unease in his voice was unsettling, but there was something else in his tone that made my skin crawl. It wasn't just fear. It was regret.

I opened my mouth to speak, but before I could get a word out, the ground trembled again—stronger this time. And this time, it wasn't just a ripple in the sand. It was as if the earth itself had taken a deep breath and was holding it in.

The wind kicked up suddenly, howling like a banshee, throwing sand into my eyes and blinding me for a moment. My heart pounded in my chest as I stumbled backward, blinking the sand away. The moonlight was all but gone, swallowed by a dark cloud that had rolled in without warning.

"Get back!" Gabriel shouted, his voice sharp with panic. He grabbed my arm, yanking me away from the pit. I didn't argue, didn't even think about resisting. There was something in his voice—something so raw and urgent—that I found myself moving without questioning.

We stumbled away from the excavation site, the sand beneath our feet shifting as if it, too, were alive, trying to pull us back. I could hear something in the distance now—a low, rhythmic thudding, almost like footsteps—but the sound wasn't steady. It echoed, bouncing off the dunes like a wave crashing in a storm.

"Gabriel," I gasped, trying to catch my breath. "What's happening?"

He didn't answer. His eyes were fixed on the pit, and for a moment, I thought he was going to run back toward it, but then he froze. His gaze flicked to the shadows beyond us, where the night seemed to thicken, and I realized with sudden clarity that the danger wasn't just coming from the earth below—it was coming from everywhere.

The thudding grew louder, closer, until I could feel it in my chest. The sound of something... someone... was coming. And we weren't alone anymore.

I thought it was just a momentary flicker in the air—something caught on the edges of my mind. But then I saw it. In the distance, far beyond the excavation site, something moved, just a blur of shadow against the backdrop of the desert. It wasn't the wind. No, the wind had become a still silence, as if nature itself had held its breath.

Gabriel's grip tightened on my arm, pulling me a few steps further back from the pit. His eyes were wide, but not with panic. No, there was something deeper, more primal, in the way his gaze darted to the darkness beyond. It was like he could see something I couldn't—a shape, a presence, something that had no business being here.

"Get in the tent," he ordered, his voice clipped, urgent. The authority in it was so starkly different from his usual demeanor that I almost didn't recognize him. "Now."

I wanted to argue, to question, but the sudden rush of unease choked the words before they could leave my mouth. Instead, I just nodded and turned, stumbling over the uneven sand beneath my feet as I made my way back toward the tent. My pulse was a drumbeat in my ears, too loud, too insistent. The night felt heavier than it should have, like the desert itself was about to swallow me whole.

By the time I reached the tent, Gabriel was already inside, pacing like a caged animal. His hands were clenched at his sides, the muscles in his jaw working overtime as if he was trying to keep whatever was building up inside him from escaping. I knew better than to interrupt his thoughts. Gabriel had always been one to keep his cards close to his chest, but this was different. The very air in the tent felt charged now, thick with whatever it was he was hiding.

I sank down onto a chair, watching him move back and forth like a clock with the springs coming loose. I didn't know how long we sat in silence, the only sound the occasional creak of the fabric in the wind. And then it happened.

A sound—loud and jagged—pierced the stillness. It came from the pit, from the place we'd unearthed, and it wasn't a groan or a rumble. It was something else. Something far worse. It was a voice.

It rose from the ground in an agonized wail, tearing through the desert like a thing from another time. I froze, the hairs on the back of my neck standing straight. Gabriel's face went ashen, the color draining from his features as if that wailing voice had sucked every bit of life out of him.

He turned slowly, his eyes locking with mine, and for the first time in all the time I had known him, there was nothing but pure terror in his gaze.

"It's awake," he whispered. "And it's angry."

I didn't need to ask what he meant. The trembling in his voice told me everything I needed to know. The thing we had uncovered was no longer just a forgotten relic. It was a living, breathing thing—something that had been buried for a reason. A reason we hadn't even begun to understand.

Suddenly, the wind outside howled again, louder this time. But this wasn't the same breeze I had felt earlier, the one that fluttered the edges of the tent. This was something different, something unnatural. It rattled the canvas, causing the tent to shake on its frame. A cold chill swept through the fabric, and I realized I could see my breath.

"What's happening?" I asked, my voice barely more than a whisper.

Gabriel didn't answer right away. He was staring out the small slit in the tent, his eyes wide and unfocused, like he was trying to see something in the night that he knew he shouldn't.

And then, I heard it.

A low, guttural growl that vibrated through the air, filling the silence. I didn't need to look to know it was coming from the pit. The sound was inescapable, as though the earth itself was trying to tear itself open to unleash whatever lay beneath.

"We're not alone," Gabriel said, his voice ragged. He didn't look at me, but I saw his hands trembling. "They've found us."

"Who?" I demanded, standing up now, my own fear edging into my voice. "What the hell is happening?"

Gabriel's gaze snapped to mine, his eyes dark with something close to despair. "The ones who were here before us. The ones who buried it. They never intended for anyone to find it."

"But why? What's in there?" I felt a sharp sting of panic, but I tried to steady myself. "Why are we still here?"

Gabriel looked at me then, really looked at me, and I saw something break in him. Whatever it was he had been trying to keep back—the walls he'd built up so high—cracked, just a little.

"I didn't think it would happen," he said quietly, as if confessing a sin. "I thought the legends were just that—legends. I didn't think…"

The ground beneath us rumbled again, but this time it was different. It was like the earth was shaking to its core, as if something was pushing its way to the surface with terrible force. A roar, a deep, bone-rattling noise echoed through the air.

I didn't think. I just ran.

I bolted for the door of the tent, throwing it open with enough force to nearly tear it off its hinges. I barely caught my footing before I was outside, my feet slipping in the sand as the sky above cracked open with the sound of thunder. But it wasn't the storm that made my heart stop. No. It was the shape that emerged from the darkness, tall and imposing, moving as though it were part of the wind itself.

A figure, dark and almost formless, rising from the pit. And it was coming straight toward us.

Chapter 3: The Desert's Secret

The floor beneath me seemed to sway, a trick of the mind or something more sinister, I couldn't tell. My fingers tingled with the remnants of the gemstone's touch, the light of it still flickering behind my eyelids. Each breath I took felt too shallow, as though the air was thinner here, in this tomb of forgotten time.

Gabriel was still beside me, his presence oddly comforting. He'd been silent ever since I first laid eyes on the artifact, his expression unreadable, a quiet observer to the chaos I'd just experienced. He had that knack, I thought—saying nothing and yet making it clear he knew far more than he let on. It irked me, that air of knowing, but I was too stunned to confront him just yet. I took another deep breath, letting it settle my racing pulse.

"You're sure this is it?" I asked, my voice hoarse, like I'd been shouting into the wind for hours. The words felt too soft in the cavernous, dark space, swallowed almost immediately by the sandstone walls that stretched impossibly high above us.

"Yes," Gabriel answered. His voice was steady, too steady. "The artifact was meant to be kept hidden. Whoever finds it is bound to its curse."

"Great." I forced a dry laugh, shaking my head. "Just what I needed. Another curse. Are we sure this isn't just an old rock with a good story attached?"

Gabriel's gaze met mine, and for the first time since we arrived, there was something vulnerable there. Something raw. I didn't like it. I preferred the confident mask he usually wore, the quiet man who seemed always a few steps ahead of everyone else, especially me. But right now, I saw the cracks.

"You're not going to like what happens next," he said, as though speaking to a petulant child.

I narrowed my eyes. "You've got to be kidding me. You came all the way out here to tell me that? I don't even like what's happening now."

He didn't smile, didn't flinch. Just stood up slowly, offering me a hand—steady, firm, without expectation. I hesitated but took it, rising to my feet. His fingers lingered for a moment longer than necessary, sending an unexpected warmth up my arm. That, too, irked me, but I pushed the feeling down. There were far more pressing matters to deal with.

"You're right," he said, his tone light but weighted with something unsaid. "You're not going to like it at all."

We both turned toward the artifact again, the gemstone now resting innocently on a stone pedestal. Its glow had dimmed since I touched it, but I could still see it, still feel it. As though it were watching us, waiting for something. Or perhaps that was just my overactive imagination.

"Why not just leave it here?" I asked. "Turn around, pretend we didn't see anything. It'll be our little secret."

Gabriel looked at me, and I could tell he was considering the option, weighing it against whatever fate had already been set in motion. His lips tightened, eyes flicking back to the gemstone as if the decision had already been made.

"I wish it were that easy," he said, his voice now filled with an edge of finality. "But once the artifact is touched, it's activated. There's no turning back."

I exhaled sharply. Of course, there was no turning back. I should've known. Nothing in my life had ever been that simple. If there was one thing I was good at, it was making things complicated.

"Why did you bring me here, then?" I asked, trying to mask the frustration that bubbled just beneath the surface. "You didn't think to give me a heads-up before I got myself tangled in this mess?"

Gabriel studied me for a long moment, his gaze steady, almost too steady, before he answered. "Because I couldn't do it alone."

A soft laugh bubbled from my chest before I could stop it. "I'm sorry, did you just say you need my help?"

The quiet exasperation in his eyes matched my own. "Yes," he said. "Whether you want to or not, you've been chosen. And so have I."

I blinked, not sure if I was hearing him correctly. "Chosen for what? To curse each other to a slow and miserable death? Because I've got some serious doubts about my qualifications for that."

Gabriel's lips curled into the faintest smile, but it didn't reach his eyes. "It's not about death. It's about the song."

"The song?"

"Yes," he said, and now there was something different in his voice. A low, almost reverent tone, as though speaking of something far more sacred than I could understand. "The gemstone... it's tied to a melody. One that we're meant to find and sing. A song that can save, or destroy, everything."

I stared at him, trying to digest his words. My pulse quickened, not from fear—though I should've been afraid—but from the simple, raw truth in his voice. As crazy as it sounded, I believed him. Something deep in me stirred at the thought of it. The song.

I looked back at the gemstone, its glow flickering again, stronger now. It was almost as if it were... waiting. Waiting for me.

"Alright, then." I straightened, my mind spinning with the weight of what he was saying. "Let's hear it. What's the plan?"

Gabriel's hand brushed against mine as he reached for the artifact. His eyes were fixed on it, dark and intent. "We find the song. And pray we're not too late."

The air around us hummed, like an orchestra tuning itself for a grand performance, but the music was muted, almost a whisper just beyond hearing. Gabriel's eyes, dark and unreadable, remained on me as if he were waiting for something—a reaction, a decision, or perhaps an apology. For a brief, fleeting moment, I wished I could shake off the sensation that something was terribly wrong. But the pull of the gemstone—the pulse of it, deep and resonant in my chest—refused to be ignored.

"Do you ever wish you'd stayed in bed?" I asked, my voice a little too sharp for my liking.

Gabriel didn't respond right away, his gaze flicking from me to the gemstone, as if he were searching for some answer in its shifting light. "I don't have that luxury," he said finally, his tone dry. "Neither of us do."

I turned away from him, not wanting to acknowledge the wave of unease that washed over me. The chamber around us felt... off, as though the walls themselves were waiting. Every inch of this place seemed to breathe with the same faint energy that was radiating from the gemstone. It was suffocating, this eerie calm before the storm.

"We're not supposed to be here, are we?" I muttered, mostly to myself, but Gabriel heard me nonetheless.

"No," he said softly, his voice lowering as if the very stone around us might overhear. "We're not. And that's the problem."

The weight of his words settled like a stone in my stomach. I hated the way he said it—like he knew something I didn't. And maybe, just maybe, that's what irked me most about Gabriel. He never let anyone see his hand. Always a card short of a full deck, just enough to leave you questioning.

I exhaled slowly, trying to push the discomfort down. There had to be a logical explanation for all of this. An artifact that could curse and control? Sure, fine, no big deal. I was well-versed in the bizarre and inexplicable, after all. But this felt different. It wasn't just some story, some ancient tale spun for tourists with too much time on their hands. No, this was something else. Something that reached into the core of me and twisted.

"I didn't sign up for this," I muttered under my breath, and Gabriel chuckled.

"Funny," he said, not even sparing me a glance. "Neither did I."

His words hung between us, sharp and thick with an unspoken history that I wasn't sure I wanted to know about. I wasn't even sure I wanted to ask. My eyes dropped to the gemstone again, its pulsing light growing in intensity, as if it recognized me. I shivered.

"What are we supposed to do now?" I asked, my tone quieter, less sure.

"We find the song," Gabriel said, his eyes narrowing as he turned toward the artifact. "The one that's tied to it. The one that can either fix everything... or destroy us all."

I swallowed hard, trying to suppress the sudden spike of panic in my chest. "And how exactly do we do that?"

"I wish I knew," he said, a flicker of frustration creeping into his voice. "But we have no choice. We're bound to it now."

"I'm sorry," I said, shaking my head. "What exactly do you mean by 'bound'? I didn't sign any contracts when I touched it. I didn't even think about it, Gabriel."

He took a deep breath, like he was steadying himself. When he spoke again, his voice was lower, his tone tinged with something I couldn't quite place. "You don't need to sign anything when something like this finds you. It knows. It chooses. And you, whether you like it or not, have been chosen."

I blinked, struggling to process the gravity of his words. "Chosen for what? To be some... sacrifice? Some puppet in a play I don't understand?"

"Not exactly," Gabriel said, his expression flickering for a brief moment before he masked it again. "You and I both have roles to play. The artifact doesn't give us the luxury of choice, only the illusion of it."

My mind raced, every fiber of my being trying to break free from the words he was saying, but they were suffocating. The illusion of choice. The artifact. The song. It was all too much, too overwhelming. And then I remembered something—something from the vision I'd seen when I touched the gemstone. It was a song, faint and distant, like a whisper carried on the wind. It had to be the key.

I looked back at Gabriel, my thoughts churning. "What if we can't find it? What if we fail?"

"Then everything goes to hell," Gabriel replied simply, his voice almost too calm. "And we don't get the luxury of time to figure it out. We start now."

I nodded, despite the fear tightening in my chest. There was no other choice. He was right. Time wasn't on our side. It never was.

"Okay," I said, forcing a steadiness into my voice. "Let's get started, then. But don't think I'm doing this for you, Gabriel."

A ghost of a smile tugged at the corner of his mouth, but it didn't quite reach his eyes. "I wouldn't expect you to. But I'm glad you're doing it anyway."

I turned on my heel, facing the chamber's entrance with a sense of grim resolve settling over me. The door back to the real world was just a few steps away, but it might as well have been on the other side of the planet. The world beyond it was one I didn't know anymore. The artifacts, the curses, the song—it was all part of a puzzle I hadn't been meant to solve.

But now, it seemed, I had no choice.

The words hung in the air like a bad joke no one had the nerve to laugh at. The curse. It was so much more than that. The images I'd seen—violent, fleeting flashes of a world long lost—were more than just remnants of some ancient past. They were a warning. A warning that clung to me like the desert dust that never really leaves your skin, no matter how many showers you take.

Gabriel rose slowly, brushing the dust off his pants as if the weight of the moment wasn't enough to make him want to shake the entire room. He didn't speak right away, and I realized, with a jolt, that I didn't know why he was here. Why had he brought me to this godforsaken place? What did he expect me to do with this? A curse? A song? A treasure chest full of doom?

"What exactly are we looking for, Gabriel?" I asked, the words sharp but tremulous. "What does this thing want from us?"

He didn't answer at first. Instead, he turned his back to me, his hands clasped tightly behind his back. The muscles in his shoulders tensed as if he were holding something in—something heavy, something that wanted to break free. I watched the way his jaw clenched, the tightness in his posture, and for the first time, I understood how much he was lying to me.

"I didn't want you to get involved," he said, his voice tight with something else now—regret, perhaps, or maybe just the crushing weight of whatever burden he carried. "But you were always going to be pulled in. It was never a question of if, only when."

I crossed my arms, unwilling to let him off the hook so easily. "You sound like a bad fortune cookie," I said, keeping my tone light to mask the way my chest was tightening. "I don't do 'destiny,' Gabriel. So, you'll have to explain to me how I ended up on this crazy train you've got running."

His head turned slowly, his gaze piercing through me like a needle, sharp and unflinching. There was a flicker of something in his eyes—something dangerous, but more than that, something familiar. It unsettled me more than I cared to admit.

"Maybe I wasn't completely honest with you," he said, his voice softening. "I didn't think you'd believe me if I told you the truth."

"Try me," I shot back, feeling a surge of defiance course through me. "You know I'm not exactly the kind of person to roll over and accept fairy tale endings, Gabriel."

He didn't respond immediately, just stood there, his gaze now fixed on the glowing gemstone that still hummed faintly in the corner of the chamber. The light pulsed with a rhythm I could almost feel in my bones. It was unsettling, like a heartbeat that wasn't my own.

"I brought you here because," Gabriel started slowly, as though testing the weight of his own words, "you're the only one who can stop it."

I froze. "Stop what?"

"The curse," he replied, his voice steady, but his eyes—his eyes betrayed him. "It's already begun. And it won't stop until it has what it wants. The artifact—the gemstone—it's more than just a relic. It's the last key to a world that's been locked away for centuries."

I took a step back, trying to process everything he was telling me. The room spun a little, my thoughts swirling like sand caught in a gust of wind. This was too much. This was insane. My logical brain was working overtime, trying to find a way to wrap this all in something neat and tidy, but it refused to make sense.

"And what does it want?" I managed to say, my voice barely more than a whisper. I wasn't sure I wanted to hear the answer.

Gabriel's eyes met mine, and for a moment, I thought I saw something flicker in the depths of them—a hint of something that wasn't just guarded, but... afraid.

"It wants you," he said simply, the words hanging in the air like smoke from a fire you couldn't escape. "The song. The bloodline. Everything."

For a moment, I couldn't breathe. His words hit me with the force of a freight train. "My bloodline? What the hell does that mean? I don't have some magic ancestor or long-lost royal family behind me, Gabriel. I'm just a—"

He cut me off, his voice low but urgent. "No, you don't understand. Your family—it's not what you think. The curse, it was meant for someone like you. You are the key."

The room felt smaller now, the walls closing in. My heart pounded in my chest, and the air seemed too thick, too hot. Everything about this felt wrong, but I couldn't deny the pull I felt toward that gemstone. It was a connection I couldn't explain, a force I couldn't resist.

"Why me?" I demanded, shaking my head as if it would all somehow make sense if I just asked the question again. "Why am I the one who has to deal with this?"

Gabriel's face softened, but only for a second. "Because you're the one who's supposed to break it."

"The curse?" I asked incredulously.

"The curse," he confirmed, his voice barely above a whisper. "The queen, the song... everything is tied to your bloodline. You're the last of them, whether you like it or not."

I stood there, trying to process the words, but nothing seemed to add up. My mind raced, and every fiber of my being screamed at me to run, to get out of this room, away from Gabriel and whatever madness he was pulling me into.

"Okay, I need a second," I said, holding up a hand. "I... I can't think straight with you standing there, dropping bombs like that. Give me a minute."

Gabriel didn't move, his gaze fixed on me with a strange intensity. "There's no time, Audrey," he said, the urgency creeping back into his voice. "The moment you touched the gemstone, you activated it. The song is waking up. And if we don't find it, if we don't stop it—"

Before he could finish, a deafening sound echoed through the chamber, like a thousand voices rising in unison, a chorus of ancient agony.

The gemstone flared to life, its pulse erratic now, and the floor beneath us trembled.

"We don't have a minute," Gabriel whispered.

And that was when I knew we were already too late.

Chapter 4: A Song in the Dark

The air in the forgotten chamber grew thick as Amara's voice lingered in the silence like a memory you can't quite place. She stood in the center of the room, bathed in the dim, flickering light of our lanterns, her skin the color of dusk just before the storm. Her beauty was unsettling—too perfect, like a sculpture that had once been alive and now held only echoes of humanity. She wore no armor, no weaponry, yet the presence she exuded felt like a force in itself. Her long, dark hair cascaded down her back like liquid night, and her eyes—deep, ancient—pierced through me as if they were reading the very marrow of my bones.

The song that had been tugging at my senses, pulling me into this place, seemed to hum from her lips, low and languorous. I shivered despite the warmth of the room, instinctively taking a step back.

"You're the last one?" Gabriel's voice broke through the air, rough and impatient. He never liked the unknown—never trusted anything that couldn't be dissected and understood. And this woman, standing so unnervingly calm amidst the ruins of a lost civilization, certainly wasn't something he could wrap his mind around.

Amara's lips curved into a faint smile, one that held no humor. "The last," she said, her voice carrying a weight that made it feel like she was speaking a truth long buried beneath layers of forgotten time.

I felt it then, a cold whisper brushing the back of my neck. Not just the weight of her words, but something older, something that pulsed beneath the floorboards of this crumbling place. The artifact we sought—it wasn't just some relic. It had a pulse of its own, alive in a way I couldn't fully grasp. It was calling to me, just like the song.

Gabriel shifted beside me, his hand instinctively resting on the hilt of his sword, a motion so practiced it was almost unconscious. He didn't trust her, and I couldn't say I blamed him. There was something in the air, something about the way the shadows seemed to bend around her, like she was woven into the fabric of this place. But my gaze, despite its better judgment, kept drifting back to her—toward the power she exuded.

"You claim I have the gift," I said, my voice betraying none of the unease that churned inside me. I knew better than to reveal weakness. I'd learned that long ago. "But gifts come with a cost, you say. What exactly does that mean?"

Amara's eyes flickered with something unreadable—whether it was regret, pity, or simply the hint of a secret she'd chosen not to share, I couldn't tell. She took a step closer, her movements so fluid it was as though the air itself parted for her. "The artifact you seek, Lyra... it was never meant for one such as you."

The words, sharp and like a slap, hit me harder than I expected. I straightened, fighting the sting that shot through my chest.

"Never meant for me?" I scoffed, resisting the urge to flinch. "You don't even know me."

"Ah, but I do," Amara said, and I could hear the faintest tremor in her voice, one that betrayed her calm. "In all the ways that truly matter."

I wasn't sure whether she was referring to some ancient power of hers or simply the uncomfortable weight of her gaze. Either way, I wasn't going to let her intimidate me.

"Then tell me, Amara," Gabriel interrupted, his tone sharp, slicing through the tension. "If you know so much, why hide the artifact away? Why protect it with riddles and cryptic songs? What is it really?"

She didn't answer him at first. Her gaze drifted past me, towards the darkened alcove at the far end of the chamber, where the faintest glimmer of something—gold, maybe, or just the glint of reflection—caught the light. Her eyes softened, though not with warmth, but with something more akin to sorrow. "The artifact is not just a thing. It is a part of me," she said quietly, as if to herself.

The room seemed to breathe with her words. The stones underfoot groaned, the walls shifted ever so slightly, as though the ruin itself were alive. I took another step forward, the air growing colder as I neared her. She held my gaze, not with challenge, but with something that felt like understanding—or perhaps pity.

"You've felt it, haven't you?" she asked, her voice so soft it seemed to come from somewhere deep inside the earth itself. "The pull. The song. The calling."

I swallowed hard. Of course, I had felt it—the strange, seductive hum that had led me to this place, to her. But I hadn't thought it would be like this. A force, ancient and woven into the bones of this place. She wasn't just a guardian. She was a part of it, perhaps even more so than I had first thought.

"I'm not like you," I said, more to myself than to her. "I don't want to be."

Amara's lips twisted into something that could almost have been a smile, though it was fleeting and sad. "I didn't say you were," she replied softly. "But the artifact... it chooses, Lyra. And it's already chosen you."

I felt a strange shiver at her words, one that was far colder than the temperature of the chamber. My pulse quickened, and I turned to Gabriel, but his expression was unreadable—his eyes narrowed, calculating.

He didn't trust her. And frankly, I wasn't sure I did either.

But something was happening, something beyond both of us. We had crossed the threshold, and there was no turning back now.

I had always been a firm believer in the idea that the truth had a certain weight to it, that it couldn't be so easily manipulated or hidden. But standing in the presence of Amara, I started to question whether I had been wrong. The tension between us was thick, like smoke that didn't dissipate, hanging in the air and curling around my lungs.

I didn't know why I had come here—why I was standing before her. The artifact was supposed to be a means to an end, a tool to be wielded, not a decision to be made. But Amara seemed to hold all the answers to questions I had yet to ask. The way she looked at me, it was like she already knew everything about me—every decision, every mistake, every doubt. And I hated it.

"You speak of gifts," I said, my voice still shaky, but steady enough to mask the unease that was gnawing at my insides. "I didn't ask for this, Amara. I didn't ask for any of it."

Her lips twitched, the smallest ghost of a smile crossing her face. "No one ever does. That is the burden of a gift." She turned toward the dark alcove in the back of the chamber, where the faintest flicker of gold caught the light. "The artifact waits for you, Lyra. But it will not be kind."

"I'm not interested in whatever game you're playing," Gabriel said, his voice low, his hand on the hilt of his sword. He stood a few steps behind me, like a shadow that would strike the moment the air shifted.

Amara's eyes darted to him, and I could almost feel the amusement in her gaze. She wasn't afraid of him, or of anything for that matter. "You misunderstand," she said, her voice soft, almost coaxing. "It is not a game. The artifact... it does not yield easily. It is a creature unto itself, as old as the world. And it will choose you, whether you want it to or not."

I wanted to argue, to tell her that I didn't need her cryptic riddles, but the words caught in my throat. There was something undeniable in the way she spoke—something dangerous and alluring that made it impossible to look away.

"I thought I was here to collect an object," I said, my tone betraying none of the internal chaos that roiled beneath my skin. "Not... whatever this is."

Her gaze softened, and I could almost believe she felt pity for me. "It is more than an object. It is a relic of power, yes, but it is also a part of something greater—a force that cannot be contained. You are too close now to walk away, Lyra. There is no turning back."

I felt it then—a shift in the atmosphere, something heavy settling over me like the weight of the world. It was no longer just the artifact that called to me, but something in the very walls of the chamber itself, something ancient that thrummed beneath the surface. My pulse quickened, and the song—no longer a whisper but a relentless pull—wrapped itself around my mind, urging me forward.

Gabriel's hand twitched at his sword, his gaze still locked on Amara, but he seemed to be listening, too. He had always been the pragmatic one, but even he couldn't ignore the force that seemed to pulse from the very stones beneath our feet.

I didn't know what to say, what to do. The truth was, I felt both drawn to this place and repelled by it. The artifact was something I had come for, yes—but the power that radiated from it, from Amara, was something else entirely.

"You still don't understand," Amara said, her voice a thread that wove its way into my thoughts. "You have no idea what you're dealing with. The artifact was never meant for one like you, Lyra. It was created for a specific purpose—one that even I cannot unravel. But you? You were chosen. You are the key."

"The key to what?" I managed to ask, the words tasting foreign on my tongue.

Her gaze grew distant, and for the first time, I saw something in her eyes that wasn't pity, but something deeper—darker, perhaps.

"To a door that has been locked for eons. A door that should never be opened."

I felt the ground beneath my feet tremble, faint but unmistakable, like the stirrings of something buried long ago. There was a pulse now—more than the song, more than the whispering wind. It was in my chest, beating in sync with something older than time itself.

"I can't take it back," she continued, her voice quieter now. "None of us can. And you, Lyra, you are standing at the precipice. What lies beyond the door, no one knows. But once it's opened, there is no going back."

I swallowed hard. "Then why don't you stop me?"

Amara didn't respond at first. She merely watched me, her expression unreadable. I wasn't sure if she pitied me or if I was simply part of some cruel design, but the words that came next sent a chill down my spine.

"Because you are already beyond saving." She nodded toward the alcove where the artifact lay hidden. "But you will not be alone in this. Not anymore."

I turned to Gabriel, but he was staring at the darkened corner, his eyes narrowed in thought. He was no longer the warrior ready to strike; he was a man trying to make sense of a world that had just shifted beneath him. The confidence that had once radiated from him was gone, replaced by uncertainty—and fear.

"You don't have to do this," Gabriel said, his voice strained. "We can walk away."

But I already knew. I could feel it, in the marrow of my bones. There was no walking away—not from this, not from what we had already started. The artifact had chosen, and I had already crossed the point of no return.

I had always prided myself on being able to read people—their gestures, their pauses, the subtle shifts in their eyes—but Amara wasn't like anyone I'd ever encountered. She didn't speak the way people did. Her words didn't just pass through the air; they settled in it, like invisible weights that I couldn't shake off. She moved with an eerie calm, as though the ruins weren't decaying around us but were simply a place she had always been. And yet, despite everything I had come here for, I wasn't sure if I was ready to know what lay behind those eyes.

"I don't need your pity," I snapped, the bitterness of my own voice surprising me. Maybe it was the helplessness I felt—the nagging suspicion that I was already in too deep, tangled in a web I didn't know how to escape.

Amara's lips quirked into a smile that wasn't quite a smile. "It's not pity, Lyra. It's understanding. The artifact has chosen you, and no matter how much you may fight it, it will not let you go." She paused, letting her words hang in the air like smoke. "It is part of you now, just as you are part of it."

The words sunk deep, an unsettling realization crawling beneath my skin. The idea of being bound to something so powerful—so unknown—was not comforting. It felt like being handed a beautiful, deadly weapon and being told, with a smile, that you must learn to wield it, whether you wanted to or not.

Gabriel was quieter now, his brow furrowed, his hand still hovering at the sword's hilt but not drawing it. He was listening, calculating. But there was something else in his eyes, too—a growing wariness, something primal that told me he wasn't just afraid of Amara. He was afraid of what we were walking into.

I turned to face him. "We don't have to do this," I said, my voice low, but there was an edge to it I didn't recognize. "We can leave. No one's forcing us to stay here."

Gabriel's jaw tightened, and for a moment, I saw the old warrior, the one who had always walked the line between confidence and pragmatism. He'd been the one to pull me back when I wanted to rush in, the one to ground me when the chaos threatened to swallow me whole. But now, he hesitated. "If we leave, Lyra, we leave with nothing but the weight of what we could have found."

It wasn't the answer I wanted to hear. I had thought he'd argue, tell me we could walk away and that the mission—our mission—was bigger than this. But now his voice carried something else. The same pull I had felt when I first set foot in this place, when the song had first whispered my name.

Amara's gaze flickered between us, and then she spoke again, her voice soft, like she was revealing a secret that only the two of us could hear. "It's not about finding. It's about becoming."

I shuddered. The thought of becoming a part of something that I couldn't understand, that no one understood, was terrifying. And yet, something inside me yearned for it—the power, the knowledge, the unspoken promise that this journey was meant for me, and maybe no one else.

"What do you mean, becoming?" I asked, my voice a little too sharp, a little too desperate.

"The artifact is not just a thing," Amara explained, taking a deliberate step closer. The air between us thickened, charged. "It is a bond, an extension of something beyond the physical. It binds its chosen to it, body and soul. But only if they are worthy. Only if they can carry its weight."

"And what happens if I'm not worthy?" I challenged, trying to sound braver than I felt.

Her lips parted in a soft sigh, a sound that almost felt like regret. "Then you will be consumed. The weight will crush you, and you will fade away. Lost to time, forgotten, like the rest before you."

I glanced at Gabriel, his face hard, unreadable. He didn't look at me—he couldn't. His eyes were locked on Amara, trying to piece together the mystery of her words. She was like a mirror, reflecting something in him that I didn't understand. But it was there, that same fatal pull.

"I didn't sign up for this," I muttered under my breath, barely loud enough for Gabriel to hear.

"You never do," Amara responded softly, her voice not unkind, but inevitably resigned. "None of us do. That is the curse of the chosen. But it is also the gift."

The weight of her words settled between us like an unspoken truth. Gabriel finally spoke, his voice barely more than a growl. "I don't like this. I don't like her. And I sure as hell don't trust this… artifact."

Amara's smile deepened, though it didn't reach her eyes. "Trust is a luxury in places like this."

I stood frozen, torn between wanting to run and needing to know what lay beyond that dark alcove, beyond Amara's cryptic words. I could feel the pulse now, stronger, as if it was calling me—not just pulling me forward but dragging me toward the unknown.

Gabriel looked at me, his eyes dark with conflict. He didn't speak, but his gaze said everything I needed to hear. He was going to follow me, no matter what.

We weren't leaving.

The floor beneath our feet groaned, a low, warning rumble, and the temperature dropped a few degrees. The song, which had been quiet until now, intensified again, swirling around us like a living thing, a sound that made my skin prickle with anticipation and dread. Something was happening. The artifact—whatever it was—was waking up.

"Do you hear that?" I asked, my voice barely audible over the growing hum in the air.

Gabriel didn't answer, but his gaze flickered to the shadows ahead. I saw it then—something moving just at the edge of my vision, a shape too dark to make out fully. The light from our lanterns flickered, casting long, sharp shadows against the walls. And for the first time since I had stepped foot in these ruins, I felt the unmistakable sensation of being watched.

It was too late. There was no turning back now.

Chapter 5: The Mark of the Ancients

The mark burned as if the ink had been tattooed with heat instead of ink, its delicate lines curling like ancient script on my wrist, luminous and raw in the dim light. I hadn't asked for any of this—no artifact, no arcane bind, no glowing mark that set me apart. Yet here I was, in the middle of this mess, tangled in something far older than me, and far more dangerous than I'd ever thought possible. The odd thing? Despite the irritation, there was something about it that felt oddly... right. Like it belonged.

Gabriel wasn't wrong, though. That much I could admit. The weight of the mark pressed on me—both figuratively and literally. It was like a declaration, a signpost for those who dealt in relics of the forbidden, the cursed, the forgotten. They'd be able to sense it, feel it hum like a radio frequency tuned to the wrong channel. And once they did, there would be no running. The hunt would begin.

Still, I wasn't about to sit back and let this thing—whatever it was—control me. There was a stubborn streak in me that Gabriel often mistook for recklessness, and though I'd let him assume the worst, I wasn't as rash as he believed. I'd learned the hard way that survival meant thinking beyond the immediate panic. I wasn't about to let the mark decide my fate.

"What do we do now?" I asked, my voice sharper than I intended.

Gabriel shifted beside me, his hand sliding over the top of his head, fingers raking through messy hair. He exhaled like it was a long, drawn-out frustration rather than a simple breath.

"Now?" His lips twisted into a grimace. "Now, you stay low. No more running around trying to get answers from every half-baked historian you meet. No more digging into whatever cursed nonsense this is." He pointed at my wrist, his face a mask of irritation. "I told you to leave it alone."

His words didn't land as harshly as he wanted them to. I'd known Gabriel long enough to read between his lines. The anger, the sharp edges of his tongue—it was all a defense mechanism. And for some reason, it felt more personal tonight, like I'd stepped on something tender without realizing it. There was no getting past that tone, but there was no mistaking it either. Gabriel cared. In his own way.

"Look, I get it," I said, trying to keep my voice steady, even though the frustration was starting to boil over. "But the problem is, it's not something I can just ignore. This thing—" I held up my wrist, "—is attached to me. It's part of me now."

He turned sharply, the muscles in his jaw tightening. The way he stared at the mark made me wonder if he wasn't just pissed off, but actually scared. Scared for me. Maybe even for himself.

"Maybe that's the real problem," Gabriel muttered, more to himself than to me. "You're always trying to take on the world, one stupid decision at a time. But this?" He shook his head. "This is bigger than anything you've ever dealt with."

I bristled. "What's that supposed to mean?"

He didn't answer immediately. Instead, he took a slow, deliberate step back, his eyes scanning the dark corners of the room as if he were looking for an escape. Maybe he was. I wasn't sure.

When he spoke again, his voice was lower, edged with something like caution.

"You don't know what's out there, Mara. And you sure as hell don't know what you've just invited into your life. It's not just treasure hunters you're going to need to worry about. It's the things that have been waiting for someone like you." He pointed again at my wrist, his fingers trembling slightly. "People have died over this kind of power. People have disappeared."

The air between us thickened, each word settling like dust in the room. I had never heard Gabriel like this before. There was something raw and unspoken in his tone, something that made my pulse skip. He wasn't just being the jaded mercenary. He wasn't just giving me his usual 'don't get involved' spiel. There was a genuine fear there. And it wasn't just for me. It was for the both of us.

I pulled my sleeve down, hiding the mark from view. The tension crackled in the air, heavy and oppressive. We both knew there was no walking away from this. Not now. Not with the mark already branded into my skin.

"So what's the plan?" I asked quietly. "You've been around the block a few times, Gabriel. What do we do next?"

He was silent for a long moment, his gaze flickering to the window. There was something there in his eyes—an unreadable mixture of conflict and resolve, like he knew more than he was willing to say. But finally, after a beat that stretched too long, he answered.

"We find Amara."

His words were simple. Almost too simple. But beneath the surface, I could hear the weight of them, feel the urgency behind them. I had no illusions about Amara. She was wrapped up in this whole mess too, but she knew things. She had answers. If anyone could help me figure out what the mark meant—or more importantly, how to control it—it was her.

I sighed, rubbing my temples. "Great. Let's go see the ancient scholar who's always a step ahead of us, but never quite enough to save our asses."

Gabriel gave a half-smile, but it didn't reach his eyes. "You don't have to like it. But if we're going to get out of this alive, she's our best shot."

With a reluctant nod, I pulled my jacket tighter, feeling the weight of the night settling in my bones. There was no turning back now. The mark on my wrist had already set everything into motion.

The streetlights flickered above us, casting pools of golden light onto the cracked sidewalk. It was past midnight, and the city of New Orleans had begun to shed its tourist-filled skin, revealing the quieter, darker corners where the real magic happened—or at least where I was starting to think the real trouble would find me. Gabriel was ahead, his broad shoulders blocking out most of the light, but I could still see the faint outline of his jaw clenching in irritation. He hadn't said a word since we left the apartment, but the tension radiating from him made up for the silence.

"I'm not saying it's your fault," I ventured, trying to break the thick silence between us. "But if I hadn't discovered the artifact, you'd probably still be drinking cheap bourbon in some dark dive bar, avoiding whatever trouble you saw coming. So, there's that."

Gabriel's eyes narrowed, and I could practically hear the snark forming on his tongue before he shot me a glance over his shoulder.

"Don't get smug, Mara. That's a one-way ticket to a broken nose and a bad hangover." His tone was dry, but the hint of amusement behind it caught me off guard. He was irritated, but not as irritable as he usually got when I pushed him. He was something else tonight, something I couldn't put my finger on. The mark on my wrist felt like a third, unwelcome presence between us, an invisible force pushing us into territory we hadn't intended to enter.

"What, no sharp retort?" I teased, quickening my pace until I was walking beside him. "Maybe that artifact's rubbing off on you."

"Maybe it's rubbing off on you," Gabriel muttered. "You're the one who's carrying around a glowing target for the entire underworld."

I shot him a look, but he didn't meet my gaze. He was keeping his distance—physically and emotionally—and I wasn't sure which one bothered me more. We rounded a corner, and the worn brick buildings of the French Quarter came into view, casting shadows that felt like they could swallow us whole.

The streets here had a different energy, a quiet pulse of the city's ancient magic lingering in the air, thick with stories and secrets. In the distance, I saw the flickering neon of a sign for a bar—one of those places that had seen better days but still attracted the occasional lost soul looking for an escape. Gabriel didn't even break his stride. He just kept walking, leading me down the path to Amara's shop.

"You think Amara knows what the mark is?" I asked, my voice quieter now, threading through the still air like a secret I wasn't sure I wanted to hear the answer to. "How she can stop it from... doing whatever it's going to do?"

Gabriel's jaw tightened again, and I could feel him holding something back. The problem with Gabriel was that he was always withholding—always keeping a piece of himself locked up, like a house with doors that only opened if you had the right key. Most of the time, I didn't care enough to find that key. But tonight was different. Tonight, I could feel the wall he was building between us, and it made me want to knock it down.

"Amara knows things," Gabriel said finally, his voice low and flat. "But I don't trust her. She has her own agenda, and you're a means to an end for her. That's all. I'm not saying she's dangerous, but..."

"But she's dangerous," I finished for him.

Gabriel didn't deny it. He didn't need to.

"She won't help you unless there's something in it for her," he added, his voice edged with a bitterness I hadn't expected. "And that's not something I'm sure you can afford."

I narrowed my eyes, piecing together the tension in his words. "What aren't you telling me, Gabriel? What's going on between you two?"

He looked over at me then, his expression guarded. "Nothing," he said quickly, too quickly. "It's just... business. You don't need to know."

But that wasn't the answer I needed. "Gabriel," I pressed, my tone sharp, "if there's something you're not telling me, now's the time."

He stopped walking abruptly, turning to face me so quickly that I almost ran into him. The intensity in his eyes was like a physical blow—raw, unfiltered, and full of something I couldn't place. For a moment, I thought he was going to say something, something that would explain everything. But instead, he just shook his head, as if giving up on trying to explain.

"Fine," he said, exhaling slowly as he raked a hand through his hair. "You want the truth? Amara and I... we've crossed paths before. She's not someone I can just trust because she knows about ancient artifacts and curses. She's got her own secrets, and the last time we worked together, it didn't exactly go smoothly."

I stared at him, waiting for more, but he fell silent again, his lips pressed into a thin line. I didn't know if he was holding back for my benefit or because he wasn't ready to face whatever had happened between them. But whatever it was, it was clear it wasn't something either of us was prepared to deal with tonight.

"Great," I muttered, "so now we're dealing with some personal history between you two as well? Fantastic."

Gabriel exhaled, turning to resume walking. "Keep it together, Mara. We don't have the luxury of letting anything distract us."

I fell into step beside him, my thoughts spinning with the new layer of complexity he'd added to our already chaotic situation. Amara wasn't just a scholar; she was a player in this game too, and I had no idea whether she was going to be a help or another complication. But either way, the clock was ticking, and the mark on my wrist was only getting stronger.

We finally reached the door of Amara's shop—an old, weathered building tucked away at the end of a quiet street, where the shadows seemed to stretch just a little too long, and the air smelled like incense, books, and the faintest hint of danger. Gabriel didn't hesitate; he knocked twice, firmly, before stepping back. I stood beside him, waiting, the weight of the mark settling deeper into my skin with every passing second.

The door creaked open slowly, and there, framed in the dim light of the shop's interior, stood Amara. Her dark eyes flicked over us, unreadable, before her lips curled into a knowing smile.

"You're late," she said, her voice smooth like velvet, with just a hint of something... sharper beneath it. "Come in."

The door to Amara's shop creaked open, releasing a gust of air that smelled faintly of aged paper and something herbal, almost medicinal. The interior was as dim as I remembered, rows upon rows of bookshelves crammed with dusty tomes and glass jars filled with things I preferred not to identify. The kind of place that could make you feel like you were lost in time, or worse, like time was lost in you. The walls were lined with paintings of abstract shapes—some looked like maps, others like cryptic symbols—and there was a faint hum in the air, like static from a radio station only a few people knew how to tune into.

Amara stood in the doorway, her figure silhouetted by the soft golden glow spilling from the shop behind her. She wore a loose, dark robe, the kind that suggested mystery without trying too hard. Her eyes, sharp and intense, flicked over Gabriel before they landed on me, lingering for a moment too long. A slow smile spread across her face, as though she'd been expecting us all along.

"Do come in," she said, her voice smooth, like warm honey drizzled over sharp edges. "I've been waiting."

"Somehow, I don't think that's a good thing," Gabriel muttered, stepping past her without waiting for an invitation. His eyes scanned the room quickly, as if checking for hidden dangers, though I wasn't sure whether he was more concerned about the artifacts or Amara herself. He clearly didn't trust her, and something told me that his mistrust was more than a passing concern.

I followed him into the shop, the door creaking shut behind me. The air inside was thick with the scent of herbs and incense, almost suffocating in its richness. Amara's gaze flicked briefly to the mark on my wrist, and I could feel her scrutiny. There was a moment of stillness, like the world had held its breath, before she spoke again, her voice softer now.

"Quite the find you have there, Mara." Her tone was almost... indulgent, as if she were toying with the idea of sharing a secret, but not just yet.

I tugged my sleeve down, hiding the mark, though I could feel its warmth against my skin, as though it were pressing against me, reminding me that it was still there, that it wasn't going anywhere. "What is it?" I asked, not willing to beat around the bush anymore. "And why is it attached to me?"

Amara's smile didn't fade, but there was something calculating in the way she studied me. "You really don't know, do you?" she mused, her voice filled with a touch of something like amusement, but there was also a quiet weight behind her words, something deeper. "That's both a blessing and a curse."

I didn't like the sound of that. Gabriel shifted next to me, his posture tense, but he didn't interrupt. Amara moved past us with an effortless grace, her fingers brushing the spines of the books as she walked. She was leading us somewhere, but I wasn't sure where. Part of me wanted to demand answers, but I also knew that pushing too hard might make her shut down entirely. So I waited.

After a few beats, Amara stopped in front of a low wooden table, its surface cluttered with a mix of scrolls, books, and small wooden carvings. There, in the center, was a book bound in leather—old leather, the kind that had been worn soft from age and use. She flipped it open, her fingers pausing at the first page.

"It's called the Mark of the Ancients," she said, her voice low. "And it's not something you can simply ignore. It binds you to the artifact, yes, but it also marks you for something far more dangerous."

I crossed my arms, trying to hold myself together, though my heart rate was picking up. "What does it do? Why is it glowing?"

Amara didn't immediately respond. Instead, she traced her finger along the page, her eyes scanning the text. Gabriel was still beside me, his arms crossed over his chest, but there was a tension in him now, a subtle shift that I couldn't place. He was listening intently, despite himself.

"Most people who come into contact with the artifact—well, they don't survive," she finally said, her voice heavy with the weight of history. "But you're different. This mark... it's not just a symbol of possession. It's a gateway. And that's what's so dangerous. It connects you to forces that have been waiting for centuries. You're marked now, not just as the artifact's keeper, but as a player in a game that's been unfolding long before you were born."

I could feel the air in the room thicken as the words sank in. A gateway? What kind of forces? And why me? Of all the people in the world, why had it been me to find the artifact? I hadn't asked for any of this.

"So, what now?" I asked, keeping my voice steady even though my pulse was quickening. "How do I get rid of it?"

Amara turned to face me, her eyes dark, unreadable. "You can't," she said simply. "Once it marks you, it's with you for life. But you can control it. If you're willing to learn how."

"Control it?" Gabriel cut in, his voice edged with skepticism. "What does that even mean? How do you control something like this?"

Amara's lips curled into a wry smile. "That's the real question, isn't it? How much are you willing to give up to learn what it can do? Because the mark—it will demand things of you. Things you might not be ready for."

I swallowed hard, my throat suddenly dry. "What kind of things?"

But before Amara could answer, the door to the shop slammed open behind us, and a figure stepped into the dim light. I froze, my eyes locking onto the stranger who had just appeared in the doorway. It was a man, tall and broad-shouldered, dressed in dark clothing that looked too well-fitted for this part of the city. His gaze swept over us, cold and calculating, before settling on Amara.

"Well, well," he said, his voice smooth but with an edge that sent a shiver down my spine. "It looks like I've arrived just in time."

Chapter 6: The First Attack

The morning sun cut through the haze of the city like a blade through silk. It should have been the kind of day where you could linger over a cup of coffee, let the warmth of it seep into your bones as the streets hummed with the usual blend of chaos and hope. But then the air changed, thickened, and every instinct I had screamed that something was wrong.

I hadn't even heard them at first. Not until the crack of gunfire split the silence, sharp and jarring, making my stomach drop to the floor. A sharp sting of adrenaline surged through me, followed by the metallic taste of dread. I shoved myself into motion, the pulse of the city, of life, echoing in my veins. The coffee I'd been cradling moments before now felt miles away, out of place in the madness unfolding around me.

My heart slammed against my ribs as I sprinted through the narrow alleyways of a neighborhood that was both familiar and yet, suddenly, unrecognizable. It was like the world was holding its breath, waiting for the next thing to fall.

The men came out of nowhere—silent, shadows moving with precision, their faces masked by scarves, their eyes nothing more than cold slits of purpose. Mercenaries. The term felt too small for the presence they carried with them. But there was no time to dwell on that. I dove behind an old stone wall, feeling the rough texture scrape against my palms, trying to steady my breath.

Gabriel was already there, crouched in the shadows. His dark eyes flicked toward me, and I couldn't read the storm that raged within them. He didn't ask what I was doing here. Didn't question how I'd gotten involved in whatever mess had just spilled over the streets. His focus never wavered from the enemy ahead.

"Keep low," he muttered, his voice low and steady, the only thing in the chaos that seemed remotely calm. "We don't need more attention than necessary."

I nodded, pressing myself against the stone, trying to make myself invisible. But my mind... my mind was a different story. It was alive, buzzing with the energy of something I couldn't control, something that had always lurked within me but that I had spent years trying to keep buried.

Gabriel's sharp gaze darted to the men advancing on us. There were six, moving in tandem, like clockwork. Each step was deliberate, each motion measured. I could hear their low voices, too low for me to catch the words, but I didn't need to. Their presence spoke volumes. They were professionals, trained to get in and get out without leaving a trace.

"Do you trust me?" Gabriel's voice was tight, taut like a bowstring ready to snap.

I didn't need to think about it. The answer was simple. "Yes."

It wasn't the kind of trust I gave lightly, but with him... somehow, it felt different. That should have scared me.

His lips twitched into something that might have been a smile if not for the situation we found ourselves in. "Then follow my lead."

The ground seemed to shift beneath my feet as the energy around me twisted, pulling at my limbs like a magnet. I resisted it, but the pull was impossible to ignore.

"Are you ready for this?" he asked.

My heartbeat thundered in my chest, but my voice came out steady. "Always."

Gabriel didn't hesitate. He sprang from his hiding spot, moving with a fluidity that made him seem almost otherworldly. I followed, my instincts kicking in as I let go of the fear that had always held me back. I didn't have time for hesitation. Not anymore.

The first strike came from Gabriel, swift and brutal, his fist connecting with the mercenary's jaw with a sickening crack. The man crumpled to the ground, his body limp. No time for mercy, no time for second thoughts. He had a job to do, and so did I.

I raised my hand, the ground beneath me groaning as if it was coming to life. The bones of the long-dead creatures buried in the sand—remnants of lives long forgotten—shifted and rose at my command. I could feel the weight of it, the cost of it, deep in my bones. But there was no other choice.

The first of the mercenaries to approach me was a tall man with a scar running down his cheek. He lunged, his knife gleaming in the early morning light, but before he could reach me, the earth beneath him cracked open, sending a thick, jagged bone from an ancient creature shooting upward. It pierced his side with an ease that made my stomach twist. He let out a strangled scream, his weapon slipping from his grasp.

I felt the rush of power surge through me, the bones shifting and twisting to my will, each movement precise, calculated, deadly. This was what I had always feared. This was the darkness within me that I had tried to ignore. But in that moment, as the mercenary's life slipped away, I knew there was no going back.

The others hesitated, looking at me as though I was something unnatural. As though they had just realized the depth of what they were dealing with. I didn't have the luxury of letting them think too long. My fingers twitched, and the earth obeyed.

One by one, they fell.

When it was over, silence descended like a heavy fog. Gabriel was standing over the last of the fallen, his chest heaving with exertion, but his eyes never left me.

His gaze lingered, searching, calculating. "You really are dangerous," he said, his voice unreadable.

I didn't flinch. I couldn't. The words hit me like a punch to the gut, but there was no time for weakness. "You didn't know?" I asked, a hint of humor threading through my tone despite the chaos around us.

Gabriel's lips pressed together in something that could have been a smirk, but he didn't reply. Instead, he turned, his footsteps steady as he moved toward the street, leaving me with the weight of his words and the stillness of the aftermath.

The sun had risen fully by then, casting a pale light over the carnage. The world was quiet once more, but I knew, deep down, that nothing would ever be the same.

The city breathed, still humming from the fight but unaware of the storm that was about to hit. Gabriel and I stood in the quiet aftermath, the world around us a patchwork of dust, shattered glass, and the smell of blood mixing with the fading scent of freshly baked bread from a nearby bakery. A few blocks away, a jazz band had started up, their trumpet blaring through the soft murmur of the city. But here, in this sliver of the world, it felt as though everything had stopped moving.

Gabriel's gaze was sharp, slicing through the space between us. His eyes were still calculating, assessing, like I was some kind of experiment he hadn't quite figured out yet. I felt the weight of his silence pressing down on me, like he was trying to read something between the lines that wasn't there. But I wasn't an open book, not to him, not to anyone.

"Well," I said, breaking the silence, "you know what they say about appearances." My voice came out smoother than I felt, the humor barely masking the tension gnawing at me. "Never judge a book by its cover."

His lips twitched, just the barest hint of a smile. But it didn't reach his eyes, those cold, calculating eyes. "I'm not judging. I'm... surprised." His voice was low, edged with something I couldn't quite place.

I looked down at the chaos around us. Bodies scattered like broken dolls, the remnants of a battle that should have never been ours. "We need to get out of here," I said, my tone shifting, becoming all business. "There's no telling how many more of them are out there, or if they were even the only ones. We can't stay in one place too long."

Gabriel nodded, his face as unreadable as ever. But there was something in the way he moved that gave me pause. It was the way he adjusted his jacket, a simple motion, but the kind that spoke of a man who had seen more than his fair share of dangerous situations and knew exactly how to handle them. It was like his entire body was on alert, every muscle poised for the next fight.

"Stay close," he said, his voice steady. "And keep your head down."

I wanted to ask where we were going. How we were supposed to escape when we'd just made a bloody mess of the place. But I kept my mouth shut. Gabriel wasn't the kind of man who would explain things to you. He'd show you. He'd act first and talk later. And there was no time for anything else.

We moved quickly, slipping into a nearby alleyway that reeked of stale cigarette smoke and the faint, lingering scent of burnt coffee. The walls were tagged with graffiti, the vibrant colors a stark contrast to the grim reality we were in. In a different time, I might have stopped and admired the art, but not now. Now, all I could think about was how we were going to make it out of this.

As we walked in silence, my mind was racing. The bones. I could feel them stirring inside me, like they were calling to me. It was as though they were hungry, eager to rise again and claim what was theirs. And I was the one who'd given them life. The one who had wielded that power without even knowing what it meant. It was the kind of power that made you feel both invincible and completely out of control. I couldn't afford to think about it right now. Not with Gabriel beside me, his presence a constant reminder that I didn't understand what I was capable of—and that terrified me.

"How long have you been doing this?" I asked, the question slipping out before I could stop it. My voice was barely above a whisper, like I was afraid that speaking any louder would break the fragile tension that hung between us. "The... fighting. The mercenaries. You're good. Really good."

Gabriel didn't look at me as he answered. His eyes stayed fixed ahead, scanning the shadows. "Longer than I care to remember." He paused, then added, almost as an afterthought, "Too long, in fact."

"Well," I said, forcing a little humor into my voice, "I guess that makes two of us."

He shot me a quick look, and for a second, I thought I might see a crack in that cold exterior of his. But no. He was too guarded for that. "I didn't ask for your help," he said, his voice clipped.

"I didn't exactly ask for this life, either," I shot back, my irritation flaring just a little. "But here we are, right?"

For a moment, we walked in silence again, the tension between us thick enough to slice with a knife.

I wasn't sure how much longer I could keep up the charade. The charade of pretending that I wasn't scared. That I hadn't just done something... unforgivable. The bones. I could feel them, echoing in my mind, reminding me of the cost. It wasn't just the mercenaries who were dangerous. It was me.

Gabriel finally broke the silence again, his voice quieter this time, almost reluctant. "You don't know what you're dealing with, do you?"

I stopped walking, the words striking me harder than I wanted to admit. "What do you mean?" I asked, my voice barely a whisper. "You think I don't know danger when I see it?"

He turned to face me, his gaze intense, burning into mine. "No," he said, his voice dark, almost too honest. "I think you have no idea what you're capable of. And that's dangerous. For you. For everyone."

I opened my mouth to respond, but no words came out. What could I say to that? That he was wrong? That I wasn't as dangerous as he thought? I couldn't. Because deep down, I knew he was right. I had no idea.

And that made me dangerous.

We walked in silence for several blocks, the only sound the faint hum of traffic, punctuated by the occasional rattle of a subway train beneath the cracked pavement. The city felt far too big for what had just happened, like the whole of it was trying to ignore the fact that we'd just made it bleed.

I could feel Gabriel's presence beside me, like a shadow I couldn't shake, and I hated that my heart started to race whenever he moved. I wasn't sure if it was because he scared me or because he fascinated me—maybe a little of both. Whatever it was, it was a feeling I didn't like. Not because of him, necessarily. But because it made me realize just how much I had to learn, and how much I was still pretending I didn't need to.

"I need you to understand something," Gabriel said, breaking the silence like the crack of a whip. His voice was steady but carried an edge to it that made me wonder just how far he was willing to push. "You don't get to play hero here. You don't get to just throw bones at people and think you're saving anyone."

I didn't flinch, even though his words hit me harder than I'd like to admit. "I'm not saving anyone," I shot back. "I'm just trying not to die."

He gave me a sharp look, as though he was trying to figure me out, but that was something neither of us had time for. I turned away, my hand instinctively reaching for the pocket where I kept my phone, only to realize I'd left it back in the alley where everything had gone down. Great. Just great.

"Do you think we're done here?" Gabriel asked, his eyes narrowing as if the very thought of being out of the woods was laughable. "This was just the beginning."

His words settled over me like a heavy weight, and I couldn't shake the image of those cold, merciless eyes staring at me through their scarves, the faces of the mercenaries still etched into my mind. Whoever they were, whatever they wanted, we were just the appetizer, the warm-up act before the real show.

"You're right," I muttered. "We're not done. But for now, I need to get off the street."

Gabriel didn't argue. He was used to this, I realized. He was used to running, hiding, moving like a ghost through places like this, cities that offered no refuge. He was like the shadows he seemed to weave through so effortlessly, a man of secrets wrapped in his own isolation.

We ducked into a diner at the corner, a place that smelled like stale coffee and grilled cheese sandwiches, the kind of diner that locals swore by but that tourists never dared enter. It was the perfect kind of place to blend in when you needed to disappear. The waitress gave us a cursory glance as we slid into a booth by the window. No words, no questions, just a tired nod. The kind of service that made you feel like you'd been there before, even if you hadn't.

The smell of bacon grease mixed with something else—a sense of comfort that felt wrong in the moment. Nothing about this felt comforting. Not the coffee. Not the soft clink of silverware on plates. Not the man sitting across from me, his eyes still narrowed, studying me like I was a puzzle he was trying to crack.

"So," Gabriel started, his voice low, the sharp edge gone, replaced by something far more dangerous: patience. "How much longer are you going to pretend you don't know what you are?"

I leaned back, crossing my arms over my chest. "I don't know what you're talking about."

"Don't lie to me," he said. His eyes softened slightly, but it didn't make his words any less cutting. "You know what you can do. I saw it. And so did they."

I looked out the window, watching the cars pass by in a blur, wishing I could just disappear into the asphalt. Wishing I could forget how it had felt to call the bones from the earth, to make them move and shift like they were alive, to feel the weight of it thrumming beneath my skin.

"It's not like that," I said finally, my voice quieter than I'd intended. "I didn't ask for this. I never wanted it."

He was silent for a moment, studying me with that same intensity that had been there when he first saw me use that power. Then he spoke, his tone almost too soft. "That's the problem. You're running from it, and it's only going to get worse the longer you pretend you don't have control."

"I have control," I snapped, leaning forward. "I don't need you to tell me what I have."

Gabriel exhaled slowly, the hint of a sigh caught in his chest. "Fine. Keep thinking that."

But the thing was, I didn't want to think about it. I didn't want to think about what I could do, what I might have done to those mercenaries if I hadn't pulled back, if I hadn't stopped myself. It had been too easy. I hadn't even hesitated. And that terrified me.

"Someone's going to come looking for us," I said, changing the subject as quickly as I could. My pulse was already racing again. My skin prickled with the knowledge that every second we spent here was one where we could be found.

Gabriel didn't respond right away. His eyes flicked to the door, the glass window beside it reflecting our image like some sort of twisted omen. I could see the muscles in his jaw tighten, could feel the tension building in his frame. He was always calculating, always assessing, and whatever he was seeing, it wasn't good.

"You're not wrong," he said, and for a split second, I thought I saw something flicker in his eyes. "But that's why I'm not sticking around."

I opened my mouth to protest, but the words died on my tongue when the door of the diner swung open with a screech that could have been heard a mile away. Every head in the place turned, but it was the three men that stepped inside that made my stomach drop.

They were taller than the average person, dressed in dark coats that blended into the shadows of the diner, their movements precise, measured. They weren't just looking for us—they were expecting us. And I knew, right then, that we weren't just running anymore.

We were being hunted.

And Gabriel had no intention of sticking around.

Chapter 7: A Tenuous Alliance

The city smelt of rain before it even started, a heavy, pregnant air that made the streets gleam with the promise of a storm. Gabriel and I stood at the edge of the alley, the dull hum of the city moving around us like a living thing. We were, as usual, on opposite sides of the same argument, my voice rising and his falling into an impatient growl.

"I told you we shouldn't have come here in the first place," I snapped, fingers digging into the strap of my bag. My gaze shifted to the narrow path ahead, the neon signs from nearby bars flickering like distant beacons. "But no, you just had to go running after the job like a dog after a bone."

Gabriel scoffed, running a hand through his tousled hair. He had that look again—the one that made him seem too handsome for his own good, too aloof, too much like someone who never got dirty. "We wouldn't be in this mess if you hadn't played the hero. How many times do I have to remind you? You don't get to save people, Mia. You're not a knight in shining armor."

I narrowed my eyes. The rain, thick and warm, began to fall in earnest now, the first heavy droplets hitting the ground like a gentle applause, making the city's worn pavement shimmer. "Oh, so now I'm the problem? Not you, chasing after leads like you're on some grand treasure hunt."

"Better than being reckless. You never think—just jump into things without a second thought." He crossed his arms, his jaw tight. The words, sharp and cutting, hung in the air between us. "Do you even hear yourself? You don't have a plan. You're all instinct and no strategy."

My pulse quickened, a mix of frustration and something else. Something that gnawed at the edge of my mind, making it hard to think clearly. "Maybe I don't need a plan. Maybe I'm just trying to do something good for once." The words tasted bitter in my mouth, like I was trying to convince myself as much as him.

"Doing good isn't always enough. It's about surviving. That's what matters." He stepped closer, his voice lowering into a dangerous whisper. "And if you keep getting in the way, we'll both be dead before we even get close to finishing this."

I knew he was right. But God, I hated hearing it from him. Gabriel had this way of making everything sound so final, as if his world view was the only one worth having. I took a breath, trying to push past the weight of his words, but it didn't quite work. Instead, I felt the silence settle between us like an uncomfortable companion, the kind you can't shake no matter how hard you try.

He shifted his weight, glancing over his shoulder toward the fading light of the city, as if the skyline held answers I wasn't privy to. "I'm not saying you're useless, Mia. I'm saying you need to be smarter about how you play this game." He caught my eye, a spark of something I couldn't place flickering behind his guarded expression. "I need you alive, all right? That's the bottom line."

I swallowed hard, the words tumbling out of me before I could stop them. "I'm alive, Gabriel. Barely. But I am." It was a confession, one I didn't expect to make, and the admission felt raw, like peeling back skin to expose something fragile underneath. "I just don't want to go through all this alone."

The words hung there for a moment, heavy, as if the world had briefly stopped to listen. Gabriel didn't say anything at first, his eyes dark and unreadable, but then something shifted. Not much, but enough. He nodded once, sharply, his gaze flicking to the street again. "You won't be alone. But don't think that means I won't tell you when you're wrong."

I couldn't help the small laugh that escaped my lips, wry and bitter. "How generous of you."

His lips twitched in a half-smile, though it didn't reach his eyes. "It's a burden I bear."

The rain had turned from a gentle patter to a steady downpour, the kind that soaked you to the bone in seconds. I took a step back, brushing the wet strands of hair away from my face, my shoes squelching on the sidewalk. "So what now?" I asked, wiping the water off my jacket. "Do we just stand here arguing until we drown?"

Gabriel studied me for a beat, then his expression softened, just slightly. "I don't think that's how it works, no." He pushed a hand through his wet hair, his eyes flicking toward the entrance to the alley. "We keep moving. We find the next piece of the puzzle. And we pray it's enough to keep us out of trouble."

I glanced up at him, feeling the weight of the unspoken words between us. "Do you ever stop to think about what happens if we fail?"

He shrugged, his nonchalance a mask for the uncertainty I knew he wasn't showing. "Failure's not an option, Mia. At least not today."

I didn't respond to that. It didn't need a response. Instead, I turned toward the street, pulling my jacket tighter around me against the cold, letting the rhythm of my steps pull me into the direction we both knew we had to go. Gabriel followed, the sound of his footsteps falling into sync with mine, the rain creating a wall of sound around us. Neither of us spoke again, but the silence wasn't as unbearable this time. There was a subtle, unspoken understanding between us now—a fragile truce. And that, I realized, was the closest we'd come to finding common ground.

The rain had finally stopped, but the air felt thick with humidity, a wet blanket of heat that clung to my skin as we moved through the city's forgotten streets. Gabriel, of course, walked like he owned every inch of this place. His stride was long, measured, as if each step had purpose, each movement a calculated maneuver. It was so different from my own, a mixture of haste and hesitation, always shifting between wanting to be anywhere but here and knowing there was no other choice.

I caught his gaze as we passed under the dim glow of a streetlight, the neon signs overhead casting an electric wash of pinks and greens across his face. He gave me a look that was half skepticism, half something else—something deeper, more inscrutable. I raised an eyebrow, the challenge in my posture more for my own amusement than anything else.

"You sure you're not just tired of me?" I asked, a playful tone hiding the tightness in my chest. I hated how often I had to swallow that knot of unease when it came to him. He was the kind of person who made everything seem effortless, while I was just... trying to keep my footing in a world that constantly shifted beneath me.

Gabriel didn't even flinch, his voice smooth and detached. "It's not you I'm tired of, Mia. It's everything else." He cast a glance up at the towering buildings around us, their facades cracked and worn, their windows glowing faintly from within. "I'm starting to wonder if anything in this city is worth saving."

"Nothing's worth saving if you're not in it for the long haul," I said, folding my arms across my chest. I hated how true that sounded. My mind flashed to my earlier argument with Gabriel, his cold words still ringing in my ears. The man was a master of isolation. He could freeze you out without even trying. It was a talent, really, how effortlessly he did it.

Gabriel glanced over at me, eyes sharp like he'd been waiting for me to let something slip. "You think you're in this for the long haul? You're just here for the thrill, Mia. And when it's over, you'll be gone, same as always."

I could feel the weight of his words, like stones dropping into my gut. There it was again. That assumption. The one that made everything feel like a temporary arrangement. Like I was the unreliable one, the flighty one, the one who never stuck around.

But this time, I didn't bite. Instead, I turned the conversation around. "What about you, Gabriel? You seem to have an aversion to the idea of sticking around. Ever wonder why?"

He stopped walking then, just for a second, his hand brushing against the side of a graffiti-covered wall as if the action gave him pause. For a brief moment, I caught the flicker of vulnerability—something fleeting, like a shadow crossing his face—but it was gone before I could process it.

"I don't stick around because sticking around is what gets people killed," he said, and the words were so flat, so certain, that they almost didn't sound like they came from him. "It's not about trust or loyalty. It's about surviving."

"Survival," I echoed, feeling the irony like a punch in the gut. "I guess we're both in it for that, then. But for some reason, I'm still trying to figure out why you think I'm the problem."

Gabriel's lips quirked, like he was trying to suppress a smile. "You're a lot of things, Mia. But 'problem' isn't one of them." His voice softened, just a touch. "You just... make things more complicated than they need to be. You want answers. You want to understand everything. I don't care about that. I care about getting to the end."

"And what happens when you reach the end?" I asked, my words cutting through the haze of his indifference. "Do you just walk away, Gabriel? Leave everything in the dust? What's the point of surviving if you've lost everything that made it worth it in the first place?"

There was a long pause. The city's ambient hum—the distant sounds of car horns, sirens, and music from a nearby bar—filled the silence between us. Gabriel looked up, his eyes scanning the darkened horizon as if the answers were written somewhere out there, just beyond the flickering lights of the street.

"I'm not the type to get sentimental," he finally said, his voice a low murmur. "But I'm not stupid either. There's always a price. And sometimes, the cost of survival is more than you can afford."

I had no words for that. What do you say to someone who views the world like it's a series of transactions, each more expensive than the last?

Before I could respond, a shadow shifted on the corner ahead, and I felt my muscles tense instinctively. Gabriel's hand shot out, gripping my wrist with surprising force, pulling me to a stop.

"Stay behind me," he muttered, his gaze flicking over to the figure that had emerged from the alley.

I didn't argue. Whatever was coming toward us—whatever shadow it was that Gabriel had sensed long before I did—wasn't something we wanted to face head-on. Not yet, anyway.

The figure drew closer, the dim glow of the streetlights barely illuminating a familiar face. Amara. Of course. She was always lurking, always watching, as though she had nothing better to do than observe our failed attempts at getting along.

"Is this your version of an intervention?" I asked, half-laughing, half-annoyed, my body still coiled in readiness.

Amara's lips curled up in that infuriating way, a smirk that spoke of too many secrets. "I'd say it's more of a reminder. You two are more connected than you think. Whether you like it or not." She took a step forward, her voice a smooth whisper. "I do enjoy the banter, though. Explosive, but necessary."

Amara's presence had that same unnerving quality it always did, like she knew the future but wasn't quite ready to reveal it. I shifted my weight, glancing over at Gabriel, whose expression had gone almost unreadable. Of course, Amara would show up now—right when we were at the peak of our discomfort with each other. She always had perfect timing.

"Explosive, but necessary?" I asked, trying to sound more casual than I felt. "Well, isn't that charming. What, exactly, are we necessary for, Amara? More of your cryptic little missions?"

She tilted her head, her dark eyes glinting with amusement. "Let's just say the storm you two are brewing will eventually clear the air. But you'll need to keep at it for a little while longer."

"Great," Gabriel muttered under his breath, clearly annoyed. "More vagueness. Just what I needed."

I could feel the sarcasm hanging in the air like a cloud, heavy and thick. Amara was no stranger to vague answers. She reveled in it, like she enjoyed leaving us in the dark while she pulled the strings from some unseen corner.

"I don't know about you two," Amara continued, her voice syrupy sweet with a hint of something darker beneath it, "but I'm getting bored of watching the two of you clash. It's amusing, yes, but we're running out of time."

Gabriel shot her a glare, but it had little effect. Amara was a force of nature, untouchable, like the storm she so often invoked. The sort of person who could melt into the shadows as easily as she could show up at the most inconvenient moment and expect you to follow her wherever she led.

"Out of time for what?" I demanded. "You're going to tell us, right? Because I'm getting the sense that you're about to drop another bombshell and walk away before we can do anything about it."

Amara's lips curved into something between a smirk and a smile, her expression unreadable. "You'll know soon enough, Mia. Both of you will."

I glanced at Gabriel, who was studying Amara with an intensity that bordered on discomfort. His jaw was clenched, his fists at his sides, like he was ready to punch something or someone—preferably her, no doubt.

"We'll know soon enough, huh?" Gabriel said, voice low and laced with skepticism. "That's exactly what we need right now, isn't it? More secrets, more waiting. Well, I'm done waiting."

I saw the twitch in his jaw, the frustration building in him. It was almost as if the very act of waiting was against his nature. Gabriel was the kind of person who needed action. He needed results.

And then there was me—the one who felt a strange mix of dread and anticipation swirling around every word, every glance. Gabriel had made me feel like I was in the wrong for wanting answers. He made me feel reckless for questioning everything around us. But there was something in the air tonight, something unspoken, that made me feel like I wasn't just reacting to him—I was reacting to everything.

Amara sighed dramatically, a delicate little noise that only made me want to roll my eyes. "Honestly, if you two weren't so stubborn, we could get this over with already. But, well, here we are."

Her eyes met mine, and for a second, the weight of them felt heavier than the damp street beneath our feet. "You're going to need each other more than you think, Mia. More than Gabriel here is willing to admit."

"I don't need anyone," Gabriel said quickly, turning away, his voice a cold slice in the night air.

But Amara wasn't done. She rarely was.

"Remember that the next time you're standing at a crossroads," she said cryptically, a wicked gleam dancing in her eyes. "Because it won't be just your survival on the line anymore."

With that, she turned on her heel, disappearing as quickly as she had arrived, her presence evaporating into the misty shadows that clung to the alley.

I didn't say anything immediately. The silence between Gabriel and me was thick, suffocating. My brain was too full of Amara's words—too full of the idea that we were both caught in something much bigger than either of us could understand. But neither of us had the luxury of walking away. Not now. Not after everything we'd been through.

I felt a surge of irritation, and my mouth betrayed me. "Well, that was enlightening."

Gabriel didn't respond right away, but I could feel his tension in the air around me. He was like a coiled spring, barely holding himself together. It was almost like he was trying to convince himself that this was all a waste of time, that there was no reason to take Amara seriously, but I saw the shift in his eyes. The uncertainty. The part of him that wanted to shut out anything that might force him to rely on someone else.

"You've got a strange way of dealing with pressure," he finally said, his voice tight. "Poking at everything until it falls apart."

"Maybe," I replied, my gaze hardening. "But it's better than pretending like everything's fine when it's obviously not."

The look he gave me was like fire and ice—sharp, cutting, and undeniably magnetic. "Maybe you're right. But sometimes, Mia, not everything's meant to be fixed. Some things are just broken."

The words hung in the air between us, charged, the city's pulse beating around us as if in sync with the tension building between us.

A sudden sound caught my attention—footsteps, sharp and fast. My body tensed. Something was wrong.

We weren't alone anymore.

I barely had time to process the shift before Gabriel was already moving, pulling me behind him as he scanned the surroundings with military precision. The hairs on the back of my neck stood up, and I instinctively reached for the small knife I kept tucked in my jacket.

The sound of approaching footsteps grew louder, heavier. I couldn't see anything through the rain-soaked night, but I could feel the danger creeping closer.

And then, just as I took a step forward, ready to face whatever was coming, the figure stepped into the light.

It wasn't Amara.

It was someone worse. Someone who had no business being here.

Someone I knew all too well.

Chapter 8: The City of Whispers

The city stretched before me like a forgotten dream—half-crumbling walls draped in the desert's dusty fingers, old stone towers etched with stories that no one had bothered to translate in years. It was the kind of place that felt like it was both living and dying, all at once. I could almost hear the ghosts whispering beneath the weight of the sand. Even Gabriel, who was as hard as the rocks surrounding us, didn't seem immune to the quiet urgency that gripped the place. His jaw was tight, his eyes scanning the horizon as if waiting for something to spring from the shadows.

We walked in silence, the crunch of our boots on the dry earth loud in the stillness. The streets were narrow, winding, the buildings leaning in on us, like they were listening to our every step. I didn't dare look up. There was something about the sky here—so wide and empty, like it was holding its breath for the storm it knew was coming.

My hand brushed against Gabriel's. A fleeting touch, but it lingered, a silent acknowledgment of the strange bond that had been forming between us ever since we'd stepped foot on this cursed land. He didn't pull away, but neither did he look at me. His focus was elsewhere—on the shadows creeping through the alleyways, on the shifting silhouettes that seemed to haunt every corner of this ancient city. I couldn't blame him. We were far from alone here. The city was alive in its own strange way.

"Is it just me," I said, my voice low, "or is the air here… different?"

Gabriel didn't respond immediately, but I could see the muscle in his neck twitch, the way his hand gripped his weapon a little tighter. He wasn't much for words—especially when they had no immediate use. But he did nod, as if confirming the silent agreement that this place wasn't just unwelcoming; it was suffocating. The desert had a way of making you feel like you didn't belong, like you were some trespasser who was about to pay for your ignorance.

We rounded a corner, and the light shifted, throwing long, eerie shadows across the path. I could feel the weight of the city pressing in on me, a pressure in my chest that wasn't entirely from the heat. It was as though the walls themselves were watching us, waiting for us to slip up. A wrong move here could cost you everything, I was sure of it.

"There's something wrong about this place," I said, glancing at Gabriel. He was already looking at me, his dark eyes narrowed. I hated how well he could read me. It made me feel like there was nothing left to hide.

"Careful, Seraphina," he said, his voice clipped. "People here don't appreciate outsiders asking too many questions."

I raised an eyebrow. "You sound like you know that from experience."

He didn't answer. He didn't need to. I could see the past written in his tense posture, in the way his eyes flicked to every shadow, every potential threat. Gabriel wasn't just any wanderer; he was someone who'd survived here. But even that didn't make him an expert. Not in this city. Not in the desert.

We kept walking, but the silence between us thickened. It wasn't just the weight of the city that unnerved me. It was the way Gabriel was starting to behave, the way he seemed... different. More human, somehow. More reachable. I couldn't put my finger on it, but the distance that had always been there between us was beginning to shrink. Maybe it was the shared fear of being in a place so ancient and full of secrets, or maybe it was the fact that neither of us trusted this place enough to face it alone. Whatever it was, the fact remained: We were in this together now, whether we liked it or not.

I turned my attention back to the surroundings, and that's when I saw it—a flicker of movement ahead, just on the edge of the streetlamp's glow. My heart stuttered in my chest, and I took a step closer to Gabriel, pressing my shoulder to his. He didn't flinch, but his hand was already moving towards the hilt of his blade, his body tense with the same recognition I had felt. There was something here. Something watching.

The city wasn't just empty. It was alive in the shadows.

A low hum rose in the distance, a sound that was more felt than heard. It vibrated through the ground, a pulse that matched my racing heart. I couldn't place it, but it sent a chill crawling up my spine. Gabriel's lips pressed into a thin line, and his eyes darted around, searching for the source. I could see his every muscle coiled, ready to spring into action.

"Stay close," he muttered, his voice rough, as though the words had been dragged from him against his will.

I didn't argue. The hum grew louder, a strange resonance that seemed to fill the entire street, vibrating beneath my feet. And then, from the shadows, a figure emerged. Tall, cloaked in darkness, with only the faintest glint of metal visible beneath its hood. I could see nothing of its face, but I could feel its gaze—cold, unyielding, like it was looking straight through me.

Gabriel stepped forward, his body blocking mine, but I wasn't afraid. Not of the figure. Not of the danger I knew was coming. No, I was afraid of the quiet, the way it held us, the way it wrapped around us, pulling us deeper into this city of whispers. And I could hear the truth in the hum now—it wasn't just the desert wind. It was the sound of something old, something angry, waiting for us to make the wrong move. Something that had been buried for too long.

"Who are you?" I asked, my voice steady despite the chaos building in my chest. I didn't expect an answer. And I didn't get one. Instead, the figure tilted its head slightly, as if considering me. And then it spoke, its voice a low rasp, like gravel scraping across stone.

"The city remembers," it said. And with that, it was gone, swallowed up by the shadows once again.

The city loomed before us, still and silent, as if suspended in time. Its ancient walls, weathered and cracked, seemed to sag under the weight of their own secrets. The desert sun had begun to set, casting long, trembling shadows that crept across the stone. Even the breeze, usually a welcome relief from the heat, felt like a breath held too long—stale, as though the land itself was waiting for something. But for what? That was the question gnawing at me, an itch I couldn't quite scratch.

Gabriel and I moved like shadows, careful not to break the silence that seemed to seep into every crack of the city. I wanted to break it, wanted to talk—ask him about the figure we'd seen, about the hum that had vibrated through my bones—but he wasn't one for questions. At least not the kind that didn't have immediate answers. So, we kept walking, our footsteps muffled by the shifting sands at the edges of the street. The only sound between us was the distant echo of the hum, a low vibration that seemed to follow us, always just beyond reach.

"What do you think it meant?" I finally asked, my voice cutting through the oppressive quiet. Gabriel didn't even flinch. He had an uncanny ability to remain still, to stand on the edge of chaos without so much as a twitch of his hand. It unnerved me sometimes. More than sometimes, if I were honest.

"The city remembers," he repeated, his voice just above a murmur. "Remember what? That's the part that worries me."

I couldn't argue with that. There was a tension in the air, a sense that something was about to snap. I felt it in my skin, the hairs on my arms standing to attention, every instinct telling me to keep moving, to keep my eyes wide open. But we couldn't rush. This was the kind of place where every corner turned, every alleyway glanced down, could reveal something far more dangerous than we were prepared for. Gabriel had taught me that much: slow and steady, and never, ever let your guard down.

We rounded another bend, and the street opened up into a small square. At the center stood an old fountain, its waters long since dried up, leaving only a shell of what it once was. The stone was cracked, weathered by years of neglect, and yet the intricate carvings on its surface were still visible—lines of ancient symbols I didn't recognize, their meaning lost to the ages. I stepped closer, my boots crunching against the gravel as I reached out to trace the markings with my fingers.

"What is this place?" I muttered to myself, though I didn't really expect an answer. I'd already learned that everything here was a puzzle, each piece hidden in plain sight, daring you to look closer.

Gabriel's voice came from behind me, sharp and direct. "Don't touch anything."

I jerked my hand back, surprised by the vehemence in his tone. It wasn't like him to sound so... emotional. I turned, and for the first time since we'd entered the city, I saw a flicker of something in his eyes—fear, maybe? No, it wasn't fear, but something close to it. He didn't want to admit it, not even to himself, but this city had gotten under his skin.

"I'm fine," I said, brushing off the moment, trying to make light of it. "I was just... curious."

He didn't reply, his jaw tight as he scanned the area, his gaze sharp, alert. There was a tension in the air now, a thickness that settled between us, and the sound of the hum grew louder, closer.

I glanced around, trying to pinpoint the source, but all I could see were the same half-buried structures, the same crumbling walls. It was as if the city was closing in on us, making its presence known in the most subtle of ways.

"It's here," Gabriel said, his voice low, almost inaudible. "Somewhere in the city."

I frowned. "What is?"

He didn't answer immediately, but his hand was on the hilt of his blade again, his stance shifting as though preparing for something. He was getting agitated, and I didn't like it. He was usually the one who remained calm, who had all the answers. But now, in this city, it was like he was just as lost as I was.

"It's been waiting," he muttered, more to himself than to me. "We shouldn't be here."

I shook my head, dismissing his words. "We've been over this. We have to be here. This is the only place left to go."

His eyes met mine then, and for the briefest of moments, I saw the weight of everything he'd been carrying. He was used to being alone, to fighting battles without anyone by his side. This city, though, was different. It had a way of pulling you in, of making you question everything you thought you knew.

"You don't understand," he said, his voice barely above a whisper. "This place... it takes things from you. Pieces of who you are."

I frowned, not understanding. "What does that mean?"

But Gabriel didn't answer. He was already moving, stepping away from the fountain and pulling me along with him. There was a sense of urgency in his movements now, a quickness to his step that told me something had changed. Something in him had shifted. I didn't know what it was, but it was as though we were running out of time, and the city knew it.

We didn't get far before the ground beneath us began to tremble, faint at first, like a distant rumble of thunder. But then it grew, the vibrations rattling through my bones. I stumbled, my heart pounding in my chest, and Gabriel grabbed my arm, steadying me. His grip was tight, but his eyes were wide, focused on something ahead.

It was then I saw it—a figure, cloaked in darkness, emerging from the shadows of an alleyway. Its movements were slow, deliberate, as if it were savoring the moment. I could feel its eyes on me, though I couldn't see its face. The hum was almost deafening now, filling my ears, blocking out everything else.

Gabriel's voice was a harsh whisper. "Stay behind me."

But it was too late. The figure was already moving toward us. And this time, there would be no running.

I could feel the figure drawing closer, its presence unmistakable now, like the air had thickened with the weight of its gaze. The hum had intensified, vibrating through the soles of my boots, my bones. It wasn't just an annoyance anymore; it was a force, something ancient and dark, like a promise that something was about to be unleashed.

Gabriel's grip on my arm tightened, but I could see the subtle tremor in his hand. For a moment, I thought I saw a flash of doubt in his eyes, something that spoke of long-forgotten fears, of past mistakes. But before I could ask, the figure in the shadows moved again, a graceful glide toward us that was almost hypnotic in its fluidity.

I couldn't make out its features, only the outline of its figure, shrouded in darkness. It was tall—taller than Gabriel—and its movements were unnervingly smooth, as if it wasn't entirely bound by the same rules of gravity that we were.

"Stay behind me," Gabriel whispered again, his voice harsh, edged with the kind of urgency that made the hairs on the back of my neck stand up.

I didn't have time to argue. There was no time for anything other than action. The figure stopped a few paces away, and the hum that had been creeping under my skin became deafening. It was so loud now that I felt it in my teeth, in the pit of my stomach. Like it was inside me, filling up every corner of my body. I swallowed hard, trying to steady my breath.

The air felt charged, like the city itself was waiting for something to snap.

"Who are you?" I asked, forcing the words out despite the tightness in my chest.

The figure tilted its head slightly, and though its face was hidden beneath the deep folds of its cloak, I could feel its eyes on me. Cold, ancient eyes. I wasn't sure if it had eyes at all, if it even had a face, but I knew it was looking at me. And I knew it could see right through me.

"Not who," it said, its voice low and resonant, like it was speaking from the depths of the earth itself. The words seemed to wrap around me, pulling me deeper into something I didn't fully understand. "What."

I frowned, confused. "What?"

The figure took a step forward, and I instinctively took a step back, the gravel crunching beneath my feet. Gabriel moved in front of me, his hand on the hilt of his blade. But even he didn't seem entirely sure of his next move. He was staring at the figure like it was the embodiment of every nightmare he'd ever had, like he was facing something far worse than any threat he had ever encountered.

"You've come for it, haven't you?" the figure continued, its voice growing colder. "For what it holds. The city remembers... and it will take what it is owed."

The weight of its words hit me like a physical blow. My heart skipped a beat. What was this thing talking about? What did it mean, 'what it holds'? What could this city possibly owe, and to whom?

Gabriel stepped forward then, his voice steady but filled with something dangerous, something that made the air crackle with tension. "We didn't come for anything. We're just passing through."

The figure didn't respond immediately. Instead, it seemed to consider Gabriel, then me, as if weighing our souls in a single glance. I could feel the pulse of its gaze, cold and calculating, and for a moment, I wondered if it was judging us, measuring us against some standard we didn't even understand.

Then it spoke again, and its voice was like the scraping of stone against stone. "You will leave this city with nothing, or you will leave it with everything. But it will take its toll."

The ground beneath us trembled again, more violently this time. My knees buckled, and I reached for Gabriel's arm to steady myself. The hum grew louder, almost unbearable now, and for a brief moment, I thought I could hear something else beneath it—voices, whispers, murmurs, like a hundred souls begging to be released.

Suddenly, the figure lunged. It was impossibly fast, closing the distance between us in the blink of an eye. I gasped, instinctively pulling back, but Gabriel's arm was already around me, pulling me behind him, his blade drawn and ready.

But the figure didn't attack. It stopped inches from Gabriel, its face still hidden. I could feel the heat of its presence, a heat that made the air feel like it was thickening, suffocating us both.

It reached out with one long, slender hand, and for a moment, I thought it might touch Gabriel's chest, press into him like some kind of dark, probing force. But it didn't. Instead, it opened its hand, palm up, and a small shard of something glowed in the darkness. A stone, I thought at first, but no—this wasn't a stone.

This was something alive.

"What is that?" I whispered, unable to look away from the object that hovered between the figure's fingers. It was the color of blood, glowing faintly, pulsating with an unnatural rhythm. It felt alive, like it had a heartbeat of its own.

The figure didn't answer, just extended the shard closer, offering it to Gabriel.

"You must take it," the figure rasped, its voice low and full of warning. "Only then can you leave."

Gabriel hesitated, his hand twitching near his blade, but he didn't make a move. His eyes flicked from the shard to the figure and back again, weighing his options. I could see his mind working, the gears turning, the calculation in his eyes. He wasn't foolish enough to trust the thing, but neither was he foolish enough to refuse it outright.

"I don't want your gift," he said, his voice hard, sharp.

The figure's lips parted, but instead of words, a low, guttural sound escaped from deep within its chest. It wasn't a laugh, but it might as well have been. It was a sound of knowing, of something far older than time itself, something that had seen everything and understood nothing.

"You do not have a choice," it said softly.

And then, before either of us could react, the shard pulsed with light, and the city around us seemed to tremble. The stone walls, the broken buildings, the sand beneath our feet—all of it seemed to shudder in unison. I heard a voice, faint at first, then clearer and clearer, until it filled my ears like a scream.

And then the ground gave way.
I was falling.

Chapter 9: The Curse Revealed

The old warehouse on Seventh Street smelled of rust and dust, the air thick with the remnants of forgotten decades. It was quiet enough to hear the faint hum of electricity from the overhead lights, flickering sporadically as though the building itself was unsure of what it had become. I stood in the middle of it, staring at the artifact—an ancient, jagged stone pulsing with an eerie green glow. It sat atop a cracked pedestal, surrounded by dust motes that danced in the dim light like the ghosts of those who had come before us. My fingers itched to touch it, even though I knew better.

Gabriel stood a few feet behind me, his dark eyes narrowed, always on edge. He had warned me—repeatedly—that this wasn't our battle. But as usual, I didn't listen. Some things, like instinct and fate, aren't so easily avoided. If it was a fight we needed to win to break the curse, then so be it.

"It's not just a relic," Gabriel continued, his voice a low growl of frustration. "It's a trap. You think we can just waltz in, claim it, and walk out?"

I shifted, not taking my eyes off the stone. "I've never been good at waltzing."

The tension in Gabriel's shoulders didn't ease. He was always so serious, so earnest. His presence was like a thunderstorm, constant and threatening, and yet, it made him impossible to ignore. There was something in the way he stood there, hands clenched at his sides, his jaw tight, that made it clear he didn't trust me, not fully. Not yet. I could hardly blame him. Trust wasn't a luxury we could afford, not when we were dealing with the kind of power the curse held.

"I know you don't believe in fate, but I do," Gabriel said, his gaze hard. "This thing, this curse—it's not something we can just solve by breaking a few rules. You're playing with forces you can't even begin to understand."

"And you think I don't know that?" I snapped, spinning to face him. "You think I didn't feel the weight of it the moment I stepped into that library and saw the first warning in the old texts? You think I didn't feel the chains tightening around my wrists every time we got closer to this damn stone?" My voice wavered, but I didn't care. "But what choice do I have? Walk away and leave it to someone else?"

Gabriel's eyes softened, just for a moment, before hardening again. "If we don't do this the right way, we're both dead, Lyra. You know that. The curse has already begun to take its toll. You don't think it's after us?"

The memory of the first sign—an inexplicable fire that burned down half the block, leaving nothing but ash in its wake—flashed through my mind. It had been subtle at first, the whispers and strange occurrences. But it had grown, feeding off our every move, tightening its grip around everything we loved. I didn't need him to remind me. I knew the cost.

The question was whether it would be worth it. The artifact was the only key to breaking the curse. I didn't understand why, but I knew it was true. The elders had warned us—talked about a sacrifice, one that neither Gabriel nor I was prepared to make. That, I knew for sure.

"We don't have time to second-guess," I said, my voice low but resolute. "We've come this far. And we're going to finish it."

Gabriel's lips parted, his expression somewhere between a sigh and a curse, before he ran a hand through his hair. "Fine. But you're not doing it alone."

A chill swept through me at his words, and I glanced over my shoulder at him, suddenly aware of the weight of the moment. His decision had been made—he was as bound to this as I was.

But there was something in his eyes that I couldn't quite read, a hesitation buried beneath the surface of his unwavering determination.

The curse wasn't just about us. It wasn't just about saving ourselves or breaking free of a shadow that followed us every waking moment. It was about the city—about everything we had lost.

As Gabriel stepped closer, his boots thudding against the wooden floor, I felt the air shift again, thickening with an energy I couldn't quite place. A door creaked open somewhere deeper in the warehouse, though there was no one else here. It was the kind of noise that made the hairs on the back of your neck stand up.

And then the whisper came.

I stiffened, my heart skipping a beat. It wasn't in my head. It was real—an echo that floated through the space, barely audible at first, but growing stronger with each passing moment.

Come closer... come closer, Lyra...

The voice was serpentine, sweet like honey, but with a darkness coiled beneath it. I knew what it was—what it wanted.

I reached for the artifact before I could stop myself, my fingers brushing the surface of the stone, the coldness of it shocking against my skin.

Too late, the voice said. You're already mine.

The floor beneath me groaned, the very foundation of the warehouse shaking as if the building itself was alive and aware of the danger. My pulse raced, and I yanked my hand back, but it was too late. The green glow from the stone flared brighter, brighter until it was blinding.

And then it stopped.

The whisper faded. The shaking ceased.

I stood there, gasping, heart pounding as if I had just outrun a thousand ghosts. Gabriel was beside me in an instant, his hand on my arm, his voice barely a murmur in the sudden silence.

"What did you do?"

I swallowed hard, trying to regain my bearings. "I think... I think I just made it angry."

The air around us buzzed, thick with the hum of ancient energy, as if the very walls of the warehouse were alive and listening. Gabriel's hand tightened on my arm, his grip firm but not unkind. His jaw was clenched, and I could feel the heat radiating off him, his temper rising faster than I could control my own.

"You shouldn't have touched it," he muttered, his voice low, but carrying that warning I had heard so many times before. The frustration in his tone made my teeth grind together. He wasn't wrong—part of me knew it—but there was something inside me that refused to retreat, to back away from what had already begun. I had made my choice.

I turned slowly, looking up at him, my expression unreadable, but the glint in my eyes was unmistakable. "If we're going to survive this, Gabriel, I need to do it my way."

The tension between us was a living thing now, crawling across the space, almost palpable. Gabriel's lips pressed into a tight line, his brow furrowed as if the weight of my words didn't quite sink in. He wasn't used to me—this version of me, the one who didn't second-guess every decision. The one who didn't shrink from the storm.

"You always say that," he replied, his tone quieter now, almost tender, despite the sharpness that still lingered. "But sometimes, Lyra, your way isn't enough."

I wanted to argue, to tell him that I didn't care, but the truth was, deep down, I felt the same uncertainty creeping in. I had no idea what I was doing. The artifact, the curse—it was bigger than both of us. And the further I reached into it, the more it felt like I was slipping, losing my grip.

Before I could answer, the air around us shifted again, the tension crackling as the stone at the center of the room pulsed brighter, its green glow filling the space, casting eerie shadows on the walls. The hum intensified, vibrating through the floor and up my spine, each wave of sound like the beat of a drum, a heartbeat that didn't belong to me.

"We've woken something," Gabriel said, his voice barely above a whisper, his eyes narrowing at the artifact as if it were the source of all their troubles.

The ground beneath us groaned, the creaking sound of old wood protesting against something heavier than gravity. For a moment, I thought I saw movement in the shadows—a figure, dark and fleeting, slipping between the cracks in the walls. I blinked, and it was gone.

"This is no ordinary curse," I muttered, as much to myself as to Gabriel. "It's... alive."

We both knew what that meant. The artifacts, the curses, the whispers—the city's elders had warned us of this very thing. The curse wasn't a simple spell that could be undone by incantations or breaking a few rules. No, it had roots that burrowed deep into the very fabric of the city, feeding off its history, its pain, its regrets.

Gabriel stepped closer, the heat of his body pressing against mine as his hand found the hilt of the dagger at his waist. It was a gesture of preparation, but something about the way he moved felt too rehearsed, like he had made peace with what was coming. His dark eyes flickered with something I couldn't quite name, a mix of resolve and fear.

"I don't think we can control this anymore," he said quietly, his voice nearly lost in the pulse of the artifact. "Whatever we've unleashed—it's not going to let us go without a fight."

The words hit me like a punch to the gut. I had been hoping—praying—that we could still find a way out, that the artifact, despite its power, could be managed. But as Gabriel spoke, I knew it was too late for that. We were already too far in.

My eyes flicked back to the glowing stone, its pulse steady now, slow but insistent. The air felt thicker, heavier, like I was breathing underwater, each inhale a struggle to maintain composure. And then it happened.

The ground cracked. A loud, deafening snap of splintering wood filled the space, and the pedestal holding the artifact shattered into pieces, sending fragments of ancient stone skittering across the floor. A dark shadow, thick and swirling like smoke, began to rise from the broken stone, coiling around us, twisting and warping the very air itself.

Gabriel grabbed my arm, pulling me back, but the shadow seemed to have a life of its own, advancing, pressing in from all sides. It felt cold—so cold—that the chill cut through to my bones. And then, as if it were mocking us, the voice returned.

You think you can break the chains? You think you can win?

I fought the urge to recoil, but the words settled deep into my chest, an echo that wouldn't let go. It wasn't just a voice—it was a presence, an awareness, a deep, malevolent thing that seemed to be everywhere, filling every corner of the room, wrapping itself around my thoughts like a vine.

Gabriel's grip tightened, his breath steady despite the chaos that was unfolding around us. "Stay close," he said, his voice hoarse, strained.

The darkness pressed in, thickening, surrounding us, but I held my ground. This wasn't a fight we could run from. There was nowhere left to hide.

The shadow lunged forward, its form shifting and changing with terrifying speed. I barely had time to react before Gabriel shoved me out of its path, his body taking the brunt of the blow as he collided with the floor. His grunt of pain echoed through the room, but he was already scrambling back to his feet, his face a mask of determination.

I reached for the dagger at my belt, my fingers finding the hilt, my grip firm despite the tremor in my hands. This was it. There was no turning back now. The artifact had chosen its side. And whether I was ready or not, I was about to make my stand.

"Gabriel—" I started, but the words were lost as the darkness swirled around us once more, its cold tendrils reaching for everything we were, everything we had ever been.

And in that moment, I realized something terrifying. It wasn't just the city that was cursed. It was us.

The shadow writhed, taking form with unnatural speed, its edges jagged like broken glass. It was less like a creature and more like the embodiment of something terrible, something ancient. Gabriel's face paled as the darkness swarmed closer, folding itself around us, a suffocating force that made the air feel thick and brittle. My heart hammered against my ribcage, the weight of the moment pressing down so heavily that for a split second, I almost forgot how to breathe.

I had expected power, yes, but not like this. This felt wrong—like we were trespassing in a space where no living thing was meant to stand. And yet, here we were, trapped between the past and the present, with no clear way forward except through the storm of everything we had unearthed.

"Lyra, listen to me—" Gabriel started, his voice strained, his hand moving to my shoulder, shaking me slightly, like he was trying to get through to me. But his words died before they could form. He didn't need to say anything. He was terrified, and I knew why.

Because so was I.

There was no rationalizing our way out of this. The stone's glow had faded, but the curse remained, pulsing like the sickening beat of a drum too deep for the ear to hear. And the figure that stood before us now—no longer just a swirling mass but a man, or something like one—stepped forward, eyes gleaming with malevolent hunger.

"You should have stayed away," the creature spoke, its voice laced with venom, heavy with centuries of malice. Its mouth didn't move the way a human's would, but somehow the words still struck as clearly as if they had been shouted in our faces. "The artifact was never meant to be claimed."

It wasn't a voice I could place, not human, not entirely. It was both ancient and new, familiar and foreign all at once, like hearing a song that haunted your dreams but was always just beyond your reach.

I took a breath, steadying myself. "Well, too bad for you. We're here now," I said, my voice shaking despite my attempt at bravado. I didn't even recognize the sound of my own words, as if they were coming from a stranger's mouth.

Gabriel shifted beside me, his eyes flicking to the shadow with the kind of instinct that said this battle wasn't something I could win alone. "We need to destroy it. Now."

But the shadow only laughed, a sound that was as cold as it was chilling, like the scrape of a thousand nails on a chalkboard. "Destroy it? Do you even understand what you've unleashed? You think you have the power to break this curse, but you will only feed it."

My pulse quickened, the weight of its words settling in, heavy like stone. My hands, shaking slightly, reached for the hilt of my dagger, but I hesitated. What was the point? What did any of this mean? We hadn't even begun to comprehend the full scope of the curse, and now we were supposed to destroy it?

"I've heard your warning," I said, forcing my voice to remain steady, "but we're not backing down."

The creature didn't respond immediately. It moved, fluid and unnatural, its limbs stretching in ways that defied all reason. It stepped forward, closer now, until I could feel the pull of its presence like a magnet, tugging at the very air around us. The space felt smaller, as though the walls themselves were closing in, squeezing tighter with every passing second.

And then, with a sudden flick of its wrist, it cast something at us—a rush of shadow, faster than I could react, wrapping around Gabriel's arm and pulling him forward. He grunted, caught off guard, but his reflexes were quick. He twisted, throwing the force off just enough to avoid being fully engulfed. But I could see the strain in his eyes, the realization that this wasn't something we could just muscle through.

"Gabriel!" I shouted, but it felt hollow, swallowed by the room's dark, oppressive silence.

Before I could do anything, the creature raised its hand again, and this time, the shadow lashed out toward me. I barely dodged it, the cold tendrils brushing my side, and I hissed in pain as a burn of ice seared through my skin. It wasn't physical, not entirely—it was deeper, a coldness that seemed to gnaw at my very soul.

"Stop!" I yelled, my voice rising in desperation. "Just tell me what you want!"

The creature paused, its gleaming eyes locking onto mine with an intensity that made my skin crawl. Its mouth twisted into something that wasn't quite a smile, but it was no less cruel for it.

"What I want, Lyra, is what you have already given me." Its voice, low and menacing, filled every corner of the room. "You are the sacrifice. You, or someone else."

The words hit me like a punch to the gut. I staggered back, blinking hard as the meaning behind its cryptic statement settled in. I thought about the elders' warnings, the mysterious texts, the whispers that had followed us from the start. The curse had never been just a curse. It had always been about power, about control, about a price—one we hadn't realized we would have to pay.

I swallowed hard, my mind racing. "You're lying," I shot back, even though I knew deep down that I wasn't certain of anything anymore.

The creature only smiled again, this time wider, its teeth sharp like jagged shards of glass.

"I am not lying," it said, its tone almost soothing, as though it were trying to lull me into a false sense of security. "But you will understand soon enough. There is no escape from what is already here."

Gabriel made a sudden move, breaking free from the shadow's grasp and lunging toward me. But it was too late—before he could reach me, the creature's form surged forward, enveloping him in a shroud of darkness.

I froze, my heart pounding in my ears, as Gabriel's desperate shout was swallowed by the abyss. The shadow twisted tighter, until I could no longer see him—until it was as if he had been erased from existence.

And in that moment, I understood the terrifying truth. The curse wasn't just about us. It was a game—and we were the pieces.

Chapter 10: Secrets in the Sand

The heat of the late afternoon sun beat down on the ancient ruins, its rays sharp enough to make the very air shimmer. A gust of wind swept through the dry sand, stirring up tiny eddies that danced in front of me like ghosts, whispering the secrets of this forgotten world. I had been standing there for what felt like an eternity, my boots pressed deep into the sand, the weight of Gabriel's confession settling heavily in my chest. I had asked the question, but hearing the answer... it was like swallowing a stone. His past wasn't the tale of a man in search of gold or fame, but something far more personal, far more tangled. He had come here, to this place, to find a piece of himself—one he hadn't even known he was missing until it was already lost.

I let the wind tug at the edges of my jacket, trying to cool the sudden flush creeping across my skin. My mind was a tangled mess, replaying his words over and over again. "What's yours?" Gabriel had asked, his voice low, almost teasing, but there had been a quiet challenge in it too—something daring me to admit what I had come here for. And I didn't have an answer. Not one that would make any sense, at least.

I shifted my weight from one foot to the other, taking in the sight of the ruins around us. They stood like ancient sentinels, stoic and silent, a witness to countless years of time slipping by unnoticed. I could feel the weight of their presence pressing on me, as if the stones themselves were waiting for me to make a decision. As if they knew something I didn't. And maybe they did. Maybe I had been blind to everything that had led me here, to this moment, to this confrontation with Gabriel.

His eyes—those dark, unreadable eyes—hadn't given anything away when I'd first demanded the truth. His lips had barely parted, the lines of his face tense, but he hadn't flinched. I knew him well enough by now to know that nothing rattled him. At least, nothing that he wasn't prepared for. His past? That had been buried deeper than any of the treasures he was after. But I had asked for it, and now the air between us felt thick with the weight of his history—one that was darker, more complicated than I had imagined.

I took a slow, steadying breath and glanced back at him. He was still there, standing a few feet away, his stance casual, but the tension in his shoulders told a different story. He wasn't the treasure hunter I had imagined, the charming rogue who could talk his way out of anything. No, he was something more—something harder to define. And suddenly, everything that had brought me here felt like a lie.

"So," I said, my voice quieter than I intended, the words trembling as they left my lips. "You didn't come for the treasure. Not really."

He met my gaze, and for a brief moment, I saw something flicker in those dark eyes—something that made my pulse skip. Was it regret? Longing? I couldn't quite place it, but it was there, hidden in the depths of his stare, and it was enough to make me question everything.

"I came for a piece of something that's been missing for a long time," he admitted, the words slow and deliberate. His tone was steady, but I could hear the undercurrent of something more—something raw. "What I find along the way... that's just a bonus."

I couldn't help but scoff, shaking my head. "A bonus? You're telling me you've spent years of your life—your whole damn career—chasing after something for 'a bonus'? That's a little hard to believe, even for you."

Gabriel's lips curved into a wry smile, the kind that usually made my insides flutter. But today, it only made my stomach tighten with something that wasn't quite frustration but wasn't exactly curiosity either. "Believe it or not, I'm not interested in your opinion on that," he said, his voice carrying that sharp edge of humor I couldn't quite ignore.

I shifted, my eyes narrowing as I met his gaze. The air between us was thick, pulsing with unsaid words and unasked questions. Gabriel's eyes never left mine, and I suddenly realized something: the truth wasn't something he was willing to give me freely. Not now, not when the stakes were so high. There was more to his story—something deeper, something that had nothing to do with me but everything to do with why he had been drawn to this place. I just didn't know what it was yet.

I felt the prickling at the back of my neck, the sense that I was being drawn into something far more dangerous than I had bargained for. And despite all my instincts telling me to walk away, to leave this place behind, I knew I wasn't going anywhere. Not now. Not when everything I thought I knew about this man was starting to unravel in front of me.

"So," I said again, my voice steadier this time, "what do you expect to find, Gabriel? What's buried in the sand that's so important to you?"

Gabriel hesitated, his eyes flickering briefly to the ruins around us. I followed his gaze, but all I saw were crumbling stones and the dust of forgotten time. Whatever it was he was searching for—whatever this was really about—it wasn't in the ground at our feet. It was something else. Something buried deeper than any artifact could explain.

He didn't answer at first. Instead, he turned, walking a few steps away from me, his back to the ruins, the horizon stretching out before him like a promise. I didn't move, didn't breathe, waiting for him to speak.

And then, almost too quietly to hear, he said, "What if I told you it wasn't a thing I was after? What if I told you it was something... someone?"

The words hit me like a wave, and suddenly, the air was charged with a new kind of tension. My heart skipped. "Someone?" I repeated, half-laughing, half-breathless. "Are you telling me you've been chasing shadows this whole time?"

Gabriel didn't laugh. He didn't even smile. He simply turned to face me, his eyes burning with an intensity I hadn't seen before. "Maybe," he said, his voice dropping to a whisper. "But some shadows are worth chasing."

I could feel the weight of his words pressing against me, the space between us charged with something heavy, something real. The wind carried the faintest scent of saltwater from the distant shore, a reminder that we weren't alone out here in this forgotten corner of the city. There were other people, other lives, other stories—stories I hadn't bothered to learn before now. But Gabriel's silence was louder than anything around us. His eyes didn't soften, didn't look away. They just locked onto me, unwavering, like he was daring me to unravel the puzzle he'd carefully built around himself.

I thought about what he'd said—what if it wasn't about the thing at all? What if it was about someone? His past, tangled and complicated, had always been a quiet shadow behind his actions, his smile, his unpredictable nature. But now, his words hung in the air like a confession that had been years in the making, waiting for me to finally catch on. I wanted to laugh. I wanted to walk away, pretend none of this mattered. But the truth was, I wasn't ready to turn my back on this—not on him, not now.

"Well, Gabriel," I said, the words slipping out before I had a chance to stop them, "if this is about someone, I think you might've picked the wrong city to find them." My voice cracked a little at the end, and I hated myself for it. I'd always prided myself on my ability to keep things cool, especially when I was faced with... well, whatever this was. But there was something about Gabriel's gaze, something about the way he stood there, that made everything inside of me turn upside down.

He didn't laugh at my attempt to mask the vulnerability creeping up my spine. Instead, his lips curled into a smile that didn't quite reach his eyes. "You think so?" he asked, his tone almost playful, though it was laced with something sharper.

"Yeah," I shot back, forcing my shoulders to relax. "I mean, New York isn't exactly the place for soul-searching, is it? There's a Starbucks on every corner, for heaven's sake. I don't think any self-respecting ghost would be caught dead here."

Gabriel's chuckle was low, almost like a growl, but it didn't sound mocking. It sounded... approving. "You always talk like that?" he asked, stepping closer. Too close, I realized too late, as the heat from his body registered against mine.

"Only when I'm trying to keep things light," I said, swallowing hard as my heart picked up its pace. "Look, you've got your reasons, I get it. But this—" I motioned vaguely at the ruins, the forgotten parts of the city we were standing in, "—this is too much. You're not going to find whatever it is you're looking for here."

He raised an eyebrow, his gaze steady as if he were trying to read me. The silence stretched out between us again, thick and uncomfortable. "Is that what you really think?"

I opened my mouth to respond, but nothing came out. The truth was, I didn't know what I thought anymore. I didn't know whether I was supposed to be mad at him for keeping things from me or if I was just mad at myself for letting him get so close. The worst part? I couldn't bring myself to walk away. Not yet. Not with this secret hanging in the air like an unfinished story.

"I don't know what I think," I finally admitted, my voice softer now, more honest than I'd intended. "I don't know you, Gabriel.

Not really. You're not some treasure hunter, some man with a map to some mythical thing. You're... you're someone who's trying to fix something." I took a step back, suddenly aware of the space between us, the crackling tension that had always been there, just waiting for the right moment to unravel. "And you've made me part of that. But I don't even know if I'm supposed to be helping you anymore."

Gabriel didn't answer right away. Instead, he looked down at the ground, his eyes tracing the lines of the ancient stones beneath our feet. The moment felt... almost fragile, like if either of us said the wrong thing, it would all shatter. I could hear the distant hum of the city in the background, a reminder that we weren't the only ones caught in this dance of words and silence. But in that moment, it felt like we were the only two people left in the world.

Finally, Gabriel spoke, his voice low and thoughtful. "You think I'm trying to fix something?"

"Isn't that what this is about?" I asked, my tone sharp but uncertain. "What else could it be?"

He glanced up at me, his eyes flickering with something—a mix of surprise and something else I couldn't place. "Maybe," he said, his voice slower now, almost hesitant, "maybe I'm just trying to put a few pieces back together. Maybe what I'm looking for isn't some grand treasure. Maybe it's just... a piece of a person that I lost."

The words hit me like a sudden gust of wind, sharp and unexpected. For a moment, I couldn't breathe. His confession was so personal, so raw, that it made my chest tighten with an unfamiliar ache. I opened my mouth to say something—anything—but nothing came out. I had never seen Gabriel like this. The man who had always been so confident, so in control, was suddenly human in a way that made my heart stutter.

But before I could gather my thoughts, before I could even try to make sense of what he had just said, there was a rustle in the distance—a sound that didn't belong. My head snapped to the side, every instinct suddenly on high alert. Gabriel's expression shifted, his eyes narrowing as he scanned the horizon, the air between us suddenly crackling with something else—something dangerous.

"Do you hear that?" I whispered, my voice barely audible.

Gabriel didn't answer. Instead, he took a step closer, his body tense, every muscle coiled like a spring ready to snap. He reached for something in his jacket, his movements quick and deliberate. Something in the way he held himself told me that whatever was out there, it wasn't a random passerby or a curious tourist. No, this was something far more serious—and we were in the middle of it.

I swallowed, my heartbeat pounding in my ears. Whatever secret Gabriel was hiding, whatever ghosts he was chasing, it was all about to collide with the present—and we weren't prepared for it.

The city stretched out before us, a jagged line of steel and glass that seemed to pulse with its own heartbeat, indifferent to the quiet confrontation unfolding in its shadow. The scent of old brick and the salty tang of the bay filled the air, mingling with the hum of life that carried on obliviously. But Gabriel's words clung to the space between us like thick fog, refusing to lift, refusing to fade. He hadn't said anything outright, but the weight of what he hadn't said pressed down on me more than any confession could have.

"Everyone has their reasons," he had told me, the words leaving his lips as if they were nothing at all. But I could hear the undertone, the weight beneath them. What was his reason? What was so personal that it made him risk everything—his career, his secrets, his heart? Was it worth the endless pursuit, this thing, this person, that seemed to haunt his every step?

I turned, my gaze drawn to the abandoned warehouse nearby, the cracked windows staring back at me like hollow eyes. We were in the Lower East Side now, far from the gleaming towers and manicured streets where everything was polished and primed for show. Here, the city felt real. The grime, the grit, the raw edges of it all made the questions in my mind feel even sharper, as if the city itself was urging me to dig deeper. To stop pretending I didn't already know the answer.

Gabriel was still standing there, his back to me now, but I could sense the tension in him—the way he held himself, like a man on the edge of something he wasn't ready to face. His fingers twitched at his side, as if they were itching for something, a weapon, a clue, maybe even the truth, but he didn't speak.

I took a step closer, the dirt crunching beneath my boots, feeling the familiar weight of the city's underbelly press in around me. "So, what now?" I asked, the words sliding out with more bite than I'd intended. "You're not going to leave me hanging, are you? After all that cryptic crap about ghosts and pieces of people?"

His eyes flicked back to mine, and for a moment, I swore I saw something vulnerable in them, something I hadn't expected. But it was gone before I could grasp it, replaced by that impenetrable mask he'd perfected over the years. "I didn't ask for your help," he said, his voice low, but not unkind. "But you've got yourself tangled up in this now. Whether you like it or not."

I didn't like it. Not one bit. I had come here looking for something—closure, answers, maybe even a way out of my own tangled mess of a life—and now I was stuck in the middle of his. And worse, I didn't know if I wanted out anymore.

I crossed my arms, frustration bubbling up inside me. "You don't get to drop a bomb like that and then walk away like it's nothing. You're hiding something. And I've been through enough in my life to know that there's no such thing as 'nothing.' So if you want me to stay out of it, you better start telling me what the hell is going on."

Gabriel didn't respond immediately. Instead, he turned and walked a few steps toward the crumbling remnants of a brick wall, his hands shoved deep into his pockets. The streetlights flickered faintly in the distance, the soft buzz adding to the stillness of the night. "I'm looking for something that can't be found in a map or a ledger," he said finally, his voice barely above a whisper. "It's not about treasure or fame. It's about answers. About finding something that's been buried too long."

I could feel my pulse quicken at his words, a mix of dread and curiosity curling deep in my stomach. "What answers?"

Gabriel's eyes met mine, the flicker of vulnerability flashing again. "Something from my past. Something I thought I could bury forever."

I didn't move. I couldn't. His words lingered in the air between us like a dare, something I wasn't sure I was ready to face. "A person?" I ventured.

His jaw clenched, but he didn't look away. "Yes," he said, the word sharp, almost regretful. "Someone I lost."

The quiet lingered between us, hanging like a thick fog that refused to lift. I had asked the question, and now the weight of his answer settled over me like an anchor, dragging me deeper into a mystery I hadn't been prepared for. But there was no walking away from it now. Not after everything. Not after the way his eyes had flickered when he spoke about the loss. I understood loss. I had lived through it. But this... this felt different. This was the kind of loss that left scars that ran deeper than skin, deeper than memory. It was a wound that never quite healed.

"You're trying to bring them back," I said, the realization dawning on me as if the pieces were finally falling into place. "You think finding whatever's tied to this artifact will bring them back."

Gabriel didn't flinch. Instead, he looked at me, the weight of his gaze anchoring me in place. "You don't know what it's like," he said softly, almost too softly. "To lose someone and not be able to fix it. Not being able to do a damn thing except chase after shadows."

I didn't have the words to respond. He had just opened up a door, a door I wasn't sure I wanted to walk through, but I couldn't stop myself. The air around us was thick with tension, but I could feel the pull toward him, a gravitational force I had no control over. It wasn't just the mystery or the danger—it was him. He had a way of making everything feel like it was both important and pointless all at once.

Before I could gather myself, a noise broke through the silence, a sharp sound that didn't belong. Gabriel's eyes snapped toward the street, his entire body going rigid as his hand reached under his jacket.

"Stay behind me," he ordered, his voice low, the urgency in it slicing through the air like a warning.

I didn't ask questions. I didn't have time to. I ducked behind him just as something—someone—moved in the shadows ahead. It wasn't a person I recognized, but it didn't matter. Whatever Gabriel was tangled in, whatever ghosts he was chasing, they were about to catch up with us.

And I had no idea how to run.

Chapter 11: The Songstress's Warning

The air in the dimly lit room hung heavy, the sound of Amara's voice curling around us like smoke. Her melody, once soft and lilting, had turned sharp and jagged, its rhythm quickening, as though she could sense something we couldn't. Her dark eyes flicked toward the doorway, where Gabriel stood, his figure outlined by the faint light from the corridor. He wasn't one for theatrics, and though his expression remained unreadable, I could see the tension in the tight set of his jaw.

"Do you understand?" Amara's voice cracked the silence again, brittle now, like ice shattering on the floor. Her fingers trembled on the strings of the lute, her gaze darting between Gabriel and me. "There's no time left. The betrayal has already begun. He is already among us." Her words were riddled with a desperate edge, the weight of them pressing down on me like an anchor in a stormy sea.

I shifted on my feet, uneasy, but unwilling to break her gaze. It felt like she was speaking from some far-off place, as if she knew something I didn't. Something none of us could comprehend.

"You're not making any sense." Gabriel's voice was cold, his words crisp and deliberate, but I saw the flicker of doubt in his eyes, barely perceptible. He had always been the one to trust facts and actions over whispered promises and vague warnings. "What betrayal? Who's betraying whom, Amara?"

Amara's lips curled into something like a smile, though it lacked humor, and her eyes grew distant, as though she was looking beyond him, beyond the walls of the room, into the very heart of the city itself. "You don't know him the way I do," she said, almost to herself, before refocusing on Gabriel. "The truth has been right in front of you all along, but you've refused to see it."

Her words hit harder than I expected, twisting in my chest. She was right, in a way. Gabriel had always been cautious, skeptical—qualities I admired in him, especially now. But there were things we couldn't ignore anymore, things that would haunt us long after Amara's song had faded into the night.

I stepped forward, unable to keep quiet any longer. "What exactly are you warning us about, Amara?" I didn't mean for the question to sound so sharp, but the weight of the moment—of everything I couldn't quite piece together—was too much to bear.

Her eyes softened for a moment, then quickly darkened. "You want answers? Then listen." Her fingers strummed one last, final, haunting note, and the room seemed to hold its breath. "You've been deceived, both of you. By someone you trust. Someone close."

Gabriel stiffened. His eyes flickered toward me, his brow furrowing in suspicion. "That's a dangerous accusation."

"Is it?" Amara's voice was a taunt now, and her lips quirked upward. "Is it any more dangerous than living a lie, Gabriel? You, who have been deceived by the one you least suspect?"

The tension in the room stretched taut, like a wire pulled too tight, ready to snap. I could see Gabriel's mind working, his sharp eyes flicking between me and Amara, assessing, calculating. But I didn't need to be a genius to know he wouldn't let this go. Not now. Not when he had spent so long building walls around himself. Gabriel was many things—smart, calculated, relentless—but he was not one to let his guard down easily, especially when someone like Amara was involved.

"I don't believe you," he said, his voice hard. "This is nothing more than a manipulation. A way to make us doubt what we've worked so hard to build."

Amara laughed, but it wasn't a laugh filled with mirth. It was bitter, as if she had already accepted her fate. "Doubt is a powerful thing. And you'll need it, Gabriel. You'll need to question everything. Because soon, there will be no place left to run." She looked at me, her eyes narrowing as if she could see through my very soul. "You, too. You've been part of this, whether you realize it or not."

I recoiled at the implication, a cold wave of unease washing over me. "I don't know what you're talking about."

But she didn't answer. Instead, she stood, her gaze lingering for one more moment before she turned and walked toward the window, her silhouette bathed in the pale light of the moon. She paused, looking out over the city, as though it held the answers we were searching for, as though she could see all its secrets laid bare before her.

"I don't expect you to believe me now," she said softly, her voice a whisper in the quiet room. "But when the time comes, you'll understand. You'll have no choice but to face the truth."

And with that, she was gone, slipping out the door as silently as she had come.

Gabriel didn't move for a long moment, his eyes still on the door she had just exited, his face hard as stone. But I could see the shift in him—the subtle change that Amara's words had caused. His mind, always calculating, was already turning over possibilities, strategies. He was just as unsure as I was, though he would never admit it.

"Do you believe her?" I asked, though I wasn't sure if I wanted to hear the answer.

Gabriel's gaze met mine, and for the first time in a long while, I saw something raw there. Something vulnerable. "I don't know," he muttered, more to himself than to me. "But I'm starting to think that maybe we've been blind to something. Something right in front of us."

The weight of his words hung in the air like a thundercloud, and I felt it settle in my chest, heavy and unrelenting.

The city was quieter now, the gentle hum of late-night traffic the only reminder that we weren't the only ones still awake. I stood by the window, watching the occasional car glide down the slick streets, its headlights carving jagged streaks of light that reflected off the wet asphalt. The sky above was a deep ink blue, heavy with the promise of rain, but nothing seemed to move except for the flickering neon signs across the street and the occasional shadow that passed by. Even the usual noise of the city felt muffled, as if it too were holding its breath, waiting for something to break the silence.

Gabriel had disappeared into the other room, his footsteps hard and determined, and I was left standing in the quiet of the aftermath, the air thick with the weight of everything that had been said. Amara's warning echoed in my mind, her words twisting like vines, choking out any rational thought. A betrayal. Someone close. How close? And who? It was a question I couldn't shake, even as my mind rebelled against it. We had come so far, fought so hard to get here, and now, this.

I ran my fingers through my hair, frustration curling in my chest. It wasn't like me to second-guess everything, to let the murky waters of suspicion creep into my thoughts, but Amara had a way of planting doubt like a seed and watching it grow.

I leaned against the windowsill, staring out at the city that felt like it was both too close and too far. What had she meant?

The click of a door latch interrupted my thoughts. Gabriel stepped back into the room, his expression unreadable, but I saw the sharp edge of concern in his eyes. He'd been on edge since the moment we'd crossed paths with Amara, his instincts set to fight, to reject anything that threatened the fragile balance we had. He was a man of action, of reason—and now, that same reason was failing him.

"I checked," he said, voice tight. "There's nothing new. Nothing unusual. No one's been in or out of the building since we came back. No signals, no wires, no nothing."

I wanted to believe him, wanted to dismiss the gnawing feeling in my gut that kept urging me to dig deeper. But the truth, as much as I hated it, was that I couldn't shake the feeling that Amara's words had hit too close to home. There was something beneath the surface, something lurking in the shadows, waiting for the right moment to reveal itself.

"Are you sure?" I asked, my voice softer than I intended.

He nodded, his jaw working in the silence. "We've been through this before. Whatever she's trying to sell, it's not worth buying."

"I'm not so sure," I said, more to myself than to him.

Gabriel's eyes narrowed, and for a moment, the world seemed to still. "You don't believe her, do you?"

I hesitated. The truth was, I wasn't sure what to believe anymore. But what I did know was that Amara had never been one for idle threats. There was something unsettlingly real in the way she'd spoken, as if the pieces of the puzzle were already laid out before her.

"She knows something," I muttered, more to myself than to him. "Maybe more than she's letting on."

He crossed the room in two quick strides, standing in front of me with that focused intensity that could burn holes through concrete. "She's playing you, just like she played everyone else. If there's a betrayal, it's hers. She's just trying to get inside your head, make you doubt everything."

I could see the conviction in his eyes, the quiet anger that bubbled beneath the surface. But there was something else there, something that made me question his certainty. He wasn't the type to let emotions cloud his judgment, and I knew better than to buy into the first thing that came my way. But this felt different.

"I don't know." I sighed, raking a hand through my hair. "I've seen it before. People like her, they always know when something's off. They have this way of sensing danger. And right now, danger is exactly what we're dealing with."

Gabriel's shoulders tensed, and I could feel the unspoken argument brewing between us. I didn't want to doubt him, didn't want to question the years of trust we'd built between us. But the gnawing sensation in my gut refused to fade, growing stronger with every passing second.

"You're playing her game." Gabriel's voice was low, dangerously calm. "You're letting her twist your mind, make you second-guess everything we've done, everything we've built."

I shook my head, frustration bubbling up again. "You don't understand. There's something we're missing, Gabriel. Something we haven't seen. I need to figure out what it is before it's too late."

"You're chasing shadows."

I glared at him. "And you're blind to the ones right in front of you."

The silence between us crackled, thick and uncomfortable. It wasn't just Amara's warning that had shifted things; it was the fact that we were both holding pieces of a puzzle that didn't quite fit together, and neither of us knew what the final picture looked like. Gabriel's confidence was rattling against the edges of my growing doubt, and it felt like we were standing on a precipice, each of us unwilling to take the first step in a direction we might not be able to come back from.

Finally, Gabriel spoke, his voice quieter now, tinged with something that resembled resignation. "What do you want me to do, then?"

I looked at him, my gaze steady. "Help me figure it out. Help me find the pieces we've missed. Because, right now, I think we're running out of time."

He didn't answer right away, but I saw the flicker of something in his eyes, a softening, a shift. Maybe he didn't believe Amara's warning, but I knew he believed in me—and that was enough to start the next chapter of whatever it was we were walking into.

The night stretched out before us like a darkened street, endless and uncertain. Gabriel didn't speak as we made our way down the quiet hallway, the sound of our footsteps muffled by the thick carpet. The tension between us was palpable, hanging in the air like a storm that hadn't yet broken. I kept my head down, refusing to meet his gaze. The silence was both a comfort and a strain, a fragile thread holding everything together. But I knew that thread was fraying, and it wouldn't be long before it snapped.

We stepped into the dimly lit office, where the city's glow outside painted everything in shades of orange and black. The scent of old books and stale coffee lingered in the air, a constant reminder of the hours we'd spent here, piecing together the puzzle that had become our lives. But now, the puzzle felt different. It felt like something had been moved, something important, and I was suddenly unsure if I could fit the pieces together again.

"I don't trust her." Gabriel's voice cut through the silence, firm and final, like a judge's gavel. He paced around the room, as if trying to shake the unease that had settled in his chest. "She's playing us, trying to get inside our heads."

I crossed the room slowly, moving toward the desk, my fingers brushing over the surface as if the wood itself could provide answers. "She's not wrong about everything, though," I said quietly. "What she said—it's not something just anyone could pull out of thin air."

Gabriel stopped pacing, turning to face me, his eyes narrowing as if he could see into the very depths of my thoughts. "You're letting her get to you. She's good at that, I'll give her credit. But there's no truth in it. We've been through enough, faced enough to know when someone's just trying to stir up chaos."

His words stung, but not in the way I expected. I had always admired Gabriel's strength, his ability to shut down doubts and distractions. But tonight, the cracks in his armor seemed to show, and I wasn't sure I liked what I saw. His certainty, once so reliable, now felt like a fragile shell. And I could see the toll it had taken on him.

"I can't ignore it," I whispered, more to myself than to him. "I can't pretend there's nothing there."

Gabriel's expression hardened, and for a moment, I thought he was going to argue with me again. But instead, he sighed, rubbing his temples as though the weight of the conversation was more than he could bear. "If you really believe her, then what? Where does that leave us? In a city full of lies and betrayals, who do we trust?"

I didn't have an answer for that. How could I? I barely trusted myself anymore. But the words Amara had spoken still echoed in my mind, a haunting refrain I couldn't shake. There was a truth in what she said, one that gnawed at the edges of my mind, making me question everything—everyone.

"I don't know," I said at last, the words feeling hollow even as they left my lips. "But I think we need to find out. Whatever she's hiding, whatever she knows, it's only a matter of time before it comes to light."

Gabriel's gaze softened, just for a moment, before it hardened again, his stance shifting into something defensive. "We don't have time to chase shadows, not when we're so close to the end."

And just like that, I felt the first stirrings of something even darker than Amara's cryptic warning. It wasn't the feeling of impending doom—it was something far more dangerous. Something I hadn't anticipated. For the first time, I wondered if Gabriel was hiding something, too. If his certainty was not just a shield against the world but a way to bury something he wasn't ready to face. The idea lodged itself in my chest, sharp and unrelenting.

The sharp chime of my phone broke the tension, its tone slicing through the room like a blade. I glanced at the screen, half-expecting another cryptic message from Amara, but it wasn't her name that flashed across the display. It was an unknown number. My pulse quickened, the blood in my veins suddenly ice-cold. I could feel Gabriel's eyes on me, but I couldn't take my gaze away from the screen.

"Answer it," he said quietly, his voice low and cautious.

I hesitated, my thumb hovering over the screen. There was a moment—just a heartbeat—where I debated letting it go to voicemail. But something about the timing of the call, the way the air felt like it was holding its breath, made me press accept.

"Hello?" I said, my voice steady but laced with an edge of suspicion.

A voice—deep, smooth, and strangely familiar—came through the line, sending a shiver down my spine. "I think it's time we had a little chat."

I stiffened. "Who is this?"

There was a pause, and then the voice laughed—a soft, almost mocking sound. "Let's just say I know someone who's very interested in your little investigation. Someone who might have a few answers for you."

I looked at Gabriel, but he was already moving toward the window, his back to me as he stared out into the night. "What do you want?" I demanded, my grip tightening around the phone.

"You already know," the voice replied. "But just in case you're still unsure, let me give you a hint. There's more at play here than you realize. And if you want to stay one step ahead, you'll need to trust the right people. Starting with me."

Before I could respond, the line went dead, leaving nothing but the hollow buzz of silence. I lowered the phone, my breath catching in my throat. Gabriel turned, his eyes narrowing as he saw the look on my face.

"What did they say?" he asked, his voice suddenly more serious, more guarded.

I swallowed hard, forcing the words past the lump in my throat. "Someone's watching us. And they know more than we do."

Gabriel's gaze flickered, the briefest hint of something dark crossing his features. "Who was it?"

I shook my head, uncertainty swirling inside me like a storm. "I don't know. But I'm starting to think we might be in deeper than we ever imagined."

The room felt smaller now, the walls closing in with a sense of impending danger. Whatever had been set in motion, whatever had begun to unravel, it was only just the beginning.

Chapter 12: The First Betrayal

The city stretched before me in jagged lines of steel and glass, the streets tangled in a never-ending web of neon lights and the exhaust fumes of cars that never seemed to stop moving. Philadelphia at 4 a.m. had a pulse all its own, somewhere between the anxious hum of early risers and the silent reverie of those who hadn't yet gone to bed. I stood on the balcony of my apartment, my fingers wrapped tightly around the railing, eyes trained on the skyline. If there were any answers to be found in this chaotic mess of a city, they would be somewhere beneath the streets I walked every day, somewhere hidden in plain sight.

It had been hours since Gabriel's disappearance, but the sting of betrayal still seared at my ribs. It wasn't just the artifact—though that had been a significant blow—but the fact that I hadn't seen it coming. Gabriel had been my partner in everything: in the quiet, hazy moments where we would sit together and sip coffee on a Sunday morning, his fingers brushing against mine with such effortless grace, as if he were made to fit into my world. But now? Now he was gone, vanished into the Philadelphia night, along with the artifact that had tied us both together in ways I still hadn't fully understood.

I exhaled, my breath forming a fog against the cool air. My apartment was dark, save for the weak glow of the streetlights casting shadows against the walls. It felt colder than it should have, colder than I expected. And yet, it wasn't the temperature that made my teeth chatter—it was the gnawing sensation in the pit of my stomach. Gabriel had taken the artifact, sure. I saw him slip it into his coat pocket before he kissed me goodnight, told me he'd be back before morning. And yet, when I woke to find him gone, I also woke to the unmistakable pull of the artifact—a tugging sensation, like something ancient and powerful calling me to find it, to understand it, to make it mine.

That pull. It was familiar, yet foreign. It wasn't something I could describe in simple terms—it wasn't hunger or fear. It was more visceral than that. More real. Like a magnetic force pulling me toward the one thing I knew I couldn't trust, even if it whispered promises of power I couldn't quite ignore.

I paced the floor of my living room, trying to make sense of the jagged pieces of my reality. Gabriel had always been secretive about certain things, sure. But this? This was different. He didn't just take the artifact—he took it and disappeared. There had to be something more at play here. Maybe it was my intuition, or maybe it was the nagging thought that Gabriel was never truly mine to begin with. He was always a little too distant, a little too enigmatic, his eyes always darting to places I couldn't follow.

And then there was the matter of the artifact itself. I should have known better than to trust something so volatile, so unpredictable. Its power was undeniable, but its nature was dangerous. Gabriel had always been fascinated by it—too fascinated, I'd thought at times. He'd talked about it like it held the key to something more, something that could change everything. But what if it had changed him first? What if he'd been so consumed by it that he'd walked into the night as a different person, someone I couldn't recognize?

The sound of a door creaking open behind me startled me. I spun around, but there was no one there. Just the faint echo of a footstep, too soft to be real, too quiet to be anything other than a figment of my mind.

I closed my eyes, breathing in deeply. My hands trembled, but not from fear. The artifact had always had this effect on me—the closer I got to it, the more I could feel its power, its weight pressing down on me. The pull was undeniable. But if Gabriel had taken it, then why was I feeling it now? Why had I woken up with the sense that something was terribly wrong, something I couldn't quite name?

I glanced toward the kitchen table, where the remnants of my last meal lay—half-eaten pizza, a glass of cheap wine, the kind of night I thought I could forget. Gabriel and I had shared that meal together, laughing at something trivial, something meaningless. It seemed like a lifetime ago. And yet, that piece of him—the one who had sat across from me, wearing that devil-may-care grin—was still here, in the way I kept thinking about him, in the way I couldn't stop chasing the feeling that something was missing.

I shook my head, pushing the thoughts aside. I needed to focus. There had to be an explanation. I couldn't afford to get lost in the same cycle of guilt and confusion that had kept me from seeing Gabriel for what he truly was. I had to find him. I had to find the artifact before it consumed me as well.

I grabbed my coat from the back of the chair and yanked it on, the cold fabric brushing against my skin like a warning. The door clicked shut behind me, and I stepped into the night, the streets of Philadelphia sprawling before me like a puzzle I was determined to solve. I didn't know where Gabriel had gone, but I was certain of one thing: I wouldn't stop until I found him—and until I understood the truth of what we had both been chasing.

The streets felt different now, as if the city itself were in on the secret I was too slow to grasp. I had wandered far from my apartment, the cold nipping at my skin despite the wool coat I had thrown on in haste. The city lights blurred into soft halos in the distance, casting long shadows across the sidewalk. Philadelphia at this hour had a way of feeling both endless and intimate—like a place that knew all your secrets but wasn't about to tell anyone else. It wasn't until I found myself standing on a corner near 9th and Callowhill that I realized I hadn't consciously decided to come here. But the sensation of being pulled here, of having something in me guiding my steps like a current in a dark river, was as undeniable as it was unsettling.

There, tucked between a row of unremarkable brownstones, stood a familiar building—an old pub with dimmed windows and peeling paint on its sign. The O'Malley & Co. Tavern. A relic from a past I had tried to forget, and yet there it was, standing as a silent reminder of all the tangled webs I had weaved in my search for answers about the artifact.

I hadn't come here in years.

My phone buzzed in my pocket, a sharp reminder of how disconnected I had become from everyone else. The name on the screen was unmistakable: Ben. He was one of the few people who knew about my connection to Gabriel, the artifact, and the sort of underground world we had gotten ourselves entangled in. A world where magic wasn't a story, but a reality that hummed through the city's veins, kept hidden behind layers of bureaucracy, bureaucracy, and the strange secrecy that came with living on the fringes of society.

I answered, my voice strained. "Ben."

"You're still looking for him, aren't you?" His voice was steady, but I could hear the weariness in it, the weight of his own thoughts pressing down on him. He'd warned me before, but I hadn't listened.

"I'm not done yet," I replied. My fingers tightened around the phone, my grip tightening as if I could hold onto the conversation, hold onto the answers he might give me, even if it was just for a moment.

"I told you. You can't keep following this. Not now. It's bigger than you think."

"Bigger than I think?" I laughed, though it came out more as a bitter chuckle than anything remotely funny. "I thought I was the one trying to keep everything from going to hell in a handbasket. But somehow, you're saying I'm missing the point?"

There was a long pause on the other end of the line. I could almost hear him debating whether or not to continue. Finally, he spoke again, quieter this time. "I'm saying, when you go looking for something you can't control, you risk losing everything you care about."

I froze, my breath catching in my throat. Gabriel. That's what he meant. I had been so focused on finding him, on tracking the artifact, that I hadn't thought about what it would cost me in the end. And yet, the pull of it—the pull of him—was something I couldn't shake.

"I'm fine," I said, but even to my own ears, it sounded hollow. It wasn't enough to reassure him. Or to reassure myself.

"Be careful," Ben added, his voice low, almost like a prayer. "You're getting too close to something you won't be able to escape from. If you need me, I'm around." The line went silent after that, leaving me with only the thrum of my heartbeat in my ears.

I tucked the phone away, the unease settling deeper in my bones. Ben had always been pragmatic, a voice of reason when I had none. But reason, it seemed, was a luxury I no longer had.

Turning away from the pub, I made my way down a narrow alley. The brick walls on either side seemed to press in, closing off any sense of escape. I had learned to trust my instincts—those deep, quiet moments when the hairs on the back of your neck stand up and you know you're being watched. But even with that warning, I didn't see the figure emerge from the shadows until he was almost on top of me.

"Still looking for him, huh?"

I jumped back, the sudden appearance of the stranger enough to make my pulse race. My breath hitched as my eyes darted across his face, trying to place him. He was tall, with a face I didn't quite recognize but couldn't quite forget either. His dark hair was just long enough to be tousled, his eyes hard and unfathomable.

"I could ask you the same thing," I retorted, my voice sharp, even if my stomach twisted at the way his gaze seemed to pierce right through me.

His smile was slow, knowing. "Don't play coy. You've been looking for him since the moment you woke up."

I stiffened. "Who are you?"

"A friend." He stepped closer, his movements smooth and deliberate. "Or maybe more like an acquaintance. A fellow traveler on a road you've yet to understand."

"I'm not in the mood for riddles," I snapped. "What do you want?"

He held his hands up, as if surrendering, but there was a slight twitch of a smile on his lips, the kind that didn't quite reach his eyes. "I'm just here to make sure you don't go running off and get yourself killed."

"Is that supposed to be comforting?"

"You're about to learn just how much danger you're really in." His voice dropped to a whisper, but his words were heavy, as though they carried more weight than I could bear in that moment. "The artifact isn't just a thing, you know. It has a life of its own. And Gabriel? Well, he's more involved in all of this than you've been led to believe."

My heart skipped a beat, a knot tightening in my chest. I had always known there was something more to Gabriel's obsession with the artifact, but hearing it confirmed—hearing the stranger's words sink in—made the ground feel less stable under my feet.

The man studied me for a moment, his gaze calculating, like he was trying to decide whether or not to trust me. Or whether or not it mattered. "You've made your choice. Now you need to deal with the consequences. But I'll be seeing you again soon. And trust me, when you do find Gabriel, you won't like what you find."

Before I could react, he was gone, slipping back into the shadows like a ghost. And for a long time after, I just stood there, alone in the alley, with nothing but the sound of my own racing thoughts.

I walked in circles, the city's lights streaking through the fog like a blur of bright colors painting the air. The night had taken on a strange weight, heavy with expectation, like the pause before a storm. And maybe it was the weight of that anticipation—of what I didn't understand—that was making the world feel so distorted. Or maybe it was just the pull of the artifact again, that low hum in the back of my mind that never quite went away. The longer I stood in the street, the stronger it grew, a soft pressure between my ribs that seemed to vibrate with a force I couldn't explain.

I turned a corner onto Pine Street, shoving my hands deeper into my pockets, but nothing seemed to settle. There was a sharpness in the air that had nothing to do with the chill. It was almost as if the city itself were holding its breath.

The stranger's words echoed in my head. *The artifact isn't just a thing. It has a life of its own.* The more I thought about it, the less I understood. I had spent years around magic, always aware of its capricious nature, but this? This felt different. There was something in the way the stranger spoke—like he wasn't warning me just about Gabriel or the artifact. He was warning me about myself.

And then, as if summoned by my thoughts, my phone buzzed again. This time, it wasn't Ben. It wasn't Gabriel. It wasn't even an unknown number. It was her.

I didn't even have to look at the screen. I knew exactly who it was.

I answered it with a simple, "What do you want, Lila?"

Her laugh came through the line, smooth and sweet, though I could hear the edges of it fray under the tension. "Well, aren't we grumpy tonight? I just wanted to see how you're holding up, considering the circumstances."

I could picture her perfectly, that razor-sharp smile of hers, the one that always made me wonder how many secrets she was hiding behind it. Lila and I had never been friends—far from it. She was the type who saw everything as a game, one she always won. She never hesitated to play dirty if it meant getting what she wanted, and what she wanted was usually something dangerous. Something I couldn't afford to give her.

"I'm fine," I said, though the words tasted like ash. "I'm dealing with things."

Lila was quiet for a moment, her voice like silk as she spoke again. "You know, you're always so evasive. It's almost cute. Almost." There was a faint clicking sound in the background—maybe the sharp tap of her nails on something, maybe something else—but it was enough to make my nerves prickle.

"What do you want?" I repeated, harsher this time.

"Honestly? I want the same thing I've always wanted: control. And now, you've made it far more interesting for me. That artifact—well, let's just say it's become necessary for both of us. If you understand what I mean."

I didn't need her to elaborate. I could feel the weight of her words pressing down on me like a heavy stone. Lila wasn't someone who would stop at just one thing. She had always wanted to be the one pulling the strings behind the scenes. And with Gabriel gone, I knew it wouldn't be long before she tried to use the artifact against me. Or worse, against anyone else she could manipulate.

"I'm not giving it to you," I said, though my voice lacked the conviction I wanted it to have.

Lila's voice softened, almost sweet, but it only made the warning in it that much clearer. "Oh, sweetie, you misunderstand me. I'm not asking. I'm telling you."

There was a soft click as she ended the call, and the weight of her threat lingered in the space between the ringing silence and my own breathing. I glanced up at the row of lights strung along the sidewalk, the soft amber glow of old lamps casting shadows that made the streets look like a faded painting. Something about that glow felt off, as if I were walking through a memory, but not my own.

I had barely taken a step forward when a figure emerged from the darkness, startling me enough that I stumbled back. My pulse quickened, but then I recognized him—Ben. He stood in the doorway of a nearby shop, hands shoved deep into his coat pockets, looking like a man who had been waiting for far too long.

"Didn't expect to see you here," I said, trying to steady my breath as I approached him.

He gave me one of those sharp, wry smiles of his, the kind he wore when he was about to say something that made my skin prickle. "I think you're going to need some help. And I'm the only one who's going to be able to give it to you."

I folded my arms across my chest, suspicion curling in my gut. "Help with what?"

"The artifact. The situation. Gabriel." Ben's eyes flicked toward the street, his gaze sharp, scanning. "Lila's not the only one you need to worry about right now."

"Tell me something I don't know," I shot back. "I'm already being pulled in too many directions. Gabriel's gone, and I'm stuck chasing a ghost."

He didn't seem fazed by my frustration. Instead, his expression turned more serious, his voice lower. "The artifact has a way of making people disappear, but it also has a way of making things... appear. And not all of them are friendly."

I frowned. "What are you talking about?"

Ben hesitated, clearly weighing his words. "I'm saying, there's more to the artifact than we've realized. And you're not the only one it's calling to. If Gabriel thinks he's hidden it, he's wrong. Someone else is already on his trail."

My heart skipped a beat. "Who?"

He didn't answer right away. Instead, his eyes narrowed as he peered into the shadows, his gaze sharpening on something I couldn't see. And then, as if the night itself had decided to play its hand, I heard it—a sound, faint but unmistakable. A whisper in the wind, and then a footstep echoing from the alley behind us.

Ben's jaw tightened, and for the first time, I saw genuine fear flicker across his face.

"We're not alone," he muttered.

Before I could ask anything else, the world around me shifted—everything felt too still, too quiet. I glanced over my shoulder just as the figure stepped out of the darkness, a glint of something silver flashing in their hand.

"Guess who found you first?"

Chapter 13: A Bond Forged in Fire

The sky had darkened by the time Gabriel stumbled through the door, his figure a silhouette against the dim light spilling from the kitchen. His coat, once pristine, was now torn, stained with what I hoped was nothing worse than mud. His hands—those hands, which had once swept over me with such calculated tenderness—were now trembling. Not from the cold, but from the weight of a burden I wasn't sure I was ready to understand.

I dropped the book I hadn't been reading and stood frozen, my feet unwilling to move. His chest heaved in shallow breaths, the air catching in his throat as if every inhale was a struggle. His jaw, set so often with unspoken things, was clenched now, the muscle twitching under the strain. He tried to make his way toward the couch, but his legs seemed to give out from under him, and he collapsed—no, crumpled—onto the soft cushions as if the weight of the world had finally broken him.

I should've been angry, perhaps. Should've demanded explanations for the silence, for the lies, for the way he had ghosted me in the days leading up to this moment. But as I looked at him, a storm of emotions churned in my chest. Hurt. Confusion. Something I couldn't name. It took every ounce of restraint I had not to rush over and do something—anything—to fix whatever was broken between us. But what if it wasn't broken? What if it was something else altogether? Something I couldn't yet see.

"Gabriel?" The name left my lips before I could stop it, my voice a hesitant whisper in the empty space between us. I wasn't sure what I expected—apologies? Excuses? Maybe even the same bravado he wore like armor every time we crossed paths. But instead, he simply raised his head, those eyes—normally so impenetrable—filled with an emotion I wasn't sure I wanted to face. Fear. Or something close to it.

He laughed, a hollow sound that didn't belong to him. It reminded me of the kind of laugh someone gives after they've just survived something that should have killed them. "Did you think I'd just waltz back in and tell you everything? Just like that?" He gestured vaguely to the room, a grimace twisting his features. "It's not that simple."

I took a step closer, the floor creaking under my weight, and his gaze flickered to my shoes before darting back to the far wall, avoiding me. But it wasn't in the usual way—a practiced evasion—but more like a desperate attempt to shield himself. From me? From himself? The difference was too thin to tell.

"Then why come back at all?" I asked, trying to mask the hurt in my voice with a sharp edge of accusation. "Why not stay gone if everything's so complicated?"

His eyes softened—just the slightest, but it was there. And then he exhaled, a long, drawn-out breath as if the words he was about to say had been held in for far too long. "Because it's too complicated," he finally admitted, the admission raw, unrefined. "And I needed to make sure you were still alive."

I froze, my blood running cold. "What do you mean?" I managed to get out, though my voice felt foreign in my mouth.

Gabriel raised a hand, and for the first time in days, I saw the true exhaustion in his posture. His shoulder slumped, and I realized then just how much weight he had been carrying. The kind of weight I hadn't even begun to understand.

"There was an ambush," he said slowly, as though testing each word. "I was targeted. For the artifact. And when they tried to take it, something happened. I... I didn't expect it. But I couldn't let go. I couldn't." His eyes locked onto mine, intense and pleading. "It protected me. I don't know how. But it's like it woke up when I needed it."

The words felt like a blow. The artifact—that artifact—had always been a strange mystery, a relic whose history was shrouded in rumors and lies. But to hear Gabriel speak of it like this, as though it had its own will, its own power, was something else entirely.

"You're telling me you've been using it all along?" I asked, the disbelief thick in my throat.

His lips twitched in a semblance of a smile. "No. Not using it. I didn't choose it, not really. It was... It's more like it chose me."

There it was again—the word I hated most. Chosen. As if we were all at the mercy of something greater than us. Something we didn't understand, couldn't control. Something that had its own agenda. And now Gabriel, the man who had been the center of my world for months, was telling me that he had no more power over it than I did.

"I don't know what's going on, Gabriel," I said, my voice barely above a whisper. "I want to believe you. But—"

He cut me off, leaning forward in a movement so fast it startled me. "I don't expect you to believe me. Not yet." His eyes burned with a fire I couldn't ignore. "But I need you to. Because I can't fix this alone. Not anymore."

Something inside me shifted then, a quiet realization that despite everything—despite the anger, the hurt, the lies—he was still asking me to be part of something larger than both of us. Something that was far from over.

I didn't know if I could forgive him. Not yet. But I knew, with painful clarity, that whatever came next, I couldn't walk away. Not from him. Not from us.

I wanted to say something, anything, to break the tension that had settled between us like a heavy fog. But no words seemed to fit, nothing felt real enough to describe the whirlwind of confusion, anger, and inexplicable affection swirling inside me. Instead, I just stood there, watching him, unable to look away, as he collapsed further into the couch, a grimace overtaking his face as his body seemed to shut down from the sheer force of his ordeal.

The remnants of his previous charm—so smooth, so poised—were now obscured by a man who appeared dangerously vulnerable. His perfect, calculated self-assurance had cracked open like a shell, revealing the raw, bleeding edges beneath. It should've been a moment of triumph for me. After all, this was the man who had always made me feel like an afterthought, something to be swayed, something to be won over. Yet here he was, broken and exposed, and all I could think was that I didn't know how to fix it—or even if I could.

"Are you just going to sit there?" he asked, his voice rough, ragged, as if the effort of speaking might actually hurt him. It was a challenge, more of a command than a plea, but the pain in his eyes stripped it of any force. He wasn't asking for anything from me; not really. He wasn't looking for forgiveness or understanding. He just needed me to stay. To listen. And God help me, I wasn't sure if I could.

I didn't move right away, but I could feel the heaviness in the air pressing down on me, the air thick with unspoken things. Finally, I dragged a chair from the small dining table across the room and sat facing him, our knees nearly touching. The proximity should have made things worse, but somehow, it didn't. Instead, it felt like the most natural thing in the world, as if we had been pulled together by some invisible force. Maybe we had been. I didn't know anymore.

"How?" I asked, the single syllable hanging between us. "How did this happen? How did you happen?"

He winced, as if the question physically hurt, but his gaze didn't waver. "It wasn't supposed to," he said, his voice barely above a whisper, a confession. "The artifact—it's not something I can control, not really. It's..." He trailed off, running a hand through his disheveled hair, the sharp lines of his face softening as if he were trying to piece together a puzzle that didn't quite fit. "I thought I could handle it. I thought I could keep it buried—keep everyone else from realizing how dangerous it really is."

I crossed my arms, leaning forward. "And now?"

"Now I'm just trying to figure out how not to kill everyone I care about," he replied, his voice dry and humorless.

I blinked at him, taken aback by the bluntness of it. He was always so guarded, so careful with his words, and yet here he was, laying everything out on the table like it was nothing. As if, in this moment, there was no pretense. No game. Just the man beneath the armor, raw and exposed.

"You think that's going to happen?" I asked, my tone softening despite myself.

His lips curled into a sad semblance of a smile, and for a moment, I saw the spark of the man I'd once known—the one who could charm his way through anything. But it was fleeting, vanishing as quickly as it came. "I think it's a possibility." His gaze met mine, holding it, daring me to challenge him. "I think I'm running out of time, and I'm running out of options."

It was the first time he'd admitted any weakness, and I hated the way it made me feel. As though all this time, I had been looking at him with the wrong eyes—eyes that saw nothing but strength, power, and untouchability. Now, I couldn't ignore the truth.

"I didn't know what I was getting myself into," he added, more quietly now, his voice almost a whisper. "I thought I could keep it under control. That's why I left. I thought you'd be safer if I stayed away."

The confession hit me like a tidal wave, crashing over the barriers I had so carefully built between us. "So, you left to protect me?" I repeated, the words tasting foreign on my tongue. "You thought it would be safer if I was just... alone?"

He looked away, his eyes flicking to the floor as if the weight of my words was too much for him. "I didn't want you involved in this. But now, I don't know if it matters anymore."

The silence stretched out, thick and suffocating, and I found myself grappling with the impossible decision in front of me. This wasn't some simple misunderstanding, some bad date gone wrong. This was bigger. Much bigger. And somehow, despite everything—despite the lies, the distance, the tangled mess we were now wading through—I couldn't let go. I couldn't walk away from him, not when everything in me was screaming that this was something I needed to understand. That we needed to understand it—together.

"I'm not going anywhere," I said finally, my voice firm, though I wasn't sure I believed it. "You can't expect me to just let you deal with this alone."

Gabriel's eyes met mine, and for a moment, the storm that had been raging between us settled. There was something almost... relieved in his gaze. "You don't have to, you know. But it's not going to be easy."

I smiled, a bit wry, a bit weary. "When has anything with you ever been easy?"

He returned my smile, the ghost of the man I had once known flickering back into place. "Touché."

And for the first time in a long time, I felt the tight knot in my chest loosen, just a little. Because if I was going to be caught up in this whirlwind, I might as well be tangled in it with someone who had a better chance of survival than most. Even if that someone was more dangerous than I'd ever imagined.

I barely slept that night, the stillness of the apartment pressing in on me like the weight of a thousand unsaid words. Every time I closed my eyes, I saw Gabriel's face—haunted, weary, vulnerable in a way I hadn't thought possible. And with each image, I felt myself unraveling further, as if something inside me was being pulled in different directions, each tug stronger than the last.

I hadn't asked for this. I hadn't signed up for any of it. Gabriel's world was chaos, and I had been foolish to think I could live in it without becoming tangled. Yet, here I was, wide awake, my mind spinning in circles I couldn't quite follow.

By morning, he was gone. His absence hit me with a strange finality, like the silence after a storm when the world has settled but everything feels... different. His things were still scattered around the apartment—his jacket slung over the chair, the half-drunk glass of whiskey on the counter—but there was no trace of him. No note, no explanation.

I couldn't decide whether I should be relieved or frustrated. Maybe both.

I tried to focus on something else—anything else—but it felt like I was chasing shadows, unable to settle my thoughts long enough to make sense of the mess Gabriel had left behind. The artifact, his cryptic words, the way he had looked at me—like he was begging for my trust, yet offering none of his own in return. I couldn't shake the feeling that I was standing at the edge of something dangerous, something I couldn't see yet, but I could feel it in my bones.

The apartment had started to feel suffocating, the four walls pressing in like a trap, so I decided to take a walk. The city was alive with the usual noise—the hum of traffic, the chatter of people hurrying to work, the distant sound of a street performer playing jazz on a corner. It was New Orleans, after all. A place where chaos thrived in the best possible way, where secrets could be hidden in plain sight, and nobody batted an eye. But today, it felt like a charade.

I wandered down to the French Quarter, hoping that the rhythm of the city would ground me, at least for a moment. The cobblestone streets were slick with the remnants of a morning rain, the air thick with the earthy scent of damp stone and coffee brewing from nearby cafés. There was something intoxicating about the city—the way it felt like it belonged to another time, yet still buzzed with the energy of the present. It was easy to lose yourself here. And maybe that was what I needed.

I stopped outside one of the small antique shops, gazing at the trinkets in the window. Old books, tarnished jewelry, glass vials filled with unknown liquids. The shopkeeper, a woman with a face like weathered wood, smiled at me from inside the shop, her eyes knowing, as if she could see right through me. She always had that look about her, like she could read the stories people kept hidden in their eyes.

"Looking for something in particular?" she asked, her voice low, raspy like old velvet.

I shook my head, stepping closer to the glass. "Just browsing."

Her eyes flicked to the street behind me, and then back to me, her smile widening. "It's not what you're looking for, is it? It's what you're running from."

I stilled, caught off guard by the sharpness of her observation. The woman's gaze was unshifting, a knowing gleam dancing in the corners of her eyes. I was about to turn away, muttering some excuse, when the sound of a car screeching to a halt shattered the moment. A black sedan had stopped right in front of the shop, the engine still idling loudly, the driver's side window rolled down.

I didn't need to see who was inside. I already knew.

Gabriel.

My heart skipped a beat, and my instinct was to run—just to turn on my heel and disappear into the crowd. But I didn't. I stayed there, frozen in place, as the door to the sedan opened and he stepped out, his body language stiff, his face unreadable.

He caught my gaze almost immediately, his eyes scanning me with that same intensity I had learned to hate—and yet, I couldn't help but feel the pull. It was as if the universe had decided we were tethered to each other, no matter how much we tried to escape.

He approached slowly, his boots tapping against the wet pavement, his expression guarded, like a man walking into enemy territory. When he finally stopped in front of me, there was a long moment of silence, the world holding its breath as I waited for him to speak.

"Are you okay?" he asked, the words coming out softer than I expected.

I blinked, caught off guard by the simple question. Okay? It felt like a question that shouldn't matter, not when there was so much more at stake. Not when there were things we both were pretending didn't exist.

"Why didn't you tell me the truth?" I asked, my voice sharp, though I wasn't sure who I was angrier with. Him? Or myself for ever believing him in the first place.

Gabriel's gaze flickered to the shopkeeper, who stood inside watching us with a knowing smirk, and then back to me. His jaw tightened, but there was something vulnerable in his expression now—something I wasn't used to seeing.

"I couldn't," he replied, his voice a low rasp. "Because the truth is... it's worse than you think. And I didn't want you involved."

I opened my mouth to respond, but before I could, a voice—cold and unfamiliar—cut through the air.

"Is everything alright here?"

I turned, my stomach dropping as two men in dark suits appeared from the shadows, their eyes cold, their postures stiff. I didn't need to ask who they were. The look in their eyes told me everything I needed to know. They were here for Gabriel. And for some reason, they weren't going to leave without him.

"Gabriel," I murmured, my breath catching in my throat. "What's going on?"

His face hardened as he stepped between me and the men, his eyes flicking to me with an unspoken warning. "You need to leave," he said, his voice low but urgent. "Now."

But it was too late. One of the men stepped forward, his gaze narrowing. "No one's going anywhere," he said, his voice like ice. "Not until we're finished."

And just like that, everything I thought I knew about this twisted world unraveled in front of me.

Chapter 14: Shadows of the Past

I leaned against the cool granite of the railing, the city sprawling below me, its heartbeat a dull murmur of distant traffic, flickering streetlights, and the occasional honk of a horn, cutting through the otherwise silent night. New York was a city that never let you forget it existed. A city with its own mind, it whispered and yelled, all at once, demanding your attention.

Amara's words echoed in my mind, like the softest of melodies clinging to the edge of memory. She had told her story with a quiet ferocity, as though every word was a weight lifted, yet bound to her forever. She had been a queen, once—long before the city below us had ever been conceived. But her reign had ended in the cruelest of fates, for the curse that gripped her was older than the stone beneath my feet.

Her eyes had gleamed with the weight of centuries when she spoke, the flicker of flames dancing in the depths of her pupils, memories of a life long gone flickering with each word. "I was not always this," she had said, a slight tremor in her voice, as though even now, the bitter taste of that ancient curse lingered on her tongue. "The artifact you found—that was meant for someone else, someone... not me. But fate, cruel as it is, decided otherwise. And now, here I remain, bound to this life I never asked for."

There had been a pause, one thick with regret, then she'd continued, softer, as if the weight of it all had drained her once more. "Eternal life. It is not a gift. It is a prison."

I had thought of Gabriel then, standing stiff and guarded, his brow furrowed as though he could piece together the puzzle in front of him with his usual sharpness. But there was no clarity here, no black-and-white answers to his questions, only shades of gray. Amara's curse was not something that could be solved with a punchline or a clever word. It was raw, unrelenting, and, in some strange way, I could feel the edges of it gnawing at my own soul. Maybe it was her eyes—so full of sorrow—and the rawness of her truth. Or maybe it was the way she carried herself, like a woman who had lived lifetimes, seen kingdoms rise and fall, and had watched people she loved vanish in the blink of an eye.

She had stepped forward then, as if the weight of her revelation was not enough to anchor her in place. "It is not just the curse that haunts me," she had murmured, "but the knowledge that I was never meant to be."

I hadn't known what to say. What could I say? The silence between us had stretched like a canyon, deep and filled with unseen dangers. Gabriel had been the first to speak, his voice cutting through the tension like a blade.

"We can't trust her," he'd said flatly, eyes narrowed, the muscles of his jaw working with suppressed emotion.

I had felt the words like a slap to my chest, my heart stuttering in response. "Why?" I had asked before I could stop myself, my voice quieter than I intended, yet defiant.

"Because," Gabriel had said, the word laced with a raw bitterness I hadn't expected, "no one is what they seem. Not in this game." He glanced at me, his expression tight, unreadable. "Especially not her."

I wanted to argue with him, to tell him that this wasn't the same, that Amara was different, but I knew—deep down—I wasn't just defending her because she had told me her story. I wasn't just defending her because of that glimpse of vulnerability she had given me. No, I was defending her because I could feel the truth of her words, as if the curse she bore was something we all carried, even if we didn't recognize it yet.

There was a moment of silence between us, the only sound the hum of the city far below. Amara had stepped back, her hands clasped together in front of her, her gaze fixed on the dark skyline.

"It doesn't matter if you trust me," she had said softly, her voice betraying no emotion. "The curse doesn't care what you believe. It will consume you all the same."

I had wanted to reach out to her, to offer something—anything—because in that moment, I had understood something crucial about her. This wasn't a choice. This wasn't a path she had walked willingly. The curse had shaped her, bound her to a fate she hadn't asked for, and it was as much a part of her now as her own breath.

"Don't," Gabriel had said sharply, his gaze on me now, intense and unyielding. "You're making a mistake. She's dangerous."

But was she? Was the curse she carried truly something that would consume us all, or was it the very thing that made her a victim in this twisted dance we'd found ourselves caught up in?

I wasn't sure. All I knew was that standing there, in the silence of the night, I felt the sting of a truth I didn't want to admit: I wasn't just drawn to her because of her past. I was drawn to her because, in some way, I recognized the darkness inside her. It was a mirror. A mirror I didn't want to look into, but couldn't tear my eyes away from.

The night felt colder as the city's neon glow painted long shadows across the concrete streets. The hum of late-night traffic blended with the distant clamor of sirens, the pulse of the city vibrating in the marrow of my bones. Despite the noise, I felt oddly detached, like the world around me was happening just out of reach, like a movie I was supposed to be watching but couldn't quite focus on.

Amara's presence lingered in the air, thick and charged, as if the tension she carried had woven itself into the very fabric of the night. Gabriel, still standing beside me, was tense—his posture rigid, his gaze trained on her every movement, as if ready for a confrontation. His words, sharp and unwavering, had seared through the quiet like a blade, but they hadn't shaken me the way I'd expected. Something in me resisted his suspicion, a quiet voice urging me to trust my instincts.

"You really believe her, don't you?" Gabriel's voice cut through the stillness, his tone rougher than usual. The question wasn't one of curiosity—it was an accusation, veiled in disbelief. His eyes, usually so calm, now carried a storm in their depths, a tempest that he clearly hadn't figured out how to navigate.

"I don't know," I admitted, leaning against the stone wall of the building, watching Amara as she turned her back on us, her silhouette framed by the city lights. "But I can feel it. There's something... real about her story. It's like she's not just telling us what happened. She's showing us the weight of it. How it's shaped her."

Gabriel's lips curled into something that wasn't quite a smile, but more of a half-formed sneer. "You mean you're buying her pity party? She's a queen cursed to live forever. So what? She's not the only one with baggage."

I shook my head, frustrated by his dismissal. "You don't get it, Gabriel. She's not trying to make us feel sorry for her. She's trying to make us understand."

"Understand what?" His voice was low, dangerous. "That she's been alive too long and now she wants sympathy? Or that she's just waiting for her chance to use us for whatever ends she's got in mind?"

I stood up straighter, resisting the urge to snap at him. He was angry, and I didn't know why, but it felt personal. "You're not hearing her, Gabriel. She's not using anyone. She's trapped, just like the rest of us. You think we're free? You think I'm free?" The words slipped out before I could stop them, and I felt them land between us, sharp and raw.

His eyes widened, his expression softening for just a fraction of a second before his mask slid back into place. "You think she's trapped like you?"

I hesitated, the weight of his question sinking in. Did I? Maybe. But the comparison wasn't quite right. Amara's curse was eternal, an ancient tether that bound her to a life she hadn't chosen. Mine was different, less tangible, but no less real. It was the weight of all the choices I hadn't made, all the roads I hadn't taken. The little cracks in my life that had started to widen, letting in the cold, until I couldn't ignore them anymore.

"I think we're all trapped in one way or another," I finally said, the bitterness I hadn't realized was there bleeding into my voice. "But that doesn't mean we can't still try to figure out how to live with it."

Gabriel looked at me, his eyes searching my face, as though trying to read the unspoken words behind mine. But then his gaze flickered toward Amara, still standing silently, her back turned to us, her posture rigid with something I couldn't quite name.

"What if we can't?" he asked, his voice suddenly quiet, almost pained.

The vulnerability in his question took me off guard. He was always the unflappable one, the rock that never cracked. The thought of him questioning whether anything could be salvaged—whether any of us could break free from the things that held us—sent a ripple of doubt through me. But I couldn't let it land. Not yet. Not when I still had faith that there was something in all of this worth believing in.

"Then we fight," I said, my voice firm now, a quiet resolve settling over me. "We fight until we find something that makes it worth it."

There was a long silence between us. Gabriel didn't answer, and I didn't know if I wanted him to. The words we were dancing around—about Amara, about the curse, about whatever the hell this was—felt too large to tackle all at once.

Finally, he spoke, his voice a little softer, but still laced with that edge I'd grown used to. "I'm not going to let her drag us down with her."

"I don't think she will," I replied, the words escaping before I could fully consider them. And then I realized, in the space between us, I wasn't sure if I meant Amara or myself.

Gabriel's eyes narrowed again, but he didn't press further. He simply turned, walking away from me, his long strides eating up the distance. He didn't look back, but I could feel the weight of his doubt, his protectiveness, lingering like a storm cloud on the edge of my thoughts.

Amara didn't flinch when he left. She was too still, her form almost indistinguishable from the shadows around her, as though she had been part of the city itself all along.

I took a step toward her, drawn by something I couldn't explain—some strange magnetism, or maybe just the pull of an unanswered question.

"You don't have to do this alone," I said, my voice steady, though I wasn't sure where the words came from. Maybe they were for her. Maybe they were for me.

She turned then, her expression unreadable, but there was something in the way she held herself, something ancient and knowing. "We never do, do we?"

I wanted to ask her what she meant, but before I could, the sound of footsteps approaching—familiar ones—interrupted the moment. Gabriel's shadow loomed over us, and his expression made it clear that this conversation was far from over.

And neither was the one that had begun with Amara.

The streets of the city seemed to hold their breath as we stood in the uneasy silence. The warmth of the night air pressed in around us, thick and humid, but there was no comfort in it, just a sense of foreboding. Even the distant roar of the subway felt like an intrusion, a jarring reminder of the world that continued to spin while we teetered on the edge of something we couldn't quite understand. I glanced at Gabriel, the words unsaid between us heavy in the space we occupied. There were no answers in his eyes, just a storm of conflict that seemed to pull at him, twisting the familiar calm I had once relied on into something foreign.

"Where are we going with this?" His voice, hoarse and taut, cut through the stillness, his words finally breaking the silence that had stretched on far too long. The question wasn't aimed at anyone, but it landed between us like a grenade, its echo vibrating through the empty streets.

I watched Amara, her profile a study in quiet resignation, her back turned toward us as she stared out over the city. The lines of her face seemed carved from stone, yet there was a vulnerability there, one that neither Gabriel nor I could quite place.

"The truth?" I said, my voice louder than I intended, a harshness creeping into it as I finally found the courage to speak. "I think we're all trying to figure out the truth here. The real truth. About her, about us, and... what happens next."

Gabriel snorted, the sound bitter. "And you think she's going to give us that? After everything?"

"Maybe she's not the one who's hiding the truth," I shot back, the words out before I could stop them, the sting of his mistrust digging deeper than I cared to admit.

Gabriel turned sharply, his eyes blazing with frustration. "You don't get it, do you? You really don't see it, do you? She's not some innocent bystander in this. She's not someone to save. She's a damn liar, and I don't trust anything that comes out of her mouth."

I opened my mouth to retort, but then Amara spoke, her voice cutting through the tension like a hot knife through butter. "You don't trust me because you don't want to."

Her words were soft, but there was a steeliness in them, an edge that made me pause. I had expected her to remain silent, to let Gabriel's accusations slide by unnoticed, but instead, she stood tall, her shoulders squared against whatever storm Gabriel had just unleashed.

"I don't trust you because I've been burned before," Gabriel bit out. His fists were clenched at his sides, his jaw tight, but there was an underlying sadness in his tone that I hadn't expected. "And I don't need another lesson in heartbreak."

I felt the air between us crackle as I took a step toward him. "That's not what this is about, Gabe."

"Oh, really?" he snapped, his gaze flicking between me and Amara, his eyes narrowing. "Because right now, it sure feels like it. She's weaving a story, playing the martyr. She's not some broken queen waiting to be saved—she's playing a game. And we're her pawns."

Amara didn't flinch at the accusation. She just looked at him, her expression unreadable, her eyes the color of dusk, full of shadows and secrets.

"No," she said, her voice barely above a whisper. "You're not pawns. You're just... caught in the middle of a much larger game."

There was a heaviness in the words, something that felt like a warning. But Gabriel, never one for subtlety, didn't take it as one. He stepped forward, his gaze hard, like he was daring her to say more.

"Then tell us," he challenged, his voice a mixture of anger and exhaustion. "Tell us everything. If you're not a threat, if we're not just your little chess pieces, then tell us the truth. All of it. What are we really dealing with here?"

The words hung in the air, weighty and pressing, like a balloon just waiting to burst. Amara's face softened, the hard edges of her expression melting into something closer to sorrow, something that I couldn't quite name. She turned her head slightly, looking out over the city again, her gaze unfocused.

"I've already told you more than I should," she said quietly. "The artifact—this cursed thing—isn't just a relic of the past. It's... connected to something much older, much darker than you can imagine. Something that spans centuries. And no matter how much we fight, no matter how many lives it takes... it will never let go."

Gabriel's lips tightened into a grim line, and he crossed his arms over his chest. "What, now you want us to take up the mantle? Fight your battle for you?"

"No," Amara said, her voice suddenly sharp, cutting through his doubt. "But you're already in it. Whether you like it or not."

The truth of her words settled over us like a cold fog, thick and choking. I watched Gabriel closely, his jaw working as if he was trying to decide if he should press further or retreat. He wasn't the type to back down from a challenge, but even I could see how much this was eating at him. The weight of the past, the lingering doubts about Amara, the way everything seemed to be spiraling out of control...

"I don't believe you," he muttered, almost to himself.

Amara's smile was small, almost sad. "That's the problem, isn't it? You can't. You won't. Not until it's too late."

The words echoed in my mind, swirling like a storm that I couldn't outrun. And just as I thought I might say something to counter them, the shrill ring of my phone cut through the night air. My heart skipped a beat as I pulled it from my pocket, the display lighting up with an unfamiliar number.

"Who's calling this late?" I murmured, but as I swiped the screen to answer, my breath hitched in my chest.

"Whatever you do, don't trust her," came the voice on the other end, low and panicked.

The line went dead before I could respond. My fingers trembled as I stared at the screen, but the sense of dread that had been building in my chest took root.

I didn't need to look at Gabriel or Amara to know that whatever was happening, whatever game we were caught in—it was only just beginning.

Chapter 15: The Sands Will Rise

The city had been holding its breath for weeks, the streets humming with a tension that made every step feel heavier, every breath a little more shallow. The air felt thicker in the evenings now, like the humidity had settled in and refused to leave. I wasn't sure if it was the heat or the fact that the mark on my wrist had started to pulse again, but something about the city felt different. Like it was holding onto a secret just beyond my reach.

I stood at the corner of Fourth and Spring, the lights of the café across the street casting a golden haze on the cobblestones. The aroma of strong coffee, baked goods, and a faint trace of lavender from the garden shop down the street mingled in the air, and I inhaled deeply, trying to steady myself. Gabriel was waiting inside, his presence as palpable as the steam rising from his mug.

I had no intention of running into him today—not because I didn't want to see him, but because everything was changing, and the changes were too fast, too overwhelming. But the curse had other plans, and it wasn't interested in playing nice.

The mark on my wrist had flared to life the moment I'd stepped out of my apartment that morning. It burned beneath my sleeve, a scorching reminder of the artifact's growing power and the relentless pull it had on me. Gabriel and I were still pretending like we had time. Like there was a tomorrow where we could take this slow. But I knew better. Time was slipping through our fingers, fast and relentless like the tide.

I rubbed at my wrist, the skin heated beneath the faint black ink that had appeared there months ago. I still hadn't gotten used to it, this curse that had claimed me the moment I laid eyes on that artifact. I'd thought, naively, that it was just an old relic. But no, it was something else entirely—a key, a marker, a harbinger of whatever darkness was lurking just beyond our reality.

I crossed the street slowly, my sneakers slapping against the sidewalk, the rhythm a small comfort as the city around me buzzed with life. It was the middle of the day, but the crowd felt different now. Maybe it was just my paranoia, but I could swear everyone was watching me. Eyes flicked away too quickly, whispers barely concealed behind the hum of the busy street. I didn't need to look up to know they were there—shadows that followed me, waiting for the moment I would slip.

When I reached the door to the café, I pushed it open, the soft chime of the bell above greeting me. Gabriel was sitting at our usual spot by the window, his gaze lifting just as the door clicked shut behind me. His dark eyes met mine, and something inside me twisted in response—a mixture of guilt, relief, and something else that I wasn't ready to name.

He had been my anchor for so long now, though neither of us had asked for this strange connection, this bond forged by a curse neither of us fully understood. When I sat down across from him, the weight of our shared silence felt heavier than any conversation we could have had. We had tried talking it out a hundred times, but the words never came. Instead, we existed in this delicate dance of proximity and tension, each of us pretending like we had control over the thing that was unraveling our lives.

"How are you holding up?" Gabriel's voice was soft, but it carried that undertone of urgency that had become so familiar in the weeks since the mark had appeared on my wrist.

"I'm fine," I lied, rubbing the back of my neck as I leaned into the chair, trying to ignore the fact that I was lying to him, and worse, to myself.

"You're not fine." His brow furrowed, and for a moment, I saw the frustration flash across his face. The kind of frustration that came from knowing something was wrong but not knowing how to fix it. "You're pushing yourself too hard. We don't even know what this curse really is yet, and you're out here running around like it's just another Tuesday."

I forced a smile, trying to keep the weight of everything from crashing down. "It's not like I have a choice. It's not going to wait around for us to figure it out. You know that better than anyone."

Gabriel sighed and ran a hand through his dark hair, the messiness of it just one of the many things that made him impossible to ignore. "I know," he muttered. "But we need to stop pretending we're in control. This thing—it's not going to let us go, not unless we stop running from it." He leaned in slightly, his voice dropping to a near whisper. "We're not the only ones searching for answers, you know."

My pulse quickened at his words, the hairs on the back of my neck standing up. "What do you mean?"

"There are others," he said, glancing around the café briefly before meeting my eyes again, his expression hardening. "I've been looking into the artifact, the curse—it's not the only one. There are others like it, and whoever is behind this, they're not done with us yet."

I leaned back in my chair, the reality of his words settling over me like a cold shadow. I had known there were risks when I picked up that artifact, but this? This was something I wasn't prepared for.

"Great," I muttered, the bite in my voice more from the fear gnawing at me than anything else. "So now we're not just dealing with a curse—we're dealing with a whole group of people who want to make our lives miserable."

Gabriel didn't answer at first, just looked at me with that intensity that was both a comfort and a warning. "Exactly. And it's only a matter of time before they come for us."

I could feel the weight of the moment press down, the knowledge that whatever had been waiting in the shadows was coming closer, and there was nothing we could do to stop it. Not yet, anyway.

The café was quieter now, the hum of conversations softened by the distant sound of traffic outside. I tried to focus on the flickering candle on our table, but it was hard to concentrate with the feeling of being watched, an unsettling sensation that made the hairs on the back of my neck stand at attention. Gabriel's gaze never left me, but there was a certain wariness in it, like we were both trying to figure out where to go next without either of us giving away too much.

"You can't keep doing this," he said, his voice low but firm, his fingers drumming lightly on the rim of his cup. "You're not invincible, you know. This curse—it's draining you, piece by piece. You have to let me help you."

I leaned back in my chair, giving him a smile I didn't feel. "Let you help?" I repeated, cocking an eyebrow. "You make it sound so easy."

Gabriel's lips tightened, the lines of his jaw sharp with the tension that had been building between us for weeks. It was as if every conversation we had lately was a little bit too loaded, a little too important. Neither of us wanted to confront the truth, but we both knew it was there, lurking beneath the surface.

"I'm not saying it's going to be easy. But nothing worth doing ever is," he shot back, his voice just a bit too rough, like it had been scraped raw. "And you're not alone in this anymore, despite how much you seem to want it that way."

It wasn't the first time he'd said that, though it felt sharper this time, as if he was testing the waters for something deeper. Something I wasn't sure I was ready for. "You know, Gabriel, I don't need a knight in shining armor. I don't even need a sidekick. All I need is for this damn curse to stop trying to eat me alive."

"Maybe what you need is for someone to care enough to try," he shot back, his voice cracking slightly, his eyes softening in spite of himself. "You've been trying to carry all of this by yourself for too long, and you're wearing yourself out. Look at you."

I glanced at my reflection in the window, noting how pale I'd become, how the dark circles under my eyes seemed permanent. The burn on my wrist flared again, a reminder of the constant pressure building beneath my skin.

I pressed my lips together, the frustration rising in my chest like a storm ready to burst. "You think I don't know that? You think I don't feel it?" The words left me in a rush, spilling out before I could stop them. "I'm not stupid, Gabriel. I'm trying to keep everyone safe—especially you. You think you're the only one who's noticed the way this thing is changing me? The way it's... making me into something I'm not? I can't drag you into this. Not when I'm not sure I'll even survive it."

Gabriel didn't flinch, his eyes locked on mine with an intensity that sent a shiver down my spine. "We're already in this, whether you like it or not. And I'm not going anywhere. Not until we figure this out. Together."

The silence between us stretched, and I felt my breath hitch in my throat. I opened my mouth to argue—because of course I wanted to argue—but nothing came out. The air felt too thick, the weight of what we were both avoiding too heavy to dismiss with a joke or a snarky comment.

The curse was pushing us closer together in ways neither of us had anticipated. At first, it was the mark, a strange little symbol etched into my skin that hadn't made sense until the day it started to burn. The artifact that had brought us together in the first place—it was pulling me in, calling me with a magnetic force that made me want to fight it, even as I was drawn to it. The problem was, I wasn't sure I could fight much longer.

Gabriel reached across the table, his hand hovering just above mine. "I know you think you're protecting me by keeping your distance, but you're wrong," he said, his voice quiet but resolute. "I'm not going to let you go through this alone. Not anymore."

I could feel his warmth just inches from my skin, and the way the air between us seemed to hum with something electric. I had spent so many years keeping people at arm's length, convinced I was better off alone. But Gabriel was breaking down every wall I'd built. And that terrified me more than anything else.

Before I could say anything, the door of the café swung open with a sudden rush of cold air, a gust that sent the scent of rain and city dust through the room. I didn't have to look up to know something was wrong. There was a shift in the energy, a crackle that spread across the room like a live wire.

Gabriel's hand stilled above mine, and we both turned to see the figure standing just inside the door. Tall, cloaked in a dark coat, the stranger's face was partially obscured by the collar, but the glint of something sharp—something metallic—caught the light. My heart skipped a beat.

Without a word, the figure stepped inside, their gaze scanning the room before locking onto me. It wasn't a casual glance, either. No, this was a look of recognition, one that made my skin crawl, and I knew—deep down—that this wasn't some passerby.

Gabriel stiffened across from me, his body language going taut as the stranger approached our table with deliberate slowness. He didn't seem interested in anyone else in the room—just me. And that wasn't a good sign.

"Looks like the past finally caught up to you," the figure said, their voice low, gravelly, the accent clipped with an unfamiliar sharpness. It was a voice that made me feel like I was about to be drawn into something far darker than I had ever imagined.

Gabriel moved instinctively, his hand reaching for something under the table—his phone, his keys, I wasn't sure. But before he could react, the stranger raised a gloved hand, stopping him in his tracks. "Don't," the voice commanded, and there was something in that word, something chilling, that made my chest tighten.

I was on the edge now, that fine line between the ordinary world I had known and the nightmare I had tried to outrun. And there was no turning back.

The stranger's eyes never left me, and the air around us seemed to freeze, suspended in some delicate, precarious moment that stretched long enough to make my skin prickle with unease. I shifted in my seat, trying to stay casual, but every instinct in my body was screaming for me to get up, run, do something—anything—but there was nowhere to go. The café felt suddenly too small, too quiet, as if the world outside had been muffled by the weight of what was unfolding.

Gabriel's hand was still hovering over the table, but he hadn't moved. His jaw was clenched tight, the muscles beneath his skin working with tension. He didn't speak, didn't make a sound—his stillness was a warning, one I wasn't sure how to read, but it was there, unmistakable. We were in this together, but even now, there was something he wasn't saying. Something just out of reach.

"You've been looking for me," the figure said, their voice like cold steel cutting through the thick silence. Their words were slow, deliberate, and every syllable felt like a threat, even without the threat itself.

I tried not to let my heart pound louder than it already was, but the burning mark on my wrist flared again, sharper this time, making my breath catch in my throat. Gabriel must've seen the shift in me, because his eyes flicked to my wrist before narrowing in suspicion.

"Who are you?" I forced the words out, keeping my tone steady, even though I felt anything but steady.

The stranger didn't answer immediately. Instead, they seemed to study me with that same unnerving gaze, as though they were sizing up a puzzle they were eager to solve. Finally, they took a step closer, the soles of their boots barely making a sound against the old wood of the floor.

"I think you know exactly who I am," they said, each word dripping with quiet menace. "But I'm willing to remind you." They reached into their coat and pulled out a small object, something glinting in the dim light of the café.

I didn't need to look closely to know what it was—another artifact, another piece of this sickening puzzle that had been pulling me deeper into its web. The sight of it made my stomach drop, and I felt a pang of frustration rise within me. How many of these damn things were there?

Gabriel shifted in his seat, his voice low but full of command. "Put it down."

But the stranger didn't even acknowledge him. Instead, they turned their gaze back to me, a faint smirk playing on their lips. "I know what you've been doing, searching for answers, trying to outrun your fate." They clicked their tongue, a sound so disapproving that it made my teeth clench. "It's cute, really. But the curse isn't going to break itself, is it?"

I narrowed my eyes, taking a slow breath, trying to force my mind to focus. The mark burned again, hotter this time, as if it were answering some unseen call. I pressed my hand against it, but it only made the sensation worse, the heat crawling up my arm, spreading like wildfire.

"What do you want?" I asked, my voice sharp now, the frustration and fear in me cutting through the calm exterior I was trying to maintain.

The stranger leaned in closer, their voice barely above a whisper as they spoke directly to me, like they were telling me a secret I wasn't ready to hear. "You're not the only one cursed, you know. Not the only one who's been chosen to carry this burden."

I shook my head, the confusion laced with a growing dread. "What are you talking about?"

The smirk widened, but it was bitter, mocking. "You think you're special? You think you're the only one who's been marked by the artifact?" The figure raised the object in their hand again, the glint of it catching the light. "You're not. You're just another pawn in a game that's been going on far longer than you realize."

The words hung in the air like a storm cloud, thick with implications I couldn't quite grasp. Gabriel's hand tightened into a fist on the table, but he remained silent, watching me closely. The tension between the three of us crackled, a sharp electricity that made the very air feel alive with danger.

I wasn't sure what to do. This wasn't just some random encounter—this was something bigger, something that went beyond the artifacts and the curses. Whoever this person was, they knew things I didn't, things that could change everything. And as much as I hated to admit it, I was in over my head.

"Why are you here?" I finally asked, the words tasting bitter as I said them. "What do you want from me?"

The stranger didn't answer right away. Instead, they took a step back, their eyes flicking to the door, as though they were checking for something. For someone. It was subtle, but I caught it, and the hair on the back of my neck stood on end.

"You're asking the wrong question," they said, their voice lowering to a cold murmur. "The real question is—what are you willing to sacrifice to break this curse?"

Before I could respond, a sudden, sharp noise broke the moment—a crash, followed by the sound of running footsteps coming from the back of the café. Instinctively, Gabriel and I both stood, our bodies going tense, ready for whatever was coming. The stranger barely moved, their focus unwavering, as if they had expected this.

And then, out of the corner of my eye, I saw it. A figure emerging from the shadows at the back of the room. Tall. Unfamiliar. And dressed entirely in black.

The stranger turned toward them, a barely perceptible nod, and for a split second, I wondered if I'd made a terrible mistake by coming here today.

The figure at the back of the room pulled something from their coat. My heart skipped a beat.

In that moment, I realized we were no longer the only ones in control of our fate.

Chapter 16: The Serpent's Call

The moonlight was sharp against the desert, painting the endless sea of sand with an eerie glow. It made everything feel surreal, like we were the last two souls on earth, trapped in a world where the rules of time and space no longer applied. The air was thick with the scent of dust and something else, something that clung to the back of my throat, bitter and metallic. I could taste it even as I tried to steady my breath, to quiet the frantic beating of my heart.

Gabriel's hand, still wrapped tightly around mine, pulled me further from the now still serpent-like creature, its massive form lying motionless in the sand. I didn't trust that it was dead. Not for a second. Not after what I'd felt—those ancient, cruel threads of power binding it to something far beyond us, something I was starting to fear might be even older than the desert itself.

"Is it...?" I began, my voice trailing off. It felt impossible to articulate the feeling in my chest, the unsettling certainty that something bigger than us had just been set into motion.

Gabriel didn't answer right away. His eyes were fixed on the creature, the lines of his face drawn tight. I could see the way his fingers flexed, itching for his sword again, even though the fight was over—or at least, that's what he thought. I could feel his tension, a tautness between us that wasn't entirely about the creature at all. He was waiting for something. The question was, what?

"Not yet," he muttered under his breath, finally releasing my hand and taking a step forward, his boots sinking slightly into the sand with each movement. He unsheathed his sword with a fluid motion, its cold steel catching the moonlight. It was beautiful in its deadly simplicity, a weapon of both grace and precision.

I took a breath, trying to settle my nerves. Gabriel was always so sure of himself, so controlled, that it was easy to forget how unpredictable he could be. But in the silence that had descended, something felt off. The crack in the earth, the way the sands had shifted, and now... now this creature. It was almost as if we had stirred something that was better left undisturbed.

"You don't think it's dead, do you?" I asked, finally finding my voice.

He didn't answer right away. Instead, his eyes flicked to me, the sharp edge of his gaze cutting through the space between us like a blade. "You're not afraid?" he asked, his words coming out slower than usual.

It wasn't a challenge, but it felt like one. It always did with Gabriel. He had a way of making you question things, to make you doubt whether you really understood the situation or if you were just playing along with a story someone else had already written. It was maddening.

I lifted my chin, meeting his gaze without flinching. "No," I said simply. "I'm not afraid." I wasn't. At least, not in the way he was asking. Fear was a tool, something I had learned to use, something I had learned to bend to my will. There was something deeper in me now, something old and vast, like the desert itself. I could feel it swirling just beneath the surface, waiting for the right moment. And somehow, I knew that moment was coming.

Gabriel's eyes softened, just for a fraction of a second. It was so quick that I almost thought I imagined it, but it was there. And then it was gone, replaced by the same cold calculation that always made him seem so distant. "Stay close," he said, his voice low and firm.

I nodded, although the warning in his tone was unnecessary. There was no part of me that wasn't already aware of the danger. Every inch of my skin tingled with the knowledge that something was coming for us, something that was far worse than a serpent bound by a forgotten spell.

As Gabriel moved closer to the creature, I let my power stretch out again, reaching for the threads that still hummed faintly beneath the surface of the sand. The air felt thick with the weight of it—an ancient power, one that had been dormant for far too long. It was like a drumbeat, a pulse, resonating beneath the earth. I closed my eyes, allowing the vibrations to wash over me. The creature's death was just the beginning.

"I don't know what we've just awoken," I said quietly, my voice almost drowned out by the wind that picked up around us. It swirled the sand into the air, carrying with it the scent of something rotten. Something that had been dead far longer than it should have.

Gabriel didn't respond immediately. Instead, he crouched down next to the serpent's body, running his fingers lightly along the coiled form, his face set in a mask of concentration. His sword was still in his other hand, but he didn't seem to think he would need it. His posture was defensive, cautious, but there was something about his stillness that unnerved me.

"I don't like this," he muttered, more to himself than to me.

Neither did I. I could feel it in my bones—the faintest whisper of danger that had been set loose by that ancient power, by the artifact we had uncovered. I had no idea what it was, only that we were both part of something far larger than we could comprehend.

"I think it's watching us," I said, my voice almost a whisper.

Gabriel's eyes snapped to mine, his jaw tightening. He rose to his feet quickly, moving back toward me, his sword now raised defensively.

And that's when it happened.

The wind howled like a forgotten ghost, and the desert stretched endlessly before us, its vastness now feeling suffocating instead of liberating. I could hear my own breath, shallow and quick, in the stillness that followed the creature's collapse. The air tasted of salt and earth, as if the desert itself were reminding us of how small we really were, how powerless.

Gabriel was staring at me, his eyes narrow and unreadable, but there was something in them that made me uneasy. A spark. Recognition. Fear, maybe, but a kind of respect that I didn't quite know how to handle. It wasn't often that someone like him—someone who had spent years carving his reputation in the underworld—looked at me like I was more than just a complication. And yet, here we were, in the middle of nowhere, and I could feel the shift. I wasn't just some rookie on a dangerous mission anymore. I wasn't the girl who had no idea what she was doing. I had power, and he knew it.

"So, now what?" I asked, finally breaking the silence, my voice a little too loud in the quiet.

Gabriel didn't answer right away, his gaze flicking to the snake-like creature's remains. It was strange. I expected it to decay or disappear, like some mythical thing bound by a spell. But it didn't. It just lay there, its massive form sprawled across the sand like it had been there for centuries, untouched and unwilling to fade into the past where it belonged.

He sheathed his sword, still not looking at me. "We wait."

My eyebrow arched, the sarcasm almost too heavy to resist. "Wait for what, exactly? A miracle? An apology?"

"Lyra," he said, turning his head just enough to give me that look—the one that said he was trying to be patient, but only because he was tired of my nonsense. "There are things you don't understand."

"Like what?" I shot back, my voice unsteady, even though I wanted to sound more confident. "What's the play here, Gabriel? I don't even know why we're standing around. That thing's dead. Let's go."

He paused, a rare flicker of something softer crossing his face. Then it was gone, like sand in the wind. "The thing that we woke up... it's not the only one."

A shiver crawled up my spine, but I refused to let it show. Instead, I crossed my arms over my chest and glared at him, as if it could make him explain what in the hell he was talking about. "So we woke up an ancient snake, and now we're waiting for... what? An army of them?"

Gabriel didn't answer, his focus still on the remains of the creature. His eyes were distant, his jaw clenched as if he were measuring something invisible in the air between us. For a second, I almost believed we were back in the city, and I was just an ordinary girl arguing with him over the next step in some overly complicated mission. But it wasn't like that. And that was the part I was beginning to understand—the part that had been gnawing at me since we first set foot in this place. Gabriel wasn't just some mercenary. He was part of something bigger. Something far older than either of us.

A cold breeze swept through the dunes, raising the sand in little swirls that danced like spirits. The creature's form seemed to ripple in the light, and for a moment, I could've sworn I saw it twitch. But that was impossible. There was no way...

I stepped back, my eyes narrowing. "You didn't tell me everything, Gabriel. What aren't you saying?"

His eyes flicked to mine, but he didn't answer immediately. He just stood there, a sentinel in the desert, the weight of everything he hadn't said pressing in on me. I wanted to scream at him, demand answers, but that would have been a waste of breath. If there was one thing I knew about Gabriel, it was that he didn't play by the same rules as everyone else. And right now, those rules weren't even on the table.

"I'll tell you when it's time," he finally said, his voice like gravel. "Right now, we need to get out of here. The artifact—"

"The artifact," I repeated, cutting him off. "Is that what this is really about? Not the snake, not the ritual, but some damn relic?"

Gabriel stiffened, a flicker of annoyance flashing across his face. But he didn't try to shut me down. Instead, he exhaled sharply, taking a few steps away from the creature's remains, as if it were contagious.

"It's not just a relic," he said, his tone softer now. But that didn't make it any less intense. "It's a key. To something bigger."

Something bigger. I swallowed hard, the weight of his words pressing against my chest. I had felt it—the pull, the connection to whatever lay beneath the sands. The artifact had called to me. But I hadn't realized it was leading to something far darker, far more dangerous than I could have imagined. And I sure as hell hadn't expected Gabriel to be tangled in whatever it was. He was the kind of guy who thrived in chaos, sure, but even he looked like he was treading water now, unsure of where this was going.

I took a step toward him, my gaze fixed on his profile. "You can't just leave me in the dark like this. Not anymore."

Gabriel glanced at me, the tension in his features momentarily breaking. "I'm not leaving you in the dark. I'm just not letting you walk into it blind."

I didn't trust him. Not completely. But right now, I wasn't sure I had any other choice. We were in this together, whether we liked it or not.

"Fine," I said, biting back the rest of my frustration. "But we move fast. And you better start talking, Gabriel. Because the last thing I need is more mysteries."

He met my gaze with a brief, inscrutable look. And then, without another word, he began walking, the sand shifting under his boots, his silhouette swallowed by the night.

And I followed, because what else was there to do?

We moved through the desert with the kind of silence that felt heavy, like the ground itself was holding its breath. Gabriel was ahead, his dark figure cutting through the dunes with purposeful steps, the weight of whatever we had just unleashed hanging over him like an unwelcome shadow. The further we got from the serpent's remains, the more I felt the odd pull of something unfamiliar—a sensation that lingered in my chest, just under my ribs, as though the artifact was still calling to me.

I glanced at Gabriel's back, noting the stiffness in his shoulders. He always carried himself like a man on the verge of breaking, but now it was different. There was something fragile in his gait, like he was waiting for the ground to give way beneath him at any moment. It made me wonder how much of this mess was planned, and how much was pure, bloody luck.

"You know," I said, my voice carrying over the wind, "if I didn't know better, I'd say you were the one who wasn't telling the truth here."

Gabriel didn't respond right away. He kept moving, his boots leaving deep imprints in the sand that were quickly swallowed up by the shifting grains. But I knew he heard me. He always heard me, even when he pretended not to.

"I didn't say anything because there's nothing you can do about it," he finally said, his words clipped. "It's not about trust, Lyra. It's about survival."

I rolled my eyes. Survival. As if we weren't already deep in the mess, hurtling toward whatever disaster we'd awakened. But I didn't argue. Not yet. We had more important things to focus on—like getting out of this godforsaken desert alive.

We were almost at the edge of the dunes when I saw it. A flicker of movement on the horizon, small at first, barely noticeable. But it was there, a distortion in the air. Not a mirage, not the usual dance of heatwaves. No, this felt different. It was wrong in a way I couldn't explain, like the air itself was holding its breath, waiting for something to crack.

"Gabriel," I said, my voice urgent.

He paused, his hand instinctively moving to the hilt of his sword. The flickering light seemed to pulse, like it was alive, like it was drawing us in.

"I see it," he said quietly, his eyes narrowing as he studied the strange anomaly in the distance. "Stay close."

I took a step forward, drawn by something I couldn't quite place. The pull was there again, more insistent this time, a magnetic force that tugged at the very marrow of my bones. It wasn't just the artifact this time. It was something deeper, something older. It was as if the desert itself was speaking to me, whispering in a language I had long since forgotten but knew all too well.

We moved cautiously toward the flickering, our senses heightened, every step measured. The desert stretched endlessly before us, an unforgiving landscape of nothingness that seemed to press in on all sides. It was hard to say whether the sense of dread was coming from the land itself or from whatever was waiting ahead.

When we reached it, the sight that greeted us was nothing short of strange. The flickering light revealed an enormous, blackened stone, half-buried in the sand. It was smooth, almost too perfect for its surroundings, its surface unmarred by the ravages of time or weather. And at its base, half-hidden beneath the stone, was something that made my stomach lurch. A symbol—carved into the rock, ancient and intricate, its edges sharp and defined as if it had been made just moments ago.

I crouched down, my fingers brushing the smooth surface of the stone. I could feel the heat radiating off of it, and the pulse beneath my fingertips. It was alive, like the serpent. Like the artifact. Like something that had been waiting for centuries to be found.

"Is this...?" I trailed off, my voice catching in the weight of the realization.

Gabriel didn't answer right away, his gaze fixed on the stone, his jaw clenched in that way he had when he was hiding something. But the moment stretched, and he finally spoke, his voice softer now, almost like a confession.

"It's a doorway," he said quietly. "A portal. To something much worse than what we've already unleashed."

The words hung between us like a curse. A portal? To what? I felt the weight of his statement settle over me, the enormity of it sinking into my bones like a slow poison. A portal. We hadn't just woken up the serpent, then. We had opened a door to something else entirely.

"What are we supposed to do with it?" I asked, my voice suddenly feeling very small in the vast desert around us.

Gabriel didn't respond right away. Instead, he stepped forward, his fingers tracing the symbol with a care that made my stomach turn. He seemed... reverent, almost. As if he knew exactly what he was looking at, what it meant. And I hated him for it. I hated that he was so calm when everything around us was falling apart. I hated that he had answers and was withholding them from me.

"It's not about what we do with it," he said, his voice low, gravelly. "It's about what's already been set into motion. The question is whether we're strong enough to close it."

Before I could respond, the ground beneath us trembled again, not like before, but with purpose—like the very earth was shaking in warning. The air turned colder, and I could feel the pulse beneath my fingertips intensify, a steady hum that reverberated through my chest.

And then I saw it. A figure, barely visible at first, but growing clearer as the wind began to whip through the desert, a shadow coming to life, pulling itself from the depths of the earth like a specter.

It was human, or at least it looked human. But there was something wrong about it, something unnatural. The air around it shimmered, bending and distorting as if the figure were pulling reality itself into a new shape.

And in that moment, I knew: the portal hadn't just opened. It had been waiting for us to step through. And now, we had no choice but to follow.

Chapter 17: Whispers of Betrayal

The city hummed with its usual energy, the night air thick with the scent of rain that never quite fell. The sidewalks shimmered under the harsh light of street lamps, reflecting every passing shadow, every hurried footstep, as if the concrete itself was holding onto secrets. I walked beneath the canopy of indifferent buildings, my mind buzzing with Amara's words, each syllable gnawing at me. I'd thought I was used to feeling exposed, but this—this was different. There was something about the way she said it, the way her lips curled around the promise of a price, that made me feel like I was standing at the edge of something I couldn't quite see.

Gabriel's silence beside me was palpable, a weight pressing down on the space between us. I could feel his distrust like a wall between us, even as his presence was a comfort. He hadn't said a word since we left Amara, his brow furrowed, his hands restless at his sides. It was obvious to me now—he was waiting for me to break, to crumble under the pressure of whatever it was that was hanging over us. And I wanted to, so badly. I wanted to lean into him, to feel the warmth of his steady gaze, but the words he hadn't said were louder than any comfort he could offer.

"You think she's lying?" I asked, not sure why the question felt so loaded in my mouth.

He didn't answer right away, his eyes scanning the alleyways around us, ever vigilant, ever cautious. Finally, his voice broke through the tension. "She's not telling us everything. She never does." His gaze flickered to mine, his lips tight. "You know that."

I knew it. There was always something about Amara that made me uneasy, a sharp edge hidden beneath her polished exterior. She had the kind of beauty that made people want to trust her, to lean into her calm, measured words. But I was starting to suspect that her serenity was just a veneer for something darker, something that didn't quite sit right with the way she watched us, like a cat eyeing its prey.

I wanted to argue, to tell him he was wrong. But the truth was, I wasn't sure anymore. The artifact was choosing me. She'd said it, and there was no taking it back. That idea, however, felt like a jagged pill lodged somewhere in my chest. What did it mean for me? What price would I have to pay for its favor? Amara's warning echoed in my mind like a curse.

"Do you think I can control it?" The question slipped out before I had a chance to stop it. Gabriel stopped walking, his gaze intense as he turned toward me. There was something unreadable in his eyes, something that made me feel like I was standing in the middle of an open field, exposed and vulnerable.

"I think..." His voice trailed off, and for a moment, I thought he might say something soft, something reassuring. But then his expression hardened, and the words that came out felt like they had been forged in a furnace of frustration. "I think it's not about control. It's about surviving it."

Surviving. That word had a weight to it, a truth that settled deep in my bones. If I was going to survive whatever this was, I needed to make sure I didn't lose myself in the process. And yet, with every step I took toward the unknown, I felt that very part of myself slipping further away. I could feel the pull of the artifact inside me, twisting, beckoning, demanding attention. It was as if it was alive, its power wrapping itself around my thoughts, my actions. But I had to hold on. I had to keep it together, no matter what.

"We need answers," I said, more to myself than to Gabriel, as I turned and started walking again. The rain still hadn't fallen, but the city felt heavier, like it was holding its breath. "We need to find out more about this artifact. Before it's too late."

Gabriel nodded without a word, falling into step beside me. There was a quiet understanding between us now, a shared urgency that wasn't voiced but understood. We had to figure this out. But where could we start? Who could we trust in a city full of whispers and lies?

The answer, I realized, was staring me right in the face.

Amara.

She knew more than she let on. She had to. And if I was going to make it through this, if I was going to survive the test that was coming, I had to get to the heart of whatever game she was playing. I had to make her tell me everything.

"Let's pay her another visit," I said, my voice more determined than I felt. Gabriel's eyes met mine, his face unreadable, but his nod was all the answer I needed.

We didn't speak as we turned back toward Amara's place. The streets seemed quieter now, the world around us narrowing, closing in. Every step felt like we were walking toward something inevitable, something we couldn't avoid, no matter how hard we tried.

I didn't know what I was walking into. But I did know this: whatever Amara was hiding, I was going to find it.

The city stretched out before us like a sprawling web of secrets, each shadow cast by the streetlights a potential clue, each alley a path to something I couldn't quite name. Gabriel and I moved through it as if we were both out of place, both aware of the weight hanging between us like an unspoken question. His silence was a kind of armor, an impenetrable shield that made it impossible to tell whether he was lost in thought or lost in me. I hated that I couldn't figure it out, but then again, I wasn't much better off.

"I'll take the alley," I murmured, nodding toward the narrow passage that ran parallel to the street.

Gabriel didn't respond, but his steps faltered for just a beat—long enough for me to feel the slight hesitation in the air.

"You think this is a good idea?" he asked, his voice low, but sharp. It wasn't so much the words as the way they cut through the cool night, the tension that slid into them, thick as smoke.

"I think we need to be ready for anything," I replied, my gaze skimming the darkened corners. My instincts were pulling me in two directions—one toward the cryptic woman who seemed to know more than she let on, the other to the unease that had wrapped itself tightly around my chest ever since she'd spoken. "And right now, that means getting answers. We can't afford to waste time, Gabriel."

He exhaled, a soft chuckle escaping him before he spoke again. "No, we really can't. That's why we're sneaking around at midnight like a couple of burglars."

"Doesn't that make it more fun?" I shot back with a grin, attempting to cut through the tension with humor, though it tasted a little too bitter on my tongue. He didn't smile, but his gaze softened ever so slightly, a flicker of recognition that, yes, I knew exactly how ridiculous we must look.

"We've got to be careful, Lyra," he said finally, the warning so subtle I almost missed it.

"I am careful," I snapped, the defensive edge to my voice surprising even me. But then I sighed, letting the sharpness drain out. "I'm trying to be careful."

The alley narrowed further, the walls of crumbling brick pressing in like a reminder of how far we had strayed from the comfort of daylight. I could taste the dampness of it in the air, the promise of a storm that wasn't quite here yet but was edging closer by the second. Something about it felt heavy—like the whole world was holding its breath.

Gabriel walked slightly ahead of me now, his shoulders tense, and I could tell he was already listening for sounds in the dark, the faintest creak of a door, the scuffle of shoes on wet pavement. He was always one step ahead, always five seconds from drawing his blade and making his way through whatever obstacle was in our path.

But I wasn't always the one waiting to follow. I was getting better at doing the unexpected.

"So what happens now?" I asked, trying to push past the thickening fog of doubt in my own head.

Gabriel didn't immediately answer, and I wasn't sure if he was waiting for me to figure it out or if he simply didn't have the words. But the silence stretched long enough that I took a sharp breath and let it out slowly, watching my exhale fog the night.

"We go back to Amara," he said eventually, the words as blunt as they were inevitable. "We find out what she's really after."

"Agreed," I said, though I wasn't sure which of us was more wary of her. Maybe that was part of the danger—she had a way of making you question everything, of making you want to trust her even when your gut screamed at you to run in the opposite direction.

The alley eventually opened up to a small courtyard, a tucked-away corner of the city that felt like it existed only for those who knew to find it. The buildings here were older, their stone facades draped in ivy, the air a little heavier with the scent of forgotten memories. In the center, a fountain stood, long since dry, its stone basin cracked from years of neglect. No one bothered to come here. It was too out of the way, too close to things most people didn't want to see.

A soft shuffle of feet broke the silence, and I froze. Gabriel's hand shot out, grabbing my arm in a quiet but firm hold, his body going still. He wasn't worried about what was in the shadows; it was what wasn't in them that made him uneasy.

"You feel that?" he whispered.

I nodded, my pulse picking up pace as I glanced around. "Like something's waiting for us?"

Gabriel's lips curled into a tight smile, though his eyes never left the surrounding darkness. "More like it's been waiting for a long time."

I didn't need to ask him what he meant. We'd both felt it, that undercurrent of tension, that familiar sense that we weren't alone, even though there was no one in sight. The air seemed to hum with it, thick and oppressive.

Before I could say anything else, a figure emerged from the shadows—a woman, her face obscured by a hood, her movements deliberate. She didn't need to announce herself. She was already a part of the night, as much a fixture in this world as the stone and brick around us.

"You came back," she said, her voice a low, almost melodic whisper that carried a thread of something ancient beneath it. It wasn't a question. It was a statement. A truth.

"Of course," I said, trying to keep my voice steady, though I could feel the weight of her gaze even through the shadows. "We've got more questions. And I think it's time you answered them."

For a moment, she didn't respond, simply standing there in the darkness, a figure both familiar and foreign. Then she stepped forward, closer, until I could almost feel the weight of her presence pressing against me. "You're brave," she said, her tone almost approving, though there was a sharpness to it. "But courage doesn't always protect you, Lyra."

I swallowed hard, every instinct telling me to step back, to run, but I forced myself to stand still. "Neither does silence."

The woman's lips curled into something that could've been a smile or a warning—perhaps both. But as she stepped closer, I knew she wasn't done with us yet.

The silence between us grew thicker as we moved further into the courtyard. Gabriel kept his pace steady, as if he was prepared for whatever the night threw at us, but I could feel the tension mounting in his shoulders, the pulse of uncertainty in his grip. The woman standing before us hadn't moved since she first spoke, her figure still cloaked in shadow, as though she were part of the city itself—some relic of forgotten streets and long-past secrets.

"You still haven't answered," I said, my voice sharper than I intended. The words tasted too much like an ultimatum, but I couldn't help it. I was done waiting. "What is it you're hiding, Amara?"

She tilted her head slightly, the faintest glint of amusement flickering beneath the hood, and for a moment, I wondered if we were both playing a dangerous game of chess, our pieces poised, our moves deliberate. The moment stretched longer than it should have, thick with the weight of unspoken truths.

"What I hide is not for your eyes, Lyra," she replied, her voice a low murmur that barely cut through the night air. "What you seek is far more dangerous than you realize. There are things that cannot be undone once seen."

I couldn't help the shiver that crawled up my spine. It was the same warning she'd given before—the same words she had used to dangle the truth just beyond my reach. And now, there was an undeniable edge to her voice, a tension that I hadn't heard before. It felt like a promise and a threat wrapped in one.

Gabriel's hand twitched at his side, and I could feel his unease spreading through the air like wildfire. "You've been withholding something," he said, his tone steady but strained, the sharpness of his gaze never leaving Amara's figure. "And it's about time you told us everything."

Amara's gaze slid to Gabriel, her expression unreadable. The flicker of amusement had vanished, replaced by something colder, more calculating. The kind of look that made your bones feel too tight for your skin.

"Very well," she said, stepping forward, closer now, until the shadows seemed to part in deference to her presence. Her voice dropped to a near-whisper, the words cutting through the night like a blade. "The artifact you so desperately cling to, Lyra... It is not just a relic. It is a key."

A key to what, I wondered, but I couldn't ask. My mind was already scrambling to make sense of the weight of her words. Gabriel took a step forward, his hand finally resting on the hilt of his blade. "What do you mean, a key?"

Amara's lips curled into a smile that didn't reach her eyes. "A key to the breach," she said, the words slowly unfurling in the space between us like smoke.

A cold knot twisted in my stomach, tightening with every passing second. "A breach?" I echoed, my voice betraying me with the slightest tremor. "What do you mean by that?"

Her smile faded, and her eyes darkened. "A breach into the unknown. A doorway to a place that is neither here nor there. And you, Lyra," she said, her gaze flicking to me, "are the one meant to open it."

The words hit like a punch to the gut. I took a step back, feeling the air leave my lungs as my thoughts scrambled to catch up. The artifact was more than I thought—more than I could have ever imagined. It wasn't just a tool or a weapon. It was a threshold, a doorway to something that shouldn't exist. And I was supposed to open it.

I couldn't breathe.

Gabriel's voice, sharp and direct, sliced through the thickening tension. "You've been using us. All this time, you've known what this is, and you've been manipulating her." His finger jabbed toward me as if that made it worse. "And now you expect us to walk into whatever trap this is without question?"

Amara didn't flinch. She didn't seem surprised by his accusation at all. If anything, there was a strange calm in her eyes, as if she knew something we didn't—something we weren't ready to face.

"I've never been your enemy, Gabriel," she said, her voice steady. "But I am not your ally either. The forces at play here are far beyond any of us. This isn't about trust; it's about survival."

I couldn't help but scoff. "Survival? You expect me to believe this is for my survival?"

Her eyes hardened, the faintest flicker of something fierce and dangerous behind them. "It's the only chance you have, Lyra. The artifact has chosen you because you are the one who can wield it. And whether you like it or not, you don't have a choice anymore."

The words sent a cold shiver through me, and I felt the ground beneath me tilt ever so slightly, as if the world itself was shifting. This wasn't just about me anymore. It wasn't about my journey, my quest, or whatever vague purpose I thought I was fulfilling. This was something far larger, something that I couldn't control.

Gabriel's grip on his blade tightened. "I think you're lying. I think there's more to this, and you're hiding it."

Amara didn't answer right away, her eyes flicking between us. Then, she said something so softly that it barely registered. "It's already too late."

Too late. The words dropped into the space between us like stones sinking into water, sending ripples through the quiet of the courtyard. I turned to look at Gabriel, hoping for some hint of reassurance, some sign that we hadn't just walked into something from which there was no return.

But there was no reassurance. Only a dark realization that we were already too deep in this to turn back.

And that's when I heard it.

A soft scraping sound, like metal against stone, followed by the unmistakable hiss of something—or someone—moving in the shadows.

I froze.

Then, as if on cue, something—no, someone—stepped out from the darkness.

And I realized too late that this was only the beginning.

Chapter 18: The Dunes of Forgotten Time

The air, thick with the scent of sand and something else—something ancient—pressed against my skin as the sun began its slow descent, melting into the horizon like a bruised peach. The dunes, now soft and muted under the dying light, rolled out in perfect symmetry, each one a silent sentinel guarding the secrets of an age older than the world itself. I squinted into the expanse before me, feeling the weight of it all—the desert, Gabriel, the tension crackling between us like static, a storm waiting to break.

I hadn't meant to come here. I'd never asked for this cursed desert, this puzzle of forgotten time. But there we were, the heat of the day seeping into my bones, and the nightfall creeping on us like a lover's kiss—smooth, cold, and far too intimate. Gabriel moved beside me, his boots sinking into the warm sand, his usual bravado gone, replaced by a quiet uncertainty. There were no words between us, none that felt right. Every time I opened my mouth, something kept me from speaking the truth. Maybe I didn't know what it was. Maybe I was scared to find out.

He watched me from the corner of his eye, as though waiting for a sign, a crack in my facade. We'd come to the desert to find something. Or perhaps to lose ourselves. He said it was for the artifact, something old and powerful that the world was better off forgetting. But in truth, we were both searching for something we couldn't articulate, at least not yet.

The first stars began to twinkle above us, pinpricks of light that seemed to hold answers in their ancient gaze. I could feel their pull, like threads woven into the very fabric of my soul, drawing me forward, urging me on. The path ahead shimmered in the dark, not like a mirage, but like a memory trying to reach out to me.

"You always know where to go," Gabriel's voice broke through the silence, low and laden with curiosity. He stepped closer, his shadow merging with mine under the rising moon. "How?"

I glanced at him, caught off guard by the softness of his tone. The words were out before I could stop them.

"I follow the stars."

He raised an eyebrow, skepticism flickering across his face like the first spark of a fire. "The stars? So, what, you're some sort of celestial navigator now?"

I smirked, the corner of my mouth twitching as I fought back the urge to laugh. It was the kind of laugh that could break the tension, that could shatter the invisible wall we'd built between us in the wake of our shared silence. But there was no time for that, not now. Not with everything hanging in the balance.

"Something like that," I muttered, my gaze flicking toward the sky. "The stars don't lie. They've seen it all."

He didn't respond immediately, the silence between us thickening. It wasn't uncomfortable, though. No, it was familiar. The kind of silence that only comes when two people have been through enough together to understand each other without the need for words. But Gabriel wasn't a man to sit with discomfort for long. Not when he could cut through it with his sharp tongue.

"So you're telling me that the stars are guiding us, then?" He scoffed, but there was no malice in it. Just a challenge, a game he liked to play. "I thought it was supposed to be some treasure we're after. Not an ancient map in the sky."

I didn't answer right away. Instead, I let the night stretch out around us, the cool breeze pulling at my hair, sending the scent of desert flowers and distant rain in my direction. This was the moment, the pause before something irrevocable would happen. What, I wasn't sure. But I could feel it.

"You don't believe me," I said softly, my voice barely rising above the rustling of the wind through the sand. "But you will."

Gabriel's laughter was dry, a sound that scraped against the quiet like a blade against stone. "Will I?"

I let my gaze drift across the horizon, my eyes narrowing as the path before me began to shimmer with a soft, silvery glow. "You will," I said again, the certainty in my voice surprising even me. "In time."

For a moment, he said nothing. He stood there, watching me with that inscrutable expression on his face, and I could almost hear the gears turning in his mind. Was he thinking of turning back? Of questioning everything we'd fought for up until this point?

"Alright," he said, his voice reluctant but resigned. "Lead the way."

And I did. Every step felt heavier than the last, but the stars—my stars—whispered to me, guiding me, pulling me forward. The path they illuminated grew clearer with each passing second, a thread winding its way through the desert as if the very earth itself were unfolding before me. Gabriel followed silently, his presence a shadow at my back, a force I couldn't escape even if I wanted to.

It wasn't until we reached the crest of the next dune that the full weight of what we were walking into hit me. The desert had no mercy. It was full of secrets—secrets that had waited for centuries, buried beneath layers of time and sand, waiting for the right moment to be uncovered. I could feel the pulse of it in the air, a strange vibration that hummed beneath the earth, as though the land itself had a heartbeat. And in that moment, I realized something I hadn't let myself acknowledge before. We weren't just searching for an artifact. No. We were searching for something far deeper, far older than anything I could have imagined.

And it was waiting for us, just beyond the next dune.

The silence between us stretched as we climbed the next ridge, the weight of it pressing in on my chest. Gabriel's presence behind me, the soft sound of his boots shifting in the sand, was like a shadow I could never escape. He wasn't the type to leave someone alone, even when he should. I could feel his eyes on me, the flicker of something that wasn't just curiosity anymore. It was suspicion, a quiet search for something I wasn't ready to give. I had learned long ago that people like Gabriel didn't ask questions unless they intended to get answers—answers that often came with a price.

But I didn't have answers for him, not real ones. Not the ones that would make sense. I wasn't sure I could explain what the stars had shown me, or how they whispered their secrets into my veins, pulling me along like a marionette in some ancient dance. The night was becoming something else now, darker, thicker. Even the stars seemed to flicker with a kind of urgency, their gleaming faces full of a warning I couldn't decipher. It was as if they knew something I didn't—knew what waited for us ahead and how we would respond to it.

"You know," Gabriel said, breaking the silence with a wry twist of his lips, "I thought this would be more dramatic. You know, mystical tombs and deadly traps. The whole Indiana Jones thing."

I glanced at him over my shoulder, a small laugh escaping me despite the tension gnawing at my insides. "You wanted traps?"

"I wanted something," he muttered, kicking at the sand. "This—this endless stretch of dunes is... anti-climactic."

"There's nothing anticlimactic about it," I said, my voice soft but firm. "The desert doesn't care for your drama."

He snorted, the sound familiar and oddly comforting, like a reminder that we'd been through worse, even if it didn't feel like it. "Fair enough."

It wasn't much of a conversation, but it was enough to keep the silence from swallowing us whole. For a moment, the hum of tension between us dulled, and I allowed myself the luxury of a breath. Maybe it was the desert playing tricks on my mind, or maybe it was just the sheer isolation of the place, but I felt a strange sense of closeness with Gabriel in that moment. It wasn't comfortable. It wasn't safe. But it was something.

The moon hung low now, painting the sand with a pale silver sheen. The light was softer, kinder than the harsh sun of the day, but there was an eerie stillness in the night, as if even the desert knew something important was about to unfold. We reached the crest of the dune, and I stopped, my feet planted firmly in the soft sand, my gaze fixed on the horizon.

There, just beyond the next set of dunes, was something different. Something unnatural. A dark shape, jagged and imposing against the quiet landscape. It was a ruin, but not one that had been forgotten by time—it was a thing that had been deliberately hidden. Its twisted stone walls seemed to reach for the sky, as if begging for the heavens to answer their silent cry.

I could feel it in my bones, the pull of it. The desert had led me here, to this place, and now it was time. Gabriel had fallen silent behind me, his steps halting as he noticed what I had.

"What the hell is that?" His voice was low, almost reverent, as if the very air around us had thickened with danger.

I didn't answer immediately. Instead, I took a step forward, my feet sinking into the sand with a soft crunch. My heartbeat quickened, a strange sense of inevitability settling in my chest. I knew I had to go forward. But Gabriel—well, Gabriel wasn't the type to follow anyone blindly, especially me.

"You sure about this?" he asked, his voice steady but laced with something else. Something I couldn't quite place.

"I'm sure," I said, turning to look at him for the first time in what felt like ages. "We've come this far. Might as well see it through."

He didn't say anything to that, just gave me a look that was too sharp, too knowing. As if he understood something I didn't.

"You always say that," he muttered, more to himself than to me. "And it's always a terrible idea."

I ignored the jab. The desert wasn't the place for petty insults or sarcasm. Not tonight. There was something bigger at play here. Something neither of us could control.

We crested the next dune, and that's when the full extent of the ruin came into view. It wasn't just any ruin—it was a temple. Ancient and weathered, its stone walls crumbled in places, but in others, they stood tall and proud, defiant against the winds and the passage of time. The sand around it had been carefully swept away, as though someone—or something—had worked to keep the desert from reclaiming it. A shadow of movement flickered at the edge of my vision, too fast to be certain, but enough to make my heart skip a beat.

I felt Gabriel's hand on my arm before I realized he'd moved. His touch was firm, his grip more insistent than I was used to. His eyes were narrowed, scanning the area around us with that predatory alertness I knew so well.

"Something's not right," he said, his voice tight with warning.

I nodded slowly. "I know."

The moonlight flickered, and the shadows seemed to stretch just a little longer than they should have. The sand shifted beneath my feet, and for a split second, I thought I saw something move—just out of the corner of my eye.

But it was too late. The ground beneath us gave way with a soft tremor, and I felt myself stumbling forward, towards the edge of the ancient temple.

The earth beneath my feet shifted, a ripple of ancient energy pulsing through the ground like a heartbeat, steady and unyielding. I could feel it in my bones, a deep resonance that sent shivers up my spine. It wasn't just the sand that moved—it was the desert itself, shifting around us, reacting to our presence. I could see Gabriel's eyes, sharp and searching, scanning the temple's crumbling façade as if it held the answers to every question he'd ever asked.

"You sure this is the place?" he asked, his voice low, as if the ruins themselves could hear us.

I didn't answer immediately, not because I didn't want to, but because the words felt trapped somewhere between my thoughts and the truth. Yes, this was the place—the place the stars had been whispering to me about. But the truth, as always, was a bit more complicated than that. I could feel the pull of it, an invisible thread tugging me forward, as if the ruins themselves had been waiting for me. The sense of familiarity, of something forgotten and long buried, wrapped around me like an old, tattered blanket.

I had known, somehow, that this was where we would end up. The stars had shown me this path long before we'd set foot in the desert. And now, standing on the threshold of whatever lay beyond the shattered stone, I felt the weight of it. The weight of everything. The choices I had made. The path I had taken. And Gabriel. Always Gabriel.

"I'm sure," I said finally, stepping forward with more confidence than I felt. I glanced back at him, catching the uncertain look in his eyes, the one that said he was ready to bolt but wouldn't, not yet. "You can turn back, you know. You don't have to be here."

Gabriel's expression didn't change, though I caught the faintest flicker of something—was it relief?—before he masked it with a smirk.

"Wouldn't dream of it," he replied, though I saw the flicker of hesitation in his eyes. He didn't want to admit that there was something compelling about this place, something that was pulling him in too. Whatever it was, it wasn't just my journey anymore.

The moment stretched, thick and heavy between us. And then, like the inevitable collision of two storm fronts, the ground beneath us rumbled.

Not a warning rumble, not a casual shifting of the earth, but the kind of rumble that promised something more. Something old and forgotten. I could feel Gabriel's breath catch in his throat as he stepped back, but I didn't move. I couldn't. The temple was calling me, its shadowed halls beckoning with a promise of answers I wasn't sure I was ready for.

"It's... it's alive," Gabriel murmured, his voice tight, strained with disbelief. "This place, it's alive."

I didn't have the words to disagree. It wasn't the stone that was alive—it was something else, something deeper, older. The temple, the very land around us, was more than just a structure. It was a sentinel, standing guard over something forgotten, buried beneath the sands of time. I had known it in my gut, from the moment I saw the first shimmer of light in the night sky, that this place was alive with secrets. And now, the desert was shaking off its centuries of dust, eager to reveal what had been hidden.

The rumble grew louder, sharper, and then, without warning, the earth beneath our feet split open.

I gasped, my hands instinctively reaching for Gabriel, but the ground opened too quickly, swallowing the distance between us. We were falling.

It was too fast to even process, too sudden to react. One moment, we were standing on solid ground, and the next, we were plunging into darkness, the walls of the earth collapsing in on us with a sickening speed. The wind howled in my ears, sand swirling up around me like a storm, blinding and deafening.

I heard Gabriel's shout, raw and frantic, just before we hit the ground.

It wasn't the soft, sandy earth I expected. No, it was cold, slick stone, sharp enough to tear through flesh, and I felt my body slam against it with a force that took the breath right out of me. Pain exploded in my ribs, and I gasped for air, my arms flailing to find purchase in the disorienting darkness.

Somehow, I managed to roll to my side, my hand grasping for anything—anything that would stop me from slipping further into the abyss. The echoes of our fall still rang in my ears, the sound of our bodies scraping against the stone walls, the sound of something ancient and powerful stirring in the depths below.

"Gabriel?" I croaked, my voice hoarse, barely audible over the rush of adrenaline pounding in my ears. My fingers scraped along the stone, searching, finding nothing but empty space and jagged edges.

"Here," he gasped, his voice coming from somewhere nearby, rough but alive. "I'm here."

I pushed myself upright, my body screaming in protest, and reached for him, finding his arm, his hand. The moment my fingers brushed his skin, he pulled me toward him, holding me with an intensity that was almost frantic.

"We're not alone," he whispered urgently. His breath was hot against my ear, but his voice was shaky, filled with something I couldn't name.

I opened my mouth to speak, but before I could, the air around us shifted. The temperature dropped, the scent of earth and dust replaced by something metallic, sharp. And then, just beyond the blackness, a pair of eyes glinted.

Bright. Unblinking. Watching us.

The ground trembled again, and I realized, with a sickening certainty, that this wasn't just the desert stirring.

It was something far worse.

Something alive.

Chapter 19: The Chamber of Echoes

The first tremor ran through the ground beneath my boots, like a whisper of something ancient, something that had been waiting for this moment, for me, to step too close to the secrets hidden in the walls. It was as if the room, the entire building, had been holding its breath—and now, it was releasing a slow, deliberate exhale. My fingers tightened around the artifact, its cold surface pressing into the soft skin beneath my palm. It was as if it knew what was coming.

Amara didn't seem to notice the quiver in the stone beneath us. Her focus was entirely on the glyphs, her fingers tracing the symbols with reverence. There was something unsettling about how easily she moved among the ancient markings, as if they were old friends rather than cryptic warnings. I couldn't make out much, the symbols too intricate and foreign to my eyes, but one thing was clear: this place was alive. The air itself seemed to hum, vibrating with energy that I could feel deep in my bones.

"It's strange," I muttered, stepping closer, "how they can make these walls feel like they're watching you. Can you feel it?"

Amara didn't look up. She was lost in the flow of history, but her lips curved slightly, a smirk that didn't quite match the intensity of her voice when she spoke.

"Oh, I feel it," she said softly. "They're watching us all the time. Waiting."

Her words wrapped around me, threading themselves into my thoughts. It wasn't just the walls, though. The atmosphere, thick with dust and the weight of centuries, seemed to grow heavier with each passing second. The temperature dropped, and I instinctively pulled my jacket tighter around my shoulders. My breath caught in the chill, small clouds of mist forming in the air with every exhale. A part of me wanted to reach out, to touch the glyphs she was studying so intently, to make sense of them. But something held me back—an almost primal sense of self-preservation. There was power here. Dark, hungry power that had outlasted its creators and was only waiting for the next soul to step forward and claim it.

"You're not scared of this place, are you?" I asked, half-smiling, trying to mask the unease in my own voice.

Amara glanced over at me then, her eyes gleaming with something I couldn't quite define. "Fear is an inconvenience," she said, voice clipped. "I've learned to ignore it."

I couldn't argue with that. She was a woman who had spent her life chasing the impossible, chasing things most people wouldn't even dare to dream of. And I? I had simply stumbled into this world, feet unsure, heart still racing from the first discovery, the first clue that had led us here.

The sudden echo of footsteps snapped me back into the present, sharp and deliberate, coming from somewhere deep within the winding halls of the chamber. The sound was muffled at first, as if the walls themselves were trying to swallow it up. But the more it reverberated, the clearer it became, until it was unmistakable: someone—or something—was coming toward us.

I froze, the weight of the artifact pressing painfully against my chest, and looked at Amara, who had already straightened, her expression unreadable. Her fingers moved to the small satchel at her waist, pulling out a leather-bound journal. She flipped through it with practiced ease, her eyes skimming over the pages as though searching for something specific.

"What is it?" I asked, unable to mask the edge in my voice.

She glanced up from the journal, eyes narrow and focused. "I'm trying to figure out who it is."

My heart began to beat faster, matching the rising tension in the air. The footsteps grew louder, closer. I could feel them reverberating in my own chest now, each step like a drumbeat. They weren't just coming down the hall anymore—they were heading for us.

"Should we hide?" I whispered, suddenly aware of how exposed we were in the center of this hidden chamber.

Amara's lips pressed together in a thin line. "If it's who I think it is, hiding won't help."

I opened my mouth to respond, but just then, a figure appeared in the doorway. Tall, cloaked in shadows, its features hidden in the dim light. The figure took a step forward, and with each movement, the air around us seemed to crackle, thickening with some sort of charged energy that made my skin prickle.

There was something unnervingly familiar about the silhouette, but I couldn't place it—until the figure stepped into the pale glow of the chamber's faint illumination, and then I saw the eyes.

Cold. Empty. Like twin mirrors reflecting nothing but darkness.

My breath hitched in my throat. "No..."

Amara's reaction was immediate. She stepped between me and the figure, her posture protective, almost as if she were ready to block an attack. The energy around her shifted, darkening in an instant.

"You," she said, her voice tight with the undercurrent of a long-held grudge. "I thought I'd finally outrun you."

The figure tilted its head, as if considering her words. Then, without warning, a low, guttural laugh echoed through the chamber. It was soft, yet bone-chilling, filling the space with a sense of predatory amusement.

"You can't outrun destiny," the figure said, its voice smooth and cold as ice.

I felt a shiver crawl up my spine. Whoever this was, whatever this was, it was no longer just about the artifact or the cryptic glyphs on the walls. Something much darker had come to claim what it had lost.

The figure in the doorway didn't move for a long moment. It was like it was waiting for us to process the weight of its presence, letting the silence stretch between us, suffocating in its heaviness. Amara didn't flinch. She didn't even blink, her eyes fixed on the shape in front of her, studying it with a cold intensity that I could almost feel.

I didn't know who this person was, but I could tell, from the way they stood there, like an immovable force in the dim light, that they weren't here for small talk. The smile—the twisted, predatory smile that curled at the edge of the figure's lips—sent a jolt of cold fear rushing through me. It was the kind of smile you only saw in bad movies, the ones where you knew, even before the villain spoke, that something irreversible was about to happen.

"Do you know who I am?" the figure asked, its voice smooth, dripping with an arrogance that stung. There was no urgency in its tone, no need to rush, as if time were a luxury it could afford.

Amara didn't answer right away. She just took a small step forward, her hand still hovering near the satchel at her waist, where something sharp and glinting was concealed.

"Don't be coy," she said, her voice light, almost casual, as though they were old friends. "You've never been good at pretending to be someone else, Malric."

Malric.

The name bounced around in my skull, sending shockwaves of confusion and realization rushing through me. I didn't know who this was—not really—but that name, the way it felt in the air, sent a chill racing down my spine. Something about it was familiar in the worst way possible, like hearing your name whispered in the dark when you're sure you're the only one awake.

"You," I said, blinking hard, trying to sort through the fog of disorientation. "You're the one who—"

"Yes," Malric interrupted, a sharp, cutting tone that sliced through my thoughts like a blade. "I'm the one who's been playing with your fate from the very beginning." He stepped closer, his eyes never leaving Amara. "And I will be the one to end it."

The words hung in the air, heavy and laden with the kind of promise that made my stomach churn. I could almost feel the room closing in on me, the stone walls pressing tighter, the low hum of energy from the artifact in my chest now pulsing with an urgency I couldn't ignore. It was like the room had shifted, as though the stone and air around us had suddenly grown too small, too narrow for the moment we were caught in. The chamber seemed to be leaning in, listening, like it was as much a participant in this twisted reunion as any of us.

"You really think you're going to get away with this?" Amara's voice, though steady, held a bite to it that was foreign, even to me. I had never seen her so... controlled, like she was holding something back, something volatile that could explode at any moment. She stood tall, unflinching, as if challenging him to make a move.

Malric's smile grew wider, almost amused by her defiance. "I'm not here to get away with anything," he said, as though explaining a simple concept to a child. "I'm here to finish what I started."

I took a small, instinctive step back, trying to make sense of the storm brewing in the room. The walls seemed to echo the tension, as though the very stones remembered the ancient conflict that had begun here—whatever that had been. A betrayal, a vengeance. It felt like we were standing at the eye of a storm that had been building for centuries.

Amara, for all her poise, looked like she was fighting against a tide that could swallow her whole. But there was something else there, a crack in her calm demeanor, a flicker of something beneath the surface that I didn't quite understand.

"Malric," she said, the name tasting like acid on her tongue. "You're not even close to understanding how this ends. You're just a cog in the machine. A very unimportant cog."

Malric tilted his head, his gaze narrowing. The faintest flicker of irritation crossed his face, but it was gone in an instant, replaced by that unnerving calm. "Do you really think your pet artifact can protect you?" he sneered, his eyes drifting over to the object pressing against my chest, as if it were some trinket rather than the source of all this madness.

Something shifted in the air—an electric crackle that hummed just beneath the surface—and the artifact pulsed in response. My fingers tightened around it, and suddenly, the weight of it was more than just physical. It was a burden, a power that demanded attention. I had no idea what I was supposed to do with it, but I knew one thing for sure: it wasn't meant to stay in my hands for long.

"I don't need protection," I muttered, more to myself than to him. But even as the words left my mouth, I realized how ridiculous they sounded. No one in their right mind would step into a room with someone like Malric and claim they didn't need protection.

Amara turned to me then, her eyes softening ever so slightly, and for a brief moment, I saw something human in her. It was fleeting, almost imperceptible, but it was there.

"You're wrong," she said quietly, but her words were directed at Malric, not me. "You've never been anything more than a shadow. And shadows always fade."

Malric's expression twisted into something dark, something feral. "We'll see," he said, voice low and dangerous.

Then, as if to punctuate his words, the room trembled again, a violent shake that seemed to reverberate through my bones. The walls groaned, the air thickened, and the artifact against my chest flared with sudden light, so bright I had to squint. The chamber was no longer just a place—it was alive, and it was reacting to something. Something big.

I didn't know how long I had before the room swallowed us whole. I didn't know how much longer the fragile thread of control we were hanging by could hold. But one thing was certain: whatever Malric thought was coming next, we were already too deep to back out now.

The sound of footsteps grew louder, each step a drumbeat echoing down the narrow corridor leading deeper into the chamber. It wasn't the hurried scurrying of someone caught off guard—it was deliberate, measured, as though whoever was coming had all the time in the world to arrive. The tension in the air was thickening, coiling around my lungs with every breath I took. I could feel it—the undeniable pull of something ancient and dangerous hanging just out of reach, like a storm cloud gathering just beyond the horizon.

"Amara..." I whispered, but the word barely escaped my throat. My mouth was dry, the weight of the moment settling over me like a suffocating blanket. "What happens now?"

She didn't respond at first. She was still standing there, the small satchel at her waist now hanging loosely, forgotten. Her fingers brushed over the journal she had been thumbing through earlier, but her gaze was fixed on the figure advancing toward us with a slow, deliberate purpose.

"I told you," Amara said, her voice quiet but sharp, "This is where it ends."

Malric was not someone who would be swayed by words. I could feel that much, the coldness radiating from him, wrapping around us like a shroud. The air between us was charged now, a strange energy crackling, and the walls, those damned glyphs, seemed to be pressing in from every angle. I could almost hear their ancient whispers, the low hum of their stories of betrayal and vengeance. Whatever had happened here, whatever dark forces had carved these symbols into the stone, they were still alive. Still waiting.

"You think you have control of this place," Malric said, his voice smooth, calculated. "But control is an illusion. Power is the only truth."

There was no bravado in his words, no grandstanding. It was a simple statement, one that made my skin crawl, because there was an undeniable ring of truth to it. Amara's defiance, my own hesitation, it didn't matter in the grand scheme of things. Power wasn't something we could simply fight. It was something we had to survive.

Amara finally looked at me, her eyes narrowing as if weighing something in the pit of her stomach. There was a flicker there—doubt? Fear? It was gone too quickly for me to be sure. But it was enough to make my stomach drop. Whatever she was hiding, it was starting to feel like there were more stakes in this than I had bargained for.

The footsteps had stopped now, and in the stillness, it was as though the chamber had fallen silent. Malric's figure was solid, unmoving, like a shadow cast by the walls themselves.

"You think this is all there is?" he asked, gesturing toward the walls. "You think these glyphs, these cryptic symbols, hold the answers?" His eyes flicked toward the artifact, pulsing against my chest, the glow from its surface intensifying.

The light flared, making me wince as it pushed against the darkness. I had no idea how or why it was reacting like this, but I could feel its energy winding tighter, pressing into me like it was responding to Malric's words. Was it choosing sides? Was it waiting to be used?

"You're mistaken," he said softly, eyes gleaming with something almost amused. "These walls tell the truth, but you don't want to hear it. None of you do."

Amara took a step toward him, her posture rigid, defiant. "You don't get to decide what we want. Not anymore."

The tension crackled in the air between them, thick and suffocating. I could feel the weight of history—centuries of betrayal, of vengeance—pressing against me, trying to crush my resolve. But Amara wasn't backing down. Not even a little.

I swallowed hard, the uncertainty creeping in again. This wasn't just about an artifact. This wasn't just about deciphering ancient glyphs. This was about something far bigger.

"Why did you bring me here?" I blurted, my voice shaking slightly despite my best attempts to hold it steady. "What do you want from me?"

Malric's smile never reached his eyes. It was more of a knowing twist of the lips, like he was amused by my ignorance. "I've already told you. The question isn't what I want—it's what you are willing to sacrifice."

The last word hung in the air, like a threat, but more than that. A promise. Something unavoidable.

I wanted to turn away from him. To look at anything else. But my eyes stayed locked on his, as if some invisible force was keeping me tethered to this moment, to this darkness he represented.

"I don't know what you think I'm capable of," I said, trying to force the tremor from my voice, "but I'm not afraid of you."

"Fear isn't the point," Malric said. He was standing just a few feet from us now, so close I could feel the heat radiating off him, a magnetic pull that seemed to draw everything toward him. "You will fear what happens when you finally understand the price of what you hold in your hands."

Before I could respond, before I could ask him what he meant, the walls around us seemed to groan. The sound, deep and rumbling, shook the air, like the chamber itself was awakening. The glyphs shifted, a subtle movement in the stone, as if they were being rewritten.

"What did you do?" I asked, my voice sharp as the walls trembled again, harder this time, the very foundation of the chamber seeming to crack under the pressure.

Malric's eyes gleamed with a cruel satisfaction. "I haven't done anything. You have."

The chamber was changing, the walls warping in a way that sent a shiver of panic through my spine. Something was breaking, unraveling. I didn't know if it was the chamber, or us, or both, but the air was thick with the promise of something terrible.

And in that moment, I realized—the artifact had never been a tool. It was a trigger.

The glyphs, the words, the weight of the centuries—all of it had been leading to this. To me.

And there was no going back.

Chapter 20: Shadows in the Deep

The alley smelled of damp asphalt and the remnants of spilled whiskey, a pungent mix that seemed to crawl into my lungs with every breath. My boots clicked against the concrete, too loud, but it didn't matter. They were coming. I could feel them, the subtle vibrations underfoot, the shift in the air that whispered danger. There was no time for hesitation. Gabriel was a shadow beside me, his presence barely a whisper, but I could sense his unease.

The weight of the night pressed down on me like the city itself was holding its breath, waiting for something—anything—to happen. The moon hung high, shrouded behind a blanket of clouds that smothered its light, leaving only a gray glow to bathe the crumbling buildings in a sickly hue. The streets of this city had their own pulse, a slow, relentless thrum of violence and secrecy. And tonight, it felt like the pulse was about to stop altogether.

I could feel Gabriel's gaze on me. It had been months since we'd shared more than a word or two. Months since the old world had crumbled under our feet and left us stumbling into something darker, something far more dangerous. A world where I wasn't just a witness, but a participant. Gabriel had learned that the hard way. I could see the doubt in his eyes, even when he didn't speak it. He had thought I was just a woman with a past, a series of bad decisions strung together by unfortunate circumstances. I'd let him believe that. It was safer that way. But the truth... the truth was buried beneath layers of things better left untouched.

I glanced at him quickly, catching the flicker of a smirk tugging at the corner of his lips. "What?" I asked, irritation creeping into my voice.

"You look like you're about to do something... extraordinary," he said, his words barely more than a murmur, the weight of them pressing down on me like a lead weight.

The wind picked up, sharp and cold, as the first of them emerged from the shadows, their faces obscured by dark cloth, their movements fluid and practiced. They were professionals. Whoever had sent them knew exactly how to make a quiet entrance. Gabriel's hand tightened around the hilt of his blade, his muscles coiled like a spring. But I could already feel my own power stirring, the weight of it inside me, a quiet whisper at the edges of my mind.

I fought the urge to ignore it, to let it fade back into the dark corners of my thoughts. But there was no time for hesitation. The dead were rising again, this time not from some distant memory but from my own command. It wasn't something I'd asked for, something I'd ever wanted. But it was mine, just as much as the blood that ran through my veins, the hunger that had been born with me, deep in my bones.

One by one, their skeletal forms clawed their way up from the ground, their bones clicking and creaking like the sound of an old door groaning open. Their empty eye sockets glowed faintly, the faintest echo of a life that had long since passed. I turned my eyes away, just for a moment, the revulsion in my stomach threatening to overwhelm me.

"Do you always bring the dead to a fight?" Gabriel's voice was tight with disbelief, but there was something else in it, too. Something I hadn't quite put my finger on. Was it fear? Or... awe?

I didn't answer. I couldn't. The power I wielded was dangerous, a weapon with no off switch. And when I unleashed it, there was no telling who might be hurt, who might be lost. Gabriel had seen it before, in flashes, but he had no idea what it could truly do.

The first of the attackers lunged at me, a knife flashing in the moonlight. I moved instinctively, my foot sliding against the slick concrete as I twisted, grabbing the blade mid-air, my fingers curling around it with a ferocity I didn't even recognize. Before I could stop myself, I drove it into the man's ribs, the sound of steel meeting bone almost satisfying in its finality. He crumpled to the ground without a sound.

Gabriel didn't flinch, didn't even blink. Instead, he stepped forward, his sword already a blur as he dispatched the next one with a swift strike. I watched, a strange kind of admiration flickering through me despite myself. Gabriel was a fighter. There was no doubt about that.

But he wasn't me.

I could hear them before I saw them—the rest of the attackers, the ones who had been waiting in the wings, watching, learning. The streetlights flickered, casting an eerie light on their movements as they closed in, surrounding us. And still, I didn't stop. My hand rose, my fingers curling into a fist, and the dead answered the call.

The air thickened, suffocating and oppressive, as more bodies clawed their way from the ground. Their bones creaked and cracked as they formed ranks, lining up between us and the attackers. They moved with purpose, like soldiers following orders. And it was then that I realized just how much I had changed. I was no longer the woman who feared her own power, no longer the one who hesitated in the face of what she could do.

I was something else. Something darker.

Gabriel stood beside me, watching, his eyes widening as the last of the attackers fell. Silence reigned for a heartbeat, and then he turned to me. His eyes, always so steady, were now wide, filled with something I couldn't name.

"You're not who I thought you were," he said, his voice low, almost a whisper. "Not even close."

I didn't know how to answer him, how to explain what had happened, what I had become. Instead, I let my power recede, feeling the cold weight of it retreat into the corners of my mind. The silence between us stretched, thick and uncomfortable, until I finally met his gaze, forcing myself to speak.

"I never was."

The words were out before I could stop them, a truth I hadn't even meant to admit. But in that moment, standing there amid the wreckage, the truth felt like the only thing I could hold on to.

The street was quiet again, the kind of unsettling silence that follows a storm. The only sound was the soft scraping of bone against bone, as the skeletal forms I had summoned shuffled back into the shadows. The wind had picked up, sweeping through the alley like it was trying to shake off the remnants of whatever dark energy had just passed through. Gabriel stood beside me, his breath still coming in short bursts, his sword dripping with the blood of men who would never see the morning sun. But that look in his eyes—it made my stomach churn in a way I couldn't ignore.

"You're not who I thought you were," he repeated, his voice edged with something sharp and unsure. It wasn't fear, not exactly. It was... confusion, or maybe something darker, like the scent of rain before a flood. A storm. The kind that comes out of nowhere, changing everything in its wake.

I didn't know how to respond to that. How do you explain to someone that everything they think they know about you is a lie, even the parts you thought were true?

"Neither are you," I said instead, keeping my voice light, though the words came out a little colder than I intended. It wasn't just him who had changed, after all. The city had changed me. The nights here had a way of grinding you down until you forgot what it felt like to be anything other than broken. Gabriel hadn't seen that side of me—hadn't seen the parts I buried so deep they were almost unrecognizable. But tonight, in this alley, under the flickering light of an old streetlamp, there was nothing left to hide behind.

He took a step toward me, eyes narrowing in that way he had when he was about to say something profound or, more likely, ridiculously unnecessary. "I'm not the one who raised the dead."

The words came out with a slight, almost imperceptible edge, as if he were testing them, letting them hang in the air like smoke.

I couldn't help it. A laugh slipped out of me, the sound startling in the stillness. "Right. But you're the one who's been swinging that sword like you're some kind of knight in shining armor." I looked at him, my tone slipping into something softer, teasing. "You do realize I've been saving your ass, don't you?"

He smirked, though it was tight and not entirely genuine. "I never asked for saving."

"Well, tough," I shot back. "It's either that or you die. I'm not sure which option suits you best, but let me know if you've got a preference."

His smirk faltered, the smile fading as he glanced down at the bloodstains that had started to pool around his boots. I watched him for a long moment, trying to see past the layers of wariness that had built up between us, to the man I used to think I knew. The one who hadn't seen the way I was twisting in the wind, spinning out of control. Gabriel had always been steady, grounded in ways I could never be. But now? Now, he was as lost in this city as I was.

"You're right," he said after a long pause, his voice softer now, more contemplative. "I don't get to decide what happens in these streets anymore, do I?"

"No one does," I replied, glancing at the fading shapes of the skeletons, the remnants of the fight already slipping back into the earth. They would return to their graves until they were needed again. "The city's been its own beast for a long time. We're just its puppets."

Gabriel turned to face me fully now, his stance widening, his shoulders squared, the tension in his muscles unmistakable. "That's... a depressing way to look at things."

"Truth's not here to make you feel good," I said, my voice steady, but my chest tight with something I couldn't name. "You know what's coming. You know the darkness in this city, what it does to people. No one stays clean for long."

He looked at me for a beat longer than felt comfortable, his brow furrowed, like he was trying to see through all the layers I'd stacked between us. "And you?" he asked, his voice barely above a whisper. "What about you? Are you clean?"

I didn't answer immediately, because the truth was, I wasn't sure I could even see the line anymore. I used to be sure of who I was, what I wanted. I used to think I was just a woman who had gotten tangled in circumstances she couldn't control, a victim of fate or chance or bad decisions. But now? Now, I wasn't sure where the girl I used to be had gone.

The wind kicked up again, snapping my hair across my face. I wiped it away, feeling the weight of Gabriel's stare still pressing against me. "I'm not clean," I admitted finally, my voice quieter than it had been. "But I'm not what you think I am either."

Gabriel looked like he wanted to argue, like he had more questions—probably a thousand more—but he didn't. He just stood there, watching me, and for a moment, I thought I saw something shift in him. Maybe it was the realization that I wasn't the hero in his story. Maybe it was the understanding that the rules had changed, and there was no going back to the way things had been.

"I don't know what this is," he said, the words more like a confession than anything else.

"Neither do I," I replied, offering him a dry smile. "But it's ours now. So, we deal with it."

I turned to leave, my boots clicking on the pavement, a rhythm that felt somehow comforting. Behind me, I could hear Gabriel's footsteps follow, steady, unhurried. There was a part of me that wanted to tell him to stay behind, to go back to whatever life he had before all of this. But I didn't. Because I knew, deep down, that he wouldn't. He couldn't. None of us could.

The city had claimed us both now.

The streets of the city hummed around us, but in the silence that had settled between us, I could hear every little noise—the distant whir of a car engine, the faint rustle of leaves being whipped through the air, the rapid thud of Gabriel's breath. We both stood there, not speaking, not moving, as if somehow the stillness could hold back the flood of questions that hovered just out of reach.

I didn't want to look at him. Not because I feared what he might say, but because I feared what I might say back. The words I had thrown at him, half in jest, half in truth, felt hollow now. I hadn't meant to go this far, to let the darkness I kept locked away come creeping to the surface. But the city—God, it had a way of pulling the worst out of you, twisting your insides until you didn't recognize yourself anymore.

And Gabriel? Gabriel wasn't the same either. Not since we'd first met, not since he'd stepped into this mess that I called my life. Maybe he thought he could fix it, somehow. Maybe he thought he could fix me. But the truth was—he couldn't. He wouldn't.

I took a deep breath, pushing the thoughts down. No. Not now. There was no room for anything other than what was in front of us. The city had a way of crumbling the best of intentions, and Gabriel—well, he was as deep in as I was now.

"So, what now?" Gabriel finally asked, his voice a low murmur that seemed to float in the air, heavy with unsaid things.

I blinked, taken off guard. "What do you mean, 'what now?'" My tone was sharp, but only because the question hit too close to something I couldn't define. What did now even mean in a place like this?

His eyes narrowed, as if considering something before he spoke again. "You're not some... I don't know, some ghost-wrangler, are you?" He gestured vaguely at the alley, the remnants of the dead still flickering at the edges of my vision. "This—this thing you've been doing, calling them up, controlling them—it's not normal, and I need to know what's behind it. I can't keep going like this, being left in the dark."

I swallowed hard, the words threatening to slip from me—words that I hadn't spoken aloud to anyone in years. The truth, raw and bitter, clawing at my throat. But I didn't speak it. I couldn't. Instead, I raised my chin and met his gaze head-on, pushing the guilt, the need, the pull of something I didn't understand deep down inside.

"I don't control them, Gabriel," I said, forcing the words out, my voice harder than I wanted it to be. "I can call them, but they aren't mine. They just—answer."

He studied me for a moment, those too-knowing eyes of his not missing a single twitch or flicker of emotion. "Answer to what, exactly?"

I shook my head, a bitter laugh escaping my lips. "Does it really matter?"

"Yes. It matters," Gabriel said, his voice low but insistent. "I can't keep doing this without understanding what's at stake. Not if—" He stopped himself before finishing the sentence. But I heard the unspoken words loud and clear. *Not if it's me next.*

We both knew what this city did to people. What it did to those who came too close to its dark heart. I was no exception.

"Trust me, Gabriel," I said, turning away from him, not wanting to see the hurt that flickered in his expression. "You don't want to know."

The words were like a curse, slipping from me before I could pull them back. But it was the truth, and he had no idea just how right I was. The shadows of the city would devour anyone who got too close. I was a prime example of that—twisted by something I couldn't control, caught in a game I didn't even know how to play. And the worst part was, I didn't want to stop.

I started walking, the sound of my boots tapping a steady rhythm against the cracked pavement. Behind me, Gabriel's footsteps followed, his silence speaking volumes. I didn't look back. Not because I didn't care, but because I couldn't afford to care. Not in this city. Not anymore.

The next few blocks were quieter, the hum of the streetlights and the occasional passing car filling the empty air. I could feel Gabriel's presence at my back, a weight I couldn't shake, even though I wanted to. We were both too tangled up in this mess to escape, and neither of us could admit it yet. Not out loud.

Suddenly, I felt it—like a spark in the air. The hairs on the back of my neck stood up, and I instinctively reached for the power inside me, the pulse of something ancient and deadly. My fingers tingled, but it was different this time. This wasn't something I'd called. It was something else, something darker, pulling at the edges of my consciousness.

I stopped dead in my tracks, my eyes scanning the alley ahead of us. The street was eerily still, as if the city itself was holding its breath. But then I saw it—a figure, just beyond the shadows.

A woman. Tall, impossibly graceful, with hair that shimmered in the moonlight like threads of silver. Her eyes were black as midnight, and her smile—a twisted, predatory grin—sent a chill down my spine.

"Hello, darling," she said, her voice smooth like honey, but there was nothing sweet about it. "I've been waiting for you."

And just like that, everything shifted. The ground beneath my feet felt unstable, the air thick with tension. I could feel the darkness closing in, like a flood, and there was no escaping it now.

Gabriel stepped forward, but I grabbed his arm, my grip tight. "Don't," I whispered. "This isn't her."

But it was too late. The woman's smile widened, and before I could stop it, the world shifted, and we were no longer standing on the street, but somewhere else entirely. A place I couldn't recognize.

And in that moment, I realized—I had no idea what had just started.

Chapter 21: A Map of Stars

I hadn't intended to find him that night. Not like this, at least. The air was thick with the scent of jasmine and damp earth, the kind that made you forget it was a Tuesday and that you had a life outside of the moment. But then, I saw Gabriel, and time folded into itself. The glow of the lanterns he carried shimmered off the stone walls of the chamber, casting shadows that seemed to move of their own accord, like the ghosts of those who'd walked these halls before us.

The glyphs—each one meticulously carved into the ancient stone—shimmered faintly in the soft light, an invitation to something far older and far more dangerous than I could have imagined. I had been staring at them for what felt like hours, but every time I thought I'd cracked their code, the symbols would shift, or I would see something new I hadn't noticed before. It wasn't until Gabriel stood beside me that the pieces fell into place. His fingers brushed mine as he knelt, studying the map etched into the stone floor, and suddenly the lines of the constellations made sense. They weren't just patterns—they were directions. Coordinates, if you will. And each one seemed to be pointing toward a place I hadn't seen before on any map.

I could feel him watching me. I wasn't sure whether it was the heat of his gaze or the anticipation of what we were about to discover that made my pulse quicken. His breath caught when I spoke.

"I know where this leads," I whispered, almost afraid to say it out loud. As if the universe might hear me and decide to pull the rug out from under my feet.

"Do you?" Gabriel asked. His voice, usually so controlled, had a slight tremor, something unspoken in the way he leaned closer to me. "And where might that be, Amara?"

The way my name sounded when he said it—like a secret, like a puzzle piece slipping into place—made me forget the map for a moment. But the moment passed quickly, and the map called me back. It was no longer a mystery. The constellations, which had seemed so foreign only a moment ago, now fit together like the final pieces of a forgotten jigsaw puzzle. I could see the shape they formed.

"Beneath the light of Orion," I said slowly. "There's something buried there. I don't know what, but I know that it's linked to the artifact." I could feel the weight of my words settling into the air between us, heavy and undeniable.

Gabriel's eyes darkened, and I couldn't tell if it was from the shadows or something deeper, something that had been buried for years, maybe even longer. His hand gripped the edge of the stone, the muscles in his arm taut under the strain, as if he were physically holding back a storm.

"Orion," he repeated, like he had tasted the word and didn't like the way it sat on his tongue. He straightened, and for a second, I could see it—the truth that he'd been hiding, buried beneath the layers of his carefully constructed façade. I wasn't sure if it was something I should've been afraid of, but the hair on the back of my neck stood up nonetheless.

"What aren't you telling me, Gabriel?" I asked, my voice sharper than I intended. The question hung between us, both an accusation and a plea. I needed to know. The tension in the chamber was suffocating, the silence stretching longer than it should have.

He exhaled sharply, his eyes finally meeting mine. "It's not just a map," he said, his voice low. "It's a warning. It's showing us where it all began. And where it could end."

I frowned, unable to mask my confusion. "A warning? What do you mean? What happened before?"

Gabriel took a step back, hands raised in a gesture of surrender. "I'm not just a treasure hunter, Amara. I didn't come here by accident." His voice faltered, just for a moment, before he took another breath, steadying himself. "I'm a guardian. I've been tasked with protecting the artifact. I failed once before, and I'm not about to let it happen again."

The words fell from him like stones in a pond, each one sending ripples through the air. For a long, unblinking moment, I could only stare at him. The man who'd come into my life like a storm—turbulent, unpredictable, and, as I was now learning, deeply entwined in something far darker than I'd realized.

"You failed?" I managed to choke out, the words foreign on my tongue. "What do you mean, you failed?"

Gabriel didn't answer right away. He turned away, walking across the room as though he needed the distance to collect himself. The lanterns flickered, their light catching the dark glint of something hidden beneath his cool exterior.

"I was supposed to stop it," he murmured, his voice cracking as he spoke the words aloud for the first time. "I was supposed to stop the artifact from falling into the wrong hands, but... I couldn't. I wasn't strong enough."

His admission, raw and unfiltered, shattered something inside me. The man I thought I knew—so controlled, so composed—was carrying a weight I couldn't even begin to understand. And yet, the pieces clicked into place. The secrets he had guarded, the way he had evaded questions, the way he kept everything just out of reach—it wasn't because he didn't trust me. It was because he was protecting me from a truth that might destroy us both.

But I wasn't going to walk away from him. Not now. Not when we were so close to understanding everything.

"We'll figure this out," I said quietly, my voice firm despite the rush of emotions threatening to overwhelm me. "Together."

Gabriel turned back to face me, the faintest flicker of hope in his eyes. "I hope you're right, Amara. I really do."

The night stretched on, its coolness settling into the bones of the old building like a secret kept too long. Gabriel and I sat side by side on the cold stone floor, our backs pressed against the ancient walls, the flickering light from our lanterns casting jagged shadows on the floor. The map was still there, glowing faintly beneath the dust and grime of centuries. The constellations we'd uncovered, now more than just shapes and lines, seemed to pulse with something—life, maybe? It felt as if they were watching us, waiting for us to make the next move.

I couldn't quite shake the weight of Gabriel's words. Guardian. Protector. All this time, I had believed him to be just a man of calculated risk, a man who thrived on the pursuit of treasures and hidden secrets. And now I was learning that the treasures he sought weren't just for fortune—they were to protect the world from something much darker.

"You failed?" The words rolled off my tongue again, as if repeating them would somehow make more sense. It didn't. And the way his jaw clenched, the flicker of something painful in his eyes, told me he wasn't about to elaborate further anytime soon.

Gabriel shifted beside me, the silence thick between us, broken only by the sound of our breathing and the occasional crackle of the lanterns. I glanced over at him, noting how his fingers, once steady and precise, were now fidgeting with the strap of his bag as if it were the only thing anchoring him to this moment. There was something about that—about him being unravelled—something that made me want to press on. The truth tasted like smoke, heavy and elusive, but I knew we weren't going anywhere until it was dragged into the open.

"It wasn't supposed to be like this." Gabriel's voice broke through my thoughts, rough and hoarse. He finally turned to face me, his gaze intense, focused. "I had it all planned out. The artifact... It was supposed to stay hidden. In my hands. My responsibility."

I could hear the regret in his words, a deep well of it that had no bottom. For a moment, I felt like I was looking at a stranger. How many masks had he worn over the years? How many versions of himself had he kept hidden from everyone, including me? I shifted uncomfortably, my hands pressed into the cold stone beneath me. There was no escaping the tension in the air.

"What happened?" I asked, softer this time, hoping that whatever the truth was, it would finally be enough to pull us out of this suspended moment.

Gabriel's lips parted, then closed, like he was chewing on words too painful to speak. I didn't push him. Sometimes the hardest truths took time to slip past our defenses. But as the seconds stretched into minutes, I could feel the pull of something larger than either of us. Whatever the artifact was, it was tied to more than just Gabriel. It was tied to both of us.

"Once," he began, his voice barely above a whisper, "I let my guard down. I trusted the wrong person, and I let it slip. The artifact was taken from me. I failed to stop it, and... the world felt the consequences. I lost it all. My purpose. My mission. Everything." His eyes were distant now, as if the memory was something he had to step around, something sharp enough to cut him if he let it.

I wasn't sure what to say to that. What do you say to someone who's admitted that kind of failure? Who had stood in the face of everything they'd ever believed in, only to watch it unravel because of a misstep?

"I didn't come here to let history repeat itself." He was staring at me now, his gaze intense, pleading for understanding. "That's why I've been so careful. I don't want to make the same mistake again. This time, I need your help."

My heart twisted. There it was again—his vulnerability, the one thing I hadn't expected from him. I had thought I understood him. Thought I had him figured out. But now, I realized that the layers of his story were deeper than I could have imagined. Gabriel wasn't just some hardened treasure hunter. He was a man burdened by failure, and if I was honest with myself, I was starting to care more than I should.

"You want my help?" I asked, the skepticism clear in my voice. "After everything? After all the secrets you've kept from me?"

Gabriel's face softened. He sighed, rubbing a hand over his face, and for a brief moment, I saw the weight of his guilt in the sag of his shoulders. "I didn't want you to be part of this. But now, there's no turning back. You've already seen too much."

The words hit me harder than I expected. He hadn't wanted me involved. That stung more than I was willing to admit. He had kept me at arm's length, protected me from something he never thought I could understand, or maybe he had believed I wouldn't survive it. But I wasn't the kind of woman who could be easily dismissed. Not anymore.

"I've always been part of it, Gabriel," I said, standing abruptly, the rush of anger and frustration surging to the surface. "You think this is something I can just walk away from?"

He looked up at me, his eyes wide, like I had thrown a bucket of cold water on him. "Amara, this is dangerous. It's bigger than both of us."

"I know." I turned away from him, pacing the length of the room, trying to steady my breath. I didn't know what I was afraid of more—losing him or losing myself in the mess of this entire situation. "But you don't get to decide what I'm capable of. Not anymore."

Gabriel didn't argue. Instead, he watched me with that same intensity, as if he was trying to memorize the way I moved, the way I spoke. There was something in his gaze that softened as he took a step closer.

"Then help me," he said quietly. "We do this together. I don't have another choice."

I met his gaze, the weight of his words settling between us. We were in this now. Whether I liked it or not.

The silence hung between us like a thick fog, only broken by the rhythmic ticking of a clock somewhere far in the back of the chamber. I had learned, over the years, to read people by the way their hands moved, the way their eyes flickered when they spoke. But Gabriel was a puzzle I couldn't quite solve. I had thought the walls he'd built around himself were nothing more than the usual bravado of a man who wasn't used to trust, but now, I wasn't so sure. The words he'd said, about failing, about being a guardian—it was as if I had just peeled back a corner of a very old, very dangerous story.

I watched him stand, his hands still clenched at his sides, his face set in that familiar mask of calm determination. I couldn't decide if it made him more insufferable or more... human.

"So, what now?" I asked, my voice sharper than I'd intended. The words felt heavier than I could have imagined.

Gabriel turned his back to me, moving to the far wall, his fingers tracing the old, cracked stone. He didn't answer immediately, his gaze fixed on something I couldn't see. When he finally spoke, his voice was low, almost as if he was speaking to himself. "We find it before someone else does."

His words rattled me. The tension in the air, thick with ancient secrets and lingering promises, seemed to shift. "And who exactly is this 'someone else' you're talking about?" I asked, my heart pounding a little faster now.

He didn't turn to face me when he answered. "People with power. People who would stop at nothing to take it for themselves."

I walked over to where he stood, close enough to feel the heat radiating off his body, but not close enough to touch. I didn't know why, but I needed to see his face when he said what he was about to say. Something in his tone, something in his posture, told me the next words were going to change everything.

"Gabriel," I said, softer now, "what is this artifact really? What does it do?"

His jaw tightened, and I saw the flicker of something in his eyes, something dark and dangerous. The kind of look that didn't just come from the artifact or from the people after it. It came from him. From the years he'd spent guarding something he didn't fully understand himself.

"It's not what you think," he said, his voice tight. "It's not just some relic. It's—" He broke off, as though the words were too dangerous to say.

I took a deep breath, trying to keep my own nerves steady. "What do you mean, it's not just a relic?"

Gabriel turned to face me then, and there was a look in his eyes that made my heart skip a beat. "It's a key," he said, his voice like gravel. "A key to something much older than any of us. And it's a key that has the power to destroy everything if it falls into the wrong hands."

I felt the air go still, the weight of his words settling into the space between us like a thick cloud. The room seemed smaller now, the shadows pressing in on all sides. My mind raced to catch up, but the words stuck in my throat.

"Destroy everything?" I repeated, my voice a little louder than I intended. "Gabriel, what are you saying?"

He took a step closer, his eyes fixed on mine, his presence like a force field. "I'm saying that whoever controls the artifact controls the world. And if that power falls into the wrong hands—"

"Like who?" I interrupted, my heart hammering in my chest.

"Like them," he said, his gaze shifting to something beyond me, somewhere in the distance. His voice had dropped, becoming a low murmur, barely audible. "The ones who've been hunting it for years. The ones who knew exactly where it was—before I ever did."

My stomach twisted, a cold knot of fear settling low in my gut. The ones who knew. The ones who had been after it all along. I suddenly felt small, like a piece of a puzzle I wasn't sure belonged.

"You're talking about a group?" I asked, barely able to believe it.

He nodded. "A shadow organization. I've been following their trail for years. And every time I think I'm close, they slip away, leaving me with nothing but broken pieces and dead ends." He stepped back, rubbing the back of his neck in frustration. "But now... they're closer than ever."

I swallowed hard, trying to steady my breath, my thoughts. I had gotten too deep into this, deeper than I had ever imagined. My life, which had once been a calm routine of classes and research, had turned into a whirlwind of ancient languages, cryptic messages, and men with dangerous secrets.

"You think they're coming for us?" I asked, my voice barely a whisper, as if saying it out loud would make it all the more real.

Gabriel didn't hesitate. "I know they are."

I felt the weight of his words like a punch to the gut. My pulse raced, my mind scrambling for some sort of plan, some way to get out of this. But there was no easy escape. No way to just walk away. Not anymore.

"So what's our next move?" I asked, my voice steadier than I felt.

Gabriel didn't answer immediately. Instead, he looked at me for what seemed like an eternity. There was something in his eyes—a kind of quiet determination, but also a warning. A warning that whatever came next, it wasn't going to be easy.

"We find them first," he said finally, his voice cold and resolute. "Before they find us."

I nodded, trying to gather my wits, but the words felt too big for me. Find them? How? Where?

And then, just as I opened my mouth to ask, there was a noise from the far side of the chamber—a soft scuffing sound that sent a chill down my spine.

"Did you hear that?" I asked, my voice barely above a whisper.

Gabriel froze, his eyes narrowing, his posture tense as he turned slowly toward the sound.

"I did," he said, his voice low, dangerous.

And then, from the shadows at the far end of the room, a figure emerged, their face obscured by a dark hood. The air between us crackled with the kind of tension that you only felt when you were standing on the edge of something you couldn't yet understand.

The figure stepped forward, and the world held its breath.

Chapter 22: The Oasis of Illusions

The air was thick with the scent of damp earth and something sweet, something almost too delicate to be real. I could feel it in the pit of my stomach, the unease coiling tighter with each step I took. Gabriel walked beside me, his presence a solid, comforting weight. His hand brushed mine now and then, sending a spark through my veins each time, even though I was beginning to suspect nothing was as it seemed. The oasis we had stumbled upon, with its towering palm trees and crystal-clear water, was too perfect, too tranquil, to be anything other than a lie.

I wiped the sweat from my brow with the back of my hand, the heat of the desert still pressing in on us from the edges of this strange paradise. The coolness of the air around the water was deceiving, like a lover's embrace, promising comfort while hiding a darker truth. Gabriel seemed unbothered, but then, he always had an uncanny ability to mask his thoughts. We had been partners in this ridiculous quest for weeks now, and yet there were moments, like this one, when I wondered if I truly knew him at all.

"Do you hear that?" Gabriel asked, his voice low, almost conspiratorial.

I stopped, cocking my head. At first, I heard nothing but the rush of water and the soft rustling of leaves in the breeze. But then—there it was. A faint whisper, like a voice on the wind, too soft to catch but unmistakable once it reached the edge of my consciousness.

"It sounds like... singing?" I said, my voice unsure. The sound was so delicate, so haunting, it made my chest tighten.

Gabriel nodded, but his eyes were narrowed, focused on the water. "It's not singing. It's a trap. Stay sharp."

I wanted to protest, to say he was being paranoid, but something about the shimmer of the water in the afternoon sun felt off. The gentle flow of the stream—no, the river—looked too perfect, too clean. And the trees, their leaves a vibrant green that seemed almost unnatural against the burnt orange of the desert beyond... It felt as if we were intruding on a painting, a scene frozen in time, designed to lure us in with its beauty.

I glanced back at the path we had taken. The narrow trail was already obscured by sand, the desert reclaiming the ground we'd walked just moments ago. But there was no turning back. The artifact we sought, the one that had been our obsession for so long, was said to be hidden here—somewhere in the heart of this illusion. A relic of unimaginable power, buried in the very ground beneath us.

"Let's keep moving," I said, my voice steadier than I felt. Gabriel nodded and, with a barely perceptible glance, led the way.

We stepped cautiously, the soft earth beneath our feet giving way to patches of smooth stone that were warm to the touch. It wasn't long before we reached the edge of the water. The pool was impossibly clear, each stone at the bottom visible as if the water was frozen in time. The surface shimmered in the sunlight, reflecting the sky, the trees, the shadows. It was beautiful. Too beautiful.

"Is this it?" I asked, my heart skipping a beat. Was the artifact hidden here, beneath the placid surface, or had we been led astray?

Gabriel didn't answer immediately. Instead, he squatted down, dipping a hand into the water. I held my breath as his fingers brushed the surface, sending ripples through the perfect stillness.

I blinked, and suddenly, it wasn't Gabriel kneeling at the water's edge. It was me.

I gasped, stumbling back in shock. The reflection in the water was mine, but it wasn't. The woman staring back at me wore a soft, hopeful smile, her eyes bright and clear, her hair wild with the wind. But she wasn't me. Not really. I was standing here, in the flesh, yet this woman, this stranger, felt like someone I could almost be. Someone I wanted to be. Her life was simple. No endless searching. No need to fight every step of the way.

I reached for the water, instinctively, desperate to shatter the image. But my hand was stopped by Gabriel's, his grip firm around my wrist, pulling me back. "Don't touch it. It's not real."

The words cut through the fog of confusion, but the vision didn't fade. I could still see her, still feel the warmth of her life pressing in on me, tempting me.

"What is this?" I whispered, more to myself than to him.

"It's a projection," Gabriel replied. "A manifestation of what you want. What you fear."

My throat tightened as I turned away from the water, meeting his gaze. "What do you fear, then?"

He hesitated, his jaw tightening. "Everything."

The words were raw, jagged, but there was a quiet honesty in them that unsettled me. I opened my mouth to respond, but no sound came. The tension between us was palpable, suffocating, as if the air itself had thickened with unspoken truths. It wasn't just the illusion that was testing us. It was each other, too.

I had never been good at facing my fears. In the past, I'd learned to bury them, to shove them aside and keep moving forward. But standing here, surrounded by this perfect facade, I felt them pressing in—those sharp, jagged edges of doubt, of guilt, of uncertainty. And worse yet, I could feel Gabriel's own fears wrapped around mine, tangled in a knot we both had yet to untangle.

"Is that why you're always so distant?" I asked, my voice barely a whisper. "Because you're afraid?"

He met my gaze, his eyes dark and unreadable. "I'm afraid of losing everything."

The words hung in the air between us, heavy and suffocating, more potent than the illusion itself.

The words still hung in the air between us, charged with an electricity I wasn't sure I was prepared to handle. Gabriel's confession had landed like a stone thrown into a still pond, and the ripples were already widening, threatening to consume everything around us. I glanced back toward the water, the reflection still staring back at me—her face, my face, that impossibly serene smile. What had I been afraid of? The woman in the water had looked at peace, untouched by the constant battle, by the weight of choices, by the fact that every step forward felt like a sacrifice.

But Gabriel... Gabriel was something else entirely.

"Everything?" I repeated softly, half to myself. "What exactly are you afraid of losing? You've got it all—brains, charm, a ridiculous amount of patience with me." The last part slipped out without thinking, but it was true. I couldn't remember the last time I'd met someone who could deal with my brand of chaos and not immediately bail out.

His eyes, dark and heavy, studied me like I was a puzzle he couldn't solve. "You think this is about me?" His lips curved, not in a smile, but in a tight, almost painful twist. "Maybe it's more about you. What you're willing to let yourself have."

I almost laughed—more out of nervousness than humor. "And here I thought we were both just after the artifact." But the joke fell flat. I could feel it: the pressure building between us. He wasn't wrong. Maybe I hadn't been fully honest with myself. Maybe I had been running from something too. The oasis wasn't just some trick of the mind. It was holding a mirror up to us, showing us what we refused to acknowledge.

And maybe, just maybe, I was afraid of admitting that the thing I feared most wasn't the artifact itself. It was the fact that I didn't know how to be present in any of this—whether it was the damn desert or... whatever this thing was with Gabriel.

"You keep your distance. Always," I said before I could stop myself. "It's like you're afraid I'll... I don't know, crumble if I see the real you. But this," I gestured to the stillness around us, the impossibly perfect illusion of an oasis, "isn't real. And neither is whatever you're hiding."

He didn't flinch. He just stood there, his stance relaxed, like he was already expecting me to figure it out. "What if you're right? What if I am hiding something?"

I squared my shoulders, my heart racing as I tried to figure out if I was making the biggest mistake of my life or if I was finally getting it all wrong. Gabriel wasn't the kind of person who wore his emotions on his sleeve. He was careful—too careful. There was an ease to him, a charm that could disarm even the most guarded hearts, but under it was a quiet storm I knew better than to ignore.

"Then stop," I said, finally walking away from the water's edge. I was done with this fantasy. "Stop pretending like there's nothing here. I'm not asking you to explain your entire life, but—"

"Why do you care?" he cut me off, his voice sharp but low, almost in disbelief.

I froze mid-step, my back still to him. Did I care? Of course I did. More than I should. More than I was willing to admit, even to myself. I had spent too long pretending that everything was a job, that this entire mess of a journey was just about the next map, the next clue, the next damn obstacle. But it wasn't. It had never been.

I pivoted, feeling the coolness of the evening setting in as the sun dipped behind the horizon, casting a pinkish glow across the water. My chest tightened, a mixture of frustration and something else swirling inside me. "Because I'm not stupid," I said quietly. "I can see it. I've been seeing it for weeks now. Whatever it is you think I can't handle, Gabriel, I can. You don't get to keep me in the dark."

He looked at me for a long time, his eyes unreadable, before he exhaled slowly, like he had been holding his breath for far too long. And maybe, just maybe, he had. "You really don't get it, do you?"

I crossed my arms, suddenly feeling the weight of the silence pressing in between us, and I hated that. Silence was never a good sign.

"Get what?" I asked, my voice quieter now, resigned to the tension that hung heavy in the air.

Gabriel took a step closer, his eyes locking onto mine with a force that made my breath hitch. "I'm trying to protect you," he said softly. "From me."

The words hit me harder than I expected, leaving me momentarily stunned. Was he—no, that wasn't possible. "What are you talking about?" My voice was rougher than I intended, but I couldn't stop it. This wasn't how I had imagined this moment would unfold.

He shook his head, a half-smile playing at the corners of his lips. But it wasn't a smile of amusement. It was something else entirely—something more vulnerable, something more frightening. "I'm not the hero in this story, Eliza. I'm not the one who comes in and saves the day."

I wanted to laugh—because how absurd, how utterly ridiculous was that? Gabriel, the one who had led us through each challenge with an unwavering calm, the one who had kept us both alive long enough to get this far, was telling me that he was the villain? It didn't make sense.

"You're wrong." The words left my mouth before I could stop them, and I took another step forward. "We're both just... people, Gabriel. We both have baggage, we both have mistakes, but you're not a villain."

He held my gaze for a moment, then turned away, his expression closing off once more. "Maybe that's the problem."

I didn't know what to say to that. How could I? Every word felt like it was shattering something inside me. Something that had been broken long ago, but I hadn't wanted to admit it until now.

And then, as if the world had decided we'd suffered enough, the oasis around us flickered. A ripple in the air, like the surface of water disturbed by an unseen hand, and then it was gone.

In an instant, the illusion collapsed.

The air shifted as the illusion dissolved like smoke. One second, I was standing in a lush, otherworldly paradise, and the next, I was blinking against the harsh, unforgiving desert light. The water that had shimmered so enticingly now looked like a distant mirage, the palms mere shadows against the burning sand.

I swallowed hard, disoriented. "That was... weird," I muttered, wiping my damp palms on my jeans, trying to ignore the way my heart hammered in my chest. Gabriel didn't respond at first, but I could feel the tension radiating off him in waves, like a storm just waiting to break.

"So much for a little peace and quiet," I added, trying to lighten the mood. But my attempt fell flat, as it often did around Gabriel when the truth was too heavy to ignore.

He glanced over at me, his expression unreadable, but his eyes were stormier than I remembered them being. "You think this was just some trick?" His voice was rough, like he'd been holding something back for a long time. "This was the test, Eliza. The one we both failed."

I blinked, not sure if he was talking about the oasis, the map, or something deeper—something far more personal. "Failed?" I echoed, trying to process what he meant. "What exactly did we fail at, Gabriel?"

His lips parted, but he didn't speak right away. Instead, he ran a hand through his already-messy hair, the frustration in his movements palpable. "We failed to see what this was really about," he finally said. "It wasn't just about the artifact. It was about us. About you and me."

I stared at him, completely dumbfounded. "I think we're getting a little too deep into metaphor territory here, don't you?" My voice was tight, trying desperately to cover the vulnerability that threatened to creep up on me. "You're saying that this entire quest was just about us figuring out some... hidden feelings?"

Gabriel's gaze softened for a moment, and I felt something inside me flicker in response, something that threatened to unravel all the carefully constructed walls I'd built. "I'm saying that sometimes what we're running from isn't what we think it is." His tone was quieter now, almost hesitant.

My breath caught. "And what exactly are we running from, Gabriel?"

He turned away, his gaze darting across the endless stretch of sand that seemed to roll on forever. "I don't know," he muttered. "But maybe I don't need to run anymore."

I took a step closer, careful not to crowd him, not sure what exactly I was trying to say. Or if I was ready to hear what he might say next. "Is that supposed to be some kind of confession?" I asked, the words slipping out before I could stop them. The wryness in my voice was an attempt to keep the moment light, but I was too aware of the tension between us—the unspoken weight of everything left unsaid.

Gabriel didn't look at me, but his jaw clenched as he exhaled sharply. "Maybe," he replied, his voice so low I could barely hear it over the wind. "Maybe it's the beginning of one."

A sharp chill ran down my spine, but I forced myself to stand still, to not retreat into the safe distance I'd created over the weeks of traveling together. It had always been easier to keep him at arm's length, to dismiss the flickers of something more than professional respect that had risen between us. But now, with the illusion stripped away, it was harder to pretend like nothing had changed.

I opened my mouth to say something, anything, but before I could form the words, a sound broke through the desert's silence. A low rumble, almost like thunder, but too regular, too mechanical.

My heart skipped. "What the hell is that?" I asked, scanning the horizon for any sign of movement, any threat. But the landscape was eerily empty, a vast stretch of nothingness.

Gabriel's eyes narrowed, his body going tense. "Get down," he ordered, his voice sharp, the command cutting through the air. Without thinking, I dropped to the sand, instinct taking over. Gabriel followed suit, pulling me down with him. I didn't even have time to ask why. I just trusted him, because that's what I always did—trusted that he knew things I didn't, that he could see what I couldn't.

We huddled together, the desert's cool evening air biting at my exposed skin, but I didn't feel it. All I could hear was the growing noise—the unmistakable thud of something large, something mechanical, drawing closer with each passing second.

I held my breath. The sound grew louder. Closer.

"What is that?" I whispered, my voice trembling despite myself.

Gabriel's hand tightened around mine, his fingers digging into my skin like a lifeline. "We're not alone, Eliza," he said quietly, almost grimly.

And then, through the haze of dust rising in the air, I saw it—a massive, hulking vehicle, its dark silhouette outlined against the fading sun. It was like something out of a bad dream: armored, menacing, the kind of thing you'd only expect to see in movies about post-apocalyptic wastelands.

I turned to Gabriel, my pulse racing. "Who the hell are they?"

His lips were pressed into a thin line, his face unreadable. "Not who. What."

The vehicle skidded to a halt several feet from us, dust swirling around us like a storm. The sound of its engines died, leaving a deadly silence in its wake. My heart pounded as I scanned the area for any sign of movement. The air felt thick, charged with tension, and every instinct in me screamed to run. But I didn't move. I couldn't move.

From behind the vehicle, a figure emerged, tall and imposing, dressed in dark, weathered clothes. The man's face was obscured by a mask—one of those old-school gas masks, the kind you'd wear if you were preparing for war.

I had a feeling we were about to find out exactly what kind of war we had stumbled into.

Chapter 23: The Song of Sacrifice

The streets of New Orleans hummed with life, a blend of jazz, the distant chime of church bells, and the rustle of leaves in the evening breeze. Even the air, thick with humidity, held a sort of vibrancy that clung to the skin, as though the city itself were alive with secrets and stories. I had never been here before, but it felt oddly like home—an electric undercurrent that tugged at my chest, urging me forward, just as the energy of the artifact we carried seemed to call to me.

The heavy bronze relic, wrapped in the leather straps of my pack, rested against my back. Every step I took seemed to make it pulse with heat, a strange, insistent warmth that gnawed at my insides. Gabriel had warned me that it wasn't just an artifact—it was a key, and not just any key. There was power bound to it, power I didn't yet understand but could feel deep in my bones, as if it had been waiting for me to arrive. And now, there was no turning back.

Amara, walking ahead, was a stark contrast to the storm swirling within me. Her long black hair fluttered with the breeze, her eyes locked on the ground ahead of her as though she could sense something the rest of us couldn't. The song she sang under her breath had a hypnotic quality, a lilting melody that seemed to drift through the evening air, rising above the chatter of the crowded streets. Her voice was soft, almost haunting, but there was something about it that kept me rooted to the moment, like a spell cast too close to break.

The words she sang were foreign to me, the language unfamiliar, yet they resonated within me in a way I couldn't explain. Love. Loss. Sacrifice. The heavy cadence of each syllable felt like a weight pressing down on my chest, reminding me of a truth I hadn't yet come to terms with. I had to wonder—was this her story, or was it a warning? A glimpse into the future of what might befall Gabriel and me if we continued down this path?

The city, alive with music and light, seemed to blur around me as I caught the undertones of her song, the eerie pull of it wrapping around my thoughts. The vibration in my chest grew stronger, matching the pulse of the artifact. My fingers twitched, itching to reach for it, to grasp it tightly in my hand and demand it reveal itself, its purpose, its price.

A sharp laugh broke through the quiet hum of the evening, and I turned, startled. Gabriel stood a few paces behind us, his dark hair tousled, his eyes gleaming with a mixture of amusement and something far more dangerous. He had that look again—like he knew something I didn't, and wasn't about to share it anytime soon.

"You really think that song of hers is helping us?" he asked, his voice a little too light for the subject at hand.

I shot him a glance, one eyebrow arched in a challenge. "What do you mean?"

He shrugged, though his eyes never left Amara's retreating form. "She's singing about love, loss, and sacrifice. And we're about to face the kind of choice that could cost us everything. The weight of that is heavy, don't you think?"

The mention of sacrifice brought a bitter taste to my mouth. Gabriel was right, of course, but that didn't stop the tightening in my chest. The journey we had undertaken, the artifact we carried—it was all leading us to something inevitable. The final confrontation loomed ahead, a sharp, jagged cliff, and I didn't know if we would fall or fly. Or if we'd survive it at all.

I shook my head, unwilling to voice my own doubts. "We have no choice. We have to keep going."

Gabriel's lips twitched into a faint smile, the kind that never quite reached his eyes. "There's always a choice, sweetheart."

I didn't want to get into another one of our cryptic debates. Not now. Not when the city itself seemed to be leaning in, listening, waiting. There was something about New Orleans that unsettled me, the sense that the past and present were constantly at odds, clashing and colliding like two worlds not meant to exist in the same space. But here we were, walking the streets as if we belonged, as if this city hadn't witnessed a thousand other stories just like ours.

Amara's song drifted back to me, and I turned, following its pull. She was standing beneath a wrought iron arch, her hands clasped in front of her, her back straight, as if awaiting some invisible cue. The streetlights flickered above her, casting long shadows that seemed to stretch and curl like fingers reaching for something just beyond our grasp. The night air was thick with the scent of magnolia, jasmine, and something else—something metallic, sharp. It made the hairs on the back of my neck rise.

I walked toward her, feeling Gabriel's eyes on me, the weight of his unspoken words following closely behind. As I approached, Amara stopped singing and looked up, her dark eyes filled with a sadness that took me by surprise.

"Do you hear it?" she asked, her voice low, barely a whisper against the hum of the city. "The song—it's changing. The end is coming."

I swallowed hard, the tension thick between us, and nodded. "What does that mean?"

Her lips quirked upward, a smile that didn't quite reach her eyes. "It means that the end of the road is close, and you'll have to make a choice. A choice that will determine whether you live or die."

The words hit me like a slap. The artifact in my pack seemed to pulse in answer, its heat intensifying until I could hardly breathe. I looked at Gabriel, who had approached silently behind me, and saw that he was as tense as I felt. Whatever was coming, we weren't ready. Not yet.

But there was no turning back. Not now.

The city seemed to stretch endlessly in every direction, an urban labyrinth woven with narrow streets and ancient oak trees draped in Spanish moss. The humidity clung to me like a second skin, and yet, there was something intoxicating about it—the heaviness of the air, the rustle of the leaves above, the soft murmur of conversations that swirled around us. New Orleans was a city that lived in its contradictions. Bright, neon lights flickered in rhythm with the old jazz standards that echoed from bars hidden between the shadows. On the surface, it was as if the city itself danced to a tune of its own making, but beneath it, there was always something darker, something waiting for the right moment to reveal itself.

I kept my eyes ahead, my hand unconsciously tracing the outline of the artifact that had become an uncomfortable weight against my back. The leather straps chafed my shoulders, but it was nothing compared to the heat emanating from the object itself. Its power seemed to seep through every fiber of my being, tugging at my thoughts, urging me onward. It felt like a presence, a living thing with its own heartbeat, and it was getting harder to ignore.

Amara's voice broke through my thoughts, a soft hum that seemed to reverberate in the very air around us. The melody floated through the narrow streets, weaving between the cracks in the cobblestone, the faintest trace of a story we hadn't yet fully understood. Love. Loss. Sacrifice. The words were like a storm gathering on the horizon, a warning we could neither ignore nor outrun.

I glanced over at Gabriel, who was walking a few paces ahead of me. His long strides ate up the distance, his silhouette framed by the warm glow of the streetlights. The distance between us felt like a chasm now, an unspoken divide that neither of us dared to cross. He was always so sure of himself, so confident in the path we were on, but I could see the tightness in his jaw, the subtle way his hands flexed as if readying for a fight, even when there was nothing in sight. He was hiding something. I could feel it, the same way I could feel the weight of the artifact.

"Is it getting to you too?" I asked, my voice cutting through the silence between us.

He glanced over his shoulder, his dark eyes sharp but unreadable. "What's that?"

I couldn't tell if he was pretending not to know or if he was genuinely unaware of what I was talking about. Gabriel was never one to let his guard down, even with me. But I knew the truth of it. The city was shifting, the air thick with something unsaid, and I could feel his unease as much as I could feel my own.

"The artifact," I clarified, letting the weight of the words linger in the air between us. "It's changing."

He said nothing for a long moment, his gaze far away, as if trying to decipher something only he could see. Finally, he muttered, "It's not the artifact that's changing. It's us."

There was something in the way he said it—dark, loaded, as if the weight of that truth had only just dawned on him. For a second, I almost wished I hadn't asked. We were already so far into this, already so tangled in whatever web had been spun for us. The last thing I wanted was for him to look at me like I was a part of the mess.

Amara's song grew louder in the distance, and I felt the familiar pull of it, an invisible thread guiding me toward her. When I caught up with her, she was standing still, her eyes closed as if in a trance, her hands resting lightly on the handle of the sword strapped to her side. There was a sense of stillness about her, as though she had become one with the night, a part of this city, its mysteries and dangers woven into her very being.

"What's it saying?" I asked, stepping closer.

She opened her eyes slowly, meeting mine with an intensity that made my heart skip a beat. "It's not just a song," she said softly, her voice like velvet, smooth and unsettling all at once. "It's a prayer."

I frowned, not understanding. "A prayer?"

She nodded, her gaze shifting to Gabriel, who had finally caught up with us. There was something unspoken between the two of them, something I didn't quite grasp but could feel simmering under the surface. "A prayer for strength. For the ones who choose to face what lies ahead."

"And what's that, exactly?" Gabriel's voice was tight, his expression unreadable, but I saw the flicker of something—concern? Fear?—just beneath the surface.

Amara turned back toward the street ahead, her fingers brushing against the hilt of her sword. "It's the song of sacrifice. It's what happens when you realize that everything you've fought for could cost you more than you're willing to give."

I swallowed hard, trying to wrap my mind around what she was saying. Sacrifice. The word felt heavy in the air, like a stone sinking into water. My hand twitched, instinctively moving toward the artifact, as if the answer might be hidden there, somewhere beneath its polished surface. But I knew better. I wasn't going to find the answers I needed by merely touching it. The answers would come when the time was right—or when it was too late.

Gabriel's lips tightened into a thin line. "We're already too deep into this," he said, the edge of desperation creeping into his voice. "We don't have time for—"

"Time is all we have left," Amara interrupted, her voice soft but unyielding. "And it's slipping through your fingers."

I could feel the weight of her words, their truth sinking into the pit of my stomach. The confrontation was near. The choices we would have to make were coming fast, like a train barreling down a track. And I wasn't sure if we'd be able to stop it when it came time to face it.

The city of New Orleans had a pulse that seemed to sync with the rhythm of the night, a wild, untamed beat that drummed through the streets like the heart of the city itself. It was as if the air itself had absorbed the stories of centuries, each one a note in an unending symphony of life, death, and everything in between. The streets were alive, a mix of tourists wandering in search of the perfect po' boy, locals leaning out of doorways with knowing smiles, and musicians strumming their guitars like they were weaving magic into the atmosphere. But despite the vibrancy of the scene, I couldn't shake the feeling that something was lurking in the shadows—something far more sinister than the echo of a saxophone or the screech of a streetcar on its tracks.

I glanced at Gabriel, his eyes distant as we walked side by side. His jaw was set, his movements purposeful, but I knew that look. It was the one he got when he was hiding something, and he had been doing a lot of that lately. Our conversations had become increasingly sparse, reduced to terse exchanges, as if the space between us was a wall we both feared would crumble if we spoke too much.

"I'm not sure how much longer I can keep up with this," I said, breaking the silence.

Gabriel's eyes flicked to mine, and then away, as though the words were too heavy to meet directly. "You don't have a choice, do you?"

The words stung, but they were true. We were too far into this mess to back out now. The artifact—whatever it was, whatever it contained—was changing everything. Its heat was almost unbearable at times, a constant reminder that we were heading toward something that none of us could control.

Amara's song reached my ears again, drifting through the heavy air like a soft breeze, seductive in its sadness. I looked over at her, her head tilted back as if listening to the same song that seemed to play in her soul. There was something about her that unsettled me—a kind of serene confidence that seemed at odds with everything else. I wanted to ask her more, wanted to understand the secrets she was clearly carrying, but every time I tried, she slipped away, like trying to hold water in your hands.

"What's it like, then?" I asked, the question tumbling out before I could think better of it. "To know?"

Amara's gaze snapped to me, and for a brief moment, I saw something flicker behind her eyes—something that made my stomach tighten. "To know what?"

"Everything," I said, not needing to elaborate. The weight of what we were doing, what we were chasing, had become so suffocating that I couldn't pretend it didn't gnaw at me anymore. "To know what comes next. To know that we're playing with forces that could ruin us."

She didn't answer right away, just kept walking with that effortless grace that I envied. When she spoke, it was soft, as though she was choosing each word carefully. "I don't know everything," she said, her voice barely more than a whisper against the cacophony of the city. "But I know that if we keep walking, we'll reach a place where nothing is the same."

The words felt like a promise, but it was one wrapped in uncertainty and danger, like a lullaby sung in the dark.

We turned a corner and suddenly, the sound of music filled the air—a jazz band set up on a corner, its horns blaring in a discordant yet somehow perfect harmony. The crowd gathered around them, swaying and clapping, lost in the moment as the magic of New

Orleans swept them up. It should have been a welcome distraction, a balm to ease the tension that had settled into my shoulders. Instead, the vibrant energy of the city made me feel more like an intruder in a place that didn't belong to me.

"I've never liked jazz," I muttered, more to myself than to anyone else.

Gabriel raised an eyebrow. "You're kidding, right? This city was built on jazz."

"Yeah, well," I said, glancing around, "sometimes it feels like it's all a little too much. Like everyone's pretending they don't see the cracks underneath."

Amara's lips twitched, as if she was about to say something, but then her expression darkened, her gaze shifting toward the alley that opened up just beyond the crowd. Without a word, she turned toward it, walking briskly, her eyes sharp as though she had spotted something the rest of us had missed. Gabriel and I exchanged a glance before following her, our footsteps echoing against the walls of the alley.

The deeper we went, the darker it became. The sounds of the city faded, swallowed by the narrow space between buildings. The faint glow of streetlights barely reached us here, leaving us in a half-shadow that felt oppressive. I felt the hair on the back of my neck rise as if we were being watched.

Amara stopped abruptly, her head tilting as she listened to something we couldn't hear. Her eyes narrowed, her hand instinctively reaching for the hilt of her sword.

"What is it?" I whispered.

She held up a hand, signaling for silence. For a moment, everything was still—so still that I could hear my own heart thundering in my chest. Then, from the darkness ahead of us, a figure emerged. It was a man—tall, with sharp features and a presence that seemed to radiate power. His eyes glowed faintly in the dim light, an unnatural shimmer that made my blood run cold.

"You've come," the man said, his voice smooth, like honey over broken glass. "I've been waiting for you."

I instinctively took a step back, my fingers brushing against the hilt of the dagger at my side. "Who are you?"

He smiled, but it wasn't a comforting smile. It was the kind of smile that made you question every decision you'd ever made. "I'm the one who's going to make sure you understand the price of what you're holding."

The temperature in the alley seemed to drop, and the artifact at my back pulsed in response, as if it recognized the danger the man presented. Amara stepped in front of me, her stance protective but measured.

"What do you want?" Gabriel demanded, his voice tight with a threat I could feel but not quite identify.

The man's smile widened. "I want you to choose. The question is—will you make the right one?"

And then, before we could react, he vanished into the shadows.

Chapter 24: The Masked Stranger

The sun was setting behind the jagged horizon, casting long shadows across the barren stretch of desert that seemed to stretch into infinity. My boots kicked up the dry earth as I trudged beside Gabriel, the weight of the moment pressing down on my chest. Every breath felt labored, each step a reminder of how far we'd come, and how much further we had to go. Gabriel, ever the stoic presence beside me, hadn't said a word since we'd seen him—a figure, standing just on the edge of the sand, draped in shadow, his face hidden beneath a gleaming mask of gold. I could barely make out the outline of his form, but the mask gleamed like a shard of the moon, distant and unforgiving.

"Do you think he's real?" Gabriel asked, his voice a soft rasp, as if he were trying to convince himself more than me.

I shot him a sidelong glance, noting the tightness in his jaw. "Real enough to know we're here. And real enough to ask for a price."

Gabriel's eyes narrowed, his gaze drifting toward the figure. "That mask..." His words trailed off, and I could hear the unspoken hesitation in the air, thick like the dust swirling around our feet. He knew better than anyone how dangerous this was, how easily it could all go wrong. We'd chased this artifact across half the country, and now, here we were, standing on the cusp of uncovering whatever secrets lay behind the curse.

The figure didn't move. Not even the slightest twitch to acknowledge us. For all its looming presence, it was as still as the desert itself.

Gabriel shifted his weight, his hand subtly brushing the handle of the knife at his belt. I could tell his instincts were on edge. They mirrored mine. "We should turn back," he said quietly, but there was a thread of something darker woven through his words—fear, perhaps, or something else, something I wasn't ready to name.

"Turn back?" I repeated, raising an eyebrow. "We've come this far. We're not backing out now."

"I'm not backing out, but this... this doesn't feel right. We don't know who or what we're dealing with."

I took a deep breath, feeling the dry desert air scratch my throat, and adjusted my pack. It weighed heavily, pressing against my spine as if reminding me of every decision that had led me to this exact moment. Gabriel wasn't wrong. The closer we got to the stranger, the more I felt a prickle at the back of my neck, the sensation of being watched from a distance, unseen eyes tracing every movement. But this was it. This was the piece we needed. And I wasn't going to back down just because it felt... off.

We finally reached the figure, who still hadn't moved an inch. The golden mask gleamed beneath the dying sun, reflecting a thousand shades of amber and crimson. The silence stretched between us, the desert surrounding us swallowing every sound. It was as if the world had paused, waiting for something to happen.

I cleared my throat, attempting to break the tension that was slowly suffocating us. "You know why we're here," I said, my voice firm but laced with curiosity. "You know what we're after."

The figure's head tilted ever so slightly, and then, to my surprise, a low, melodic voice echoed from behind the mask, each word wrapped in a strange, almost musical cadence. "I know. And I also know that what you seek comes with a price."

I swallowed. "What kind of price?"

There was a brief pause, and then the figure stepped forward, the sand barely stirring beneath his feet. The motion was smooth, deliberate—unnerving, almost. "The truth," he said, the words carrying a weight that made my skin prickle, "is not something you can simply take. It must be earned."

I raised an eyebrow. "Earned? We've been earning it for months. What else do you want from us?"

The figure's laugh was soft, like a breath of wind over a long-forgotten grave. "You think you've earned it?" he asked, the mockery clear in his voice. "Your journey has just begun."

Gabriel's hand tightened on his knife, but I reached out to steady him. We couldn't afford to act rashly. Not now.

"Then tell us," I pressed, "what do we need to do?"

For the first time, the figure moved, his masked face tilting upward as if to stare at the sky, as if contemplating the vastness of the desert and everything it contained. When he spoke again, his voice was different—darker, as though it had descended from a place that wasn't entirely human. "You will have the truth," he said, "but it comes at the cost of your greatest fear."

I felt a cold knot settle in my stomach. "What does that mean?" I asked, though the answer already felt like it was creeping along the edges of my consciousness.

The figure didn't respond right away. Instead, he took a slow, deliberate step toward us, closing the gap between us like an inescapable tide. "You'll understand soon enough," he murmured, his voice lowering to something almost soothing, like a lullaby meant to lull you into a false sense of security. "But I must warn you: once you accept the truth, there is no turning back."

Gabriel's breath caught, a flicker of something desperate passing over his face before he quickly masked it, a tight mask of defiance taking its place. "What's the price?" he demanded, his voice no longer soft, but edged with something darker.

The figure finally reached up, one gloved hand gently tracing the golden mask, and I could almost feel the shift in the air around us—the temperature seemed to drop, the wind stilled, and the ground beneath us felt as though it was shifting.

"The price," the figure repeated, "is the cost of your soul's reckoning."

It was a warning, and we both felt it—a weight that threatened to crush us beneath the weight of its meaning.

Gabriel's grip tightened on his knife, the motion so subtle it could have been mistaken for nothing more than a nervous twitch. But I knew him too well to miss the way his knuckles paled, the way his jaw clenched even harder than it had before. The figure in the golden mask hadn't moved an inch, but I could feel the weight of his words sinking into the ground like heavy stones, their meaning settling over us with a slow, suffocating pressure.

"I don't like this," Gabriel muttered, his voice low, barely a whisper. It was the first time he'd spoken since the figure had warned us of the price we'd have to pay. "It's not just a cost. It's—" He stopped, shaking his head as if he were struggling to find the right words. "We shouldn't trust him."

"Who else do we trust?" I replied, the words coming out sharper than I intended. But the truth was, Gabriel was right. This was madness. Every instinct in my body was screaming at me to turn around, to leave this bizarre encounter behind and continue our search elsewhere. But we couldn't. The artifact, the curse—it was too important. Too many lives were at stake, and we couldn't walk away now, not when we were so close.

"Trust?" Gabriel's voice cracked, a rare edge of panic creeping into it. "He's not here to help us, Harper. He's here to trap us."

I wasn't sure if it was the rawness in his tone or the sharpness of his words that made me pause, but for the first time, I felt the tremor of doubt beneath my own resolve. This wasn't just about the artifact anymore. It was about something deeper, something darker that I couldn't quite grasp. Something Gabriel saw but I couldn't yet.

The figure behind the mask tilted his head, his movements deliberate, almost unnervingly slow. "I understand your hesitation," he said, his voice too calm for my liking, as if he were enjoying this. "But there is no escaping the price. There never is. You are standing at the edge of a choice, and once it is made, there will be no going back."

"What exactly do you mean by that?" I asked, trying to keep my voice steady. I knew better than to reveal the extent of the doubt creeping in, but it was getting harder to hold it back. "What is the price?"

For a moment, the golden mask seemed to flicker, as if something beneath it—some unspoken emotion or secret—was trying to break free. But then, it was still again. The figure's hand raised, almost languidly, and the air around us seemed to shift, as if the entire desert held its breath.

"The cost," he began, his voice dropping into an almost hypnotic cadence, "is not one of gold or silver, nor of flesh or blood. It is the very thing you hold most dear, the thing that makes you who you are."

A shiver ran down my spine, and I saw Gabriel's eyes narrow in response. His jaw tightened, but there was something in his gaze now, something more than just fear—it was a flicker of recognition. As if, suddenly, he understood what was at stake in a way that I didn't.

I took a step forward, the dry sand crunching beneath my boots. "Are you saying we have to give up our... identities?" The words sounded absurd as soon as I said them, but the figure's knowing silence seemed to confirm that absurdity.

"No," the figure said, as though answering an unspoken question. "Not your identities. Not your past. But everything you believe you control. Your certainty. Your sense of power. The illusion that you are the masters of your fate."

I swallowed, the bitter taste of dread rising in my throat. This wasn't about an artifact. This wasn't even about the curse anymore. This was about something far more personal, far more intimate. A test of will, of desire, of what we were willing to sacrifice in the name of whatever this journey had become.

Gabriel's voice cut through the air, brittle with tension. "I don't care what it costs. You can keep your damned truth."

The figure didn't react, but I felt the moment shift—like a ripple in the air, something unspoken settling between us. It wasn't surprise, exactly. More like an understanding, a quiet acknowledgment that Gabriel's resistance had been anticipated, that it was part of the game.

But my own thoughts were a whirlwind, swirling with doubt and fear. The truth had always been my driving force. But what if the truth wasn't worth the cost? What if it tore something inside me that I couldn't repair?

Gabriel and I had always worked together, even when we didn't see eye to eye. But now... now, I felt the first stirrings of a fracture between us. His fear wasn't something I had seen before, not in this form. It was raw, it was real, and it was palpable. And I wasn't sure how much of it was for him, how much was for me, and how much was for the two of us standing here, about to make a decision that would alter everything.

I turned to Gabriel, searching his face for some hint of the man I had trusted, the man I had fought beside. But his features were closed off, the mask of indifference slipping back into place. It was the mask he wore whenever things were too complicated, whenever he couldn't solve the problem with his fists or with a plan.

"This isn't about us anymore," I said softly, trying to reach through the walls he was building around himself. "It's about the people we're trying to save. This is bigger than us."

He met my gaze then, his eyes dark, haunted, but resolute. "Maybe it should be," he muttered, almost to himself.

The figure in the mask stepped forward, his body language predatory, like a lion circling its prey. "You will make the choice soon enough, and you will understand the cost of your ambition. The truth you seek is nothing compared to the truth you will become."

The words echoed in my mind long after they were spoken, reverberating like a whisper carried by the wind.

The air between Gabriel and me hummed with a strange tension, the kind you feel when you've just stepped into a room where the furniture's been rearranged but you don't know why. We stood there, neither of us daring to take the first step toward the masked figure. The golden mask reflected the fading light of the desert sun, making it look almost ethereal, like some otherworldly object dropped onto this desolate earth by a careless god. I could feel it—the weight of our decisions, the gnawing hunger of the unknown.

Gabriel was still silent beside me, his gaze flicking back and forth from the figure to the horizon, as if weighing some invisible scale. Every muscle in his body was coiled tight, ready to spring at the slightest provocation. His fear was palpable, and I could feel it gnawing at the edges of my resolve. It was the fear of losing control, of stepping into something we couldn't fight or outrun.

I took a step forward, breaking the deadlock. If Gabriel wouldn't do it, I would. "I want the truth," I said, more firmly than I felt. "What is it you want in exchange?"

The masked figure remained perfectly still, the silence stretching so long it almost felt like we were intruding on something private. Then, his voice, low and melodic, sliced through the quiet like a blade. "What do I want?" He almost seemed to laugh, but there was no humor in it. "What do I want? You should know by now. You already have the answers, but you're too afraid to face them."

I swallowed, the words curdling in my stomach. "You're telling me this is a test?" I couldn't quite suppress the bitterness creeping into my voice. "You think we're not worthy?"

The figure tilted his head slightly, as if considering me. "Not worthy. No." His voice dropped, turning almost sadistic, and it was then that I felt the full weight of the trap tightening around us. "You're not worthy yet. But you will be, if you dare to understand what I'm offering."

Gabriel's hands clenched into fists at his sides. "What's the catch? Why don't you just tell us what we need to know and be done with it?"

I could feel his anger now, rising like the dust storms we'd seen on the horizon, sweeping through him and pushing against everything he'd built up to survive this long. But the masked figure didn't flinch.

"No," the figure said, his voice suddenly sharp. "Not so easy. Not with the stakes so high. Not when you think you can control everything, that you can walk through this world and shape it with your hands. That's the mistake, isn't it? Thinking you can control your own fate." His tone was almost cruel now, each word a drop of acid sinking into our skins.

"You've lost control," he continued, as if savoring the confession. "Everything you think you know, every step you've taken, every choice you've made, has already been set into motion. The price you'll pay isn't for me to decide. It's already been decided. You've already chosen it."

I felt a sickening chill crawl up my spine. "What the hell are you talking about?" My voice was too sharp, but I couldn't help it. The weight of this encounter, the maddening uncertainty, was beginning to crack through my calm exterior.

The figure tilted his head, those golden eyes staring through the mask with an unnerving intensity. "I'm telling you this now because you need to see the truth before you choose," he said, each word like a nail being driven into the coffin of our certainty. "Once you accept the truth, you will lose everything. Your choices will no longer be yours to make. And your futures will be shaped by forces you cannot understand."

Gabriel took a step forward, suddenly moving like a coiled spring released. "We've come this far," he said, his voice hoarse but resolute. "You think we'll walk away because you're playing mind games?"

The figure didn't respond immediately, but there was something in the air now, a sudden shift in the atmosphere that made every breath feel heavy. "This isn't a game, Gabriel," he said, his voice taking on a colder, more dangerous edge. "This is the end of everything you think you know. When you make this choice, you will face the consequences—no matter what they may be."

There was a moment of silence, thick and suffocating. Gabriel stood there, frozen, his face pale beneath the harsh desert light. I could see it now—the fear, raw and palpable, spreading across his features like wildfire. And it wasn't just fear of the figure in front of us. It was something deeper. Something about the words that were being spoken, something he hadn't told me yet, something I didn't want to know.

I took a deep breath, my heart hammering in my chest. "Gabriel," I said softly, reaching out toward him. "What aren't you telling me?"

For the first time since we had met this masked stranger, Gabriel didn't answer immediately. His eyes met mine, and in them, I saw something I wasn't ready for—something broken, something irreparable. His mouth opened as if to speak, but the words never came.

The figure in the golden mask was watching us, a silent observer to our unraveling. His lips curled into something that wasn't quite a smile, but more like the ghost of one. "You should hurry," he said, his voice low and threatening. "The choice will be made for you soon enough. There's no escaping the cost."

The ground beneath us seemed to tremble slightly, as if the earth itself was reacting to the tension, and then the first stone fell—an ominous crack from somewhere in the distance. Gabriel's head snapped around, and I saw the first flicker of genuine panic in his eyes. "What the hell is happening?"

I turned toward the sound, my pulse quickening. The air felt charged, electric, like the calm before a storm. But this wasn't a storm we could escape.

The ground beneath our feet seemed to ripple like water, and then, just as I felt my breath catch in my throat, the figure stepped forward, his gloved hand reaching up, fingertips brushing the edge of his mask. Slowly, deliberately, he lifted it.

And what I saw beneath it was nothing I could have ever imagined.

Chapter 25: The Valley of Kings and Ghosts

The city buzzed beneath a sweltering heat that painted the streets in shades of sun-bleached gold and burnt orange. As I stepped into the worn, yet ever vibrant, streets of the Lower East Side, the hum of conversations mixed with the distant rumble of subway trains. The graffiti-clad walls told stories of their own—stories of rebellion, love, and loss, often scrawled in colors so bold they seemed to defy the concrete they clung to.

I was on my way to meet Gabriel, though not for any reason that could be neatly tied with a bow. There was no grand plan, no tidy outline of events. Just the odd, unexplainable pull between us, like the last knot on a tangled ball of yarn that seemed impossible to untie but essential to try.

It was there, in the dim light of a corner bar, that I found him. His figure was unmistakable—tall, angular, his presence cutting through the crowded space as if the room had to make room for him. And yet, in a way, he seemed utterly out of place, like a lost note in a song no one was quite ready to hear.

"Amara," he said, his voice low, rough in a way that made my pulse quicken, "you came."

I didn't know why I had. I should have known better than to follow whatever this was between us, but in that moment, as I stood on the precipice of everything I had ever believed to be true, I chose to step forward. What else could I do?

"You sound surprised," I replied, the words more playful than I intended, like a shield I could hide behind.

"I'm not," he answered quickly, eyes narrowing just a fraction as if trying to gauge something beyond the surface of my words. "You've always been here, Amara. Whether you admit it or not."

A faint, crooked smile tugged at my lips, but it didn't feel as natural as it used to. The air between us thickened with something unspoken—an electric charge that both terrified and thrilled me. I hadn't realized just how much I had let myself unravel since meeting him, how much of myself I had willingly surrendered in these stolen moments.

"Right," I said, shaking my head. "You're not wrong. But I'm not staying long."

His gaze softened, like he was trying to memorize every line of my face, as though he knew what came next. Something terrible, something neither of us could avoid.

The world outside the bar shifted, twisted, and collapsed into something altogether darker. Or maybe I just saw it more clearly now.

I blinked, but when I opened my eyes, the bar was gone. It was replaced by an expanse of desert—vast and silent. A dry wind swept over us, whipping up dust and sand that bit at my skin like forgotten memories. And there, ahead of us, rose the jagged, ancient tombs, their stone surfaces worn smooth by time. Ghostly figures lingered at the entrances, their forms translucent, their faces obscured by shadows.

"What the hell—" I began, but Gabriel was already a step ahead, his hand gripping my arm with an intensity that snapped me out of my panic.

"It's happening," he murmured, his voice tight, his grip unyielding. His eyes were locked on the valley, darkened by something that felt older than time itself. "The artifact. It's calling to you."

I swallowed, trying to push down the dread that rushed over me. I hadn't thought it would come to this. But as we approached the edge of the valley, I felt the weight of it all—the pull of the artifact, the way its energy hummed through the air like the tremor before a storm.

"Can you feel it?" Gabriel's voice was barely above a whisper now, his face inches from mine. His breath was hot against my skin, and the air between us seemed to thrum with a strange energy. "It's changing you."

I didn't want to admit it, but I could feel the shift—like a heavy tide pulling me deeper and deeper into the unknown. The artifact, a relic I had never fully understood, had begun to weave its hold on me. Its power seeped into my veins, turning every thought, every breath, into something more. Something dangerous.

Amara's voice pierced through the heaviness, clear and melodic. It was a song unlike any I'd ever heard—one that seemed to harmonize with the whispers of the spirits around us. The eerie figures that had once guarded the tombs now softened, their movements more fluid, less menacing. The air itself seemed to bend around us, responding to the pull of her voice.

But the deeper we ventured into the valley, the more volatile the artifact became. It was as if it were aware of Amara's song, battling against it with an energy that threatened to swallow us whole.

I could feel it. The artifact's power, like fire in my chest, was growing stronger, and I wasn't sure how much longer I could control it.

"Gabriel," I gasped, my voice trembling. I couldn't keep up this façade of control any longer. "It's too much."

He stepped closer, his hand on my shoulder grounding me. "I'm not going anywhere," he said, the conviction in his tone doing little to quell the storm inside me. "We'll get through this."

But even as he spoke, I could feel something slipping—something that was always just out of reach, just beyond my grasp. It wasn't just the artifact; it was us. There was something between us, something that neither of us could deny. And the closer we got to the heart of the valley, the more I realized that nothing—absolutely nothing—would be the same once we uncovered the truth.

The valley stretched out before us like a chasm of forgotten promises, its silence swallowing every breath I took. The spirits, now more vivid than ever, hovered just on the edge of my vision, their forms ghostly wisps that flickered like the last embers of a dying fire. I could feel them watching, waiting—anticipating the next move, the inevitable step forward that would bring us closer to whatever lay hidden in the heart of this cursed land.

Gabriel, ever the enigma, was at my side. His usual cool demeanor had shifted, something darker creeping into his expression, a vulnerability I hadn't seen before. It was as if the artifacts' pull had dug beneath his skin too, and now we were both caught in its web, struggling to find our way through the sticky strands of power, fear, and something far more dangerous.

"You're holding up well," he said, voice low, a faint glimmer of amusement playing in his eyes despite the tension in the air. "For someone who's about to lose her mind."

I couldn't help but let out a short laugh, though it was sharp and hollow. "I think that ship sailed long ago, Gabriel. I've been unhinged since the moment we stepped into this mess."

His lips quirked, but there was something tender in the way he looked at me—a strange blend of concern and admiration, the kind you get when you're watching someone walk to the edge of a cliff, all the while hoping they'll turn back before they fall. But he knew better than to speak the words out loud. Gabriel was no fool, and he certainly wasn't one to treat me like glass.

We walked in silence, the only sound between us the soft scrape of our shoes against the stony path, the rustle of wind moving through the dusty air. But as we ventured deeper, the temperature seemed to drop. A chill crept through my veins, not from the cold, but from the growing intensity of the artifact's presence. It was like a knot tightening in my chest, squeezing out the air in small, painful bursts. The artifact was alive, it had always been alive, and now it wanted something from me.

And whatever that was, it wouldn't be pretty.

Amara's voice broke through the growing tension like a lifeline, her melody shifting, the notes curling in the air like the smoke from a long-forgotten fire. Her song was more than just a sound—it was a force, a barrier against the darkness creeping around us, and for a fleeting moment, I thought we might be okay. That we might make it out of here without losing everything.

But then the ground beneath us shuddered, and the valley itself seemed to sigh in discontent. I froze, the air thick with a low, guttural hum, like something stirring deep below the earth. The tombs, once imposing and silent, now seemed to breathe with a life of their own, their stone faces etched with expressions of agony, as though they too could feel the storm building inside the valley's heart.

"We're not alone," Gabriel whispered, his voice barely audible above the thrumming sound that seemed to reverberate from the ground itself.

"I noticed," I replied, the sarcasm coming out more strained than I intended. "Any ideas on how we stop it from eating us alive?"

He didn't respond immediately, his eyes narrowing as he studied the tombs. The ancient structures seemed to shift before my very eyes, their entrances widening, shadows spilling from within like dark pools of water.

The spirits, once peaceful in their eerie dance, had grown restless. Their movements became erratic, as if they were trying to break free from the constraints of the tombs. Some whispered louder now, their voices like nails against glass, their words unintelligible, and yet, somehow, familiar. My head throbbed with the effort of trying to understand them, like a thousand pieces of a puzzle scattered just out of reach.

"What do they want?" I asked, the question hanging in the air like a cloud of smoke.

Gabriel looked at me, his gaze intense, searching for something in my eyes. For a moment, he didn't speak. Instead, he reached out, his fingers brushing against the edge of the artifact, which hung around my neck like an anchor. His touch was warm, grounding, but it sent a shock of energy through my body, one that made my blood run cold and my heart race in time with the thunder in the distance.

"The artifact," he said, his voice a little rougher now, "it's a key. But it's not just unlocking the valley. It's unlocking something inside of you."

My throat went dry, and I felt a flicker of something—something not quite fear, but something darker, something far more ancient. "What do you mean by that?"

He hesitated, his lips pressing together in a hard line, and for a second, I thought he might say something that would shatter the fragile illusion of control I'd been clinging to. But instead, he simply looked away.

"I think we're too close now," he said finally. "It's almost as if the artifact's power has chosen you."

My pulse quickened. The words hung in the air, sharp and ominous. "Chosen me?" I echoed, my voice almost lost in the wind. "That's not exactly comforting."

He didn't offer an answer. Instead, his eyes tracked the figures moving in the tombs. Their forms were becoming more solid, more defined. And in the distance, at the heart of the valley, a dark shape was beginning to materialize—something so massive, so undeniably ancient, that even the air seemed to tremble at its presence.

I had no idea how much longer I could hold on. The power of the artifact pulsed through me like a living thing, growing stronger, its demand louder. And as we moved closer to the center of the valley, the walls of my resolve started to crumble. I had a choice to make. But was I ready to face the consequences of it?

The air had become thick, oppressive, almost as though the earth itself was holding its breath. With every step deeper into the valley, the weight of the artifact's power grew heavier, a pulse beneath my skin that rattled my bones. And yet, I found myself unwilling to stop. It was as if something within me—something primal and hungry—was pushing me forward. It wanted to see what lay hidden in the depths, wanted to unlock whatever secret the valley had been keeping for centuries.

Gabriel's hand brushed mine, a fleeting touch that sent a shock through me, grounding me in a way I didn't know I needed. The connection between us was undeniable, like an anchor in a stormy sea, but I couldn't allow myself to lean too heavily on it. I couldn't afford to.

"This is madness," I muttered, trying to shake the creeping unease.

He was silent for a moment, his gaze fixed ahead, but I could feel him listening, sensing the fear that was clawing its way up my throat. I almost wished he would speak, but the words wouldn't come. So instead, we continued on, the valley yawning wider with each step, its shadows deepening, as if the earth itself was trying to swallow us whole.

The figures that had once stood still now moved in sync, their ghostly forms twisting and writhing like smoke, their whispers rising to a crescendo that made the hairs on the back of my neck stand at attention. It wasn't just the artifact that called to them—it was me. The spirits were drawn to whatever was stirring inside me, to the unraveling that was beginning to take place.

"I told you this wasn't just about the artifact," Gabriel said quietly, his voice cutting through the growing cacophony of voices.

I glanced at him, meeting his eyes for the first time in what felt like hours. His face was tense, his brow furrowed as he studied the path ahead. But his gaze softened when it reached me, a fleeting moment of tenderness that felt completely out of place amidst the madness.

"You were right," I said, my voice barely above a whisper. "It's me, isn't it?"

His lips pressed into a thin line, and for a moment, I thought he might lie. But instead, he nodded, his expression serious. "The artifact was always meant for someone. It didn't choose just anyone, Amara. It chose you."

I stopped, suddenly overwhelmed by the weight of his words. "I don't—"

"You don't have to understand it all now," he interrupted gently, though there was an edge to his voice that betrayed the urgency of the situation. "You just have to keep moving."

I swallowed hard, my throat dry. I had no idea how I was supposed to keep moving, especially when every instinct in me screamed to turn back. But something—no, someone—was counting on me. I wasn't sure who or what, but the pull of the valley, the voices of the spirits, and the oppressive weight of the artifact all had one thing in common: they demanded my attention, my obedience.

The valley opened up before us, revealing a massive stone archway, its surfaces etched with symbols I couldn't even begin to decipher. The air around it shimmered, as if the very atmosphere was charged with electricity, the hairs on the back of my neck standing at attention.

"Is this it?" I asked, my voice trembling despite my best efforts to sound calm.

Gabriel didn't respond immediately. He stepped forward, his eyes scanning the archway as though he were reading something only he could see. The closer we got, the more the artifact hummed with energy, a low, vibrating pulse that filled the air with an almost unbearable pressure.

"Whatever is on the other side," Gabriel said softly, his gaze never leaving the archway, "it won't be what you expect."

I could feel his unease, but it was mixed with something else—something deeper, something older. The valley had been built to protect whatever lay behind the arch, but why? What was so powerful that it needed to be hidden for all these centuries?

Before I could ask, the ground beneath us trembled. The tombs that lined the valley seemed to come alive, their stone faces cracking open with an eerie groan, revealing the faintest glimpse of what lay hidden inside. And that was when I saw them—figures emerging from the shadows, their eyes glowing with an unnatural light, their bodies more spectral than solid.

Gabriel's hand found mine, his grip tight, his palm warm against my freezing skin. "We have to hurry," he said, his voice low and urgent.

But it was already too late.

The figures moved toward us, their forms shifting and distorting in ways that defied logic. They were no longer just spirits—they were something else entirely, something that reached for us with the desperation of a thousand years. The artifact in my chest flared, its power responding to the surge of energy from the tombs, and I could feel my body beginning to tremble under the weight of it all.

"You have to control it, Amara," Gabriel said, his voice laced with tension. "You're the only one who can."

Control it? How could I? The power was too much, too overwhelming, and it felt like it was slipping further from my grasp with every passing second. The walls of the valley, the tombs, and the spirits—they were all closing in around us, suffocating us with their ancient demands.

I could feel the artifact's pull like a weight in my chest, a force beyond anything I had ever known. And as the figures grew closer, their forms shifting in and out of reality, I knew one thing for certain:

We weren't leaving this place without facing whatever was waiting on the other side of the arch.

And I wasn't sure if I could survive what lay beyond it.

Chapter 31: The Keeper of the Abyss

The abyss felt like a living thing, breathing beneath our feet, its darkness swirling and twisting around us, wrapping itself in the corners of my mind. Each step I took echoed unnaturally in the cavernous expanse, as if the very walls were aware of our presence. Gabriel's torch flickered like a fragile promise, the golden light trembling against the oppressive blackness that threatened to swallow us whole. His hand, warm and steady, remained just inches from mine, a subtle reassurance that despite everything, we weren't truly alone.

We moved forward, our breath shallow, as though the air itself had thickened to a point where it became a tangible force, pushing against our lungs. The whispers, those soft, slithering voices, grew louder. They weren't words exactly—just fragments, broken syllables carried on the wind. One moment, I could almost make them out, a single word pressing against the tip of my consciousness. Then, just as quickly, it would fade, replaced by another rush of sound that seemed to come from behind me, from within the stone, from places no voice should ever inhabit.

"This place is... wrong," I said, the words escaping me before I could stop them. "It feels like it wants us here. Like it's waiting for us to fail."

Gabriel didn't reply at first. He kept his eyes forward, scanning the shadows with the quiet intensity of someone who had long since learned to distrust the unknown. "The artifact... it's not just a relic, is it?" His voice was strained, as though even he could feel the weight of the air pressing in on him.

"No," I answered, though I wasn't sure myself. The artifact, the one that had been in my possession for so long now, felt different. I'd carried it through so many trials, always knowing that its power was far greater than any of us truly understood. But here, in the heart of the abyss, it thrummed against my chest like a living thing, and I couldn't shake the feeling that it had its own plans—plans that didn't necessarily align with mine.

The keeper's presence was everywhere now. Even though I couldn't see him clearly, I could feel his eyes on us, burning into me with a heat that made my skin crawl. He was more than just a guard, more than a mere protector of the artifact. There was something ancient about him, something far older than the world I knew. His very existence was a paradox—his form shifting and undulating like smoke, but those eyes, those eyes were burning with a fire that could not be extinguished. They were not the eyes of a man, or even of a god—they were the eyes of something eternal, something unyielding.

And then, just when I thought the silence might swallow us whole, his voice emerged—soft at first, like a breath of wind, then growing louder, more insistent.

"You think you can control what you do not understand?" The words wrapped around us, an intangible weight pressing on our minds. "The artifact will test you, and you will fail. You will see, little ones, what it is truly capable of."

I felt the artifact pulse again, and this time, it wasn't just in my chest. It radiated outward, a hum of power that filled every corner of the abyss, every inch of the air we breathed. The temperature dropped even further, the cold seeping into my bones, my fingertips going numb.

I could feel Gabriel's presence beside me, his warmth the only thing grounding me in that moment. "We're not turning back now," he said softly, though his voice betrayed the tightness in his throat. "We came here for a reason. We'll face whatever it throws at us."

His words were enough to steady me, but only for a moment. The keeper's form shifted again, this time coalescing into something more solid, more terrifying. His face, if it could even be called that, seemed to ripple like the surface of a pond disturbed by an unseen hand. And then, for the first time, he spoke directly to me.

"You, child of the light, you are the chosen one," he said, his voice a hiss that seemed to seep into my very soul. "But the power you seek will consume you. The artifact is not a gift—it is a curse."

The words hung in the air like poison, filling me with a dread I couldn't shake. I wanted to argue, to shout that I was in control, that I had the strength to bear whatever came my way. But deep inside, something twisted, a tiny seed of doubt that had been planted long ago. Was I truly in control? Or was I simply a pawn, another soul swept along by forces far beyond my comprehension?

Gabriel's grip tightened on my hand, a silent reminder that I wasn't alone. But even his touch couldn't erase the fear gnawing at the edges of my mind.

"We'll see about that," I muttered, my voice steady despite the chaos swirling inside me.

The keeper's laugh was a low, rumbling sound that vibrated through the ground beneath our feet. It was a sound that seemed to mock us, to challenge us to prove him wrong. And then, with a final, sweeping gesture, he faded into the shadows once more, his presence lingering like a heavy fog, the oppressive weight of his words still echoing in my mind.

The silence that followed was thick and suffocating. But it wasn't the kind of silence that brought peace—it was the kind that made your skin prickle and your heartbeat race, as though something was waiting, watching, and biding its time.

"We're not done yet," Gabriel said, his voice a little louder now, his resolve hardening in the face of the keeper's warning. "Whatever this place is, whatever it wants from us, we're going to finish this. Together."

Together. That word echoed in my mind as we moved deeper into the abyss, the darkness swallowing the light of our torch. And in that moment, I wasn't sure what lay ahead—but I knew one thing for certain: I would not face it alone.

The silence in the abyss was maddening. The whispers that had once felt like a haunting hum in the back of my mind now seemed to grow louder, stretching and contorting in the air, pressing against my eardrums as though they could reach inside me, pull apart my thoughts, and unravel whatever feeble sense of control I had left. Gabriel's steady presence beside me was the only thing that held me together, the warmth of his hand, though just a whisper of contact, an anchor in a sea of madness.

The path ahead was treacherous, jagged stone reaching out like skeletal fingers, and yet we continued, every step forward another plunge into the unknown. The torchlight wavered in the heavy air, casting grotesque shadows along the walls—shadows that seemed to move, to twitch, like the very fabric of the place was alive and aware. And at the heart of it all, the artifact pressed against my chest, a constant reminder that I wasn't just here to survive. No, I was here to face something that no one, not even Gabriel, truly understood.

"Do you feel that?" I whispered, my voice hoarse, as if the very air had stolen the moisture from my throat.

Gabriel's grip on my hand tightened, but he didn't speak. I knew he felt it too—the thrum of power, ancient and untamed, vibrating through the ground beneath our feet. The artifact, its power not just in its weight but in the way it seemed to pulse with an almost sentient hunger, resonated with the place itself. It wanted something. And I wasn't sure whether it was me it sought or if it was merely using me as a means to some far darker end.

"I don't know how much further we can go," Gabriel finally said, his voice barely above a murmur, as though the abyss itself might overhear him and strike. "But we have to. Whatever happens, we have to."

I nodded, though the chill creeping through my bones made me wonder if we were already too far gone. We had come here for a reason, for the power the artifact was rumored to hold, for the promise of something that could change everything. But with each step, it became more apparent that this place was no simple temple, no mere tomb. This was not just a test—it was a trial by fire, designed to break whoever dared step inside.

The keeper's voice echoed again, but this time, it was different. It was as though he had woven himself into the very walls, his words reverberating through the stones, curling around us like smoke.

"You think you can change the world with this?" The words came in a voice like grinding metal, scraping at my sanity. "You, who cannot even control your own fate? The artifact's power is not a gift—it is a trap. A snare meant to entangle your soul."

The weight of the keeper's words settled in the pit of my stomach like a stone. The artifact had always been powerful, but had I truly known its full scope? Or had I merely been a fool, blind to the price it exacted?

Gabriel's hand brushed mine again, steady and sure. He was my tether now, the only thing that kept me from drowning in the flood of fear and doubt that threatened to overwhelm me. "We're almost there," he said, as if he were trying to convince himself more than me. "We've made it this far. We can finish it."

The shadows seemed to thicken, coiling around us as we moved forward, the whispers now a chorus of hissing voices that slid in and out of my mind, pulling at the edges of my thoughts. But then, just when I thought we couldn't go any further, the ground before us opened up into a vast, cavernous space, and we stepped into the heart of the abyss itself.

The air here was colder than I could have imagined, so frigid it felt like it was cutting into my skin, seeping into my bones. The torchlight sputtered, struggling to cut through the darkness, and for the first time, I realized we were no longer alone. Figures moved at the periphery of the light, shadows that shifted unnaturally, too fluid to be anything human.

I wanted to speak, to ask Gabriel what we should do next, but my throat was tight, my mouth dry. Every instinct screamed at me to turn back, to flee, but there was no going back now. The keeper's voice filled the cavern, soft and sweet, like a poison poured directly into my veins.

"Do you feel it? The weight of what you carry? It is not just an object. It is a key. A key to everything and nothing. It will either break you or remake you, but it will never leave you whole."

The shadows stretched, undulating, wrapping themselves around us, and I realized with a start that the figures weren't just moving—they were watching us, circling, as if we were the prey and they the predators. My heart beat faster, my breath coming in short, sharp bursts. I could feel the pressure building, the force of the artifact's power pressing against my chest like it wanted to burst free, like it was waiting for something.

"Gabriel—" I started, but the words caught in my throat as the keeper's form appeared before us, materializing from the shadows with the same unnatural fluidity. He was no longer the whispering phantom we had seen earlier. Now, he stood before us in full, towering and vast, his eyes blazing with an infernal fire. His form was still shifting, as though reality itself refused to fully contain him, but there was no mistaking the malevolent energy that radiated from him.

"You have come this far," the keeper intoned, his voice a low, resounding echo that seemed to reverberate through the very core of the abyss. "But this is where it ends. The artifact will either bind you to its will, or it will destroy you. There is no third option."

The words hung in the air, heavy and suffocating, as though the very walls of the cavern were closing in on us. And in that moment, I realized something chilling: I wasn't here to claim power. I wasn't even here to survive. I was here to be tested. And only by surviving this trial could I hope to understand the true cost of the artifact's power.

Gabriel squeezed my hand, his voice steady as he spoke. "Then let's make sure we don't fail."

The keeper's presence hovered over us like an oppressive storm, his form a swirling mass of shadows and flickering light, constantly shifting in ways that defied logic. His eyes, however, remained fixed on us—on me—like a searing brand that refused to let go. The weight of the artifact was unbearable now, each pulse from it sending tremors through my body, as if it too was trying to break free from the chains that bound it to me.

I glanced at Gabriel, his face illuminated in the torchlight, every line etched with resolve and determination. But I saw the subtle twitch of his jaw, the slight flicker of doubt in his eyes. We were standing on the precipice of something we couldn't understand. The abyss wasn't just a place. It was a test, a riddle with no answer, and it wasn't just the artifact it sought to claim—it was us.

The keeper's voice sliced through the air, a low, resonant hum that vibrated in my chest. "You've come this far, but the path does not lead to what you think. The artifact is not what it appears. It is a mirror—a reflection of your deepest desires. What you see in it will not be what it truly is. And once it is revealed to you, there is no going back."

I stiffened, my fingers tightening around the artifact. His words rattled me, far more than I wanted to admit. What was I truly seeking? Power? Knowledge? Revenge? The line between ambition and destruction was razor-thin, and I feared, deep down, that the abyss knew this far better than I did.

"You're wrong," I said, more to myself than to him, though I knew the keeper could hear me. "This isn't about me. It's about—"

"The truth?" His laugh was a low, haunting sound, as if the keeper himself were a part of the abyss, a product of its twisted nature. "You seek the truth, but truth is not what you will find here. Truth is for the brave, for those who are willing to face themselves. But none of you—none of you—are prepared for what this truth will cost."

A shudder ran through me, one that I couldn't control, a cold fear that had nothing to do with the temperature of the air. The artifact pulsed again, its power now a jagged rhythm beneath my ribs. I felt as if it was drawing me in, tugging at something deep inside me that I couldn't quite name.

Gabriel took a step closer to me, his voice steady though there was an unmistakable tightness to it. "Whatever it is, we can handle it. We've come this far, and we're not backing down now. The artifact is ours to control, not the other way around."

The keeper's eyes flickered with something that might have been amusement—or perhaps pity. "You think you control it? You think it bends to your will? That is the greatest illusion of all. The artifact is not a tool. It is a force of nature. And you will face it—face yourself—before you ever leave this place."

I could hear my pulse in my ears, each beat louder than the last. The keeper's words clung to my mind, twisting and turning in every direction. What did he mean by that? Was the artifact a mirror of some deeper truth? If it was, what was I truly seeing when I looked at it?

"I didn't come here for illusions," I said, my voice sharper now, fueled by a surge of defiance. "I came here to face whatever this is. Whatever you are."

For a moment, there was silence. The keeper seemed to grow still, though it was hard to tell—his form was so fluid, it was like trying to pin down smoke with your hands.

Then, without warning, the shadows around us began to move. Slowly at first, a subtle shift that I could almost dismiss as the wind—until the air seemed to crack open, and from the depths of the darkness, the shapes began to emerge. Figures, long-limbed and pale, their eyes hollow, their faces featureless but for the deep, endless black that swallowed any hint of humanity. They were... watching us. Waiting.

I stumbled back, the torchlight flickering wildly as Gabriel raised his own weapon, a long, gleaming blade of strange metal. The keeper smiled—or something approximating a smile—and gestured to the figures, who stepped forward in unison, as though the command had been embedded in their very being.

"Face them," the keeper intoned, his voice rich with something that might have been dark satisfaction. "Face the truth you so desperately seek. Only then will you understand what the artifact truly holds."

I felt Gabriel's grip on my arm, his strength grounding me, but the fear in his eyes mirrored my own. "What are they?" I managed to ask, though the words felt weak and small against the vastness of the abyss.

"They are reflections," the keeper replied, his voice now lilting with mockery. "Shadows of what you fear the most. They are the first test. And once you face them, there will be no more hiding from the truth."

Before I could ask him to clarify, the figures moved. It was slow at first, deliberate, but their speed quickly escalated, until they were no longer walking—they were charging. Their eyes, black as pitch, locked on mine, and I felt a lurch in my stomach. These weren't mere apparitions. No, they were something more—a physical manifestation of something I had long feared to confront.

One of them reached out toward me, its fingers like ice, as though it could freeze time itself. I recoiled, my mind scrambling for a way to defend myself, but the artifact, that accursed object, thrummed against my chest, urging me forward.

"Gabriel!" I shouted, my voice raw with panic, but I knew even as the words left my lips that it was no use. The keeper's laughter rang out, cruel and triumphant.

And then, just as the first shadow's fingers brushed my arm, the world exploded in light.

Chapter 32: Chains of Memory

I had never been good at letting things go. Not in the traditional sense. Sure, I'd toss out old receipts, donate a worn pair of boots, or clean out a drawer that had long become a resting place for forgotten knick-knacks, but that wasn't really letting go. No, the things I struggled with were the pieces of myself, the quiet traumas and failures I couldn't shed, no matter how much time passed or how many new layers of life I built on top of them. They sat at the bottom of me, like a deep-rooted knot that, try as I might, I couldn't untangle.

That night, however, I found myself standing in the middle of a world that mirrored my worst fears, every last one of those hidden regrets swirling around me in full force. The air tasted metallic, the scent of wet stone and stale memories clinging to my skin. The walls of the abyss were alive, reflecting back all the faces I'd failed, all the times I hadn't been strong enough, all the promises broken before they even had a chance to take root.

A cacophony of voices echoed, low and haunting, creeping into my thoughts. They called me weak. They reminded me of every misstep, every moment where I wasn't the version of myself I knew I was supposed to be. I clutched my head as the weight of their words threatened to crush me.

And yet, in the midst of it all, a clear, steady voice broke through—Gabriel's.

"Lyra, it's not real. Fight it!" His words were firm, like a lifeline thrown into a stormy sea.

But what was real? Wasn't all of this a reflection of me? Didn't I carry the weight of those moments, the echoes of my past, every single day? It felt too real to be anything but the truth.

I stumbled, my legs weak beneath me, and for a moment, I thought I might collapse. Then, through the haze of my own self-doubt, I saw him—Gabriel. His silhouette cut through the darkness, like a sliver of light slicing through the shadows. He was still, unwavering, his eyes locked onto mine with a strength I envied.

"You are more than your past," he said, his voice steady and unyielding, like the calm in the eye of a storm. "You are more than this."

His words rang in my ears, cutting through the distortion of my memories. It was like a jolt of electricity, a sharp breath that split the oppressive air around me. I blinked, and the world around me shimmered, the edges of my regrets starting to blur, to fade. His voice was the thread that pulled me back from the brink, and suddenly, I remembered how to breathe.

"Lyra," he said again, his figure growing clearer as I took a tentative step forward. "This isn't you. None of this is you."

I shook my head, the remnants of those painful images lingering at the edges of my mind, trying to claw their way back in. "How can you say that? I've been... I've been a mess, Gabriel. I've hurt people, I've made mistakes that I can never fix."

Gabriel's gaze softened, but there was a strength in it that made my chest tighten. "Those things don't define you. They're just pieces of your journey. And what matters is how you choose to move forward."

For a moment, I just stood there, struggling to reconcile his words with the weight of my own history. Could I really leave all that behind? Could I somehow stop being the person who carried all that baggage, who was constantly trying to outrun the ghosts of her past?

But Gabriel's unwavering gaze held me, grounding me in a way that felt like I was finally seeing something real, something I could trust. His words weren't just a fleeting comfort—they were a challenge. A challenge to step beyond the shadows, to stop running from the parts of myself I'd buried so deeply.

As I took another step toward him, the walls around me seemed to ripple, and the voices faded into the ether. The chains of memory that had once held me so tightly began to loosen, piece by piece. I wasn't free yet, not completely, but I could feel the shift. And for the first time in a long while, I believed that maybe, just maybe, there was a way forward that didn't involve being dragged behind by everything I couldn't change.

Gabriel's hand reached out, and as I took it, I could feel the warmth of his presence, steady and real. Together, we stood at the threshold of something new—something that didn't require me to be defined by the weight of my past.

And though I knew there was still much to face, still many pieces of myself I had yet to confront, I also knew something had changed. The illusion had broken. The abyss had no more hold on me.

I had always thought of myself as someone who could compartmentalize. Life was messy, of course, but I believed I was good at sweeping the dirt under the rug and going about my business as though nothing ever lingered. But standing there, clutching Gabriel's hand as the remnants of my past swirled around me, I realized how much of it I had buried, how much I had avoided. The rug had long since burst open, and now I was forced to deal with the mess, not just the dirty laundry but the tangled threads of who I had been and who I had failed to become.

"Are you sure this is the right place to stand?" Gabriel asked, a wry smile tugging at his lips. "I mean, you look like you're about to collapse."

"I'm not collapsing," I muttered, though my legs were more than a little shaky. I glanced around. The abyss had receded somewhat, but it was still there, lurking in the corners of my vision like a darkened sky waiting to pour rain. "I'm just... thinking."

"Well, you could think while sitting," he said, his eyes twinkling with the same mischief I'd come to rely on in moments like this. "I'm not saying you have to make a break for it, but we could take a break, right?"

I shot him a look, half-amused and half-worn thin by the weight of everything that had just happened. "I'm pretty sure 'thinking' while sitting isn't going to solve whatever this mess is."

Gabriel grinned, that boyish charm never too far from his face, even in the middle of the most surreal moments. "Well, it's your mess. I'm just here for moral support."

I couldn't help it—I laughed. Not a polite, soft giggle but a real one that shook through me, down to my bones. Maybe it was the absurdity of the whole situation—the fact that I'd just faced down my deepest fears and now stood in the middle of what felt like an emotional battlefield with a guy who had become, in a very short time, the kind of person I couldn't imagine not having around. The humor, no matter how dark it was, gave me the space to breathe.

Still, despite the tension that lightened the moment, the weight of my own hesitation was hard to ignore. I looked up at Gabriel, the light from the recesses of the abyss casting long shadows across his face. "I can't help thinking... maybe I'm not the person you think I am. I mean, you saw that. That... what was that, a circus of self-doubt? My past just... laying me bare."

Gabriel cocked an eyebrow, clearly unfazed by my sudden burst of vulnerability. "You mean the collection of 'oops' and 'I should've done that better' that tried to suffocate you? It was a show, alright. But it wasn't who you are. You're still standing here. You didn't let it swallow you whole."

I scowled, not at him but at myself. "Is that supposed to make me feel better?"

"Well, it wasn't meant to be a magic fix," Gabriel said, his voice a little softer now. "I think you know you've got a lot of work to do. But, Lyra... you're still here. That counts for something."

I swallowed hard, my throat suddenly dry. I wanted to believe him. God, how I wanted to believe him. But all the self-doubt, the mess of everything I hadn't dealt with, still clung to me. I'd never been the type to believe in fairy tales or that people could change with a few kind words and a brave face. But with Gabriel? There was something about him, something so impossible and true that I couldn't quite explain. Maybe, just maybe, it wasn't too late to make a real difference.

"Alright," I said, forcing my voice to stay steady. "What now?"

Gabriel's grin returned, pulling me back into the present. "Now? Now we get out of here."

I frowned, scanning the area. "How?"

"You see those walls?" he asked, pointing to the shimmer at the edges of the abyss. "The illusions they create are as real as you let them be. If you stop believing in them, they stop having power over you."

I took a deep breath, the words catching in my throat. Stop believing. It sounded so simple, but the weight of my history, the mistakes and the people I'd failed, were never quite so easy to discard. It was like trying to let go of an old friend who had become a little too comfortable in your life—even when they were bad for you.

"I'm not sure I'm ready to stop believing," I admitted, my voice smaller than I wanted it to be. "How do you just... stop?"

Gabriel's smile softened into something more genuine, his eyes locking onto mine. "You do it one step at a time. And maybe you don't do it all at once. But you start. That's what counts. That's how you move forward."

I nodded, though I wasn't entirely sure I believed him. But maybe... maybe he was right. Maybe the fight wasn't over yet. There was still a way forward, no matter how small the steps seemed.

"Alright," I said, my voice steadier now, more certain. "One step at a time."

And as we turned away from the remnants of the abyss, I realized something I hadn't been able to admit before: it was possible to start over. Maybe I wasn't as broken as I thought. Maybe I just needed a little more time, a little more grace. And a whole lot of Gabriel by my side.

We walked through the remnants of the abyss, and for the first time in what felt like forever, the air didn't taste like regret. The space around us began to shift, each step we took pushing the darkness further away. It was strange how the simplest things—the act of putting one foot in front of the other, the rise and fall of our breath—could seem so monumental after everything that had happened. And yet, every step felt like a tiny rebellion against the weight of all the things I'd carried.

Gabriel didn't speak for a long while, but his presence was a steady anchor, the kind that grounded me, made the sharp edges of my thoughts smooth over, if only for a brief moment. I could feel him watching me, waiting for something—maybe for me to finally speak the words I'd been avoiding. The silence between us wasn't uncomfortable, though; it was like the quiet of a late-night diner, where you don't need to fill the space with chatter. It was comforting, and a little unnerving, like something big was coming, something I wasn't ready to face.

"So," Gabriel finally broke the silence, his voice light, like he was offering me a soft place to land. "How do you feel?"

I snorted, unable to help myself. "Like I just spent the last hour getting strangled by my own mind." I shook my head, the edges of the memory still sharp and jagged in my mind. "But I guess I'm... better. I think."

"Better's good," he said, his eyes twinkling as he offered me a crooked smile. "We'll take 'better.'"

I rolled my eyes but couldn't help smiling back. "I don't know about you, but I'd take a 'perfect' over 'better' any day."

"I'm afraid 'perfect' isn't on the menu," Gabriel teased, his voice turning slightly more serious. "But 'better' is a damn good start."

We continued walking, the path before us still unclear but infinitely more manageable than what we'd just left behind. But with every step, that familiar sense of unease crept back in, the uncertainty that had followed me like a shadow, clinging to me through every failure, every success. The truth was, I wasn't sure I was ready for whatever came next. Not that I had much choice in the matter.

"Do you ever wonder," I asked, breaking the silence again, "how we got here?"

Gabriel didn't respond immediately. Instead, he studied the horizon, where the first light of morning was beginning to creep across the sky, painting it in shades of deep violet and rose. "I think about that a lot," he said slowly. "About how things fall apart, and how they come back together." His eyes flicked to me, a knowing look in them. "I guess we just... show up. Even when we're broken."

I nodded, though his words hit me deeper than I cared to admit. It was strange how sometimes the simplest truths cut through you the sharpest. "Do you think we're just doomed to keep showing up until it all catches up with us?" I asked, half-joking, half-serious.

Gabriel's grin softened, and he stopped walking, turning to face me. "I don't know," he said quietly, his voice a little too serious now. "But I do know this: no one is meant to face everything alone."

I swallowed hard, the lump in my throat suddenly thick and painful. The walls I had built around myself were crumbling, brick by brick, and I wasn't sure I was ready for what would happen when they fell completely. But looking at Gabriel, I couldn't help but feel a quiet certainty that maybe—just maybe—I didn't have to do it all alone.

Before I could say anything else, something shifted. The air around us crackled, a sharp tension building in the space between us. The ground trembled slightly, and I felt the familiar sensation of a storm on the horizon, the kind that hits you without warning, leaving you with no time to brace yourself.

A dark figure appeared on the path ahead of us, silhouetted against the glowing sky. My heart leaped into my throat as it approached, its form blurry at first, like something half-formed in the shadows. But as it drew nearer, the shape began to solidify, revealing the unmistakable outline of a person.

"Who the hell is that?" I whispered, my pulse quickening.

Gabriel stiffened beside me, his eyes narrowing, and for the first time since I'd met him, I saw a flicker of something unfamiliar in his gaze—something sharp, protective, and deeply wary. He didn't answer me, but I could feel the tension building between us like a knot tightening in my chest. The figure continued to move toward us, its footsteps slow and deliberate.

And then, just as I thought it might finally speak, the ground beneath us cracked open, a loud, bone-shaking noise that sent me stumbling backward. The figure paused, just out of reach, its face still hidden in the shadows. But I knew, deep in my bones, that this was not just some random traveler on the road. No, this person was something else. And I was beginning to realize they weren't here to talk.

"Get ready," Gabriel muttered, his voice low, just above a whisper.

I didn't need him to say anything more. The air was thick with the promise of a storm. And as the figure took one final step forward, the darkness around us seemed to pulse with something dangerous, something I hadn't seen coming.

And then, before I could react, the world exploded.

Chapter 33: The Song that Binds

The chamber was bathed in a dim, golden light that flickered with every note Amara sang. The sound reverberated off the stone walls, twisting and bending in ways that no earthly melody should. It was as if the room itself was breathing, alive in a way that seemed almost wrong. I could feel the pulse of the artifact beneath my fingertips, the steady thrum of it resonating with something deep inside me, like it was calling to me—no, more than that. It was part of me now, rooted to my very soul.

Amara's voice grew louder, more urgent, each note a pleading, coaxing thing, pulling at the edges of the power I had grown so accustomed to. Her eyes never left mine, dark pools of determination, as though she could see the very thing that held me back. Her words about breaking the curse—about saving everything—hung between us, heavy and impossibly fragile. The world outside the chamber felt so distant, so irrelevant. What was waiting for me in the light beyond this stone prison? It was a vague memory, like something half-remembered from a dream I'd long forgotten.

But this... this was real.

"I don't know if I can," I whispered, the words slipping from me like the last remnants of an old life that had no place here.

Amara's gaze softened, just for a moment, before it hardened again, like the steel strings of a violin pulled taut. "You have no choice. It's always been you. The power, the curse—it's always been your burden to bear." She took a step toward me, her voice lowering, as though she were confessing something deeply personal. "It's why you're here."

My heart drummed against my ribcage, as though it, too, wanted to be part of the symphony that was building around us. The artifact hummed, vibrating in the air between us, filling every crack and corner of the room with its thick, liquid warmth. It was a strange comfort, as though the artifact itself were trying to reassure me, even as it urged me toward the precipice of something far greater than myself.

Gabriel was standing a few feet away, his eyes never leaving mine. He didn't speak, but there was an unspoken plea in his expression, something that told me he would never forgive himself if I faltered now. The weight of that unspoken truth was almost unbearable. He didn't know, not truly, how this power had become an extension of me. I couldn't just walk away from it. Not after everything.

"Amara," I said, my voice breaking through the haze of the music, "I don't know if I can give it up. It's... it's mine now." The last word was more of a confession than a statement of ownership. I had clung to the artifact like a lifeline, like a tether to something solid in a world that felt like it was made of shadows.

Her gaze flickered for the briefest moment, a crack in her composed exterior, but then she was back to her steady self, the song wrapping around us like a shroud. "It never was yours," she said, her voice low and compelling. "It's only ever been a prison, and the only way to truly free yourself is to let go."

I looked at Gabriel again, his jaw set, his eyes dark with something I couldn't quite place. Was it fear? Concern? Or was it something else entirely? My mind spun, torn between the pull of the artifact and the way it seemed to resonate with my every thought, my every heartbeat. The power coursing through me had always been a part of the curse—woven into the very fabric of who I was—but it had also become my shield, my weapon. What would I be without it?

Gabriel stepped forward now, his voice barely above a whisper. "You're not alone in this, Lyra. You don't have to carry it anymore."

The words were kind, and yet they made something in me crack open, something raw and vulnerable that I didn't want to face. He was right, wasn't he? I didn't have to carry it. I didn't have to bear the weight of this power any longer. But the thought of letting go felt like surrender, like I was giving up a part of myself that had come to define who I was.

Amara continued to sing, her voice undeterred by my hesitation, and the artifact thrummed again, sending a ripple of heat through my body. My breath caught in my throat as the room seemed to shrink, pressing in around me. The walls were closing in, the air thick with something almost unbearable.

And then I understood.

It wasn't just about the power. It was about what I had become. What I had built from this power. Who I had been before I was bound to it was a fading memory, a story that seemed irrelevant now. I had lived in the shadow of this curse for so long, I had forgotten what it meant to be free. To be myself.

And the answer, the only answer that mattered, was clear.

I stepped forward, my hand trembling slightly as I reached for the artifact, still pulsing with that strange, magnetic warmth. The music swelled, almost as if it were urging me forward, as though it knew the weight of my decision.

"I'm ready," I said, my voice quiet but firm.

The chamber fell silent. Even Amara's song seemed to pause, hanging in the air like an unfinished note.

The silence that followed my words was thick, pregnant with meaning, stretching between us like a taut wire. It was as if the chamber itself was holding its breath, waiting to see if I would do what had been asked of me, what was expected of me. My fingers hovered above the artifact, its surface cool and strangely soothing, as though it were trying to calm the storm of doubt that had begun to churn in my chest.

I had lived in the shadows of this power for so long. It had been my constant companion, my crutch, and my curse. It had whispered to me in the dark, in the quiet moments between breaths, offering me strength, a sense of purpose. And now, here I stood, on the edge of letting go. The thought sent a shiver through me, a sense of loss before I had even made the choice.

Gabriel's voice broke the silence, his words soft but filled with an unwavering belief that I wasn't sure I deserved. "Lyra, I've seen you face impossible odds before. This isn't different. You're stronger than you think."

Stronger than I think. I had heard those words before, too many times, spoken by others who didn't understand the weight I carried. They meant well, but what did strength mean in a world that had twisted me into something unrecognizable? What did it mean to be strong when your very soul was at war with itself?

I looked at Gabriel, his presence a steady anchor in the storm of my thoughts. His expression was open, trusting, as though he believed in me more than I believed in myself. The flicker of something more than friendship—something I'd tried to ignore—simmered just beneath the surface of his gaze. A tenderness that felt foreign, but not unwelcome. But now wasn't the time for that.

I turned back to the artifact, its pulsing rhythm now matching my heartbeat, a lullaby that tried to pull me back into its embrace. It was seductive, this power, this feeling of control. I had spent so long on the edge of understanding it, of mastering it, and now the idea of walking away from it felt like a betrayal of everything I had ever known.

Amara's song swelled again, the notes cascading like drops of rain, filling the room with a sense of urgency. "You must make your choice," she called, her voice still as melodic as ever, but with an edge that was unmistakable. "There is no middle ground here, Lyra. Either you give the artifact willingly, or it consumes you."

Her words struck deep, deeper than any blade ever could. The power I had so carefully cultivated, the power that had kept me alive through the darkest of days—would it really consume me if I kept it? Could I risk the unknown, the potential chaos of releasing it?

The warmth of the artifact seeped into my skin, a quiet comfort that whispered promises of untold strength, of mastery over everything around me. I could feel it—this deep, undeniable connection—pulling at my very core. It was part of me. How could I just... let it go?

"I've come too far," I murmured, more to myself than anyone else, my words feeling like a desperate plea for understanding. "I've sacrificed too much to let go now."

Gabriel took a step forward, his presence a quiet force at my side. His voice was steady, unwavering. "You haven't sacrificed yourself. Not yet. But you will if you keep holding on to this. You're not this artifact, Lyra. You're not this power. You're more than that."

His words stung, not because they were wrong, but because they held the bitter truth. I wasn't the power. I had become so wrapped up in it, in what it had made me, that I had forgotten who I was beneath it all. I wasn't just the girl who had stumbled into this cursed life. I wasn't just a vessel for the artifact's might. I was something else. Something real.

Amara's song faded, her eyes locking onto mine once again. "It's time, Lyra. You know what you have to do."

The pull of the artifact was stronger now, almost overwhelming, but beneath it, something else—something raw and real—began to rise. I could feel it in my chest, in the quiet part of me that I had ignored for too long. I had been so consumed by the need to control, to wield the power that had been thrust upon me, that I had lost sight of who I really was.

I took a deep breath, steadying myself, and for the first time, I truly felt the weight of the decision I was about to make. The artifact was not just a tool; it was a reflection of everything I had been and everything I could become. But that didn't mean I had to carry it anymore.

I lowered my hand, and as I did, the artifact seemed to pulse one final time, as if it knew it was losing its grip on me. The warmth that had filled my body evaporated, leaving behind a coldness that had nothing to do with the temperature of the room. It was a quiet emptiness, a space where the artifact had once resided, but also a space where something new could begin to grow.

"Good," Amara said softly, her voice now full of a quiet satisfaction. "You've chosen the path of freedom."

But as the weight lifted, I couldn't help but feel a tug of something else—something I hadn't expected. A sharp pang of loss, of regret. Was I making the right choice? Would I be able to live without it? Without the power that had become my shield and my sword?

Gabriel's hand found mine, warm and steady, and for the first time, I didn't feel alone in the decision I had made. He had been right. I wasn't this power. And I wasn't going to let it define me anymore.

The silence in the room felt as dense as the heavy stone walls that surrounded us. The artifact, still cradled in my trembling hand, hummed as though it was alive, a heartbeat I could feel through my skin, a pulse that was far too familiar. The very air around us seemed charged with a strange electricity, like the calm before a storm, and I realized with a sudden shock that I was the storm.

I stared down at the artifact, its smooth surface reflecting the dim light of the chamber, and wondered just how much of me had been consumed by it. It had been with me for so long, a constant presence at my side, that I had come to think of it as part of my own self. Its power had been my crutch, my shield, and as much as I hated to admit it, it had shaped me. Would I even know who I was without it?

"Amara," I said, the words coming out thick with emotion, "What happens if I don't give it up? If I keep it?"

Her eyes flickered with something like pity, but there was no judgment in her gaze—only a quiet, undeniable truth. "You'll never be free. It will bind you forever. And when it's done, when you've used every last ounce of yourself, it will take everything. It always does."

Her words were like daggers, sharp and cutting deep. I could feel the weight of them in the pit of my stomach, a hollow ache that told me she was right. It would consume me. But could I let it go? Could I sever that bond, that thread that had held me together through every trial, every darkness?

Gabriel was still standing a few steps away, his eyes never leaving me. There was a softness to his gaze now, a vulnerability that made my chest tighten. He had always been the one who believed in me, even when I couldn't believe in myself. And yet, I wasn't sure if I was ready to give up the only thing that had ever made me feel in control, the only thing that had ever made me feel like I mattered.

The music in the background, Amara's song, began to swell again, but this time it was different. The notes had taken on a sharper edge, filled with urgency. It was as if the very room was imploring me, begging me to make a decision.

"You don't need this anymore, Lyra," Gabriel's voice was quiet, almost tentative. "You're not that person anymore. You've changed."

I felt a sharp pang at his words. Changed. The thought was terrifying and exhilarating all at once. I had been hiding behind this power for so long, convincing myself that it was a part of who I was, a part of what made me whole. But Gabriel was right. I had changed. The journey, the trials, the pain—it had all carved something new inside me. Something strong. Something free.

And yet, despite everything, the idea of letting go felt like losing myself, losing everything I had fought for. "I don't know if I can," I whispered, my voice betraying the uncertainty that twisted deep inside me.

"You can," Gabriel said, his voice sure now, a fire in the steadiness of his words. "You've always had the strength to do it. This—this is the last thing holding you back. Once it's gone, you'll be free. You'll be whole."

Amara's voice pierced the silence again, this time softer, as if she were speaking directly to my soul. "The choice is yours, Lyra. But remember, the curse has always been about control. And as long as you hold onto this artifact, you will never have the power to truly control your own fate."

The words settled into me like the weight of the world. Control. That was what it had always been about, wasn't it? The need to grasp at something, anything, to keep myself from slipping into the abyss. But now, standing on the precipice, I realized that my grasp on the artifact wasn't control—it was fear.

"I'm not afraid anymore," I said, my voice stronger this time, though the tremor in my hand remained. With a deep breath, I raised the artifact above my head, the power thrumming beneath my fingertips, pulsing in time with my heartbeat. "I'm ready to let go."

The air around us seemed to hum with energy, a surge of raw power building like a tidal wave, ready to break free. Amara's eyes locked onto mine, her gaze steady as she held her breath, waiting for the final act. The weight in my chest grew heavier with each passing second, as if the entire world was waiting for me to make the impossible choice.

But just as I was about to release the artifact, the ground beneath us trembled. A low rumble reverberated through the chamber, making the walls shake with a force that sent dust and debris cascading from the ceiling. My heart lurched in my chest as the tremors grew stronger, faster, until the very foundation of the room seemed to crack beneath the force.

"Lyra, get back!" Gabriel shouted, his voice rising above the chaos.

But I couldn't move. I was frozen, my body unwilling to step away from the power that had been my anchor for so long, even as the ground beneath me split open, revealing a gaping chasm where the floor had once been solid. The artifact pulsed once more, a blinding light shooting from its core, illuminating the room in a flash of white-hot energy.

And then, with a deafening crack, the ceiling above us began to cave in. The world seemed to collapse in on itself, the air thick with dust and debris, and I felt a sharp pain sear through my chest.

Before I could even process what was happening, the light from the artifact flared so brightly that everything went black.

Chapter 34: Betrayal in the Dark

The weight of the artifact was nothing compared to the pressure bearing down on my chest as I held it, heart hammering in my ears. The cold stone beneath my feet seemed to pulse with a rhythm of its own, as if the very bones of the altar were alive, waiting for the spark that would ignite its ancient power. I could almost taste the magic in the air, thick and acrid, swirling around me like smoke. My fingers trembled as I fought to keep my grip steady, but every part of me screamed to drop it, run, do anything to escape the impending storm.

But then the figure materialized from the shadows, his presence like a storm cloud blotting out the flickering candlelight. His eyes gleamed—a pale, almost ethereal blue, too cold, too empty, like the depth of an uncharted sea. His lips curled into a slow, deliberate smile, a smile that made my skin crawl, as though he already knew everything about me, everything I feared.

"You're brave to hold it," he said, his voice as smooth and dark as silk, each word carrying a weight of malice that settled in my bones. "But foolish to think you can control it."

I wanted to tell him to go to hell, but my throat had gone dry, the words strangled by the very air itself. Instead, I turned, finding Gabriel at my side, his sword drawn in an instant, its gleam like a sliver of light in the consuming darkness.

"Stay behind me," he ordered, his voice rough but filled with an unshakable resolve.

But I couldn't move. I couldn't look away from the stranger who had appeared out of nowhere, who knew too much and yet remained a mystery in every sense. His shadow stretched long and sinister, creeping across the floor like some living thing, a harbinger of whatever evil he intended to unleash. The air grew colder still, a biting chill that wrapped itself around me, seeping through the layers of my clothes, making every muscle in my body tense.

Gabriel lunged forward, his sword a blur as it collided with the stranger's, the sound of steel against steel ringing through the room. But the stranger, unfazed, barely moved, as though the force of the blow was nothing more than a passing breeze. I saw the sharpness of his grin widen, and in that moment, I realized that Gabriel, for all his skill, was outmatched.

"Step aside, Gabriel," the stranger purred. "This doesn't concern you."

A growl rumbled deep in Gabriel's chest, but he didn't back down, keeping the stranger's blade at bay with every strike, his body a wall between me and the danger that loomed ever closer. I swallowed hard, desperate to make sense of it all. Amara had warned us, had known something was coming—but even her foresight had seemed vague, wrapped in riddles that only made sense in moments like this, when everything was falling apart.

"Lyra!" Amara's voice cracked through the chaos, her song weaving through the air like threads of light and shadow. She was standing near the far end of the room, her eyes wide with fear and urgency. "You must choose! Now!"

Choose? Choose what? My heart stuttered in my chest, the weight of the artifact suddenly too much, pulling me down, making my knees tremble. The power of it was seeping into my bones, whispering promises of strength, of control. The shadows shifted, as though they had heard Amara's plea, responding to the call of something far darker.

The stranger laughed, low and guttural, as if he were savoring the fear that bloomed in the room. "You think you can stop me, little girl? This isn't about choices. It's about destiny." He took a step forward, and the shadows seemed to follow him, twisting around his limbs like a cloak of darkness. "This world has long forgotten what it owes me. But you, Lyra," he said, his eyes narrowing, "you will remember."

I felt the artifact pulse in my hands, the power of it thrumming against my chest, urging me to listen. The air thickened with the promise of something terrible, something ancient and long-forgotten. Amara's desperate plea still echoed in my mind, but I couldn't make sense of it. What was I supposed to choose? How could I stop this madness?

Gabriel's blade rang out again, his strike failing to land as the stranger's own weapon slashed forward with terrifying speed. The impact sent Gabriel stumbling back, his stance faltering as he tried to regain control. I could see the strain in his muscles, the effort it took to keep up, and my heart clenched with the realization that we were losing. Losing everything.

And then, without thinking, I stepped forward.

The decision came unbidden, as though the artifact had made it for me. The choice was simple, and yet it terrified me. I raised the artifact high, the power in it rushing to meet the air, filling the room with a brightness that made everything else fade into shadow. The stranger froze, his eyes locking onto mine, a flicker of recognition in his gaze.

"You think you can wield it?" he sneered, but there was an edge of doubt in his voice, a crack in the façade of confidence he wore so well.

"I don't need to wield it," I replied, my voice trembling but firm. "I just need to survive it."

And in that moment, I understood what Amara had meant. The choice wasn't about power, or control, or domination. It was about surviving the darkness. Surviving him.

The artifact's pulse quickened, vibrating so violently in my hands that it almost felt like it had its own heartbeat, as though it were alive—alive and hungry. I could feel it calling to me, an insistent whisper in the back of my mind, one that seemed to grow louder with every passing second. But that voice, too, was mingled with another—a darker one, something that didn't come from the artifact itself but from the very air around us. It was thick, poisonous, wrapping itself around my chest and making it harder to breathe. The shadows were alive now, twisting, crawling like serpents across the stone floor, responding to some unseen master, and I knew that the stranger had unlocked something far more ancient than any of us had anticipated.

"Lyra, please!" Amara cried again, her voice high-pitched with panic. She was moving toward us, but each step she took seemed to be swallowed by the shadows, as though the ground itself didn't want her to reach us. She was singing now, her voice strained, words that I could barely understand, but they carried the weight of everything we had learned in the past months—the fragile balance, the power we had underestimated, the cost of this moment. "Choose, now, before it's too late!"

I glanced at Gabriel, his eyes flashing with that same fierce determination that had drawn me to him from the very beginning. But even he seemed unsure. The man before us—he wasn't just a thief, a mere mortal with ambitions that could be thwarted. No, he was something worse, something that had set its sights on the very fabric of our world. The artifact wasn't just a relic. It was the key to an ancient power, and he, with his cold eyes and eerie confidence, was here to unlock it.

"Stay back, Lyra," Gabriel warned, his voice low and full of command. But he didn't mean it. Not really. Not when I could see the fear creeping into the edges of his gaze. He knew, as I did, that this wasn't something we could fight off. Not without the artifact. And yet, it felt wrong to hold it, as though the moment I let it touch the altar—my hands clenched tighter—it would bind me to something I couldn't undo.

But the stranger—his presence was overpowering, an oppressive weight that squeezed at the edges of the room. "You really think you can stop me, girl?" he said, his smile stretching wider, more dangerous. "I've waited centuries for this, for someone like you. You think you're the hero of this little story? You're not. You're just a vessel, a pawn. And now... now, it's my turn."

The sound of his voice reverberated in my bones, a deep, hollow echo that seemed to shake the very foundation beneath us. The room felt smaller somehow, like the walls were closing in, pressing against me. The artifact hummed louder, like a frantic drumbeat in my chest, and I could feel its hunger. Whatever I was meant to do with it, the choice wasn't clear, not in the face of this man's twisted certainty.

I took a step forward, and Gabriel moved to stop me. But I raised my hand to him, silencing the protest that was about to spill from his lips. "Don't," I whispered. The words were barely audible, but I knew he heard me. I didn't need to explain. We both understood what was at stake. I wasn't just holding the artifact anymore. It had become part of me, my only defense against the growing darkness that surrounded us. If I was going to survive this, if any of us were, I had to face it—whatever it was.

The stranger laughed, a sound so cruel that it sliced through the air. "Ah, how noble. How typical. The hero who thinks she can save the world." He lifted his hand, and the shadows responded, twisting into shapes that seemed to pulse with a life of their own. "But you don't know what you're dealing with. You don't even know who I am."

The air crackled, the tension so thick now that it felt like the room was holding its breath. I swallowed hard, trying to steady myself, but the pressure was unbearable. He wasn't just a man. Not in any real sense. He was a force, an embodiment of something ancient and corrupt. And in that moment, I realized that this wasn't just about power. This was about survival—not just mine, but everyone's. Because if the stranger took control of the artifact, there would be nothing left but ruin.

"You're wrong," I said, my voice stronger than I felt. "You're not in control. Not yet."

And then, as though on cue, the shadows shifted again, moving not toward the stranger, but toward me. I flinched, my heart hammering in my chest, and for a brief, terrifying moment, I thought they might consume me whole. But they didn't. The artifact pulsed once more, brighter, warmer, and the shadows recoiled, as though repelled by some invisible force. The room stilled for a fraction of a second, and in that quiet, I felt the power of the artifact shift. It was mine to command, for now. But I knew that could change.

"You think you're the one who controls this?" the stranger sneered, his eyes narrowing as he watched the light. "I've waited too long to be stopped by someone like you."

"Then wait longer," I shot back, defiance cutting through the fear that still clawed at me. The power thrummed, and for the briefest of moments, I felt it settle within me, a rush of warmth, a comfort that filled every part of me. I wasn't the hero. I wasn't the villain. I was simply a woman, standing between him and the destruction he sought to bring.

Gabriel's voice cut through the tension, low and dangerous. "Lyra, get ready. This isn't over yet." He stepped in front of me, blade raised. And I knew he would fight to the end, not for the artifact, but for me. I wasn't the only one whose survival depended on this.

And so, standing in that ancient chamber, with darkness pressing on all sides, we prepared for the battle that would determine not just our fate, but the fate of everything we had fought for.

I could feel the artifact thrum against my chest, a low hum that seemed to match the rhythm of my pulse, and for the briefest of moments, I thought I might lose myself to it. The shadows stretched toward me, slithering across the stone like hungry snakes, eager to devour everything in their path. My breath caught as the man's cold eyes locked onto mine, as if daring me to make the wrong move. Gabriel was there, his sword gleaming in the dim light, a stark contrast to the stranger's deadly stillness. The tension in the room crackled, a silent countdown hanging over us like a sword poised to fall.

"Lyra," Gabriel's voice was steady, but I could hear the tension threading through it. "Step back. I'll handle him."

But I didn't step back. I couldn't. There was something in the air—something electric, something I couldn't explain—that tied me to the artifact. I knew, deep down, that the decision had already been made for me. It wasn't a matter of whether I wanted the power or not—it was whether I could control it long enough to stop him from destroying everything.

"I'm not going anywhere," I said, my voice trembling but firm. I wasn't sure if I was trying to convince him or myself. The shadows were closing in now, swirling around the stranger, responding to his every movement like a storm ready to break. They weren't just shadows anymore—they were alive. They whispered in a language I didn't understand, words that seemed to pull at the very fabric of the world.

The stranger stepped forward, the shadows at his heels, a slow, deliberate movement that spoke of centuries of practice, of a power he had honed and perfected. "You think you have the strength to wield it?" he asked, his voice low and mocking. "You don't. You're nothing but a girl holding a relic she doesn't understand."

His words were like needles in my skin, each one digging deeper than the last. But I wasn't about to let him see how much they stung. "And you're nothing but a thief trying to steal what doesn't belong to you."

Gabriel lunged, his sword aimed for the stranger's throat, but the man's movements were faster than I could follow. In one smooth motion, he parried Gabriel's strike, knocking him back with a force that left Gabriel stumbling, barely regaining his balance. I didn't have time to react to Gabriel's fall. The shadows were already reaching for me, curling around my ankles like icy fingers, and the air grew heavier with each passing second.

"Lyra!" Amara's voice sliced through the tension, a desperate, urgent cry. "You must choose now!"

Choose what? What did that even mean? I didn't have the luxury of thinking about it. The stranger's smirk deepened, and he reached out with one hand, his fingers brushing the air as if he were commanding it. The shadows coiled tighter, and for a moment, I couldn't breathe. They were everywhere, smothering me, squeezing the air from my lungs. And yet, the artifact in my hands pulsed in a way that made my skin tingle with heat, urging me to do something—anything—to fight back.

Before I could think, I did what felt instinctive. I held the artifact out in front of me, fingers tight around it, and felt its power surge through me. The shadows screamed, recoiling as though burned, and I felt a sudden wave of heat spread through my chest, a warmth that made my blood race and my heart pound in my ears. For the briefest of moments, I thought I might lose control, that the power of the artifact would consume me whole. But I gritted my teeth and held firm, my mind focused on one thing only: survival.

The stranger's eyes flickered with something like surprise, and then his lips curled into a snarl. "You really think that will stop me? You're a fool."

"Maybe," I said, my voice low and steady, surprising even myself. "But I'm not the one who's going to lose."

With a guttural roar, the stranger swung his sword at me, the blade slicing through the air with deadly precision. I barely had time to react. I twisted out of the way, the shadows at my feet swirling and grabbing at me like they were alive, but the artifact's power surged once again, a wave of force that threw the shadows back and sent the stranger stumbling.

I didn't hesitate. Not for a second. I knew that if I faltered, even for a moment, it would be over. This wasn't a game anymore. This wasn't some puzzle that could be solved with a few well-placed words or clever tricks. This was life or death.

The artifact pulsed again, its light blinding in the dimness, and I could feel it draw the shadows to me, feeding off the energy in the room like a predator closing in on its prey. I could feel the stranger's power too, a dark, terrible presence that pressed against me like a physical weight. It was suffocating, almost crushing, and I had to force myself to breathe. The artifact was my only lifeline, the only thing keeping me from falling into the abyss that beckoned at the edge of my vision.

But then, just as I thought I had a moment to breathe, I heard a sound—a soft, shuffling noise behind me. And then, a voice. A voice I hadn't expected. A voice that made my blood run cold.

"Lyra."

I spun around, eyes wide with shock, and there, standing in the doorway, was someone I thought I'd never see again. Someone I thought was lost to me forever. Someone who had betrayed me once, and who now... now had come back to finish what they started.

Chapter 35: The Sacrifice

I tried to inhale, but my lungs betrayed me, the air thick and strange, as if the very atmosphere had changed. The room around us was vast, stretching beyond my sight, yet the ground felt like it had been ripped away from beneath me. I could still hear the echo of Gabriel's voice, but it wasn't enough to anchor me.

"Stay with me." His words threaded through the chaos, catching me like a lifeline. I squeezed his hand, a sharp pulse of reality coursing through my fingertips. It was strange, how something so simple could feel so essential, as if our shared breath might be the only thing that could hold back whatever storm was swirling beneath our feet.

The light began to wane, retracting like the tail of a comet, leaving behind a room that was still and quiet—too quiet. The altar where I had placed the artifact was empty now, the stone smooth and unmarked. Whatever had been inside it, whatever that power had been, was gone. But my wrist burned, that familiar, searing sensation. The mark was deeper now, more intricate, as if it had fused with my skin, becoming part of me. I could feel it pulse, a rhythm that matched the erratic beat of my heart.

"What did we do?" I whispered, though I already knew the answer. The choice I had made wasn't just mine—it had been ours, Gabriel and me. His fingers tightened around mine, but he didn't say anything. We didn't need to speak. The silence was heavier than any words could be.

His voice, low and gravelly, broke the stillness. "We did what we had to. We didn't have a choice." He leaned in closer, his breath warm against my ear. "Did you feel it? The power, the shift? This is only the beginning."

I didn't want to hear it, didn't want to admit it. But I could feel it too—the weight of what we had unleashed, the consequences of our actions swirling like a storm just out of sight. The tension between us thickened, the invisible threads of our bond stretching taut, ready to snap. There was no going back now. Not after everything we had sacrificed to get here.

I looked up at him, and for the first time, I saw it—the fear that had been buried deep inside him, the uncertainty that no amount of bravado could mask. It was there, hidden beneath his usual confidence, and it mirrored my own. We had done the unthinkable. But it was done. There was no undoing it now.

His jaw clenched, and he pulled away just enough to meet my gaze. "I knew what I was walking into when I followed you here," he said, his words slow, deliberate. "I've known all along. But I didn't think it would be this... much."

I didn't know what to say. What could I say? There were no comforting words, no reassurances. We were standing on the edge of something vast and unknowable, and I had no idea what awaited us in the depths below. It was as though we had shattered the world and, in doing so, broken ourselves.

Gabriel took a step back, his gaze flickering across the chamber. There was no denying the enormity of the place now. The air was still heavy with power, thick with the residue of the artifact's magic. It clung to the stone walls, the ceiling, the floor—permeating every inch of this ancient space. I felt it, tasted it, as though it had become part of the very air I breathed. I could feel it in my veins, like fire running through my blood.

"You're not the same," he said, his voice strained. I wasn't sure if he meant me, or both of us. But I knew what he meant. I could feel the change, an unsettling new awareness that pressed against my skin, like someone whispering in my ear when no one was there.

"I know," I said, my voice tight. "Neither are you."

Gabriel shook his head, his eyes clouding with something I couldn't quite decipher. "We've crossed a line," he murmured, more to himself than to me. "There's no going back from this. We've released something... something ancient. And it's not done with us."

I felt a shiver run through me, though I didn't want to admit it. Whatever had been bound in that artifact, whatever had been waiting for centuries to be set free, was no longer contained. We had released it into the world—and it was hungry.

Suddenly, the walls around us groaned, a deep, vibrating sound that echoed through the chamber. The stone trembled, shifting beneath our feet. The mark on my wrist burned brighter, as though it were pulling me toward something, urging me to understand, to unlock whatever it was that had been waiting in the dark for so long.

"It's coming," Gabriel said, his voice hoarse, and I could hear the steel in it now, the resolve that had always been there beneath his uncertainty. He was ready for what was next, even if he wasn't sure what that would look like. "Are you ready?"

Ready. I wasn't sure if anyone could be ready for what we had unleashed. But I didn't have a choice. I had already made my decision, already sealed my fate when I placed that artifact on the altar. It wasn't just a sacrifice anymore—it was a commitment, a bond with the unknown.

I glanced at Gabriel one last time, our eyes locking in silent agreement. "Let's finish this," I said, though I wasn't sure who I was trying to convince—him, or myself.

And with that, we stepped forward into the shadows, knowing that whatever was about to unfold would demand everything from us.

The silence that followed was deafening. It settled over us like a blanket, thick and oppressive, choking out any remnants of the chaos that had just torn through the room. The flickering afterimage of the light was still embedded in my mind, each lingering spark a cruel reminder of what we had done, what we had unleashed.

I could feel Gabriel beside me, his breath sharp and uneven, the warmth of his hand a constant presence in the cold emptiness. His grip tightened, a silent plea for reassurance, or maybe for something else altogether. I wasn't sure anymore.

"Are you... are you okay?" I asked, though the question felt hollow, the words slipping from my lips like water through a sieve.

Gabriel didn't answer right away. His chest rose and fell in a steady rhythm, as though he was trying to steady himself as much as me. The burn on my wrist had dulled to a steady throb, a reminder that the power we had touched was no longer contained in that artifact. It was in us now—seeping under my skin, twisting its way into my bones, lacing itself into the very fabric of my being.

"Does it feel different to you?" His voice broke the silence, raw and strained, as he turned toward me, his eyes narrowing slightly. "The mark. It's like it's... alive."

I nodded slowly, my throat tight. "I know. It's... it's like it's part of me now."

He glanced down at my wrist, the darkened mark still pulsing with a strange, hypnotic rhythm. It was like the heartbeat of something older than time itself, beating in tandem with my own. There was no escaping it now, not really. And even though I knew that, the weight of the decision—the gravity of what we had just done—pressed harder against my chest with every passing second.

We stood there in the silence, the room around us still and motionless, as though the very air had been sucked from it, leaving only the echo of our breaths. There was something eerie about it, something that made the hairs on the back of my neck stand up. I could feel eyes on me, though no one was there. Could feel the pull of something watching, waiting for us to make the next move. And it wasn't the mark on my wrist that made me feel that way.

"It's not just us, is it?" I asked, my voice shaking slightly. "There's something else in here with us."

Gabriel's jaw tightened, and he turned his head slowly, as though listening for something. When he spoke, it was so quiet, it was almost a whisper. "I think it's just the beginning."

I didn't need him to explain further. The dread that had crept into my bones from the moment I placed the artifact on the altar had only grown stronger, the sensation of being watched by something ancient and powerful that had just been set free. Whatever had been bound inside that artifact wasn't gone. It was still here, in the air, in the walls, in us.

"Let's move," Gabriel said, his voice suddenly low and controlled, a stark contrast to the tension in the air. He was already pulling me toward the exit, his hand still firm around mine. "The longer we stay here, the more dangerous it gets."

I followed him without hesitation, though every instinct in me screamed to stay put, to not leave the safety of the chamber. But we couldn't stay here. Not anymore. The artifact was gone, its power now something that we couldn't ignore or outrun. We had already made the choice to step into the unknown; the only thing left was to keep moving forward.

The corridor outside the chamber was long, the stone walls slick with moisture, the air thick with the scent of earth and decay. It felt like walking through the belly of a forgotten beast. As we made our way through the dark, the silence enveloping us again, the weight of what we had just done began to settle in my stomach, like a stone.

"Do you think it's over?" I asked, the question barely above a whisper, my voice a thread in the thick, oppressive silence.

Gabriel didn't answer right away, his gaze fixed ahead, his jaw set in that familiar line of determination. "I don't know. But we're not getting out of this that easily. Whatever we unleashed, it's going to follow us. We can't run from it."

I wanted to tell him that he was wrong, that we could fix this, that somehow we could find a way to reverse whatever it was we had done. But I didn't. Because deep down, I knew he was right. There was no unmaking this. We had made a choice, and now we would have to live with it. Whatever came next, we would face it together.

We reached the end of the corridor, and the sudden change in the air almost knocked the breath from my lungs. The temperature had dropped, the air now frigid, biting at my skin. Gabriel's fingers dug into mine, a silent warning that whatever was waiting for us ahead, we were not prepared for it.

"Stay close," he murmured, his eyes scanning the shadows that stretched out before us. "This isn't over. Not by a long shot."

I swallowed hard, a tight knot forming in my stomach. But I didn't question him. Not now. Not after everything. The bond between us—whatever had been forged in that moment on the altar—was stronger than anything I had ever felt before. If this was a battle we had to face, then we would face it together.

We stepped into the next room, and the doors slammed shut behind us, sealing us in with whatever was lurking in the dark.

The heavy thud of the door behind us sent a tremor through my spine. It had barely closed before the darkness in the room thickened, like something alive, pressing in on all sides. The sudden absence of light left us struggling to adjust. I could barely see Gabriel's silhouette, just the outline of his broad shoulders and the sharp, almost predatory gleam of his eyes in the half-darkness. He was tense, every muscle taut, as though expecting something—anything—to leap from the shadows.

My heart thudded in my chest, but it wasn't fear that made it race. It was something else—something deeper, like the pull of an undertow, hidden beneath the calm surface of a pond. The mark on my wrist was still warm, like a spark lodged just beneath my skin, and I felt its presence in the way it hummed quietly, almost imperceptibly. It wasn't simply a symbol anymore. It had become part of me, woven into the fabric of who I was, inseparable.

Gabriel stepped forward, his hand brushing mine before pulling away again. I wanted to reach for him, to hold on, but something in the air stopped me—some primal instinct that told me to be still. We were no longer just in the room. We were part of it now, part of something that had been waiting long before either of us had stepped foot in this forsaken place.

"This doesn't feel right," I whispered, more to myself than to him.

"It wasn't supposed to," Gabriel murmured, his voice low and ragged. "We never should've come here."

I felt a shiver run down my spine, as though the walls themselves had heard him and decided to prove him right. A sound—a soft, wet scraping noise—echoed from the far corner of the room. It was almost imperceptible, but it was there, unmistakable in the otherwise suffocating silence.

"Do you hear that?" I asked, not daring to move closer to the source of the sound.

He nodded, his eyes narrowing. "We're not alone."

I could feel the words vibrating in the air around me, thick and oppressive, as though the space between us had collapsed, crushing me with its weight. A new sound joined the first—this one a rhythmic tapping, like footsteps, but they weren't ours. They were coming toward us, methodical, almost deliberate.

My breath caught in my throat. I wanted to run. I wanted to drag Gabriel out of here, back to the sunlight, back to something—anything—familiar. But the mark on my wrist burned again, a sharp, biting pain that made my knees nearly buckle. I was no longer sure where the fear was coming from. Was it the power inside me, making its presence known? Or was it something else entirely—something far older, far darker than we had anticipated?

"Stay close," Gabriel said, his voice hardening as he took a cautious step forward. "We need to find a way out of here before it finds us first."

Before I could respond, a high-pitched, shrill sound cut through the room, sharp as a knife. It made my teeth ache, reverberating in my skull. I closed my eyes, willing the sound to stop, but it only grew louder, a crescendo of terror that made my skin crawl. When I opened them again, the shadows in the room seemed to pulse, like they were breathing, shifting in unnatural ways. The walls felt closer, as if the room itself was closing in on us.

"What the hell is that?" I asked, my voice a whisper of panic.

"It's not the artifact, not directly," Gabriel said, his hand reaching for his belt, pulling free a small, jagged knife. "But we disturbed something. Something that was never meant to be disturbed. And now it's awake."

The shadows surged, coiling around us like dark tendrils, creeping closer, faster. I could feel their weight pressing against me, their presence stifling the air, stealing my breath. And then, in the midst of that oppressive darkness, a figure emerged.

It wasn't human. At least, not in the way I understood humans. The thing that moved toward us was tall, impossibly so, its limbs unnaturally long and twisted. Its face—if you could call it a face—was a blur, as if it was made from the very shadows that surrounded it. It was a distortion, a mockery of something human, a figure that didn't belong in this world.

"What the hell is that?" I gasped, my words strangled.

Gabriel's grip tightened on the knife, his body tense. "Not what. Who."

The creature—or whatever it was—took another step, and the ground beneath our feet groaned in protest. My knees felt weak, the weight of the mark on my wrist now a constant, unyielding pulse. It was as if the mark was calling to the thing, or perhaps it was calling to me.

"Who are you?" Gabriel demanded, his voice steady but strained.

The thing stopped, its long limbs folding unnaturally as it crouched down, its face still obscured. For a moment, nothing happened. Then, in a voice that scraped the air like nails on glass, it spoke.

"You've woken me," it hissed, its voice low, almost like a whisper, but it vibrated through the air, through my bones. "And now... you will pay."

And just like that, the room exploded into chaos.

The air snapped with a crackling energy, the room trembling violently, as though the very walls were about to collapse. The shadows surged toward us, thick and suffocating. I could feel Gabriel's hand on mine, tugging me back, urging me to move, but the pull of the mark, the weight of the choice I had made, held me in place. Whatever was happening now, it was connected to the power we had unleashed.

"Run!" Gabriel shouted, his voice strained. "Now!"

But I couldn't. The mark on my wrist burned with an intensity that stole my breath. And just as the figure lunged toward us, the ground beneath my feet cracked open.

Chapter 36: A Kingdom Restored

The morning sun cast a sharp light over the city, blinding in its clarity, as if the sky itself had been scrubbed clean. The streets, once buried under endless dunes, now glittered with stone and sunlight, and the wind that had whipped through the desert with a cruelty that could strip the flesh from bone had turned soft, like the breath of a lover. I felt it on my face, the warm, gentle caress of air that smelled faintly of earth and green things, things I hadn't remembered in years—things that, until moments ago, I had believed we had lost to the annals of myth.

Amara stood a few feet away, her dark hair flowing like silk, though there was nothing soft about the set of her shoulders. Even as the city around us slowly took shape, shaking off the centuries of neglect and reclaiming its ancient elegance, she was still tethered to the burden of what we had done. Her eyes were as hard as stone, reflecting the gleam of gold that now danced on the horizon. She had spoken the words that had broken the curse, but I knew her well enough to understand that the relief she should have felt had been drowned out by the weight of the cost.

I was still trying to figure out what that cost was.

"We're here, Amara," I said, my voice unrecognizable to my own ears. A strange sweetness lingered in the words, a joy that I had thought would be too far beyond reach for me, for us. "We did it. It's over."

She turned to me slowly, as if the movement took more effort than it should. Her lips quirked upward, but the smile was thin and reluctant, as though she were apologizing for the fact that it didn't quite reach her eyes. "It's over," she echoed, but the word tasted sour in her mouth.

I followed her gaze over the city, to the emerald glint of the river cutting through the heart of it, past the sprawling markets that would soon reopen their doors to traders from all over. Already, I could see the faint outlines of people gathering in the streets—whispers of the forgotten past stirring in the wind as they emerged from the shadows of their long slumber.

But there were no crowds cheering. No banners waving. No celebration beyond the silent acknowledgment of those few who were still alive, still willing to breathe beneath the weight of the restoration. It was almost like they were waiting. Waiting for the other shoe to drop, as the saying goes. They didn't know what the cost had been, not yet. But I did.

Amara shifted, her boots grinding against the stones as she began to walk toward the palace. The golden spires that crowned it shimmered against the dark sky, like the crown of some ancient deity. I wanted to follow her, to walk beside her, but there was a sense of distance that kept me back—one that I couldn't explain, but I felt in the marrow of my bones. The city might have returned, but Amara wasn't the same woman she had been. Not anymore.

I hesitated, but she didn't wait. She was already moving, striding purposefully toward the heart of the kingdom, where the ruins of the great palace still stood. We both knew that this place would hold more than just memories—it would hold the remnants of a curse, a history that couldn't be erased no matter how many stones were set back into place, no matter how many rivers ran clear again.

"Are you coming or not?" she called over her shoulder, her voice sharp and cold, the hint of warmth still buried deep beneath the surface.

It wasn't an invitation. It was a command. And though I had no right to follow her, to step back into that world we had once known, I did. I always did.

I caught up with her quickly, our steps in sync as we reached the threshold of the palace. The heavy doors, once gilded and inscribed with symbols long forgotten, creaked open with a sound that echoed through the halls like a ghost's lament. We both stopped just inside, letting our eyes adjust to the dim light filtering through the broken windows.

"This is it," Amara said softly, her voice almost lost in the air around us. "This is what we fought for."

But the grandeur of the palace did nothing to soothe the knot in my stomach. The walls were crumbling, the golden furniture cracked and dust-covered, and the air smelled faintly of decay. I could feel the pulse of something ancient beneath my feet, something that hadn't truly been banished from this place. The curse hadn't died—it had merely been forced into hiding.

I turned to her, finally able to break through the silence that had stretched between us like a vast chasm. "What happens now?"

She didn't answer immediately, her eyes tracing the remnants of the palace as though she were looking for something—or someone—she feared might still be here. "Now," she said slowly, "we rebuild. But we do it carefully. We do it differently. We can't repeat the mistakes of the past."

I nodded, though the thought of the past—of the betrayal, the loss, the curse—hung in the air between us like an uninvited guest. It was a reminder that there would be no easy redemption, no quick fix to the damage done by the artifact.

But even as I thought that, I realized the truth in her words. We had broken the curse. The land would grow again. The people would find their way back.

And we would rebuild—whatever it cost us.

The air around us felt different now, thick with possibility. The kind of possibility that lingers like the last sip of wine in a glass, leaving a bittersweet aftertaste that you can't quite shake. It was only then that I understood the true weight of the moment. The city, resplendent in the new light of dawn, held its breath, suspended in time. But Amara's eyes—those fierce, relentless eyes—betrayed the silent war waging inside her.

I followed her, keeping a few steps behind. It wasn't that I didn't want to walk beside her. She just had a way of turning every step into a march, a one-woman crusade against the past, the future, and everything in between. I respected it. Most days, I admired it. But in moments like these, I couldn't help but feel like the shadow she cast would always be longer than my own.

We made our way deeper into the palace, the coolness of the stone beneath our feet offering a stark contrast to the warmth of the city outside. The echoes of our footsteps sounded far too loud in the empty halls, reverberating off the shattered statues and broken walls. They were all remnants of a past that no longer had a place here, even if it still haunted the air we breathed. I was certain Amara could hear them too—the whispers of the past that clung to every corner like dust.

"Do you ever wonder," I began, breaking the silence that had started to press down on me, "if we're making a terrible mistake? Rebuilding all of this?"

Her eyes didn't leave the path ahead of her. "If we don't, who will?" Her words were sharp, clipped, as though she'd already had this conversation in her head a hundred times.

I caught up to her, matching her pace as we turned a corner. The high ceilings of the corridor loomed above us like an old cathedral, its splendor marred by the ravages of time. "Maybe no one," I said, the words slipping out before I could stop them. "But maybe that's okay."

Amara stopped dead in her tracks. The muscles in her neck tightened, the tension visible under her skin. "You think we should leave it to rot? To be forgotten?"

I shrugged, though I wasn't sure if I even believed my own words. "Maybe we shouldn't try so hard to bring back what we can't understand. We don't know what's here, Amara. What's waiting for us." I waved a hand toward the crumbling walls, the fallen tapestries, the broken glass that still sparkled in the faint light. "We might be setting the stage for something worse."

She let out a long breath, and for a moment, I saw a flicker of uncertainty. It was gone just as quickly, but it had been there. In her eyes. In her posture. A vulnerability that I hadn't seen in years.

"You're wrong," she said, her voice soft, almost too soft. "What's here is ours. All of it. We have the right to rebuild." Her hand tightened into a fist, but there was no anger behind it—only a determination that bordered on desperation. "This is what we fought for. What we sacrificed for."

I nodded slowly, even though I wasn't sure if I believed her. There was so much about this place, this city, that felt like it had been waiting for something. For someone. For Amara.

She turned abruptly, heading toward a set of double doors at the far end of the hall. "Come on," she said, her voice suddenly brisk, like the conversation was already over. "We have work to do."

I followed, still unsure of where this road would take us, but knowing I had no choice but to follow her down it. When we entered the room, the smell hit me first. It wasn't the dampness I had expected, but something sweeter, something intoxicating. The walls were lined with shelves upon shelves of dusty books, scrolls, and faded maps. The remnants of the ancient scholars who had once walked these halls, now only ghosts in the records they left behind.

"This is where it all started," Amara murmured, running her fingers along the spine of an old tome. "This is where the answers are."

I watched her for a long moment, wondering what exactly she was looking for. The city had come back. The power of the artifact was gone. We had succeeded in breaking the curse, hadn't we? But something still gnawed at me. A feeling in the pit of my stomach that this wasn't the end. That something else was coming.

Amara turned to me then, catching the expression on my face. Her eyes softened, just a fraction. "I know you're scared," she said, as if reading my thoughts. "But we can't stop now. Not after everything."

"I'm not scared," I said quickly, though I wasn't sure if I was trying to convince her or myself. "I just think... maybe we're not ready for what comes next."

Amara didn't reply, but her gaze held mine for a moment longer than usual. It was a silent acknowledgment of the truth we were both avoiding. She turned back to the shelves, pulling down a thick, weathered scroll. "We'll be ready," she said firmly, as if she believed it herself. "We have to be."

I didn't respond. I didn't have to. We both knew the only way out now was forward, no matter how uncertain or dangerous the road ahead seemed. Amara was right about one thing—we had fought for this. The city, the kingdom, the power—it was all ours now. The question was what we would do with it. What we would become in the process.

I just hoped we didn't lose ourselves in the process.

The silence between us thickened, laden with the unsaid. Amara's words hung in the air, a stark reminder of everything that had been sacrificed. I watched her closely, the way she held herself—like she was afraid to breathe too deeply, as if the very air might shatter the fragile peace we had claimed. She didn't need to say it. I knew. The price of breaking the curse wasn't counted in coins or blood, but in something far more elusive, far more painful. Trust. Family. Ourselves.

"Are you really ready for this?" I asked, more to myself than to her. My voice came out rougher than I intended, but Amara didn't flinch. She never did.

She paused for a moment, and I could almost feel the weight of the question pressing on her chest. Her lips parted, but no words came. Instead, she gave me a sharp, almost imperceptible nod. I wasn't sure if she was answering me, or if she was simply trying to convince herself that she was, in fact, prepared for what came next.

"You don't have to do this alone," I offered. "We can figure it out together." The words slipped out before I had a chance to really think about them. But there was something about the uncertainty in her eyes, that flicker of vulnerability, that made me want to be the one to hold her steady.

Her gaze softened, but only for a second, and then it hardened again. "I'm not alone. Not anymore. None of us are."

I nodded, though I wasn't entirely sure I believed her. Something in her tone told me that she still carried a weight, one that I couldn't even begin to understand. But I would stand beside her, whether she wanted me there or not. That much, at least, was certain.

The room around us felt colder as the sunlight began to fade, the shadows creeping in from the corners like ghosts waiting to be released. The shelves of books loomed, silent sentinels to forgotten knowledge and unspoken secrets. Amara reached for another scroll, this one older, darker, its edges frayed like the last breath of a dying civilization.

"I have to see this through," she muttered, her voice low and strained, as if the words themselves carried some kind of forbidden weight.

I stepped closer, my curiosity pulling me forward. "What is it?"

She didn't answer immediately, her fingers tracing the faded ink on the scroll with a reverence that almost seemed sacred. When she finally spoke, her voice was distant, lost in the depths of some uncharted thought. "This is the final piece. The one that will tell us what comes next."

"Is it dangerous?" The question slipped out without warning, and I immediately regretted it. She didn't need to hear the doubt in my voice, not now.

Amara looked up, her eyes locking with mine. "Everything is dangerous now."

And just like that, the silence returned, more oppressive than before. The air grew thicker, as if the world itself was holding its breath, waiting for something—or someone—to break the tension. Amara didn't look at me again, instead unfurling the scroll with a careful hand, like it might crumble to dust at the slightest touch.

I could see the way her fingers trembled ever so slightly, the only outward sign of the fear she kept buried beneath her calm exterior. She was more fragile than she let on. I had seen it before, glimpsed it in the moments when her guard slipped just enough for me to see the person she truly was—the one who had sacrificed everything for this cursed kingdom, the one who had borne the weight of a thousand years of history on her shoulders.

But now? Now, I wasn't sure who she was anymore. The woman before me was no longer just Amara, the fierce warrior and leader. She had become something else entirely, something wrapped in secrets and lies. Something I wasn't entirely sure I could trust.

"Is that it?" I asked, breaking the silence. "Is that the answer you've been looking for?"

She didn't answer. Instead, her eyes scanned the scroll, the tension in her shoulders mounting with each passing second. I could feel it too, that same uneasy anticipation, as though something was waiting just beyond the edge of our understanding, something that had been waiting for centuries to be uncovered.

Then, without warning, the room grew darker, the air growing heavier, suffocating. The temperature seemed to drop in an instant, the cold creeping into my bones, making the hairs on the back of my neck stand on end.

Amara looked up from the scroll, her face pale, her lips parted in shock. Her eyes, wide with a mixture of fear and disbelief, locked onto mine. "No," she whispered, her voice trembling.

"What is it?" I demanded, my heart racing in my chest as I stepped closer, the urgency in my tone rising with every beat.

But she couldn't answer. Instead, she turned the scroll around, and I saw it too—the words on the page were no longer written in the ancient language of the kingdom, but in something darker, something twisted. The symbols seemed to writhe on the page, shifting and rearranging themselves as if alive.

"Amara—" I started, but she didn't hear me. Her eyes were fixed, unblinking, on the scroll. And in that moment, I realized something far worse than the curse we had broken had been unleashed.

"Run," she whispered, barely audible.

But it was already too late.

Chapter 37: The Quiet Before the Storm

The city smelled of fresh rain that evening, the kind that makes the asphalt shimmer and the leaves glisten as though they're wearing tiny diamonds. It was the sort of rain that didn't ask permission to fall; it just did, sweeping through the streets in a quiet, determined procession. Gabriel and I had wandered out of our usual corners, both of us exhausted from the weight of the work we'd been doing. Every day felt like a balancing act. We'd each come to this city for different reasons, but it had somehow claimed us, slowly and without fanfare. Still, we hadn't talked about the reasons we stayed.

It was late, later than I intended, but when the night air pulled me out of the apartment, I couldn't deny the pull to walk. Gabriel's absence hung around the edges of my thoughts, and though it shouldn't have, it bothered me. He didn't like the rain. Never had. But there he was, sitting on the edge of a low stone wall, eyes fixed on something far beyond the skyline, hands shoved deep into the pockets of his worn jacket.

There was something magnetic about the way he sat—so still, like he was guarding a secret, or maybe holding onto something that was already slipping away. I wondered if he even noticed the way the world had slowed around him. The hustle and bustle of the city seemed to have quieted in reverence. Even the cars that usually hummed along the streets seemed to hold their breath as they passed.

I took a step closer, my boots tapping against the wet pavement. The sound echoed like an unspoken invitation, and he turned, just slightly, his gaze sharp and calculating. He saw me but didn't speak right away, and for a split second, the air between us felt thick, like a promise, or maybe a threat.

"Should've known you'd be out here," he finally said, his voice low, tinged with something I couldn't place. "It's quiet. I don't know what it is about nights like this..."

"I know," I said, settling next to him on the wall, the wet stone cool against my skin. "Something about it feels like the calm before a storm."

He didn't respond, but I felt the weight of his silence, like there was more he wanted to say but couldn't quite find the words. Gabriel wasn't the sort of man to speak unless there was something worth saying, and the longer I sat there beside him, the more I wondered just how much of him I hadn't uncovered yet. What did he hide beneath that quiet exterior? What was behind those eyes that rarely gave anything away?

"I hate the quiet," he muttered after a moment, his voice carrying an edge I hadn't expected. "It's... too much space. It gives people room to think about things they don't want to think about."

"You mean things like... us?" I asked, a teasing note in my voice that belied the tension tightening in my chest.

He met my gaze, and for the briefest second, I thought I saw a flicker of something softer in his eyes—something that didn't belong to the hard, determined man I had come to know. But it vanished before I could decipher it, leaving behind only the mystery.

"I mean a lot of things," he said, his voice even more distant now. He looked back out over the city, the rain tracing silver lines down the windows of the buildings. "People don't like thinking too much. It's too damn dangerous."

I wasn't sure what he meant by that. Dangerous how? Dangerous in the way it made us face the things we wanted to bury? Dangerous in the way we might have to confront the parts of ourselves we preferred to keep hidden? I didn't ask, though. The words felt too heavy, too vulnerable, and Gabriel had a way of making those kinds of conversations feel like a labyrinth, one you couldn't escape without losing a piece of yourself.

A cold gust of wind blew through the alley, cutting through the moment. I wrapped my arms around myself, pulling the collar of my jacket up against the chill, but I didn't want to leave. Not yet. I wasn't sure if it was because of the rain or because of him, but I wanted to linger, to stretch this moment out as long as I could.

"We're good at distracting ourselves, aren't we?" I said, more to fill the silence than anything else. "With work, with everything we're doing here... helping people rebuild, fixing things."

"Fixing things doesn't mean they're better," he replied, his eyes flicking back to me. "It just means they're patched up long enough to distract us from how bad they really are."

I thought about that. About the city, about the people we worked with, and about Gabriel. There were things we couldn't fix. Things we shouldn't try to fix, because once you started patching up one hole, another one opened somewhere else. And maybe, just maybe, we were both too afraid to acknowledge that there was a hole between us, one we hadn't even realized existed until now.

"You're too damn cynical for your own good," I teased, nudging him lightly with my shoulder. But my voice faltered a little, unsure if I was joking or if something else was creeping in.

"I'm not cynical," he shot back, his lips twitching into something that could have been a smile, though it didn't quite reach his eyes. "I'm just realistic."

There it was again—the push and pull between us, something invisible but undeniable, like a rope that tugged at our backs, threatening to pull us closer even as we resisted. I didn't know what to say next. We both had our walls, built up over time and through experience, and neither of us was ready to break them down. At least, not yet.

The silence stretched again, but this time, it didn't feel as heavy. It felt... inevitable. Like we were both waiting for something. I wasn't sure what that something was, but as the rain softened and the city hummed around us, I realized I wasn't so afraid of the quiet anymore. Maybe it was just the calm before the storm, but for the first time, I was starting to think that the storm might not be the worst thing to face.

And maybe, just maybe, neither of us was as ready for it as we pretended to be.

The days blurred together after that quiet evening, each one passing in the same rhythm: we woke up, we worked, we helped, we retreated into ourselves when the sun dipped below the horizon. Gabriel and I had settled into something that was neither comfortable nor uncomfortable, just a delicate balance of proximity and distance. He'd return to the apartment late, his face a little more worn, his shoulders a little more slumped, as if the weight of the city had pressed a little deeper into his bones. I'd do the same, pretending that the space between us was fine, that I was fine.

But nothing about it felt fine. The undercurrent of tension hummed constantly, threading its way through the simplest of exchanges, a quick look, a lingering touch, all those moments that should have been fleeting but instead settled in the corners of my mind like stubborn dust.

That night, as I leaned over the railing of our building's rooftop, watching the skyline blur in the distance, I couldn't help but think about the way Gabriel had looked at me after our last conversation. The city glittered below me, the yellow lights of streetlamps catching the sheen of rain on the pavement, and for the first time in a long while, it felt like we weren't alone in this city. It felt like we were part of something—too big, maybe, too dangerous, but something all the same.

The silence stretched thin between us. He was just a few feet behind me, as usual, close enough that I could feel the weight of his presence pressing in, but not enough to make him feel near. His hands were jammed into his pockets, a stance that spoke volumes, but his face was unreadable, the shadows of the evening turning him into something other than himself. He was a man who held his secrets close, and I wasn't sure if I wanted to know what they were anymore. But I couldn't shake the feeling that he was keeping something from me, something vital, and that knowledge festered like an itch I couldn't quite scratch.

"You know," I said, my voice cutting through the quiet night air, "I always thought I'd be the one to leave first."

Gabriel didn't answer immediately. His silhouette remained in place, watching the city as if it held some kind of answer that would make sense of the mess of us.

"Why?" His voice was low, a little strained, and yet somehow still calm. I almost didn't hear the hint of curiosity buried underneath.

I half-smiled, my gaze not leaving the far-off horizon. "Because I've never been the kind of person who sticks around. Not for long, anyway. I tend to move on when things get complicated."

"That's not you." The words came quicker than I expected, as though he'd been sitting on them, waiting for the right moment to let them slip out. And when they did, they landed like stones between us, heavy and real.

I blinked, caught off guard by the intensity in his voice. "What do you mean?"

He shifted, the sound of his boots scraping against the gravel roof punctuating his movement. "I've watched you work. You don't just walk away from things. You fix them. You build them, even when everything around you is falling apart." He paused, his voice barely a whisper. "You're not a quitter."

The air between us seemed to contract, and for a moment, I wondered if I was imagining it—if maybe, just maybe, the distance between us wasn't as vast as I thought.

But no. Gabriel was still a puzzle, and I was just the fool who thought I might solve it.

"I'm not sure that's the compliment you think it is," I muttered, half-grinning, because what else was there to do? His words had struck a nerve, and I hated that.

Gabriel's gaze finally left the skyline, his eyes flicking toward me. The change in him was subtle, but I caught it. That tension, that small but undeniable shift. "It's not about compliments," he said, his tone hardening just slightly. "It's about truth."

The city was never truly quiet, but tonight, the sounds of the traffic, the chatter of the pedestrians below, all seemed muffled, as if even the world outside had decided to hold its breath and wait. The quiet had stretched into something else, something tangible that pressed into me, wrapped around my ribs, and I didn't know if I wanted to breathe through it or shatter it with a few words.

And then, without warning, Gabriel closed the distance. It was a slow, deliberate motion, his boots scraping against the roof as he moved toward me. There was a kind of magnetism in his approach, a force I couldn't ignore, and before I could even gather myself, he was standing next to me, too close for comfort but close enough to make the air thick and heavy with unspoken things.

His gaze met mine, intense, unwavering. "You're right," he said softly, "about a lot of things. But you're wrong about one."

I blinked, suddenly aware of how sharply my heart was beating. "Which one?"

He reached up, his hand brushing against my arm lightly, his fingers trailing the edge of my sleeve. The touch was so casual, so unremarkable, but it hit me like a jolt of electricity, making the ground beneath me feel uncertain. "You think you're the one who's going to walk away first. But I've been watching you. You're not the one who leaves. You're the one who makes people stay."

My breath hitched in my chest, and I looked away, the words too much to digest, too much to handle right now. What was he trying to say? I couldn't make sense of it, not when everything inside me screamed to run away from the moment, from the emotions swirling around like a storm I couldn't predict.

But when I turned back to him, when our eyes met again, something shifted in the space between us. Something clicked. Something neither of us could control anymore. And that, in itself, was the most dangerous thing of all.

The city hummed around us, the soft rhythm of it filling the spaces we left in the wake of our words. But still, there was that feeling of something unsaid, a pressure building between us, unspoken but palpable, like a storm that hovered just beyond the horizon, too distant to touch but too close to ignore.

I had started to think maybe it was all in my head—the way his eyes lingered on me just a moment too long, the way his voice had dropped an octave when he spoke to me, the way he seemed to notice things about me that no one else did. But every time I tried to convince myself that I was imagining it, I would find him standing just a little too close, his body language just a little too familiar.

We'd been avoiding this for weeks now—this strange tension that had begun to grow between us. It wasn't like we were strangers. No, we knew each other all too well. But there was something more now. Something that neither of us was willing to confront.

I was still standing there, my back against the railing, trying to sort through the jumble of thoughts that twisted in my mind, when Gabriel spoke again, his voice unexpectedly soft. "You don't have to do it alone, you know."

I glanced at him, half expecting to see the usual wall of indifference he liked to keep up. But there was none of that now. Instead, there was only something like vulnerability in his gaze, a crack in the armor that was usually so impenetrable.

"I never thought I was doing it alone," I replied, my words more biting than I meant them to be. "Not really."

But the thing was, I wasn't sure if I believed that. Not anymore.

The city beneath us had transformed in the past few weeks. The devastation that had once choked the streets, the ghostly remnants of buildings that had collapsed under the weight of a crisis, had slowly started to shift. It was as if the very soul of the city was refusing to stay broken, each piece of rubble, every shattered window, a reminder of what had been lost—and yet, also a promise of what could still be found. Gabriel and I had worked alongside each other, our shoulders pressed together in that strange rhythm of two people who had been doing this too long, never asking for help but never quite managing to offer it, either.

It was hard, working like this. It had been hard from the start. But there was a strange kind of satisfaction in it too, in the way our hands would meet in passing, the brief glances we'd exchange when we weren't quite looking. Each moment was a reminder of the pull between us, the one neither of us was quite brave enough to acknowledge.

Gabriel shifted next to me, his gaze never leaving the distant skyline. His voice was quieter this time, almost hesitant, as if he had been thinking about this longer than I had. "Maybe you've convinced yourself you can do everything on your own, but I've been watching you. You don't have to. You don't have to carry it all. Not anymore."

The words struck me harder than I wanted them to. Gabriel wasn't the type to offer reassurances, not unless he meant them. And even though I was certain he was talking about more than just the work we were doing, I still couldn't shake the weight of his implication. That maybe—just maybe—there was something more to our connection than either of us had let on.

I swallowed hard, forcing myself to keep it together, keep the walls intact. "What is it you think I need from you, Gabriel?"

For a moment, he didn't respond, the air between us thick with that familiar tension. I didn't know if I wanted him to say it, didn't know if I could bear it, but I felt like I was teetering on the edge of something, something inevitable, something that had been coming for a long time.

He exhaled, slow and steady, before finally turning to look at me. And for a heartbeat, just one, the city seemed to fall away. The noise, the cars, the people walking below us—they didn't matter. All that mattered was the way his eyes held mine, dark and searching, full of a hundred unspoken things.

"I think you need someone who's not going to let you go," he said, his words simple but heavy. The honesty of it caught me off guard, rattling my cage just a little.

I looked away quickly, my heart pounding too loudly in my chest. "Don't say things like that," I said, more harshly than I meant to. "We're not—"

"I'm not trying to make this harder, I swear." His voice softened, like he was trying to take the sting out of his words, but it didn't quite work. "But it's hard to pretend, you know? It's hard to ignore what's right in front of us."

I wanted to laugh, to make a joke, to break the tension that was quickly growing unbearable, but my mouth went dry. The truth of his words hit me in a way I wasn't ready for. And so, I stayed silent, my hands gripping the cold metal of the railing, my body frozen in place.

He moved then, slowly, so I could step out of the way, his hand brushing against mine as he did. A simple touch, but the electricity of it was undeniable. It lingered long after he had taken a step back, his eyes never leaving mine.

I couldn't breathe.

"We can't keep doing this," I said, my voice barely above a whisper, even though I wasn't sure who I was trying to convince more—him or myself.

Gabriel exhaled sharply, the sound filled with frustration and something else I couldn't name. He ran a hand through his hair, his jaw tight as if he was trying to hold back something, something wild, something dangerous.

"Maybe we don't have to," he muttered, stepping away from the edge of the roof.

I didn't have time to react, didn't have time to think about what that meant, because at that very moment, the sound of a distant siren pierced the night air, followed by the unmistakable thud of an explosion that rattled the buildings around us.

My heart jumped into my throat. Without thinking, I grabbed his arm, pulling him toward the stairwell. "We need to go. Now."

He didn't protest, but his face was suddenly hard, his expression dark as the city around us seemed to crack open once again. And in that moment, I knew—whatever had been building between us, whatever storm was about to break—it had nothing on what was coming for us now.

Chapter 38: A New Threat

The sky hung heavy over the city, a brooding canvas of steel-gray clouds that seemed to mirror the tension in the air. The distant hum of traffic below was barely audible through the thick walls of Gabriel's study, yet every sound was heightened in my ears, as if the world had narrowed down to the thrum of my pulse. The room smelled faintly of tobacco and the faint tang of coffee, but it was Gabriel's silence that made it suffocating.

He stood by the window, his back rigid, gaze fixed on something far beyond the jagged skyline. His shoulders, once relaxed in the ease of the evening, were drawn tight now, as if the weight of some unspeakable truth had descended upon him. The message had arrived just moments ago, brought by a boy who looked like he'd run through the night to deliver it. And the moment Gabriel read it, the air in the room shifted. He didn't have to say anything. His eyes, dark with worry, told me everything I needed to know.

I wasn't sure if I was angry or relieved—or a mix of both. It wasn't that I wanted to be at the heart of this madness. The mark on my wrist, a twisted design that burned like fire beneath my skin, had never promised peace. Still, I'd hoped it was finally over. That we had reached the end of this long, twisting road, only for it to twist yet again.

Gabriel turned slowly, his eyes meeting mine for the first time since the message arrived. The intensity in his gaze made the hairs on the back of my neck stand on end. "It's not over," he said, his voice low, each word weighted like an anchor.

"Tell me something I don't know," I muttered, rolling my eyes in a show of bravado. But inside, there was nothing but the gnawing sensation that maybe I wasn't as prepared for what lay ahead as I thought.

The courier had been clear: the artifact's energy hadn't vanished; it had found a new host, far from here. In some ways, it felt like a betrayal. The energy had been something I thought I could control, something I had spent months studying, binding it to me with a series of rituals. But to think it could simply slip away from my grasp—well, that was a thought I wasn't willing to entertain.

Gabriel, ever the strategist, seemed to read the shift in my expression before I could even verbalize it. "It's not just the artifact. It's the host." His words were clipped, his jaw tight with the strain of restraint. "This—" he gestured to the space between us, "this is just the beginning."

I shook my head, willing the sudden dizziness away. "You think they're coming after me?"

Gabriel took a step closer, his eyes burning with that familiar intensity. "I don't think it's about you anymore," he said. "It's about power. And whoever controls it will stop at nothing to wield it."

I was still reeling from the idea of the artifact moving. But as his words sank in, they took root deep in my gut. The mark on my wrist had always been a symbol of the bond between us, between me and the power I had inherited, cursed with. But now, it felt like a branding. A target. I was tied to this in ways I didn't fully understand.

I swallowed hard, the urge to run overtaking me. But where would I go? Back to the small apartment I'd been hiding in, pretending to live a normal life? There was no such thing as normal now. My life, this life, had taken on the weight of something much darker and more dangerous. And I wasn't sure I was ready for it.

Gabriel must have sensed the turmoil crashing against the walls of my mind because his next words were softer, more carefully chosen. "You don't have to do this alone."

His voice was warm, even comforting, but I heard the underlying note of something else—something I couldn't quite place. I looked at him, really looked at him, and for the first time in months, I wondered if I ever truly knew him at all. He was always the one who had the answers, who knew exactly what move to make. But in the quiet moments, when his guard was down, I saw the vulnerability lurking just beneath the surface. The weariness. The part of him that wanted to pull away from it all, too.

I took a step back, distancing myself from the pull he had over me. "I'm not afraid of doing this alone." I didn't know if I believed it. But it sounded good. "I've been handling this—whatever this is—on my own for a long time now."

"Handling it?" Gabriel scoffed, the edge of his frustration cutting through his calm demeanor. "This isn't something you handle, not with the stakes so high. The forces at play here... they're beyond anything you've faced before."

I was about to snap back, to tell him that I didn't need his protection or his pity, but then I caught sight of the shadow that flickered across his face. There was something he wasn't telling me. Something that made the tightness in his jaw even more pronounced. Something I was too afraid to ask about.

"I'm not going anywhere, Gabriel." The words left my mouth before I could stop them. I didn't even know if I meant them. But they were out there now, hanging between us like a thread pulling taut.

Gabriel stared at me for a long moment, the muscles in his face working as he processed my words. "Then we'll deal with it together," he said finally, his tone low but determined. "But be prepared. This time, it won't just be a matter of stopping an artifact. We're dealing with something far worse."

And in that moment, as the weight of his words sank in, I knew that whatever came next—whatever threat had taken root in some faraway place—was coming for both of us.

The sound of my own heartbeat thrummed loudly in my ears as I stared at the door Gabriel had just closed behind him. The weight of the conversation—of the possibility that everything we'd fought for might crumble in the blink of an eye—hung like an oppressive fog in the air. The world beyond the narrow windows of the study felt distant, removed, as though it could never touch the raw nerve of uncertainty that now sparked beneath my skin.

I had been running from this for so long, trying to keep the world at arm's length while pretending that the storm I'd once stirred wasn't still building. But it was there, just below the surface, waiting for its chance to break through.

I shifted in my seat, restless, pulling at the fraying sleeve of my jacket. I could hear Gabriel moving quietly down the hall, no doubt preparing to leave. There were things we needed to do. People we needed to find. But I wasn't ready to move just yet. Not until I had the time to breathe, to process the relentless weight of his words.

"You're quiet," came a voice from the doorway, startling me from my thoughts. I looked up, blinking, and saw Alina leaning against the frame, arms crossed over her chest, her usual smirk tugging at the corner of her mouth. Alina had always been the one to fill the silences, to turn the tension into something sharper, something more manageable. She had that gift—of making the unbearable seem just a little less daunting.

"I'm thinking," I muttered, not entirely sure what I was thinking about, but willing to put the words out there anyway.

"Must be a pretty heavy load to silence you like that," she teased, stepping further into the room. "Usually, you're more the 'talk first, think later' type."

I snorted softly at the understatement. "Usually. But this is different."

Alina paused, her eyes narrowing in that way that made her look like she was solving a puzzle, trying to figure out which pieces fit and which ones didn't. "Different how?" she asked, the playful tone from moments before replaced by something sharper, more curious.

"The artifact's energy hasn't gone away," I explained, rubbing my thumb over the mark on my wrist, feeling the pulse of it underneath. "It's moved. To someone else. Somewhere far away. And we have no idea who it is."

She let out a low whistle, walking toward the window where Gabriel had stood only moments ago. "You're telling me that all this time, you were hoping to control it, to put it to rest, and now it's gone rogue?"

"Sounds dramatic, doesn't it?" I muttered, but I didn't feel dramatic. I felt exposed, raw in a way that had nothing to do with the physical world around me. "It's worse than that. It's as if... as if the energy has found a new home and it's biding its time, waiting."

Alina turned to me, her expression more serious now. She took a step closer, crossing the room with that quiet intensity I always admired. "Whoever this new host is, they've got a hell of a responsibility, don't they? That kind of power doesn't come without consequences. You know that."

"Yeah," I said, shifting in my chair uncomfortably. "That's the part I'm struggling to wrap my head around. We thought we were keeping it in check. But now? Now I feel like I'm holding a live grenade and I'm waiting for the fuse to burn out."

Her gaze softened, though she still carried the weight of understanding in her eyes. "You've been through worse," she said quietly. "You'll get through this too. But you're not doing it alone, you know that, right?"

I didn't know how to answer her. Part of me wanted to say that I wasn't sure how much more I could handle, how much longer I could keep pretending that I wasn't losing my grip. But instead, I just nodded, because Alina was right in one sense: I wasn't alone. Not yet, anyway.

The words had barely left her lips when the phone on the desk buzzed, its sudden shrillness slicing through the moment like a blade. I jumped, caught off guard by the sound, before I grabbed the receiver. "This is Emily," I said, trying to keep the unease out of my voice.

"Emily, it's Gabriel." His voice was sharp, tight with the urgency I had come to associate with moments like these. "We need to move quickly. I've tracked the energy, and it's already too far. They're getting closer."

I glanced at Alina, who had caught the change in my expression immediately. "Where?" I asked, my stomach twisting into a knot.

"East. To a place I thought we were safe from. We'll need to move fast, but we'll have a window of time. They don't know I'm onto them yet."

"Give me an hour," I said, my voice more sure than I felt. I hung up the phone, my thoughts racing.

Alina raised an eyebrow. "That was quick. Where to?"

I turned to face her, the weight of what we were about to do sinking in. "I'm going to find whoever this new host is, Alina. And I'm going to make sure they don't have a chance to unleash whatever this thing is."

For a moment, Alina studied me in silence, her face unreadable. Then, with a slow, deliberate motion, she reached into the pocket of her jacket and pulled out a small vial. "You won't be doing it alone," she said, her voice low and steady. "Not this time."

I didn't ask what was in the vial, didn't need to. Alina always had her own ways of preparing for the things most people wouldn't dream of. But what she said next caught me off guard.

"We'll get ahead of this. We'll beat it, whatever it is. Together."

And in that instant, I realized something I hadn't wanted to admit before: this wasn't just about the artifact anymore. It was about the people I had come to care for—the ones I couldn't afford to lose.

The city stretched beneath me like a jagged puzzle piece, its outlines softened by the late evening haze that hung low over the streets. New Orleans was never quiet, but tonight it felt like the air itself was holding its breath, waiting. As I pulled the leather jacket tighter around my shoulders, the weight of what was coming pressed against my back, pushing me forward without mercy. The mark on my wrist throbbed again, a pulse that didn't belong to me, a warning I couldn't ignore.

I looked to Alina, who was already walking ahead, her strides purposeful, the streetlights catching the glint of her silver earrings. She didn't speak as we navigated the quiet side streets, but I could feel the unspoken tension between us. Gabriel's call had made it clear: this wasn't just about finding the host; it was about controlling something that could tear this city—and maybe the world—apart if we didn't act quickly.

We made our way through the familiar chaos of Bourbon Street, the air thick with the scent of fried food, cigarettes, and the unmistakable funk of spilled beer that never quite left the cobblestone roads. Neon lights flashed above, advertising everything from overpriced Hurricanes to cheap tarot readings. But none of it mattered right now. None of it could drown out the hammering in my chest, the gnawing feeling that something was closing in on us.

"What exactly is it you think we're walking into?" Alina asked, her voice barely rising above the hum of the city. "A cult? A sorcerer on a power trip? You didn't say much on the phone, just that Gabriel's tracking something—someone."

I considered her words carefully, the cold weight of the unknown creeping up my spine. "All I know is that the energy is shifting. And it's got a life of its own. The host... whoever they are, they're already pulling strings in ways we can't predict."

"You're not making this any easier," Alina quipped, adjusting her jacket. "But then again, you never were much for reassuring."

I couldn't help but laugh, the sound a little too loud in the quiet of the night. "Who needs reassurance? I'm just trying to keep up with everything else that's happening. You wouldn't believe what it's like to be on the receiving end of something you can't control."

Alina shot me a glance, her eyes sharp despite the exhaustion that clung to her. "Yeah, well, I think we're all in the same boat now."

We moved faster, the streets narrowing as we cut through alleys, the air cooling as we neared the old warehouse district. The city's pulse felt stronger here, the hum of something ancient beneath the modern chaos. There were whispers in the city's veins—about the artifacts, about what they could do, about what they were capable of in the wrong hands. And I had no idea whose hands were holding the one we were chasing now.

When we arrived at the building—a crumbling relic wedged between an old jazz bar and a defunct speakeasy—the hairs on the back of my neck prickled. I could feel it then, a current of energy running through the cracked asphalt beneath our feet. Something was here. Something was waiting.

"Any bright ideas?" Alina asked, already moving toward the door, fingers brushing over the rusted handle.

"Don't get ahead of yourself," I warned, my voice tight. "This place might be empty, but we don't know what we're walking into."

"Are you always this cautious?" Alina raised an eyebrow, glancing back at me. "I mean, I thought you were the one who liked to dive headfirst into danger. Or did I misremember?"

"I've changed," I said dryly, though I didn't entirely believe it myself.

She didn't answer, just stepped forward and pushed the door open with a creak that felt too loud in the quiet night. Inside, the space was damp and smelled of mildew, but it was empty—or so it seemed at first. The air was thick, as though something had been waiting, like an animal at rest before pouncing. I could feel it in the pit of my stomach, a pull I couldn't ignore, the kind of sensation that told me I was standing on the edge of something far bigger than I had anticipated.

Alina stepped in beside me, her hand hovering over her belt as she scanned the space. Her fingers brushed against the smooth surface of a blade, and she sighed. "I was hoping for something a little more straightforward, you know. Maybe an old-fashioned fight, a few broken noses. But this feels... off."

I nodded, stepping carefully around the cluttered remnants of old furniture, broken bottles, and shards of glass. The shadows seemed to reach for us as we moved further into the warehouse, the faint sound of footsteps echoing faintly, as though someone—or something—was following us.

Suddenly, a flicker of light caught my eye—faint, almost imperceptible, but unmistakable. It wasn't the kind of light that came from a bulb or any natural source. It was a pulse, a brief flash that buzzed like static electricity. And before I could react, the ground beneath us shifted.

"Down!" Alina shouted, pushing me toward the floor just as the entire warehouse seemed to tremble. A sound like thunder followed, but it wasn't thunder—it was something far more dangerous. I barely had time to brace myself before the floor cracked wide open, the ground splitting open like a mouth ready to swallow us whole.

"What the hell was that?" Alina gasped, her eyes wide, her hand on her gun now.

I didn't answer. I couldn't. All I could do was watch as the darkness below us swirled, the faint glow growing brighter, coalescing into something that was neither alive nor dead. It was as if the very air had turned into a living thing, swirling and shifting like smoke.

And in the center of it all, a figure began to emerge, slow and deliberate, like a shadow breaking free from the chains of reality.

"I think we found them," I whispered, but I didn't know if the words meant anything at all.

Chapter 39: The Journey Begins Anew

I wiped the beads of sweat from my forehead, not bothering to glance at the faint smudge of dirt it left behind on my palm. The sun had long since dipped below the horizon, leaving behind a suffocating humidity that seemed to cling to everything—skin, clothes, the air itself. The old warehouse loomed before us like some half-remembered nightmare, the kind that stalks you through the quiet hours of the night, whispering secrets that make your pulse race for reasons you can't explain.

Behind me, Gabriel shifted his weight from one foot to the other, his brow furrowed as he gazed at the building. The silver of his hair caught the last vestiges of the fading light, an almost ethereal contrast against the gritty, unkempt backdrop of the Brooklyn skyline. It was the kind of evening that felt heavy with the promise of something profound—or, if you were unlucky, catastrophic.

"I can't believe we're here," I said, my voice betraying the nervous tension curling in my gut. It was a simple enough statement, but the weight of it settled like an anchor in my chest. No one ever truly expects to be in a situation like this. The artifact was too much, too dangerous. It was the kind of thing that made people disappear without a trace. And here we were, walking straight toward it.

Gabriel gave a small, tight smile, his lips barely curving in a way that made me wonder if I had imagined it. "It's a little late for second thoughts, don't you think?"

I glanced over at him, the sharpness of his words catching me off guard. It wasn't like him to be flippant, but then again, we weren't dealing with anything ordinary. A century-old artifact buried beneath layers of secrecy and betrayal, whispered about in the deepest corners of occult societies. And Gabriel had been at the center of it all. His connection to the past was too strong for him to walk away now, especially when his involvement in this was what had drawn me into its mess to begin with.

Amara's words from earlier played like a record stuck in my head, the reminder of the cost hanging in the air. "Every choice has its price." The words seemed to reverberate through the cracks of the warehouse, mocking my every step. But I couldn't back down. Not now. Not when we were so close.

I pulled the strap of my bag tighter over my shoulder, forcing my legs to move, one step at a time. The asphalt beneath us was cracked and uneven, a reflection of the decay that had long settled into this forgotten corner of the city. The world had been waiting for us, and now, the past was finally catching up with us both.

"I didn't think you'd come with me," I said quietly, glancing sideways at Gabriel. He had never been one for sentimentality, for complicating things with words that didn't matter. But then again, I'd never expected him to be so... present. Every step he took was one I had to follow, but this was no longer about chasing down a story or hunting an artifact. It was about something more—something far too deep and terrifying to fully understand.

Gabriel met my gaze, the usual guarded look in his eyes now softening just enough for me to see a flicker of something vulnerable. But it was gone as quickly as it had appeared, leaving behind only the cool exterior of the man who had never let me in.

"Did you think I would leave you to handle it alone?" he asked, his voice smooth, yet carrying a hint of something unspoken. "That's not how this works."

There was something in his words—something buried beneath the surface. It wasn't just the artifact we were after. It wasn't even just the shadowy figures who were tracking us. It was the unspoken bond we shared. Whether I wanted to admit it or not, we had crossed into a territory where loyalties were no longer about the simple things. They were about survival. About fate. And about the very real possibility that one or both of us might not make it out of this alive.

We reached the door of the warehouse, its rusted hinges groaning in protest as Gabriel pushed it open. The dim light of the street lamps barely penetrated the thick, oppressive darkness inside, and the air smelled like mildew and old metal. The only sound was the shuffle of our feet against the dust-covered floor.

"This is where it all ends," I whispered, even though I didn't believe it. Somehow, I knew that whatever we were about to face inside, this wasn't the end. It was only the beginning of something far larger than we could comprehend.

Gabriel didn't respond at first. He was too busy scanning the space, his hand resting near the holster at his side. I wondered, not for the first time, whether I could trust him. But there was no time for doubt now. The closer we got to the artifact, the clearer it became that whatever connection Gabriel had to this place, it was tangled up in far more than just our current predicament. It was as if the city itself had a pulse—a heartbeat that mirrored our own.

"I don't know what we're walking into," I said, the words slipping from my mouth before I could stop them. There was a hesitation in the air now, something palpable. I wasn't sure if it was coming from him or from me. Maybe both of us were too tangled in our own histories to see what was coming.

"I do," Gabriel said, his voice a little too steady, a little too certain.

Before I could ask him to elaborate, we heard the sound. Faint at first, but unmistakable. A creak of wood. A shuffle of feet. And then—whispers. A hundred, no, a thousand voices, all murmuring in a language I didn't understand. Not yet.

We weren't alone.

The whispers grew louder, curling around the air like tendrils of smoke, thin and insidious. I could almost taste them—sour, like the aftertaste of cheap whiskey on the back of my tongue. Gabriel had drawn his gun, his knuckles white against the cold metal, but his gaze was locked on the far end of the warehouse, where the darkness seemed to pulse with a life of its own. Every nerve in my body screamed at me to run. And yet, I stayed. Maybe I was more like him than I cared to admit—compelled by a force I couldn't explain, tied to this twisted fate by a thread that felt more like a noose every passing second.

"Do you hear that?" I asked, keeping my voice steady, even though my heart was hammering in my chest. There were too many of them, too many voices overlapping, each one layered with an edge of desperation, as if something—someone—was fighting to break free.

Gabriel's lips tightened, but he didn't respond. He didn't need to. The weight of the situation was heavy on both of us, more unspoken than any words could convey. This wasn't just about the artifact anymore; it was about something deeper, something older. And I had no idea what was lurking in the shadows, but I knew Gabriel did. The question was whether he would tell me before it was too late.

We stepped further into the warehouse, the floor creaking beneath our boots like a living thing, groaning in protest as if it, too, sensed what we were about to disturb. The whispers became clearer, but now they weren't just voices—they were murmurs, choked and suffocated, like ghosts trying to claw their way back to the world of the living.

I wasn't sure what I expected to see when we rounded the corner, but it certainly wasn't what lay ahead. The room stretched out in front of us like some macabre cathedral, its vaulted ceilings nearly lost in the darkness above. The only light came from the flickering bulb in the far corner, casting a sickly glow over the room and illuminating the stone pedestal at the center.

It wasn't the artifact itself that caught my attention first, though. It was the figure standing in front of it, draped in a cloak so black it swallowed the dim light around it.

I stopped dead in my tracks, my breath catching in my throat. There was something undeniably familiar about the figure, something that twisted in the pit of my stomach.

"Gabriel," I whispered, more to myself than to him, but he heard me anyway.

"I know," he said, his voice low, almost drowned out by the increasing hum of the voices. But the figure had already turned, and in that moment, I realized I was staring at a ghost—a ghost that had once been very much alive.

"Amara," I said, the word falling from my lips with the same reverence as a prayer.

Her eyes, now a piercing, almost unnatural shade of green, locked onto mine. She didn't speak, but there was an understanding between us—one that had always been there, buried deep beneath layers of time and mystery.

She took a step forward, her movements fluid, almost graceful, despite the stark blackness that now surrounded her. "You're here," she said, her voice like velvet, smooth but laced with something darker beneath. "You should not have come, not yet."

I could feel Gabriel's tension beside me, the way his muscles coiled like a spring, ready to snap. But I couldn't bring myself to look at him. My focus was entirely on Amara, the woman who had once guarded the artifact with a fierceness I could barely comprehend. The same woman who had just told me that this—this moment—was my story now.

"What are you doing here?" I demanded, my voice coming out stronger than I intended.

She didn't flinch, didn't react the way I expected. Instead, she smiled—a smile that didn't reach her eyes, one that seemed too practiced, too knowing. "I've done my part. The artifact is not mine to guard anymore."

"But you..." I trailed off, my mind struggling to keep up with the pieces of the puzzle that were rapidly shifting out of place. "You said you were the guardian."

"I was," she replied, her gaze drifting toward Gabriel, then back to me. "But time changes things, as you well know. You, too, are bound to it now." Her smile faded, and there was a sadness in her eyes that I hadn't seen before, an exhaustion that seemed to have settled deep in her bones.

Gabriel's voice cut through the tension, sharp as glass. "What's going on, Amara?"

She didn't immediately respond, her eyes flicking to the pedestal. It was there, glowing faintly under the dim light, that the artifact waited. It was an unassuming object—smooth, like a river stone, but there was something about it that made my skin prickle. Something ancient, something that should have stayed buried.

"Who's been protecting it now?" Gabriel asked, his tone betraying his suspicion.

Amara's lips curled into something that wasn't quite a smile but more of a grimace. "You think the artifact needs protection? No, Gabriel." Her eyes locked with his. "It has been the one protecting us."

The words hit me like a slap. "What do you mean by that?"

She turned to face the artifact fully now, and for a moment, I swore the air around us shifted, thickened, as though the very room had exhaled. "It has chosen you," she said softly, her voice echoing through the cavernous space.

"Chosen?" My voice was hoarse, barely a whisper, as the realization began to sink in.

Gabriel stepped forward, his eyes hard, intense. "What do you mean, chosen?"

But Amara's answer came not with words, but with the subtle shift of the air around the artifact. And as I stared, wide-eyed, at the glowing object before me, I knew that whatever had been guarding it for centuries, whatever had been waiting—wasn't finished yet.

The air in the warehouse seemed to thicken, as if the very walls were closing in around us, the old stones groaning under some ancient weight. It wasn't the soft scrape of the floor beneath our feet or the incessant hum of the flickering light overhead that had my skin prickling—it was the palpable sense of waiting, of something not yet revealed, but inevitably approaching. Amara's words had carved themselves into my thoughts, echoes that grew louder with each passing second.

"The artifact has chosen you."

I glanced at Gabriel, his jaw clenched, his usual composure slipping just enough for me to see the slight tremor in his hand as he gripped the gun. He wasn't afraid of much—if anything at all—but this? This was something else. It wasn't just the artifact; it was the invisible thread that bound us to it, the sense that it wasn't just a thing, but a force. A living, breathing entity waiting for us to make our move.

"So what now?" I asked, the words tumbling out of me without thought, desperate for any hint of clarity.

Amara tilted her head slightly, as if the question was beneath her. "Now, you embrace what's been set in motion." Her smile was slow and cold, a little too knowing. "You'll understand in time."

I didn't have the luxury of time. Not here. Not now.

My gaze flicked to the pedestal once again, the soft glow of the artifact casting an eerie halo on the stone beneath it. There was a promise in that glow—one I wasn't sure I was ready to face. I could feel the pull, the way it seemed to reach out toward me, as if it recognized something in me that even I couldn't yet name.

"I don't think it's you we should be worried about," Gabriel muttered under his breath. I didn't need to ask who he meant. There was something in Amara's eyes—something ancient and untouchable—that made her an enigma. She wasn't just standing in the room with us; she was part of the shadows, part of the very air we breathed.

"And what's that supposed to mean?" I snapped, frustration lacing my words. I didn't have the time to pick through Gabriel's cryptic statements. Not when there was something far worse lurking in the wings. I could feel it now—the low rumble of something waiting, something alive and angry.

Amara's eyes flashed, the faintest glimmer of amusement in her gaze. "You have no idea what you're dealing with, do you?"

I wanted to retort, wanted to make her explain, but the words died in my throat when the lights above us flickered once more, plunging us into a darkness so deep it felt as if the world had exhaled and forgotten to inhale. It was the kind of dark that clung to your skin, seeped into your bones, made you feel as if the ground beneath you was shifting.

"Gabriel," I whispered, my breath catching in my chest. My voice sounded thin in the vast space, swallowed by the silence that followed. "What's happening?"

"Stay close," he ordered, his voice like steel. It wasn't a suggestion; it was a command. And as much as I hated it, I followed it without question, stepping closer to him.

We stood in the shadows for what felt like an eternity, but no time seemed to pass at all. Then, as suddenly as the darkness had fallen, it lifted—only this time, the air was heavier, charged with an almost electric tension. And that's when I saw it.

A figure—no, not a figure, but a presence—had materialized in front of the artifact. It wasn't solid, not entirely, but it wasn't some apparition, either. It was like a shadow given form, shifting in and out of focus, its edges flickering like a flame caught in the wind. The whispers had stopped, replaced now by a low, guttural sound that made the hairs on the back of my neck stand on end. It was as if the air itself had taken a breath, waiting.

"What is that?" I asked, my voice barely more than a rasp. The figure didn't answer, but something about it felt familiar. It felt... wrong, in a way I couldn't put into words. There was no question in my mind anymore—this wasn't just an artifact. It wasn't just some piece of forgotten history. It was a beacon. A magnet for whatever that thing was.

Gabriel didn't answer me. Instead, he stepped forward, the muscles in his body taut with some unspoken intention. I wanted to stop him, to shout out for him to wait, but the words were lodged in my throat, suffocating me.

I had the sense, deep in my gut, that this moment—the one we were caught in right now—was a crossroads. One wrong move, and we would be swallowed whole.

"Amara," I said, the name more of a plea than a question. "What's going on?"

She didn't answer immediately. Instead, she took a slow step toward the figure, her gaze never leaving it. Her voice, when it came, was calm—too calm. "It's time for the truth to come to light. Everything you've been running from, all the pieces that didn't make sense...they've been leading you here."

"I'm not running from anything," I snapped, the words sharp with frustration. But she wasn't listening. She was already lost in whatever vision the figure had shown her. Whatever truth had been revealed.

Suddenly, the figure moved. Its form stretched and twisted in ways that didn't make sense, like something caught between worlds. It reached out, toward me, and I froze, my pulse thundering in my ears.

"Stay back!" Gabriel shouted, his voice finally breaking the tension. But it was too late.

The figure's hand, or what passed for a hand, brushed against my arm. A cold, bone-deep chill spread from the point of contact, a burning frost that felt as if it were seeping into my very soul.

And then, just as suddenly as it had appeared, the figure vanished.

The warehouse was silent again, save for the sound of our breathing—shallow, erratic.

But something had changed. The artifact, no longer glowing with a soft light, now pulsed with an ominous, rhythmic thrum, as if it had begun its countdown. Time had run out. And the only thing left to do was face the consequences of our choices.

I turned to Gabriel, but his expression had shifted. Gone was the determined man I had stood beside. In his place was someone who had seen something—something he wasn't ready to share.

"Gabriel?" My voice wavered, unsure now, unsure of everything.

He didn't answer.

Instead, his eyes flicked toward the far corner of the warehouse, where the shadows seemed to grow deeper, darker.

And that's when I realized—the worst part hadn't even begun.

Chapter 40: Bonds Forged in Fire

The city hummed with the kind of quiet urgency that only a place steeped in history can carry. Baltimore, with its labyrinth of narrow streets, crooked rowhouses, and the occasional flash of neon from a dive bar that seemed to exist outside the laws of time, had a way of making you feel like you were constantly on the edge of something—an unknown, a possibility, or maybe just the impending storm. It was the kind of place where things happened without asking permission, and today, as Gabriel and I navigated the crowded docks, it felt like we were being drawn into one of those things.

The salty scent of the Chesapeake Bay mixed with the burnt leather of Gabriel's jacket, a reminder of how close we had become over the past few weeks. We had stopped pretending that the world was only about the artifact, the elusive thing we had chased across states, through forgotten towns, and into dead ends. That pursuit had changed us, but in a way that felt like a delicate, invisible thread pulling us together.

Gabriel glanced over at me as we made our way past a group of dock workers hauling crates onto an aging freighter. His smile was half-hidden beneath the weight of unspoken words, the kind of smile that made you want to lean in and catch the rest of the sentence he wasn't saying. I caught myself, once again, thinking how little I knew about him. It wasn't just the history of the artifact that was unfolding between us; it was him. And that scared me more than I cared to admit.

"What's going through that head of yours?" he asked, his voice a mix of challenge and amusement, his eyes scanning the crowds, the tired hustle of the waterfront.

I fought the urge to roll my eyes. "Do you ever wonder how it is that every single time we make a plan, it immediately falls apart?" I bit back a smile, knowing he'd catch on to my sarcasm.

He looked at me sideways, eyes narrowing with the kind of familiarity that made me feel like we'd known each other a lifetime instead of just weeks. "The plan doesn't fall apart, Charlie," he said, drawing my nickname out with a smirk. "It just... adapts."

We both knew he wasn't just talking about the hunt for the artifact anymore. Our entire partnership had adapted, bent and reshaped by whatever strange pull had latched onto us from the beginning. There was a pull, no doubt about it—something deeper, messier, and, at the same time, more precise than the mechanics of a well-oiled plan. I felt it at the tips of my fingers, and when I glanced down at my wrist, the mark—the same one that had started as a faint impression, almost unnoticeable—burned hotter now, as though it had its own agenda.

"You're quiet," Gabriel added, his voice low, almost too casual. He was trying to read me. I could tell. And I had no idea if I wanted him to.

I swallowed, knowing that the truth wasn't something I could give him—not here, not now. "Just thinking."

His eyes softened for a moment before his jaw tightened. We were walking toward a warehouse, the final destination of our journey—or at least what we thought was the final stop. The wooden doors loomed ahead, marked with faded symbols and the thick grime of saltwater.

Inside, the air was thick with dust and the weight of things long forgotten. The warehouse stretched out in front of us, its rafters creaking in the soft breeze coming through the cracks in the walls. Boxes were stacked haphazardly in the corners, some toppled over as if in a hurry to be forgotten. But the moment we stepped inside, the burn in my wrist intensified.

"Something's wrong," I said, my voice barely above a whisper.

Gabriel stopped in his tracks, his hand going instinctively to the gun at his side, but not pulling it out. His senses were sharper than mine, though I had a way of knowing when the air felt wrong.

"Right," he muttered, voice tight. "But you're not the only one who's been feeling this." He rubbed the back of his neck, a gesture that betrayed his calm exterior.

We moved deeper into the warehouse, every creak of the floor beneath our boots sounding like a warning. At the far end of the room, hidden in the shadows, a figure emerged.

I didn't need to see the face to know who it was. But Gabriel's posture shifted, just slightly, enough to indicate he recognized them too.

"Didn't think you'd be the one to find me here, Gabriel," the figure said, voice low and gravelly.

I clenched my fists at my sides, fingers tingling from the pressure of the mark on my wrist. "You should have stayed hidden, Titus."

Titus didn't answer right away. Instead, he took a step forward, his heavy boots thudding on the floor, and the dim light caught his profile. His dark hair was longer than I remembered, wild, like he'd been running from something, or someone. His eyes—once sharp and calculating—seemed dulled by exhaustion.

"Don't worry, I'm not here for trouble," he said, though the words felt more like a concession than an assurance. "But the artifact? It's not just in your hands anymore, Charlie. And it's not going to stay there."

Gabriel stiffened beside me, and I knew this wasn't going to end the way we'd hoped. We had come this far, pushing our luck, clinging to the idea that we could control the chaos. But now, in the dim light of that warehouse, the weight of our quest pressed on us with a force that could no longer be ignored.

"You know what this means," Gabriel said, his voice dark with the kind of tension that only a handful of people could understand.

Titus nodded, his lips curling into something between a grimace and a smile. "I do."

The tension in the air thickened, pressing against my chest like the weight of an ocean, relentless and suffocating. Titus stood there, arms crossed over his chest, the faintest smirk playing on his lips, as if he was amused by the fact that we had come this far, only to be blindsided at the very last moment. His words hung between us, unspoken promises and threats woven into every syllable.

Gabriel's stance remained rigid beside me, his hand twitching toward the edge of his jacket, where the outline of a weapon lingered just beneath the fabric. I knew the look in his eyes—it was the same one he wore when the world had forced him into a corner, where his options were few, and none of them good. It was that dangerous calm, the kind that made you think things would be handled with cold precision, but it was only the calm before the storm.

"So, you're just going to stroll in here and drop this little bomb, Titus?" I bit back the frustration bubbling up in my throat. "Tell me, do you always show up like this? Or is this just a special occasion?"

Titus chuckled, but there was no warmth in it. His eyes, usually sharp and calculating, flickered with a trace of something I couldn't quite place. "You've got a lot of fire, Charlie. Shame it's all going to burn out before you even realize it."

I felt the hair on the back of my neck rise. It wasn't just his words. It was the way his presence felt too heavy in the room, like something was about to crack. And as much as I hated to admit it, I couldn't shake the feeling that Titus wasn't just some rogue trying to throw a wrench in our plans. There was something bigger at play—something darker.

Gabriel took a slow step forward, his eyes narrowing as he scanned the room. "Where is it, Titus? The artifact."

Titus didn't respond immediately. Instead, he took a deep breath, as though the weight of whatever had been running through his mind had caught up with him. And then, without warning, he shifted his weight, pulling something from beneath his jacket—a small, unmarked box, weathered and worn at the edges.

My heart stopped. Not because of the box itself, but because the symbol on it—the one etched into its side—was unmistakable. It was the same as the mark on my wrist.

Gabriel cursed under his breath, his eyes locked onto the box. "You're playing a dangerous game, Titus."

"I don't play," he replied, his voice quiet but edged with finality. "I survive."

There it was—the undeniable truth. Titus had never been one to play by anyone's rules, least of all ours. And that box—whatever it contained—wasn't just a clue or a piece of the puzzle. It was the heart of the storm, the thing that had set everything in motion. And now, standing in front of me, in the shadows of this forgotten warehouse, it felt like the final nail in the coffin.

I stepped closer, unable to tear my gaze away from the box. "You didn't come here to stop us. You came here to make sure we didn't get there first."

Titus's lips curled, the faintest hint of a smirk tugging at the corner of his mouth. "Smart. But you're wrong about one thing. I didn't come here to stop you. I came here to offer you a choice."

Gabriel and I exchanged a glance, but there was no time for the unspoken conversation that passed between us. The air in the warehouse seemed to pulse, like we were standing at the edge of a precipice.

"A choice?" Gabriel repeated, his voice low. "What kind of choice?"

Titus took a step forward, the box still clenched in his hand. "You can walk away, right now, and forget everything. Let it go. Live your lives. Or you can follow me, and finish what you started. But be warned—this time, there will be no turning back."

The weight of his words hung in the air like smoke, swirling and suffocating. I could feel the mark on my wrist burning even brighter, like it was pushing me toward a decision I wasn't sure I was ready to make.

Gabriel's voice was steady, but I could hear the underlying current of urgency. "Why should we trust you?"

Titus looked at him like he was amusing—like the answer was so obvious, it wasn't even worth saying. "Trust is a luxury, Gabriel. I'm offering something far more valuable than trust. I'm offering a chance to finish this, to take the power for yourselves, before it's too late."

"Power," I repeated, the word sour on my tongue. "You don't get to decide what we do with it."

Titus's eyes flicked to the mark on my wrist, and for a moment, there was something almost—genuine in his expression. "You're right. I don't. But the power of the artifact isn't something you can just control. Not without consequences."

I wanted to argue, to tell him that we had made it this far and we would finish it—whatever it was. But something inside me stilled, a voice whispering doubts I couldn't ignore. The mark was no longer just a symbol. It was alive, pulling at me, urging me toward something I couldn't yet understand.

And as I stood there, in that forgotten corner of the city where the past and present collided, I realized that whatever choice we made next, we wouldn't be able to outrun the consequences. Not this time.

Gabriel reached out, his fingers brushing mine, the simple touch grounding me when everything else felt on the edge of unraveling. The burn on my wrist flared again, and I could feel the weight of the decision hanging between us.

"I think we've already crossed the point of no return," Gabriel said softly, his gaze locking with mine. "But let's make sure we're ready for what comes next."

Titus's smirk deepened. "Good. Because what comes next, you won't be able to stop."

The words echoed in the warehouse, drowning out the noise of the city outside. And in that moment, I realized that we were no longer just chasing an artifact. We were chasing something far darker—and far more dangerous—than we could have ever imagined.

The flickering yellow light overhead did little to ease the sudden chill that had settled in my bones. The warehouse had grown even darker in the last few minutes, as if it, too, could sense the shift in the air. Titus had yet to move, the box still hanging heavily in his hand like some grotesque offering, and I realized with a jolt that I didn't know if I was ready to face whatever lay inside. Gabriel's presence next to me was a silent anchor, but his own unease was palpable, the shift in his posture signaling that we were no longer on familiar ground.

Titus had always been a wildcard—unpredictable, dangerous—but there was something else now. Something colder in his eyes, something that told me he wasn't just offering a choice. He was presenting us with a trap, wrapped in the guise of an opportunity, and I had no doubt it was one we wouldn't walk away from unscathed.

The silence stretched between us like a taut wire, and I found myself caught in the tension of it. Gabriel's hand brushed mine again, this time a touch meant to steady himself as much as me. The burn on my wrist was sharp now, a searing sensation that threatened to swallow me whole. I could feel it pulling, tugging at my very core, whispering promises of things I wasn't sure I wanted.

I glanced at Gabriel, his brow furrowed, the muscles in his jaw tight as if he were trying to hold back something dangerous, something far darker than the situation at hand. "What happens if we walk away, Titus?" I asked, my voice steadier than I felt.

Titus's eyes flicked to the box in his hands, then back to me, his lips twisting into a mocking smile. "You won't," he said simply. "You think you're in control here, but the truth is, none of us are. You can either accept that, or you can try to run, but you'll never get far."

There it was, the undercurrent of threat he'd been circling around this whole time. His words didn't land on me like a challenge but more like a curse, as though he knew something we didn't. Something that would turn the very ground beneath us into quicksand if we weren't careful.

Gabriel took a step forward, his expression unreadable now, but I could see the tension in his shoulders, the muscles coiled tight beneath his shirt. "And if we choose the third option? The one where we don't just stand here and listen to you yammer on about choices?"

Titus's grin widened, but it wasn't one of humor. It was the kind of grin that made you wonder how far you could trust someone who was about to deliver a fatal blow, only to watch you bleed out slowly. "The third option," he said slowly, savoring the moment, "is to see just how far you're willing to go to finish what you started. And trust me, it's farther than you think."

A cold gust of wind rattled the windows of the warehouse, the sudden chill making my skin prickle. The mark on my wrist flared again, a sharp, painful throb that seemed to echo in my chest. It was almost as if it was warning me, pushing me toward something

I couldn't understand—something I wasn't sure I wanted to understand.

"Enough games, Titus," I snapped, my patience worn thin. "Tell us what you want."

He glanced at the box again, and for the first time, there was a flicker of something resembling hesitation in his eyes. "I want you to see what you're really dealing with. You think you're after the artifact, but it's been following you. You've been chosen, whether you like it or not."

I felt a rush of heat in my veins, and before I could stop myself, I moved toward him. Gabriel's hand shot out to grab my arm, but I yanked away from him, driven by an instinct I couldn't quite shake. "Chosen?" I echoed, my voice shaking now. "Chosen for what?"

Titus exhaled slowly, the weight of his next words settling between us like a trap ready to spring. "Chosen to wield it, Charlie. To control it. But there's a cost. Always a cost."

I could feel Gabriel's breath catch behind me, and his voice was barely a whisper when he said, "You're lying. You're playing us."

Titus shook his head, his gaze sharp as a blade. "It's the truth. And you'll see for yourselves soon enough. Once you open that box, there's no going back."

I stared at the box, my heart pounding so loudly in my chest I thought it might shatter the fragile silence that had fallen. The mark on my wrist burned, and with each pulse, the words felt heavier, more undeniable.

Gabriel was still beside me, but I knew we were on the edge of something far more dangerous than either of us had anticipated. The power Titus spoke of—whatever it was—was real, and it was tied to me in ways I couldn't fully understand. The artifact, the mark, the weight of it all—it was all converging in this one moment, this one impossible decision.

"You really think we're just going to follow you into this?" I said, my voice shaking but defiant. "You think we're that stupid?"

Titus didn't flinch. "You don't have a choice," he said, his tone final, almost too sure. "You're already too deep. The only question is whether you'll survive the answers you find."

And then, before either of us could react, he opened the box.

The light that poured from it was blinding, a sudden explosion of brightness that felt like it was tearing through the very air. I stumbled back, my hands raised instinctively to shield my eyes, but it was no use. The glow consumed everything, swallowing up the shadows, the grime of the warehouse, and even the very air I breathed.

When the light finally faded, I blinked against the afterimage, and then I saw it—something that made the ground beneath me feel like it had cracked open.

Titus was gone.

But in his place was a shape, dark and pulsing with a strange, unnatural energy. And I knew, in that moment, that nothing—nothing—would ever be the same again.

Chapter 41: The Final Confrontation

The city felt like it was holding its breath. The skyscrapers loomed above, casting long shadows over the streets, but it wasn't the evening twilight that made the air so dense. It was the weight of what was about to unfold, pressing against me like a thousand tons of concrete. New York, with its pulsing heart of ambition, never seemed quieter, as if even the endless traffic and ceaseless chatter of pedestrians could sense the storm brewing in the air.

Gabriel stood beside me, silent and tense, his eyes scanning the horizon as though he could see the battle we were about to fight even before it had begun. His jaw was clenched, the muscles working beneath his skin, and I could feel the heat of his body next to mine, a constant, reassuring presence. The kind of presence that, in times like these, could mean the difference between life and death.

"It's here," I said, the words tasting sharp on my tongue. I didn't need to look at him to know that Gabriel was already several steps ahead in his mind, calculating the angles, the moves. That's how we worked. I would feel the threat, and he would strategize the fight. The problem with this one, though, was that I didn't have a strategy. All I had was instinct, and even that felt precariously thin against the force we were about to face.

Gabriel's gaze shifted toward me, dark eyes locking with mine. There was something in them, a softness—an unspoken promise to shield me from the worst of it. But I wasn't so sure he could. Not this time.

"Be ready," he murmured, his voice low and steady, the kind of voice that could calm storms and rattle bones in equal measure. "We're not just fighting the artifact anymore. We're fighting her."

I swallowed, the name hanging in the air like a weight. "Her," I repeated, almost tasting the bitterness on my tongue.

Clara Westbrook. The name sent a shiver down my spine every time it came up, but today, it felt like a full-body shudder. She was more than just a name now. She was the enemy. She had become the thing I dreaded most. A force of nature wrapped in human skin, a woman who had taken everything I thought I understood about the artifact and turned it into something monstrous.

"Do you think we can stop her?" I asked, my voice barely above a whisper, though I knew he'd hear every word.

His response was a sharp exhale, a brief flash of tension in his face before it smoothed out into the carefully crafted expression I was becoming too familiar with. The one that said he wasn't sure, but he wasn't going to let me see the doubt in his eyes.

"We don't have a choice." His fingers brushed mine, quick and light, but it was enough to remind me that we weren't just in this battle for the artifact. We were in this because we couldn't walk away from it. We never could.

I turned, trying to steady my breath. The city around us seemed to blur, as though reality itself was bending in anticipation of the chaos to come. The last few weeks had been a blur of running, dodging, and hiding, piecing together fragments of a puzzle that I had no idea how to complete. But it wasn't the artifact that had me twisted in knots—it was Clara. Her face, the memory of her cruel smile, the way she had manipulated the power of the artifact to bind it to her. It wasn't just about power anymore. It was about control, about bending everyone and everything to her will.

The air shifted again, a prickling sensation sweeping over my skin, the hairs on the back of my neck standing at attention. I could feel it, the weight of her presence growing closer. The streets seemed to close in around us as the sound of footsteps echoed down the alleyway ahead.

"Ready?" Gabriel asked, his voice low but sharp.

I didn't answer right away. Instead, I took a moment to gather the steadying breath that had become my ritual before every battle, before every confrontation. It wasn't about the odds anymore. It was about survival. For me, for Gabriel, and for everything we'd fought to protect.

"I'll follow your lead," I said, my words edged with the kind of resolve I hadn't known I was capable of.

Gabriel didn't say anything more. He didn't need to. With a swift, fluid motion, he led the way, his steps purposeful, as if he had already mapped the fight out in his mind, down to the last inch of ground. I followed closely behind, the rhythm of our movements synced, our connection a quiet understanding that needed no words.

As we approached the alley, the shadows deepened, the air thickening with a tension that made the hairs on my arms prickle. Clara stood at the far end, framed by the harsh light of a flickering streetlamp. Her eyes, bright and predatory, locked onto mine as though she had been waiting for this moment just as long as I had.

"Well," she said, her voice smooth and confident, as though she were enjoying the spectacle of our impending destruction. "I was wondering when you two would show up."

Her eyes narrowed, and in that instant, the air around us seemed to crackle with raw, uncontrolled power. It wasn't just the artifact anymore. Clara had fully integrated herself with it, became one with its energy. And that made her something far more dangerous than I had ever imagined.

"Let's get this over with," she added with a smile that was more like a sneer.

The ground beneath us seemed to tremble, a low rumble vibrating up from the earth itself. I could feel the weight of her energy, coiling in the air, wrapping around us, squeezing the breath out of my lungs. My heart pounded in my chest, but I wasn't going to back down now. We'd come this far.

The world around me held its breath for a moment, suspended between the present and whatever future Clara was about to dictate. Her smile, sharp and condescending, didn't falter as the space between us seemed to twist and warp with the weight of her control. The artifact thrummed behind her like a pulse in the darkness, a low hum that resonated deep in my chest, like something ancient had awakened. A force so potent, so primal, it made every hair on my body stand on end.

"Go on, then," Clara said, her voice like honey dripping from a blade. "I'm waiting."

I could feel Gabriel's body beside me, taut, ready for whatever she was planning. The familiarity of his presence was a small comfort in this swirling chaos, but it wasn't enough. It wouldn't be enough if we didn't play our cards right.

"You've gone too far," I said, my voice trembling with the quiet rage I'd been holding onto for too long. "You don't know what you're dealing with."

Clara laughed, a sound that made the air itself vibrate in disdain. "Oh, I know exactly what I'm dealing with. You're the ones who don't get it. You're still playing by rules. But I've won, haven't I?" Her eyes flared as she extended her hands toward the artifact, and the air around us seemed to bend, crackle with energy. She was no longer just a woman standing in front of me. She was a force, a conduit, and all I could do was watch as she manipulated the power she'd bound herself to.

The ground beneath us groaned as the streetlights flickered and blinked, one after another, until the entire alleyway was bathed in an unsettling, flickering half-light. My heart was racing now, thudding in my chest as I instinctively stepped forward.

Gabriel held me back with a gentle hand, his fingers like iron wrapped around my wrist. "Wait," he hissed. "Don't provoke her."

It was too late, though. I could feel the pulse of the artifact in my bones now, a distant echo of its dark promise. I had seen this power before, had felt its grip on me. But what Clara had done was so much worse. She wasn't just a victim of it; she was its master.

"You've made a mistake," Gabriel added, his voice calm, though the tension radiating off him was palpable. "You think this power will save you, but it will consume you. It's already started."

Her eyes flashed with a sharp, mocking gleam. "It's already too late for me, Gabriel. But I'm not the one who should be worried." Her smile widened as she stepped forward, almost in slow motion, as though relishing the moment. The air around us thickened, the weight of the artifact's energy pressing down on my chest. It felt like a storm was coming, but I couldn't tell from which direction.

Without warning, Clara lifted her hand, and the world seemed to stop. The energy she was manipulating bent the light, casting strange shadows against the walls as if the very laws of physics were at her command. I could see it in her face—the sheer, unfiltered delight of power. She reveled in it. She lived for it.

I had seen it in others before. The moment they tasted control, the moment they realized they could break the world to their will, the power corrupts them. And Clara had already crossed that line.

"You're nothing more than a puppet with a broken string," I shot back, my own words coming out colder than I intended. There was no way to sugarcoat this. We weren't here to negotiate. We were here to stop her. To save what was left of the world before she tore it apart.

Clara's laugh was light, almost airy, but it held a dangerous edge. "You're so predictable, Kendall. I think I'll enjoy watching you try to fight back. All of this power, and you're still the same girl from the warehouse. The one who couldn't even protect herself."

ECLIPSE GATE 351

Her words hit like a slap, and for a brief moment, I could feel the sting of her truth, even as I fought to steady my breath. I wasn't that girl anymore. The artifact had taught me that much. Gabriel had taught me that much. But even so, there was a tremor deep in my core that I couldn't shake.

Gabriel stepped forward, his eyes locked on Clara with the kind of focus that could slice through stone. He was always the tactician, the strategist, the calm in the chaos. But tonight, I could see the flicker of something else in his gaze. It wasn't just determination—it was desperation. The same desperation that gnawed at me, the same desperation that kept us from turning away.

"You're wrong," Gabriel said, his voice hard and steady. "This ends now."

The words barely left his mouth before Clara snapped her fingers, and the ground beneath us shattered with an audible crack, like a broken mirror splintering into a thousand pieces. The blast of energy hit us like a wave crashing against the shore, throwing us backward. My breath left me in a rush, the world spinning as the concrete scraped against my skin. I could feel the sting of the cuts, but there was no time to register the pain.

I pushed myself to my feet, my heart pounding in my chest as I struggled to regain my balance. Gabriel was already there, moving with a fluidity that made me wonder if he was ever truly human, or if he had been born with the same unnatural grace as the artifact itself. He was by my side, pulling me up before I even had the chance to blink.

"Stay close," he muttered, though I didn't need the reminder. We both knew what was at stake.

Clara was laughing again, but this time, there was an edge of frustration in her tone. "You think you can stop me?" she spat, her voice dripping with venom. "This power is mine, and there's nothing you can do about it."

The street around us flickered and swayed, the buildings warping like figures in a dream, as if the city itself were being torn apart by her will. But even amidst the chaos, there was one thing I knew for certain: she was underestimating us. And that would be her biggest mistake.

The air was thick with the hum of her power, the electric crackle that curled through the alley like a living thing. Clara's laughter echoed in my ears, sharp and cruel, as though she had already won. The concrete beneath our feet groaned as though even the buildings were being crushed under the weight of what she was doing. It was impossible to ignore the sheer volume of force she wielded. It wasn't just the artifact anymore—it was her. And she was using it as a puppet master uses strings.

Gabriel was already moving, his body as fluid as a panther's. He didn't hesitate—he never did. He swept me behind him in one smooth motion, positioning himself between me and Clara like a human shield, his jaw set, his eyes like steel.

"Stay down," he said through gritted teeth, his voice clipped with an edge I wasn't used to. There was a certain finality in his words. This wasn't just a fight anymore. This was a decision, a line in the sand.

I opened my mouth to protest—because that was the last thing I wanted to do, hide while Gabriel took the brunt of this—but then Clara spoke again, and the words burned through the air, like a whip crack.

"You really think you can protect her?" Clara sneered, eyes narrowing. She was toying with us, twisting the knife as she stepped forward, her presence filling the alley. "You're both so predictable. Power isn't a toy, Gabriel. It's not something you can just put down when you're tired of it."

Her hands raised again, a shimmer of violet light radiating from her palms, and I knew the moment she unleashed whatever hell she had brewing, it would be more than we could handle.

"Clara, you're wrong," Gabriel said, stepping forward with a surety I envied. "Power is nothing without control."

It was then I saw it. The flicker in her eyes. The brief hesitation before the storm, like a thunderhead gathering strength, as if she were weighing his words. For a split second, I wondered if Gabriel was right—maybe she wasn't as untouchable as she seemed. Maybe, just maybe, there was something left of the woman I had once known beneath the layers of obsession and dark power. But then the moment was gone, and the storm broke.

A blinding pulse of light erupted from Clara, and the force of it slammed into us like a freight train, sending Gabriel and me sprawling to the ground. I felt the air burn in my lungs as the world tilted sideways. My body was screaming in protest as I tried to get my bearings, but the ground beneath me felt like it was shifting, the world turning upside down.

I pushed myself up, breath coming in sharp, ragged gasps. The city around us was barely recognizable. Buildings had crumbled, their frames contorted as if the very fabric of reality was being stretched and bent. The night sky had turned an unnatural shade of green, swirling ominously above us.

I blinked, trying to focus through the haze. Gabriel was already on his feet, though his movements were slower, as if he, too, was feeling the weight of Clara's power. I could see the strain on his face, the sweat on his brow. He was holding his ground—but barely. And I wasn't sure how much longer either of us could hold on.

Clara's eyes locked onto mine again, and this time there was no trace of hesitation. "You were always the weak one, Kendall," she said, her voice soft, almost pitying. "I could have saved you. I wanted to save you. But now... well, now it's too late."

I felt the words cut deep, far deeper than I wanted to admit. She wasn't wrong. I'd always been the one who couldn't keep up. Always the one in the shadows while others took the lead. But I wasn't that girl anymore. Not since I'd learned to hold my own against the darkness. Not since Gabriel had trusted me to stand beside him, not behind him.

I gritted my teeth, pushing away the sting of her words. "Maybe you've forgotten what it feels like to fight for something that actually matters," I snapped, my voice shaky but resolute. "You think you've won, Clara? You're wrong. This ends tonight."

With a snarl, Clara snapped her fingers again, and a surge of energy shot toward me, faster than I could react. But before it reached me, Gabriel was there, standing between us, his body glowing with the force of his own power. He raised a hand, and the energy collided with his shield, shattering into sparks that fizzled out in the air.

"Gabriel—!" I started, but he didn't respond, his focus entirely on Clara, his eyes fierce with a fire I had never seen in him before. His jaw clenched, his entire body vibrating with tension as he prepared for the next wave.

Clara smirked, clearly enjoying the spectacle. "You think you can stop me with that pathetic defense? You're wasting your time."

But something was different. The very air around us seemed to tremble, as though the universe itself was holding its breath. Gabriel's hand twitched, and for the briefest of moments, there was a crack—just a sliver—of light in the darkness. I couldn't quite place it, but it was there, a fleeting moment of clarity amidst the storm.

"Maybe it's time you learned something, Clara," Gabriel said, his voice steady, carrying a finality that made the hairs on my neck stand on end. He raised his hand again, and this time, the crack of light was wider, more pronounced, like something deep inside him was awakening.

But Clara wasn't backing down. Her hands shot out, her eyes alight with a manic gleam, and the force she unleashed this time was more than anything I had felt before. The ground trembled, the air sparked with energy, and a deafening roar echoed through the alley.

I took a step forward without thinking, driven by a mix of fear and something else, something deep within me that refused to let Clara win. This wasn't just a battle for power—it was a battle for our lives, for everything we had fought for.

And just as the two forces collided—Gabriel's light against Clara's storm—the world around us exploded into blinding white, leaving me suspended in the middle of a void.

And then, the darkness swallowed everything.

Chapter 42: A Love Revealed

I leaned against the rusted rail of the balcony, my fingers grazing the peeling paint, the cool evening air tangling my hair in unruly knots. The city below pulsed with life—taxis honking, people darting across streets, and the faint hum of distant conversations rising into the twilight. But here, above it all, the world felt different, almost suspended in time. The clutter of the streets seemed so far removed from the chaos in my head. And the only sound that mattered, the only sound I could hear clearly, was Gabriel's soft breathing beside me.

The man was a puzzle. He always had been. I had never known how to fit him into the neat corners of my life, or how to reconcile the distance he kept, the way he looked at me like I was a dangerous idea that could go up in flames at any moment. But there he was, standing close enough that our shoulders brushed, the weight of everything between us finally simmering to the surface.

"I don't think you understand how much I've been avoiding this," I said, the words tumbling out without warning. I hadn't planned to say them, but it seemed I had been holding onto them for far too long. The vulnerability in the air tonight wasn't just from the city, it was from us, too.

Gabriel glanced at me, his eyes darkened with something like regret. His jaw tightened as though he was trying to hold something back, a tension I could almost taste in the air. He didn't answer at first, just stared ahead at the skyline—those ugly glass towers that stood like silent witnesses to everything we had endured.

"I don't think I understand anything about this," he finally said, voice low, almost a whisper, but filled with weight. He turned to me then, his face illuminated by the soft glow of the streetlights below, and in that light, he looked so utterly...lost. "I didn't know what to do with you, with us. It's not the kind of thing you plan for."

I let out a short, bitter laugh. "You think I planned for it?" I shook my head, trying to fight the rush of emotion threatening to flood me. "What are we doing, Gabriel? Hiding behind all this...pretend indifference, like it's easier than just admitting that this—whatever this is—has been everything."

His eyes narrowed at my words, and for a moment, I wondered if I had overstepped, but then he took a step closer. I could feel the heat from his body even though the air around us was cooling. "You think it's been easy for me?" His voice dropped an octave, his tone growing sharp. "Every moment I've been near you, I've wanted to—" He cut himself off, as if the admission was too much even for him.

I met his gaze, holding it steady. "Wanted to what, Gabriel?"

His gaze flickered, betraying a hint of something raw, something vulnerable I rarely saw in him. "Wanted to make it right. Wanted to not hurt you in the end. Because I knew...I knew I'd end up doing exactly that. Hurting you."

The words hung between us, thick as smoke. I swallowed hard, trying to keep the sting of his admission from shattering everything. I wasn't sure I could survive it.

But the longer we stood there, wrapped in the tension of everything unsaid, the more I realized how much I had needed this. This moment. His truth, raw and unfiltered. It didn't matter that it was painful. It mattered that it was real.

I reached out, my hand brushing his wrist, just the smallest touch, but it was enough. Enough to break the wall between us. Enough to make him breathe again.

"We've both been avoiding it," I whispered, my fingers lingering on his skin as if I could anchor us in that one moment, like I could make the future seem less terrifying. "But now, here we are. No more running."

Gabriel let out a breath, and for the first time in what felt like forever, his eyes softened. "I don't know how to do this, but I'm willing to try."

That was the moment everything shifted. It wasn't the fireworks or the dramatic declarations, but the quiet, hesitant promise in his words. The vulnerability he had allowed himself to show me in that instant. It was everything.

"I'll hold you to that," I said, my voice firm, yet wrapped in something tender. The weight of everything we had shared—every decision, every choice, every fractured moment—suddenly felt like it could be rebuilt. Not perfectly, but enough. Enough for us to start again.

And so we did. Slowly. The world around us faded into nothing but the sound of our breathing and the soft murmur of the city as it continued to churn. There was no grand declaration, no applause. Just the two of us, here. Present. Together.

I wanted to pull away from him, just for a moment. The intensity in his eyes, the way the city seemed to press in around us—everything felt too close. But the temptation to stay, to not break this fragile thing between us, was stronger than my desire for space. He stood there, watching me as though he could read my mind, his fingers still tracing the outline of my wrist, a touch as gentle as the breeze that swirled through the alley behind us.

"You don't have to say anything else if you're not ready," Gabriel murmured, his voice low but threaded with a quiet, determined edge. He wasn't asking for permission, not exactly. He was just offering me the space I hadn't asked for but clearly needed.

"I'm not ready to let go of this," I said, the words tumbling out before I could stop them. It was funny how simple truths could come out sounding like confessions when they had been buried for so long.

He raised an eyebrow, that familiar, mischievous look flickering in his eyes. "Then why does it feel like we're both standing at the edge of something we're too afraid to jump into?"

I shook my head, laughing softly, trying to ignore the knot that had formed in my chest. "Because we are. We're standing right at the edge, and I'm scared to even move."

"Me too," he replied simply, his voice rough, as if admitting it was the hardest part of all. "But I think I've been scared long enough."

The air between us shifted then, a quiet understanding passing between us. No grand speeches, no promises. Just the kind of connection that couldn't be faked, couldn't be denied.

But of course, nothing ever comes easy, does it? Life is always ready to throw a curveball just when you think you have a handle on things.

A car screeched in the distance, pulling me back into the moment, and my phone buzzed in my pocket. I frowned, looking down at the screen, then back at Gabriel. "I've got to—" I started, my words trailing off as I saw the name flashing across the screen.

"What is it?" Gabriel asked, stepping closer as I hesitated.

I gave him a quick look, but I could already feel the weight of the conversation creeping back in. "It's... it's work. Something urgent."

He didn't protest, but his face tightened, just enough for me to notice. I could tell he hated that, hated the idea of this moment being interrupted. He had a point, of course. This should have been ours—ours to savor, ours to explore. But reality had a funny way of intruding.

"Do you mind?" I asked, already unlocking the screen and lifting the phone to my ear. Gabriel didn't answer, his eyes locked on me in a way that made my heart do an odd little flip.

I exhaled, pressing the phone to my ear. "Hello?"

The voice on the other end was a familiar one, and instantly, the tension in my shoulders returned. "We need to talk," the voice said, a little too calmly for my liking.

I swallowed hard, trying to shake off the sudden wave of anxiety. "What is it?" I asked, keeping my voice even, though the words tasted bitter on my tongue.

"There's been a shift in the project. They're reconsidering your role in it. We need to discuss options," the voice continued.

My stomach twisted. "Are you kidding me? I've been working my ass off for weeks, and now you're telling me—"

"Calm down," the voice interjected quickly. "We're just assessing things. No decisions have been made yet. But we want you to come in for a meeting first thing tomorrow morning. You'll have all the details then."

I didn't respond right away. The adrenaline in my veins was fizzing now, my heartbeat loud in my ears. I had been caught off guard, and that never boded well.

"Fine," I muttered, ending the call with more force than necessary. I turned to Gabriel, who was watching me with a piercing, concerned look, no trace of the earlier levity in his expression.

"Well, that was..." I began, struggling for the right word, but it didn't matter. Nothing seemed to make sense right now.

He stepped closer, a hand resting lightly on my arm, his eyes still intense. "What happened?"

"I'm being pulled back in. That was my boss, telling me about some project—no, some shift in direction. I don't even know. But I have to go in tomorrow morning." I looked up at him, the weight of the world in my voice. "I thought I was done with it all, Gabriel. I thought I was finally moving forward, but now it feels like I'm stuck in the same endless loop."

He didn't say anything at first, just stared at me for a long moment. I saw the way his jaw worked, as though he was chewing on the situation, deciding what to say. Finally, he spoke, his voice low and steady.

"Maybe this is the universe reminding you that you're stronger than you think. I know you've had enough of these projects, but if anyone can turn this around, it's you."

I felt a pang of emotion twist inside me. His words weren't just an attempt at encouragement; they were a truth that felt hard to swallow. He was right.

But he wasn't wrong in another way, either. The universe hadn't been kind to me lately, and I was tired. Tired of the endless juggling, tired of the constant balancing act that came with trying to make a living, trying to stay afloat in a world that was perpetually shifting beneath me.

I sighed deeply, leaning back against the balcony railing. "I don't know if I can keep doing this. Not like this. I need something more."

Gabriel gave a slow nod, understanding more than he probably let on. "Maybe this is your chance to figure out what that 'more' is."

The apartment felt like a foreign place in the aftermath of everything. The old floorboards creaked beneath my feet as I paced back and forth, the weight of the decision I had to make pressing into my chest. Gabriel had left, though not without offering some measure of comfort. His final words before stepping out the door were still echoing in my mind. "You don't have to do this alone," he had said, his voice low but unmistakably earnest. He was right, of course. But somehow, even with all the kindness he offered, I felt utterly alone.

I could hear the faint hum of the city below, but it didn't soothe me the way it usually did. Instead, it reminded me of all the chaos that waited outside these walls—the endless responsibilities, the uncertain future, the nagging sense of never quite being in control.

The phone call from my boss had been the catalyst, but it was more than just that. It was the culmination of everything I had worked for, every late night spent grinding through projects, every sacrifice I had made to get ahead. I had climbed a ladder, only to find that the view from the top wasn't all it was cracked up to be. And now, the universe had decided to knock me back down a few rungs. The meeting tomorrow felt like the final judgment. Was I still good enough to be in the game? Or had I reached my expiration date?

I picked up the glass of wine I had left on the counter, taking a sip without much thought, the liquid cold on my tongue but offering no real relief. I set the glass down with more force than I meant to, the clink of the glass against the counter echoing in the stillness. My thoughts swirled in a dizzying pattern, as though I was watching myself from the outside—observing a woman who had it all together one minute and was unraveling the next.

And then, there was Gabriel.

I let out a short, bitter laugh. His face, his touch, the warmth of his words—nothing about him felt simple or easy. Everything about him was complicated, layered with history and things left unsaid. And yet, in those quiet moments when the world fell away, I realized I couldn't imagine walking this road without him by my side. It terrified me more than anything else.

The doorbell rang, slicing through my thoughts. I froze, unsure of who could possibly be at my door at this hour. I glanced at the clock—well past midnight.

I wasn't expecting anyone.

I hesitated, the familiar rush of adrenaline coursing through me. Maybe it was nothing. Maybe it was the neighbor again, annoyed that I hadn't picked up my package earlier. I almost ignored it, but then the doorbell rang again, longer this time, insistent.

I exhaled sharply, moving toward the door, my heart now pounding in my chest. When I opened it, I wasn't prepared for what I saw.

Gabriel stood there, drenched from head to toe. His hair stuck to his forehead, and his jacket clung to him like a second skin. He looked as though he had just come from the middle of a storm. In a way, I suppose he had.

"I—" He started, but his words faltered as if he didn't know how to continue. He was close enough that I could feel the heat radiating from his body, a contrast to the chill of the rain that clung to him.

I could see it then—the raw emotion in his eyes, the vulnerability that mirrored my own. I didn't know what to say either. It wasn't the time for declarations or apologies. All I could do was stand there, holding the door open just wide enough to let him in.

"I know I said I'd give you space," he continued, his voice rough, "but I can't do it anymore. I can't leave things like this."

I stepped back, not trusting myself to say anything, and he stepped into the apartment without waiting for an invitation. I didn't mind. It felt like we were caught in a moment that neither of us could control, and for once, I didn't want to try.

"I'm not sure what you expect from me," I said softly, my voice strained, barely a whisper. "I've got enough to deal with already. Work, this project, this whole mess of a life I've been trying to hold together."

Gabriel looked down at me, his expression softening. "I'm not asking for you to fix it. I'm not asking you to make everything okay. But I'm asking you not to run from this. Not from me."

The words hung there, heavy and meaningful, and for the first time in so long, I wasn't sure if the right thing to do was to fight back or to just let go. His presence was a balm and a threat all at once.

"I don't know how to trust anyone anymore," I admitted, the words slipping from my lips before I could stop them. "I don't even trust myself half the time."

Gabriel's face softened, and he took a step closer, as though he knew exactly how fragile I was at that moment. "Then let me teach you," he whispered. "Let me show you how to trust, not just in me, but in yourself."

His voice, so calm, so steady, felt like the only thing keeping me from shattering. I looked up at him, my heart in my throat, and for a moment, I thought that if I said yes, if I let myself fall into him, everything would finally make sense. But that was the problem, wasn't it? Nothing had ever made sense for me, not in the way I wanted it to. And the more Gabriel stood there, so close, so willing, the more I wondered if that was a reason to hold on—or a reason to run.

I opened my mouth to say something, but the words never came. A knock sounded from the window, light tapping, soft at first, but growing louder. Something instinctively told me it wasn't just the wind.

Gabriel turned sharply, his gaze going straight to the window. My stomach dropped as I saw the shadow of movement outside.

"Who is that?" Gabriel asked, his voice tight with something I couldn't place.

Before I could respond, the tap at the window turned to a thud, and the figure outside stepped forward, revealing the unmistakable silhouette of a man I thought I'd left behind forever.

Chapter 43: The Legacy of the Artifact

I hadn't expected to find peace in the desert. After everything that had happened—after the chaos, the unraveling, the way the world had seemed to spin right out of control—I imagined that the stillness would be suffocating. But there, beneath the endless sky, where the sun turned the sand into molten gold, I realized how wrong I had been. The desert wasn't empty, nor was it silent. It hummed with a pulse, a rhythm that was as ancient as time itself. I hadn't understood it before, but now, as I sat with my back pressed against the rough stone of a canyon wall, it was as though the land was breathing alongside me, its secrets whispered in the wind.

Gabriel was sitting next to me, his profile sharp against the horizon. He had his eyes closed, but I knew he was awake. He always was. His presence, once an intrusion, now felt like an anchor in the ever-shifting tide of my thoughts. In the months since the artifact had been destroyed, everything had changed—except, oddly, for Gabriel. His quiet steadiness had been a balm, the kind of comfort I didn't know I'd needed until it was there.

I glanced at him sideways. His jaw was clenched, a barely perceptible tick of tension in his shoulders that told me he was thinking, plotting, mulling over something as usual. He rarely gave anything away easily, but that was part of what had made him so infuriating—and so compelling. We'd spent so many nights after the destruction of the artifact, talking about its legacy, how it had shaped us, how it still clung to our bones, like sand slipping through your fingers no matter how hard you tried to hold on.

"You're quiet," I said softly, my voice almost lost against the vastness of the desert.

Gabriel's eyes flickered open, and he turned to look at me, a faint smile tugging at the corner of his lips. "And you're loud," he replied, his tone dry but not unkind.

I huffed, giving him a look. "I meant more... is there something on your mind? You've been brooding like a man with a thousand secrets. Are you going to keep them all to yourself, or do I get a glimpse?"

Gabriel didn't answer right away. Instead, he turned his gaze back to the horizon, watching the way the light played across the craggy peaks, the way the desert stretched out in infinite layers of sand and stone. It wasn't the kind of place you could rush through; it was a world that demanded patience, that required you to sit with your thoughts, your memories, until you had no choice but to confront them head-on.

"I'm thinking about what comes next," he said finally, his voice low and contemplative.

I raised an eyebrow, the tension in my chest tightening in spite of myself. "Next? You mean, like, after the world has ended and we've destroyed an artifact that could've torn it apart? You're worried about what's next?"

His lips curved into something resembling a grin, but it wasn't the usual teasing one I'd grown accustomed to. There was something else there—something heavier, maybe even a little vulnerable. "Yes," he said, leaning back against the wall, stretching his legs out in front of him. "I guess I'm just trying to figure out how to live with what we've done. What we've... inherited."

I looked at him, trying to read the lines of his face, the shadows that clung to him even in the bright daylight. Gabriel had always been so sure of himself, so impenetrable, but now he seemed to be struggling with something I couldn't quite name. "You mean the weight of it all," I murmured, a chill running through me as I realized how much we had lost—and how much we had never even been able to grasp.

The artifact had left a scar in the fabric of our world, but its legacy wasn't just in the destruction it had wrought. It had shaped us, bound us together in ways neither of us could have predicted. When the artifact had been destroyed, it hadn't vanished. No, it lingered—carried in the memory of the land, in the silent stories of those who had once been its guardians, and in the blood we shared, now forever marked by what we had done.

Gabriel shifted, his hand brushing against mine as he sat upright. His fingers lingered for a moment, the barest of touches, but it was enough to send a ripple of heat across my skin. "I never imagined it would come to this," he admitted, his voice almost a whisper. "I thought... I thought we were just playing at something bigger than us. But now, everything's changed. And we—"

"We're not just players anymore," I finished for him. "We're part of it. The desert, the people, the artifact... it all intertwines. And so do we."

He nodded slowly, his eyes dark with some unspoken thought. "Yeah. We do."

We sat in silence for a while after that, the weight of our words settling between us like the heavy heat of the midday sun. The desert wasn't the same as it had been before the artifact, but neither were we. There was a shift in the air, a hum that vibrated beneath my skin, and for the first time in ages, I felt something like hope. A glimmer, perhaps, that what we had lost wasn't entirely gone, that it could be rebuilt.

It was a fragile hope, like a single thread weaving its way through the tapestry of the world. But it was there. And it was enough to keep me from falling into despair. Enough to remind me that even in the wake of destruction, there could still be a chance to rebuild.

It was the kind of night that made you question whether the stars were intentionally trying to make up for the sun's indifference during the day. The air in Santa Fe was cool now, enough to make the heat of the desert a memory rather than a threat, and I found myself wandering down a narrow street, one of the old, adobe-lined alleys where the shadows clung to the edges like whispered secrets. Gabriel was nowhere to be seen—he'd gone off to meet someone, or perhaps to chase some new lead. I had stopped asking what he was doing when he disappeared into the city. I trusted him in ways that surprised me, even now.

The world felt strange tonight, more so than usual, and I wasn't sure if it was because of the way the city hummed at a different frequency after the chaos had settled, or because I was, as always, trying to put myself back together.

I turned a corner, and there she was.

A woman in a long red dress. She stood in the middle of the street like she was waiting for something—or someone. Her heels clicked against the pavement in a staccato rhythm, a stark contrast to the slow, lazy night. There was something about the way she moved—no, it was the way the air around her seemed to shimmer, as if she weren't quite part of this world. She looked like she belonged to another time, or at least to some version of the world that wasn't quite as grounded as the one I inhabited.

I stopped walking. She noticed, of course. She always noticed.

"You're out here, too, then," I said, voice low. My breath caught in my throat as I took in the strange aura that surrounded her.

"Someone has to keep the pieces from falling apart, don't you think?" she replied with a tilt of her head, a wry smile playing at the corner of her lips. "Besides, you're more like him than you realize."

I blinked, unsure how to react. "Excuse me?"

She took a step closer, her heels quiet against the street now, like she was treading on air. "I've been watching you, you know. Ever since you found the artifact. Ever since you thought it was destroyed."

I stiffened. No one had told me about her, not that I had asked. And besides, I didn't know why I was surprised. People had been watching me for as long as I could remember, some closer than others.

"Why are you here?" I asked, keeping my distance, but not enough to retreat entirely.

Her smile deepened, but it wasn't comforting. It was the kind of smile someone gives you when they know something you don't—and aren't about to tell you. "To remind you. That you're not finished."

That stopped me cold. My heart skipped a beat as the words sank in. "Not finished? With what?"

"Oh, don't be coy," she said, waving a hand dismissively. "You think the destruction of the artifact solved everything? You think it erased the legacy it left? You still have work to do."

I took a deep breath, the familiar prickling sensation of dread creeping up my spine. I'd been so sure that the nightmare was over—that we had severed the chain that had linked us to something beyond our understanding. "I don't know who you are, but I don't need riddles right now."

She leaned in, her presence suddenly overwhelming, filling the narrow space between us with an energy I couldn't shake. "You don't need them? Well, that's a shame. Because the truth? The truth will chase you until you finally face it. Whether you want to or not."

I swallowed hard, trying to summon something more substantial than my growing unease. "I don't believe you. The artifact is gone. It's finished. There's nothing more to say."

She studied me for a long moment, her eyes like the desert at dusk—full of danger, yet impossible to look away from. Then she laughed, a sound that echoed too brightly in the quiet of the street.

"You're wrong," she said, stepping back, her gaze softening ever so slightly, as though she had just decided to humor me. "Maybe you don't have to see it now. But the road you're on? It's not over. You'll figure it out. Or someone else will."

The street around me seemed to pull back, the darkness swallowing her up in an instant. One moment she was standing before me, and the next, she was gone—like a ghost or a mirage in the desert.

For a long time, I just stood there, my feet planted on the street, wondering if I had imagined the entire conversation. The night felt thicker now, the air heavier, pressing down on me like it was trying to smother something hidden in my chest.

But there was no denying it. She had left me with more than questions. She had left me with something worse—doubt.

I turned back toward the hotel, unsure of what I'd just experienced. But one thing was clear: this wasn't over. The pieces hadn't all been put together. Something—or someone—was still waiting, lurking in the shadows. And whether I liked it or not, I was going to have to face it.

By the time I made it back to the hotel, the air had cooled considerably, though my thoughts were a different kind of heat. My mind swirled with the words of the woman—stranger, enigma, messenger, I didn't know what to call her—and the nagging feeling that I hadn't yet seen the full picture. I wasn't sure if I was trying to outrun the truth or if I was simply stalling, but either way, there was something in the pit of my stomach that told me there was more coming.

I pushed open the door to my room with an almost exaggerated calm, as though the night had been just another walk down a familiar street. But nothing was familiar anymore. The familiar scent of the room—the faint floral undertones from the potpourri by the window—seemed stale now. Even the sound of the air conditioner felt too intrusive. I hadn't realized how much I relied on the illusion of quiet until it was shattered.

And then there was Gabriel.

He was seated by the window, his posture relaxed, but the way his fingers drummed against the edge of the table betrayed the tension under the surface. He looked up as I entered, his expression unreadable for a moment, and then—too quickly—he stood, his movements fluid but sharp.

"Where did you go?" he asked, his voice rough from too much silence.

I closed the door softly behind me, suddenly aware of how the space between us had grown since the artifact's destruction. The things unsaid hung thick in the air, as if we were both trying to ignore the fact that we were no longer the same people who had walked into this city weeks ago.

"I needed some air," I said, choosing my words carefully, as though there was any way to hide what had happened outside.

He frowned slightly, but I could see the flicker of something behind his eyes—was it worry? Maybe just curiosity. Either way, I wasn't interested in explaining. Not yet. Not until I had figured it out for myself.

"Did you find what you were looking for?" he asked after a beat, a dry edge to his voice. He had his own demons to wrestle, his own scars from the destruction. But even so, I couldn't help but feel like I was dodging his gaze, as though I were still carrying some invisible weight that had never been shared.

I dropped my bag onto the bed and turned to face him. "I'm not sure. I met someone."

His eyes narrowed, his expression unreadable, and I could almost see the gears turning in his head. "Who?"

"A woman," I said, my voice betraying none of the unease still coiling in my chest. "She said the artifact's destruction didn't solve everything. That the road we're on isn't over."

Gabriel's jaw tightened, and I saw a flicker of recognition, though he didn't speak right away. His hand slid into his pocket, a subconscious motion I'd seen a hundred times, a gesture that always made me feel like I was on the edge of something—something dangerous. "What else did she say?" he asked, his voice lower now, like he was threading a needle with every word.

I sighed and ran a hand through my hair. "She said I wasn't finished. That whatever we thought we'd dealt with, it's still out there. Waiting."

His eyes met mine, and for a moment, the distance between us felt like it had closed. But then it was gone again. Just as quickly. The walls went up, like they always did, and I found myself wishing I had never said anything at all.

"Well, isn't that just fantastic?" Gabriel said, his voice laced with something sharp. "You've just met some random woman in the middle of nowhere, and now you're telling me we're back to square one?"

I bristled at his tone, but the truth was, he was right. It was madness to think that everything was settled. That we had put it all behind us. The artifact had left more than just physical scars. It had planted seeds of something far more insidious—doubt, fear, the lingering knowledge that some things never truly disappear.

"Maybe we're not as done as we thought," I said, my voice steadier than I felt. "But that doesn't mean we're helpless."

Gabriel leaned against the wall, crossing his arms, a posture that mirrored my own. He didn't seem to have an answer, and in that moment, neither did I. We were both just standing there, waiting for something we couldn't name.

The silence between us stretched long enough for me to wonder whether it had become a permanent fixture of our relationship—one of those things you never really noticed until it was too late. And then, without any warning, the silence was broken.

A loud bang.

It was sharp, immediate, and so out of place that it made me jump. My heart slammed against my chest as I turned toward the window. The air outside had gone still. Too still. I was moving before I even realized it, crossing the room and flinging open the window.

Below, in the street, a figure was silhouetted in the dim light, standing unnaturally still. My pulse raced. Who was it? And what the hell was going on?

Gabriel was at my side in an instant, his expression hardening as he scanned the figure below. "We weren't supposed to be followed," he muttered, but the words felt more like an accusation than an observation.

I didn't have time to answer, not when the figure below took a step forward. The streetlights flickered, and in that brief moment, everything seemed to pause—like time itself was holding its breath. Then the figure moved again, faster this time, and before I could even register what was happening, they were gone.

The world seemed to shudder, just slightly, and then there was nothing.

Nothing except the nagging feeling that we had just crossed a line—one we wouldn't be able to uncross.

Chapter 44: A World Reborn

The sun hung low over the city, casting its fiery glow over the worn streets as if it, too, was tired of the battle for survival. I stood in the middle of the market square, the vibrant pulse of this now-rebuilt place humming around me. It was a rare moment when the dust of the past settled long enough to allow the present to breathe. People hurried about their business, their faces hopeful in a way I hadn't seen in years. And for once, it wasn't just about survival—it was about living.

The scent of fresh bread, roasted meats, and spice-filled dishes mingled in the air, urging me to pull away from the task at hand and indulge. But I had learned over the last year that indulging in distraction only led to regret. No, today was about the work. Today, we kept building. Gabriel stood beside me, a figure of quiet strength against the backdrop of our transformed world. His dark hair was ruffled by the breeze, his broad shoulders silhouetted against the sun's dying light. The months had done something to us, something more than just time. It had made us whole again, filled in the cracks where the curse had once drained us. I didn't need to look at him to know he felt the same.

We had rebuilt this city, brick by brick. The people who had once lived in the shadow of the curse now moved freely in the light of a new dawn, their eyes bright with the possibility of a future they had long thought lost. We had cleansed this place, not with the sweeping power of magic or the violence of a storm, but with patience, sweat, and the steady rhythm of labor. It wasn't glamorous, and I often wondered if that's why it felt so much more satisfying. We had done it ourselves.

I glanced down at the dirt under my boots. How many times had I walked this same ground, burdened by the weight of memories and failures? How many times had I tried to avoid it, to walk away from what I knew was always just beneath the surface? But now, everything had changed. The air was different. The people felt different. Even the land felt like it was stretching, growing, and shifting into something it had never been before. The curse that had once clung to the very soil was gone, as though it had been swept away with the dust storms of the past.

And yet, something lingered. A sense of unsettled energy that I couldn't quite name. It wasn't a bad feeling—not exactly—but it was strange, like the edges of a dream that refused to sharpen into focus. I had grown accustomed to this sensation of waiting, of feeling like we were just on the cusp of something, but the feeling was more palpable now. Maybe it was just my nerves, still too raw from the fight. Or maybe it was something else—something out of reach, something I couldn't yet grasp.

"Penny for your thoughts?" Gabriel's voice cut through my reverie, rich and low, like it always was when he spoke to me. He always seemed to know when I was lost in the tangled web of my own mind, when the past and future clashed together in a way that left me teetering on the edge of something—though I wasn't always sure what.

I turned toward him, catching a glint of mischief in his dark eyes. There was something comforting about his presence, a solid weight in a world that often felt as though it could fall apart at any moment. His hand reached for mine, fingers curling around mine with an ease that made me wonder why we hadn't always been this way, why it had taken so long for us to find each other in the chaos.

"I was just thinking about how much has changed," I said, my voice a little softer than usual. "How much more there is to do. It's like the world is waiting for us to fill in the gaps."

Gabriel gave a small chuckle, the sound so familiar it made my heart ache. "It's been waiting for us to take charge, that's for sure. It's just a good thing we don't mind getting our hands dirty."

I snorted, shaking my head. "Getting our hands dirty is practically a requirement at this point. I'm starting to think we were born for this."

"Born to rebuild, you mean?" He raised an eyebrow, an impish smile playing at the corners of his lips.

"Born to do something. Maybe rebuild. Maybe... more." I didn't say it aloud, but the thought had been gnawing at me. The city was recovering, but there was a bigger picture. A world out there still fragmented, broken in places we hadn't yet discovered. What if it wasn't just about the city? What if our role in this new world was something... grander?

Gabriel's gaze softened as if he knew exactly what I wasn't saying. "Whatever it is, we'll face it together. You and me. No more running from it. Not anymore."

The certainty in his voice steadied me, even as the prickling sensation in the back of my mind only grew stronger. There was something I was missing, some puzzle piece still out of reach. But as I stood there with him, watching the last rays of sunlight flicker across the market, I knew that whatever came next, I would face it with him by my side.

The world was changing, and we were part of it. And for the first time in a long time, I wasn't afraid of what was coming. Not as long as we had each other.

The evening air in the city felt like a promise, cool against my skin, with the soft scent of jasmine from the garden next door drifting through the open window. It was one of those nights that made you feel as if the world were holding its breath, suspended in time, as if waiting for something. The hum of the city outside was muted, as if everyone had collectively decided to pause, to simply exist in the moment. There was no rush, no urgency. It was a rare gift, and I soaked it in like a sponge.

Gabriel sat across from me, his fingers tapping a slow, rhythmic pattern on the old wooden table, the one we'd found in a long-forgotten corner of the warehouse when we first started this whole process. It wasn't much—just a battered table and mismatched chairs—but it was ours, and that was all that mattered. We didn't need much more. The other side of the room was littered with half-finished projects—blueprints for new homes, a couple of half-repaired chairs, and even some makeshift bookshelves stacked with salvaged reading materials. The room, like the city itself, was still a work in progress. But for once, it didn't feel overwhelming. It felt right.

"Tell me again why you didn't want to go to the festival tonight?" Gabriel's voice was light, teasing, but I could hear the thread of genuine curiosity beneath it. His dark eyes were intent on mine, playful, but with that familiar edge of concern. He was always looking out for me, and I couldn't decide whether it was endearing or slightly aggravating.

"I'm not much for festivals," I replied with a shrug, my fingers tracing the chipped edge of my coffee mug absentmindedly. "I prefer the quiet. The simplicity of it all. The people here... they don't need me to join them in their celebrations. They just need us to keep building. To keep showing up."

Gabriel's lips quirked up at one corner, but he didn't push me further. Instead, he leaned back in his chair, the wooden creak of the old thing mingling with the ambient sounds of the evening. His gaze softened, and for a moment, the teasing light vanished from his expression, replaced by something quieter, more contemplative.

"I get that," he murmured, his voice just low enough to carry the weight of his thoughts. "But sometimes, it's okay to stop building, you know? To just... be. To celebrate what we've accomplished."

I met his gaze, the weight of his words sinking into my chest. It was a thought that had occurred to me before, but I wasn't sure how to respond. How could I celebrate something that still felt so unfinished? Every day, there was another brick to lay, another problem to solve. How could we celebrate when so much of the world still felt like it was waiting to be fixed?

But Gabriel had a way of making me rethink things, of pushing me to see beyond my narrow lens of practicality. He had this uncanny ability to make even the most mundane moments feel like a revelation, like stepping into a world I hadn't noticed before.

"I'll think about it," I said, my voice a little quieter than I intended. "But right now... I need to get this done. There's too much left to do."

Gabriel's expression didn't falter, but I could see the shift in his eyes, the recognition that I wasn't ready to let go just yet. He didn't argue, didn't insist. Instead, he simply nodded and stood, walking over to the cluttered desk by the window, where we kept our papers and plans. His broad frame loomed over the space, his movements slow and deliberate as he examined the map we'd been working on for weeks.

"We should have more people working on the infrastructure," he said, his voice taking on a more practical tone. "The roads are holding up well enough, but we're starting to see cracks in places. The last thing we need is a setback."

I joined him at the desk, leaning over the map with him, tracing the lines of roads and buildings with my finger. There were indeed cracks—some literal, others less so. The city was strong, yes, but it was also fragile, like a building that had been reconstructed too quickly, too hastily. It was all so delicate, like something that might collapse under the weight of its own ambition.

"We've been over this," I said softly. "The resources are thin. People are still recovering, still getting back on their feet. They need us... but they also need to believe they can stand on their own, to not have us hovering over every decision."

Gabriel's eyes flickered with the same frustration I had been feeling, the struggle between giving people the space to grow and pushing them when they weren't quite ready. It was a balancing act that didn't come naturally, but it was necessary.

"I know," he said, his voice carrying the exhaustion of the last few months. "But it's hard, isn't it? Watching people stumble when we know they could do better. Watching them... wait for us to solve it all."

His words hung in the air between us, a shared burden that neither of us had quite figured out how to carry. It wasn't just about the rebuilding, the physical labor, or the strategic decisions—it was about something deeper. Something more personal.

"We can't do it for them," I whispered, my eyes meeting his. "But we can help them believe they can."

Gabriel's lips curled up at the edges, the smallest flicker of approval crossing his features. He reached over, his hand brushing mine in a simple gesture that spoke volumes more than words ever could.

"You're right," he said, his voice rough with the weight of everything we were trying to carry together. "We can help them see the possibility. We can make them believe."

For a moment, there was nothing but the sound of our breaths, the gentle rise and fall of the air between us. It wasn't easy, but it was enough. Enough to keep going. Enough to keep believing. And in that small, quiet space between us, I realized that maybe that was the most important thing of all. The belief. The conviction that we could change things, one step at a time.

The night had wrapped itself around the city like a velvet curtain, quiet and thick with promise. The streetlights flickered to life one by one, casting long, tired shadows on the cracked pavement. It was a city reborn, and I could almost taste the shift in the air, as though something ancient and forgotten was stirring beneath the surface. The hum of life was quieter now, no longer frantic or desperate, but subdued, as if the city had just exhaled after holding its breath for far too long.

Gabriel was leaning against the windowsill, his profile sharp against the moonlight that filtered through the blinds, throwing dark lines across his face. He had a way of standing like that, as if the world outside was as much a part of him as the air he breathed. It was almost maddening, how natural he looked in this place. I sometimes wondered if he ever felt as out of place as I did. He didn't talk much about it. That's the thing about Gabriel—he was a man of action, not words.

But tonight, the quiet between us was different. The space between us felt fuller, somehow, as if the weight of everything we had yet to face was pressing in. I could feel the pull of it, the urgency, like the ticking of a clock that I couldn't quite ignore.

I broke the silence, my voice steady but low, more to fill the air than to offer any real answer. "Do you ever think we'll get to a point where we stop rebuilding? When we can just live?"

Gabriel shifted, his gaze sliding over to me, but it wasn't judgment or pity in his eyes. It was understanding, the kind of understanding you get when you've seen too much and lived through too much together. He gave a slight shrug, one shoulder lifting and then dropping again. "I don't think we ever stop rebuilding. Maybe it's not about the city. Maybe it's about us. Maybe we're always rebuilding ourselves, just a little bit more with every day."

I didn't know if I agreed or not. I wasn't sure if it was the truth, or if it was just one of those things people told themselves when they didn't have any better answers. But there was something about his words, the way they settled in the room, that made me believe they could be true.

The pause stretched between us until it felt like it might snap. And then, as though the moment had decided for us, there came the unmistakable sound of footsteps approaching the front door. They weren't hurried, but there was a purpose to them. A sharpness. I stiffened instinctively, the hairs on the back of my neck rising.

Gabriel didn't move, didn't even flinch. His eyes never left mine, but there was a flicker of something else there now, a tension that I hadn't seen before. We had spent so long rebuilding, replanting hope in the cracks of this world, that it felt absurd to think someone might knock on our door now, of all times. But in this city—my city—there was no such thing as a simple knock.

The doorbell rang. One, two, three times, its sharp tone cutting through the silence of the night. I wasn't sure whether I was relieved or unnerved by the sound.

"Expecting someone?" I asked, my voice more clipped than I meant it to be.

Gabriel pushed away from the windowsill, his movements slow, measured. "Not exactly."

I stood, my eyes fixed on the door, my heart picking up its pace. There was no time for hesitation. Whoever it was, whatever this was, it had come at the worst possible moment.

"I'll get it," I said, turning toward the door. I moved quickly, my steps light against the wooden floor. I could hear Gabriel behind me, his boots heavy as they pressed into the ground, but I didn't wait for him to catch up. He had never been one to hesitate, either.

I reached the door, my hand hovering over the handle for a moment, a strange sense of dread crawling up my spine. This wasn't just any visitor. There was something in the air tonight, something heavier than the moonlit calm. I opened the door with a swift motion, my breath caught in my throat.

Standing there, framed by the dim porch light, was a figure I didn't recognize. His face was shadowed, but the silhouette of his figure was unmistakable. Tall, lean, with a posture that screamed authority, as if he were used to commanding attention. His eyes were hidden behind dark glasses, though the way he stood—shoulders squared, feet planted firmly—made it clear he wasn't just passing through.

"I need to speak with Gabriel," the man said, his voice gravelly, but not unkind.

I stepped aside, half-expecting Gabriel to appear behind me, but he didn't. I glanced back, but Gabriel was standing in the hallway, his face unreadable. It took everything I had not to look at him and make some kind of silent plea. Whatever this was, it had nothing to do with us.

"Who are you?" I asked, my voice steady even though my heart was racing in my chest. I wasn't about to let some stranger walk in without an explanation. Not tonight. Not when everything felt so fragile.

The man seemed to hesitate, just for a moment. Then, with a slight tilt of his head, he stepped into the house without waiting for an invitation. I tensed, ready to react, but before I could say anything, he spoke again.

"You might want to sit down for this," he said, his voice low, like he was about to drop a bomb. "It's about the curse. It's not over."

Chapter 45: The Endless Horizon

The city hums beneath me, a steady beat that fills the air with its rhythm, one I know as intimately as the pulse of my own veins. It's that odd kind of noise that becomes comforting after a while, the way you don't notice the traffic, or the endless chatter of voices blending into the background. The sort of noise that wraps around you like an old sweater, familiar, warm, and just tight enough to make you forget about the edges of the world you've left behind. And tonight, as I lean against the balcony railing, the city sprawls out before me—alive and restless as always. Yet, somehow, it feels like everything is still. Still, in that way that makes you feel as though the world might just pause if you let it. It's an illusion, of course. The city never stops moving, not even for a second. But in that moment, I am the only one who can breathe. The only one who knows that after everything, I've arrived.

It wasn't always like this. A year ago, the thought of being here—standing alone in a city that never sleeps, where the clamor of the world felt more like a weight than a soundtrack—would have made me laugh. But here I am, with the city whispering its secrets and the stars hanging low above me, like they're in on a joke only they know. The best part? I'm not even sure if it's a joke anymore. I didn't mean to end up here. I certainly didn't plan on it. But somehow, the city knew I needed it. And I needed it more than I ever could have imagined.

The smell of old leather and tobacco from the jacket I'm wearing lingers in the air, a reminder of who I used to be and who I've learned to become. The rough edges of the jacket rub against my skin, as though it's an extension of myself, and maybe it is. Maybe everything is, in the end. I've had time to think. Time to reflect. The kind of time you only get when you're miles away from home, thousands of decisions behind you. But there's one thing that hasn't changed. Not one single thing. Gabriel. He's the one constant, the thread running through everything—through the days I thought I'd lost, through the nights that felt too quiet, too heavy, until he pulled me into a dance where we both forgot the world and were just us. Just two people lost in something that might not make sense to anyone else, but to us, it makes everything.

I can hear his footsteps before I see him. The soft echo of his boots on the worn floorboards of the loft, a sound that's become as familiar to me as the scent of coffee in the morning. It's strange, how little things like that can carve out a place in your heart, something so simple yet so significant. Gabriel moves like he has all the time in the world. And he does, I suppose. At least for now. He doesn't rush through life like I used to, trying to outrun everything that came with it. He simply moves, with purpose but without haste, as though he knows where he's going and doesn't need to prove it to anyone.

"I thought I'd lost you," he says, his voice breaking through the quiet like the first drop of rain after a drought. I smile at the sound of his voice. It's a sound that's both steady and soft, like the deep rumble of thunder before the storm. But there's something different about it now. Something that wasn't there before. His words, always carefully measured, now feel more vulnerable than they ever have. More real. He's been thinking, too, I can tell.

"You haven't lost me," I reply, my words slipping out more easily than I expected. "I'm right here."

And I am. I really am. The last year has been nothing but a blur of moments stitched together with frayed edges—each one sharper than the last. But the truth is, I haven't gone anywhere. Not really. No matter where the road took us, no matter how far it stretched, I was always here, just waiting for the pieces to come together.

He reaches me then, standing beside me in the quiet hum of the city. He's not close enough to touch, but I can feel the warmth of his presence, like a low flame keeping the darkness at bay. For a moment, neither of us says anything. We just stand there, side by side, as the world continues its endless spin. I know he's waiting for me to speak, to give him something. A reassurance, perhaps. Or maybe he's just waiting for me to say what we've both been thinking, even though we know it won't change anything.

"I don't know where this is going," I say finally, my voice barely a whisper against the sounds of the city. "But I know I want to go there with you."

He nods, a small smile playing at the corners of his lips. "I think I'd like that."

It's a small thing. A simple thing. But in that moment, it feels like everything. The city may never stop moving, but for us, time stands still. It's an odd feeling, this peace that has settled between us. I never thought I'd find it, certainly not here, where life moves fast and hard, where the world's edges are sharp enough to cut you if you're not careful. But somehow, I've found it. With Gabriel. In the quiet of this city. In the heart of a place that doesn't ever stop, yet finally feels like home.

The sun was setting, painting the sky a wild tangle of gold and orange, turning the air heavy with the kind of stillness that only comes when the world is on the verge of something monumental. As the light waned, the city below me flickered to life—like a million tiny fireflies coming out to breathe. The chaos of the day was nothing more than a memory now. The city, always so alive, had quieted into something almost intimate, its energy shifting from frantic to peaceful, and I could almost hear it exhale. The rhythm of traffic had softened, the hum of voices muted to a background murmur that felt far away, even though it was only a few floors beneath me.

Gabriel's presence beside me was undeniable, a steady force that grounded me, even in moments when everything around us seemed like it could go up in smoke. He was always steady. Always certain. His confidence was something I had never taken for granted, and I was starting to wonder if that might have been my mistake all along.

"What's on your mind?" His voice cut through the space between us with ease, like a warm breeze.

I turned to face him, taking in the familiar lines of his face, the easy smile that had once made me question everything I thought I knew. "Just thinking," I murmured. "About how things were before... before all of this. I mean, before us."

Gabriel raised an eyebrow, his lips twitching at the corners. "Are you regretting it?" His voice was soft but had an edge to it—a challenge, something that dared me to speak the truth.

I laughed, the sound sharper than I'd intended. "I'm not regretting anything. But sometimes, I can't help but wonder if we're just two pieces trying to fit into a puzzle we can't quite see yet."

His expression softened, and for a moment, I could almost see the armor crack, just a sliver of it, enough for me to see the vulnerability lurking underneath. "Isn't that the point, though? Not knowing exactly where we're going, but knowing we want to go there together?"

It was simple, his answer. But it was so full of weight. The kind of weight that could drag you under or lift you higher, depending on how you chose to look at it. I had spent so much of my life trying to chart my own course, to make sure that every decision was deliberate and calculated. But with Gabriel, nothing had been planned. Nothing had been certain. And yet, here we were. Something I hadn't been prepared for, yet still welcomed with open arms.

"You're not wrong," I admitted, glancing down at the city below us. "I guess I've just been so used to controlling everything.

Trying to fix the broken pieces, make things fit. And sometimes, I forget that not everything has to be fixed."

He nudged my shoulder, the action simple, yet so intimate that it made my breath catch in my chest. "I've always been more of a 'go with the flow' kind of guy. But I think you've got more of that in you than you realize." His voice was light, but there was something behind it—something I couldn't quite place.

I narrowed my eyes at him, a smirk tugging at the corner of my lips. "Are you saying I've been rigid?"

"Only when you're trying to be perfect," he teased. "But that's what I like about you. You're full of surprises."

And there it was, the softness again, the same warmth that I had been trying to keep at arm's length. It was like he could read me. Could see past the walls I'd so carefully built. And instead of pushing back, instead of being unsettled, he just kept pulling me closer.

A noise from down the hall drew our attention, but I didn't need to look. I knew it was coming. The buzz of life, the people we'd tried to leave behind for just a moment, creeping back in as the world moved forward. My heart wasn't ready for it yet. Not ready to face the fallout of what had happened, of what I had done. But Gabriel's hand found mine before I could slip away into the quiet. His grip was firm, warm, and steady. Like always.

"We can't just keep running from it, can we?" I asked, the question sitting between us like a quiet ghost.

Gabriel chuckled, the sound low and knowing. "You can run all you want. But I'll always be here, waiting. And when you're ready to face it, you'll know. It won't be as scary as you think."

He was right. Of course he was. But it didn't make it any easier.

The city outside, with all its noise and confusion, was a stark contrast to the quiet that had settled between us. But still, there was something about it. Something about the way the lights shimmered like stars in a sky that would never go dark. There was something about Gabriel, too, and the way he fit into this life I had never fully understood, as though he had always belonged here. In this city, in this moment. With me.

And as we stood there together, I realized that it didn't matter whether we had all the answers. It didn't matter if the puzzle pieces didn't fit neatly. What mattered was that we were both willing to try, to see what this strange and chaotic world had in store for us. Because sometimes, the best part of a journey isn't knowing where you're going. It's knowing who you're going with. And with Gabriel, I wasn't afraid to take that next step.

The cold air from the river swirled around us, tugging at my coat like it had a mind of its own, teasing the hem of my skirt as if to remind me that this moment, for all its beauty, would slip away if I wasn't careful. The lights of the city behind us twinkled in time with the stars above, a reflection of the chaos that lived just out of view, hidden beneath a veneer of calm. I used to crave the chaos. I thought it was my birthright, a constant hum that I could live with, could conquer. But now, standing here beside Gabriel, the quiet felt like a gift, something foreign but intoxicating in its stillness.

"Hey," Gabriel's voice broke the silence, soft but certain. "You okay?"

I turned to him, our shoulders brushing, the slight pressure a tether to the world that felt both too big and too small at once. His eyes, always intense, were searching mine, as if trying to read a story I wasn't quite ready to tell. And maybe I wouldn't. Maybe I'd keep this part of me hidden, tucked away in the spaces between the beat of my heart and the rhythm of my breath. Some things weren't meant to be shared. At least, not yet.

"I'm fine," I said, brushing off the weight of his gaze. "Just... thinking. About everything."

His lips quirked, a half-smile playing at the corners of his mouth. "You think too much."

I arched an eyebrow, a wry smile forming of its own accord. "Says the guy who spends more time inside his own head than in the real world."

He laughed, low and knowing, the sound threading through the cool night like a thread of warmth. "Touché. But sometimes, it's the thinking that gets in the way. You know that, right?"

I nodded, the smile fading into something more contemplative. "I know. But the problem is, when you stop thinking, that's when the world starts catching up to you. And I'm not sure I'm ready for that yet."

Gabriel turned to face me fully, his expression softening, like he was trying to piece together the fragments of me that I didn't want to offer up. "You don't have to be ready for it. Not now. Not until you are."

The words hit me like a ton of bricks, landing somewhere in the pit of my stomach, but I didn't know whether to laugh or cry. It was that strange balance between wanting to run and wanting to stay. Gabriel, for all his strength and determination, had this way of unraveling me with just a few words, a few gestures, a quiet steadiness that I could neither fight nor resist.

But the world didn't stop. It didn't give me the luxury of taking my time. And just like that, the moment shattered, replaced by the cacophony of the city—horns blaring, voices shouting in the distance, the low hum of a thousand lives intersecting. My phone buzzed in my pocket, a reminder of the life I'd left behind in favor of something new, something I didn't yet understand.

I hesitated before pulling it out, my fingers trembling ever so slightly. But it wasn't what I expected. It wasn't a call. It was a message.

A simple string of words that stopped my heart cold:

Meet me. 2 AM. Central Park.

I swallowed, my throat suddenly dry. "Who is it?" Gabriel asked, his voice turning serious, sharp like a blade drawn in the quiet.

I didn't know how to answer. Because I didn't know the sender. Or, rather, I didn't want to know. Not like this.

"What's wrong?" Gabriel's hand was on my arm, the heat of his palm seeping through the layers of fabric, grounding me. But this was different. This wasn't a casual message. This was a summons. A reminder that no matter how far I ran, no matter how much I tried to build something new, the past was never far behind.

"It's nothing," I lied, slipping the phone back into my pocket. "Just someone from... a while ago."

Gabriel's gaze darkened, the shift in his posture telling me everything I needed to know. He wasn't buying it. And, to be honest, I wasn't sure I was either. Something in my gut twisted, like an old wound I'd long forgotten. But this—this wasn't something I was ready to face.

His voice was low when he spoke again. "We're in this together. Whatever it is, whatever comes next... you don't have to do it alone."

The sincerity in his words was almost too much. I could see the way he wanted to protect me, to shield me from whatever shadow was creeping up from my past. But I wasn't sure I wanted protecting. Not anymore. Not when it felt like every time I thought I had a grip on who I was, the world would tilt, and everything would shift out of place again.

"Let's just... not worry about it," I said quickly, the words tumbling out before I could stop them. "Not right now."

Gabriel didn't press. Instead, he just nodded, his eyes narrowing slightly as he studied me. The weight of the silence between us wasn't comfortable, but it wasn't unbearable either. It was the kind of silence that filled in the spaces where words didn't belong, where feelings were far more tangible than anything you could say.

But I could feel it. The pressure was building. The clock was ticking down. And the closer it got to midnight, the more I knew that whatever was waiting for me in that park, whatever was pulling me back to a life I thought I'd left behind, would change everything.

I tried to shake off the unease swirling in my chest, but it stuck with me, clinging like the last vestiges of a storm long after the rain had stopped falling. I wasn't ready for what would happen next. But I knew one thing for sure: it was coming. And I wasn't sure if I could outrun it this time.